TOR MURDERS

By

Dave Watson

Mirador Publishing
www.miradorpublishing.com

First Published in Great Britain 2012 by Mirador Publishing

Copyright © 2012 by Dave Watson

All right reserved. No part of this publication may be reproduced or transmitted, in any form or by any means, without permission of the publishers or author. Excepting brief quotes used in reviews.

First edition: 2012

Any reference to real names and places are purely fictional and are constructs of the author. Any offence the references produce is unintentional and in no way reflect the reality of any locations or people involved.

A copy of this work is available though the British Library.

ISBN: 978-1-908200-86-0

Mirador Publishing
Mirador
Wearne Lane
Langport
Somerset
TA10 9HB

Acknowledgements

My heartfelt thanks and gratitude to Sandra Coyne, whose support and guidance helped to define the final manuscript.

Thank you to Di Gaedtke, for her kind feedback on an early manuscript.

As always, my gratitude to Sarah and everyone at Mirador. I'm delighted to be working with such a terrific team.

1

'Now class that's the end of today's lecture. If anyone has any assignments they want me to read or mark, please leave them on the table. Oh by the way. The Chief Librarian has reminded me that several books have yet to be returned, or date extensions paid for.'

David Hare gave a deep sigh as he slumped behind his desk whilst the seminar room slowly emptied. Another day's lecturing almost complete. Some days he felt he was talking to himself and found himself wondering why students enrolled for a subject they had little interest in.

Sarah Carpenter was different. She was always the last to leave, always wanting to ask one more question. She was a breath of fresh air, but sometimes she didn't take the hint that her question had already been answered.

'Professor, you said that people still believe the Abbey to be the final resting place of King Arthur. Do you really believe that?'

David sat back in his chair and placed his hands behind his head.

'It's not for us to decide, my dear. One has to draw one's own conclusions from the evidence we have today. Which I have to say, still remains quite limited.'

'But is that your opinion? I mean, there are so many conflicting stories it's difficult to know which one to believe.'

'Sarah, my opinion is irrelevant. All you need to submit in your assignment is a précis of the facts that are presented. Historians like to keep us guessing. It helps to create both myth and interest.'

'OK thanks, Sir.' Sarah skipped out of the door and could be heard whistling as she walked down the corridor.

David shook his head and laughed to himself. Sarah had been his student for almost a year now. She was twenty-two going on sixteen. She always wore the same clothes. A low- cut wool jumper, a knee-length tartan skirt and a pair of multi- coloured trainers. There was something about the way she continually pushed back the fringe of her long blonde hair and curled the side of her lip, that made most of the male students in the class pay more attention to her than any others.

Being Professor of Ancient History at Bath University certainly had its advantages David thought to himself. Gathering his notes he bundled them into his briefcase and left the seminar room. Once outside the building he crossed the lawn between the inner sanctum of the University courtyard and the outside world. It was a beautiful sunny afternoon and a number of the female students were making the most of the good weather by sitting out on the lawn. It would have been very tempting to join them but he had a prior appointment to meet Colin Dempster at The Sceptre, a pub in the High Street.

Leaving the grounds of the University he crossed the main road and headed towards the bank to withdraw some money. Because it was lunchtime the whole area was awash with students and lecturers from the University. As a result, David had to stop to say hello to individuals or groups of people every few yards.

Having finally extracted some cash from the machine, he made his way to The Sceptre.

The dark oak frontage gave the pub the appearance of dating back to medieval times, but the date of 1755 above the main entrance was a bit of a giveaway. The flagstone floor in the porch gave way to a threadbare, stained carpet that had obviously been laid several years previously. The sparse wooden furniture stood unevenly on the sloping floor.

He found Colin Dempster seated at a small round table in the corner of the front lounge bar, surrounded by a mass of books and paperwork.

'There's hardly any room for the beers,' said David pulling up a chair opposite.

'Hello there,' Colin replied peering over his glasses. 'Yeah, sorry. I'm trying to catch up on some marking. Saves time for later because I'm supposed to be going to the cinema tonight.'

'Oh, right. What are you going to see?'

'Haven't got a clue. I'm taking young Suzie Potter. So - who cares? She's the young English lecturer who started last term.'

'Suzie Potter? She must be half your age.'

'As I said, who cares?' Colin replied raising his glass to down the remains of his first pint. 'Have you finished for the day?'

'No, I wish. I've got another lecture to give at four o'clock. The history of the Celts in Britain.'

'Sounds fun. You ought to take up Geography like me. That way you'd have a better excuse for snooping around the grounds in the summer when all the young lovelies are about.'

'You never change, do you?' said David laughing, managing to spill his Pedigree beer over the already well-stained carpet.

'Are you going to Pete's party this weekend?' Colin asked shuffling papers around the table.

'I hadn't really given it much thought. Sally is coming down for a few days, and I'd planned to take her to Glastonbury. She wants to see the Abbey and the Tor, as long as the weather's OK.'

'Oh coming down for a dirty weekend is she?'

'It's nothing like that,' David replied with a smirk on his face.

The two friends spent the next half an hour discussing the rights and wrongs of the new principal's role at the University before David downed the remains of his beer and stood up to leave.

'Sorry mate, but I've got to run. I've got to collect some books from the library before the next group of hooligans arrives. Catch you later.'

'Yeah will do. Have fun.'

David left the pub and set off back to the University. The sun had faded a little and there was a nip in the air so he placed his briefcase under his arm and dug his hands deep into the pockets of his cardigan, pulling it close. Knowing he only had half an hour to spare he quickened his pace. As he turned into the University courtyard, however, a figure stepped out blocking his way.

'Hi Pete. What's up? You look somewhat agitated.'

Pete Stanley, the Chief Librarian for Bath University, was stood under the arch leading into the courtyard. His mop of thick black hair was untidy as usual having not seen a comb in years and the rip in his jeans gave the appearance of a dog having chewed a hole in the kneecap.

'What's up? I'll tell you what's up. Half of the students in your damn classes are overdue on books they've borrowed from the library. They're making my life a misery. Can you have a word with them?'

'Sure thing, Pete,' David replied patting him on the shoulder.

'I'll drop them all an email to try and speed things up a bit,' he called, but Pete was already half way across the courtyard.

'What on earth is bugging him?' thought David to himself.

There were only two other people in the library when David entered. He walked over to the main enquiry desk where he collected the books that Pete had signed out for him and took a seat at one of the benches at the back of the library.

David sat down and started on the task of searching for the snippets of information he needed for his next class. He was so engrossed in jotting down a few bullet points he failed to notice that Pete had sat at the desk next to him until someone walked past saying his name. Toying with the pencil in his hand, David watched Pete for a few moments. The guy seemed unusually nervous today. It was so out of character for him to get upset about books being overdue, that was a common thing for any library. Even more unusual was the sight of Pete sat in the library taking notes from a book. David put his own notes away and closed the mountain of books in front of him.

'That's the first time I've seen you studying anything other than the female students,' said David trying a light hearted approach.

'Eh what? Oh yeah sure,' Pete stammered. He closed the book he was taking notes from and rested both arms across the desk as if he didn't want David to see what he'd been looking at.

'Pete. Are you OK?'

'Yeah fine. I just thought it was about time I educated myself,' he replied trying to force a grin.

'Anything interesting?'

'Err no, not really. Look I must get on. I need to finish an audit of the books in the Latin section.'

He stood up and gathered his things together before striding off. David sat back in the chair and watched him as he made his way up the staircase to where the Latin section was located. He was about to stand up when he noticed that someone had approached Pete at the top of the stairs. He didn't know the stranger but going by the level of Pete's voice it was quite obvious they were having an argument.

He watched for a few moments before both Pete and the stranger turned around, descended the stairs and headed out of the library. Gathering his own things David made his exit and stood in the doorway looking either side along the length of the corridors that encompassed the interior of the University.

Neither Pete nor the stranger, were anywhere to be seen.

David shrugged his shoulder's and took the first flight of stairs on the right up to the second level and headed towards the lecture room. The one hour weekly lecture he gave on the influence of the Celts in ancient Britain always dragged.

He would stand there, and verbally pour out lists of dates and events along with inventions and tribal history, while half the class would sit through frantically scribbling data, and the other non- interested half would draw and doodle on their pads.

He would end each lesson asking the class if there were any questions. The response was always the same. Just blank stares.

David was often left wondering why he bothered. Only a handful of the students were interested. The majority only attended his lectures because they made up the rest of their syllabus.

2

Sally's feet were killing her and her back still ached from standing on the train carrying the weekly food shopping, so the warm bath was a welcome relief. Sally Martin, thirty-one years of age, brunette, tall, slim figure, was exhausted. It had been a long and stressful week. She'd held numerous meetings trying to get people to agree to a simple proposal to help ease the traffic problems around Canary Wharf during the 2012 Olympics.

She laid back in the bath and let the warm water envelope her. The glass of wine in her hand was her second one of the evening and she'd only been home for half an hour.

She was thinking about the events of the day when a blast of 'We are the Champions' from her mobile phone brought her back to earth. She was expecting David to phone but he usually finished later.

'Hello,' she said in the sexiest voice she could muster. 'I'm naked, soaking myself in the bath. Do you want to come over and wash my back?'

'Pardon me?'

'Oh, hello, Mum.' Sally's face flushed with embarrassment as she sat up straight, sloshing water all over the floor.

'I thought it was David,' Sally stammered.

'Obviously.' Her Mum gave her a two minute lecture regarding her telephone manners.

'Sorry,' Sally replied after her mother had let off steam.

'How's Dad? Has he been up to the allotment today?'

Sally's father had retired only two months ago but her mother said he was already bored.

'Your father's fine. He's found a new friend. Some old chap who spends most of his time growing vegetables for half of the county.' Sally smiled to herself. It was her Mum's way of cracking a joke.

'Listen, I'm going up to Bath tomorrow for a couple of days to see David, and if the weather is OK we're going to spend a day in Glastonbury. As you know, I've always wanted to see the Abbey and it should be fun climbing the Tor if the weather does hold out.'

'I thought you'd already visited the Abbey. Anyhow, what's the Tor?' her mother asked sounding confused.

'Oh it's the big hill that overlooks Glastonbury. There are still remains of a church tower at the top. I'll send you some photos.'

'Alright. I'll look forward to seeing them. I just wanted to let you know that your father and I are going down to Auntie Jean's this weekend. She's not been too well again so we're going to get her out for a bit.'

'OK, that's cool. Send her my love. Tell Dad I received the newspaper clippings he sent, they were just the job.'

After saying goodbye Sally hung up and burst out laughing. She towel dried before slipping into her pyjamas and was cooking an omelette when her phone rang again. This time she checked the caller first.

'Hello David,' she laughed.

'Hey what's funny?' She told him about the conversation with her Mum.

'So is the offer still open?'

'Sorry too late. I had to ask the neighbour to come round. He was very obliging,' Sally replied with a grin.

'You will get a slap young lady.'

'Ooh promises, promises.'

'So how's your day been?'

'Oh the usual. Some people just don't see a good idea even when it's explained to them a hundred times.'

'So the new transport proposals are not going too well eh?'

'Yeah you could say that.'

'Talking about transport. What time is your train tomorrow? I'll meet you at the station.'

'I'm getting the train from King's Cross at ten-thirty so should be down around midday. Do you need me to bring anything?'

'What about that red underwear you bought when we were in Paris.'

'I meant food you idiot.'

'Ah well. It was worth a try,' he replied. He couldn't see her flushed face.

Sally enjoyed travelling on the train down to Bath but always hated the queues at the ticket office. Having eventually purchased her ticket she made her way to Platform four where she boarded the first carriage and walked through the train to the first class compartment. She felt it was always worth the extra cost as she was able to spread her reading material on a table. An avid reader, Sally enjoyed the opportunity to sit back and read the newspapers and magazines. The magazines usually supplied by her parents.

For once the train departed on time and soon the concrete horizon of the city was replaced by the open space of the countryside. Sally sat back in the chair and relaxed. It wasn't long before the motion of the train was beginning to take effect and she was having difficulty in keeping her eyes open. She woke when the train began to slow as it crawled through a remote station teaming with steam train enthusiasts.

The Somerset Bluebell was sat in a nearby platform being photographed by hundreds of onlookers. One young boy turned to look at Sally's train as it meandered past. Sally smiled and gave him a wink at which point he aimed his camera and took her photo. She waved and blew him a kiss. As the train continued forward she just managed to glimpse the boy tugging his father's arm and waving at the same time.

Sally had been so engrossed she hadn't noticed the well-dressed gentleman who had entered the compartment, and taken a seat on the other side of the train. She jumped as she looked up.

'I'm sorry. I didn't mean to disturb you,' he said apologetically.

'Oh no, that's fine. My fault. I was miles away,' Sally replied looking somewhat embarrassed.

The train slowly picked up speed as it pulled away from the station and soon the rocking of the carriage sent her back to sleep again. She dreamt she was lying on the top deck of a yacht sunbathing and the gentle sway of the ocean was caressing her every limb. A young waiter placed her drink on the table and advised her they would be mooring in a few moments. Glimpsing between the rails she could see the tiny island. The breeze was toying with the branches of the Palm trees and the tide was rolling gently up to the shoreline, caressing the white sandy beach. A calypso band were playing a reggae tune somewhere in the distance and the smell of a barbecue was caught in the breeze.

Sally woke with a start to the sound of carriage doors being opened and slammed shut and people calling out. They had arrived in Bath.

She looked around the carriage and realised she was on her own. The passenger who had joined her earlier must have already disembarked. Trying to compose her thoughts she gathered her things together and stepped off the train.

David was there waiting for her with a red carnation.

'What's that all about?' she asked laughing.

'I thought it was likely to be the only red thing I got to see this weekend.'

'You silly sod,' said Sally slapping him on the shoulder.

'You can bloody well buy me a drink now.' She leaned forward and kissed him on the lips.

'Here,' she said, handing him her sports bag. 'I'll let you carry that.'

'Why because it's heavy?' he answered putting on a sad face.

'No because I thought you might want to keep a close eye on my underwear.'

They headed towards the station exit, joining the queue of travellers. Once outside, David hailed a cab asking the driver to take them to the University.

'So how was your journey?' he asked as they settled into the back seat.

'Quite amusing really.' She told him the story of the little boy taking her photograph. Ten minutes later the cab stopped outside the main entrance to Bath University.

After signing the visitor's book and obtaining a temporary pass for the weekend, Sally was eventually allowed into the University campus and followed David up to his room. He set about making them a snack to eat whilst Sally went straight to the bedroom to unpack her weekend things.

He'd just finished washing up the breakfast plates when Sally appeared from the bedroom. She was dressed in jeans, tracksuit top and hiking boots.

'Are we going mountaineering or just visiting the Abbey?'

'The last time we went somewhere for the day, I ended up with a pair of trainers that had no soles.'

Closing the cupboard door he walked across the lounge and put his hands around her waist.

'You look lovely,' he laughed and kissed her on the cheek.

'Bugger off and get ready,' she replied grinning.

Ten minutes later, dressed in jeans, roll neck jumper and an old pair of trainers, David left his room keys in the University office. He made his way across the street to the overflow car park where Sally was already sat in his car, playing with the radio, trying to select another channel.

'Don't you go breaking my radio now,' he said tapping on the side window.

'I don't know how you listen to all that local drivel,' she replied laughing as he jumped into the driver's seat.

'I'll have you know young lady that there are people out there who listen to that day and night.'

'Yeah well, it takes all sorts I guess.'

Sally finally selected Smooth FM and turned up the volume.

The weather had been kind to them. It was a bright breezy day with a pale sun filtering through. The early bank of cloud was now starting to disperse allowing the afternoon sun's rays to push back the shadows on the surrounding countryside. David had decided they would visit Glastonbury Abbey first, then after a late lunch in the town walk from there up to the Tor. After stopping to get petrol, he let down the sunroof of his old MG and as soon as they turned off of the main Bath road, he gunned the old sports car through the country lanes.

Sally sat back in her seat and let the rush of air envelope her as she sang out loudly to a collection of old Motown hits.

'Did you bring any sweets?' David shouted pointing to his mouth.

'No I didn't and looking at your waistline lately I would say I'm doing you a favour,' she replied mockingly.

They reached the edge of Glastonbury in just under an hour where they met a queue of traffic trying to get into the town centre.

Leaving the main stream traffic at the junction to Magdalene Street they took a left turn and headed for the car park opposite the entrance to the Abbey. It was just after two o'clock and the car park was already two thirds full. David put the hood back up on the car while Sally grabbed their jackets and went in search of the ticket machine.

After purchasing a ticket, she placed it inside the windscreen before David locked the vehicle.

Crossing the road they joined the throng of people entering the grounds of Glastonbury Abbey. Sally wanted to visit the Lady Chapel and St. Dunstans Chapel first which was directly in front of them, so they followed a local guide, dressed in Tudor clothing from a bygone era. She gave them a guided tour of the Lady Chapel and provided historical information of both the Lady Chapel and St. Dunstans Chapel.

Unfolding the map they'd been given at the reception desk, Sally pointed towards the North Walk. Grabbing David's hand she pulled him in the direction of King Arthur's tomb and the High Altar.

The edge of the path along the North Walk was awash with hundreds of blooming white and yellow daffodils which Sally insisted on photographing for her mother. As they stopped to read the plaque by King Arthurs tomb Sally asked,

'Do you really believe King Arthur is buried here or is it all a myth?'

'That's the million dollar question. It all depends on whether you believe in fairy tale fiction or plain fact.'

'So what's your call?' Sally asked slipping her arm around his.

'Personally I think he may have existed. There are a lot of books written about King Arthur's exploits. Maybe there's something in it.'

'That's a typical kop out answer from a Professor.'

'Yeah. I suppose it is,' he said laughing, and led her towards King Edgar's Chapel.

After listening to an audio tape of the history surrounding the Chapel they came across the entrance to the grounds of Abbey House. They both stopped to peer through the railing. The gated entrance was locked and a display sign stated that the grounds belonged to a private estate. Stopping to admire the house that stood some hundred yards back from the gated entrance Sally observed the man standing on the steps to the main entrance. Although he was some distance away she recognised the man immediately.

'What's wrong Sally?' David asked seeing her stare through the gate.

She pointed before answering.

'That's the man who was on the train.'

David continued to look through the railing at the entrance to Abbey House and at the figure now entering the front door.

'You can't say for certain that it was him,' said David. 'I mean, you did say that you fell asleep for a while.'

'But no one else was in my carriage.'

'Sal, you can't be certain of that. OK, you saw no one else in the compartment, but there were probably two hundred people on that train. In any case, what does it matter?'

'I know. It's just that he gives me the creeps.'

'But you've only met him once, and spoken briefly.'

'You know I've always been a good judge of character,' Sally replied standing her ground. 'There's something fishy about that man.'

3

Penny Westbrook heard the front door slam and listened to Michael's footsteps as he strode down the hall towards the library at the back of the house. She knew he was having one of his tantrums as soon as he walked in the room. The ruddy complexion of his cheeks, and the way he puffed out his chest, were both signs she knew well.

'Bloody tourists! They stand there gawping through the damn gates looking at us as if we're animals in a bloody zoo.'

'I'm sure no one was gawping at you,' Penny replied putting her book down on her lap.

'Are you calling me a liar? I suppose you think I'm making the whole damn story up.'

Penny closed her book, placed it on the reading table and walked across the room to where Michael was stood with his hands on his hips.

'Give me a cuddle. You know the doctor said you shouldn't get so worked up.'

'That's easy for him to say,' replied Michael whose temper was already beginning to recede as Penny ran her fingers through his hair. She knew how to control him.

'People will always look through the gate. They always have. You forget we live in a mansion compared to most of the tourists out there. They're only jealous.'

'Hmm, well that might be the case. I just don't like it.'

'Shush.' She began to nibble his neck. 'It's not important.'

Having calmed him down, she sat him in the sofa whilst she mixed him a gin and tonic and slipped one of his tranquilisers into the glass. Ten minutes later he was sleeping like a baby, curled up on the couch. Penny looked down on the man she had married only six years ago. How he had changed. His mood swings were becoming unpredictable and more regular. She wasn't sure how much longer she could handle the situation without obtaining some form of prescription from the doctor for herself. She knew he was taking drugs but so far she had failed to find out where he was getting his supply from.

Retrieving her book from the reading table she walked out of the library and crossed the hall into the kitchen closing the door quietly behind her.

Abbey House, being located on the edge of Glastonbury Abbey and visible by tourists was always going to attract onlookers. On top of that, tourists paid to visit the adjoining Chapel which helped to pay towards the upkeep of the property. As Michael's depression got worse he had begun to hate all visitors and thought that everyone was spying on him. Penny on the other hand enjoyed seeing people around the place. The more people around usually meant more income.

She poured herself a cup of tea and went back to her book. She knew she only had a couple of hours of peace and quiet until the tranquilisers wore off and Michael would be stomping around the house again.

The property had been left to Michael by his father but it was really too big for just two people. Penny had tried to persuade Michael to sell it but he refused. Dating back to the 1830s it offered eighteen bedrooms, some of which his father used to hire out. Today parts of the building had fallen into disrepair and were closed off as there wasn't sufficient income for repairs. Being set in several acres of grounds overlooking the ruins of Glastonbury Abbey, the house still attracted a number of tourists each year. The main attraction being the adjoining Chapel. The local vicar would hold services there at specific times throughout the year with the proceeds going towards the restoration of the house and local community projects.

Penny had always wanted to open the house as a bed and breakfast establishment but Michael wouldn't hear of it. He could just about put up with strangers walking around the grounds. He certainly didn't want them in the house. Most days, the only sound in the house came from the builders who were working on some of the restorations.

Jenny Stevens, their housemaid, had been living in Abbey House for three years and knew how Penny would always calm Michael down.

Michael's ranting and raving had become a daily occurrence and she had learnt to keep out of his way when he was in one of his moods. Having overheard the earlier conversation between Penny and Michael she had waited until Penny had left the library.

Hearing the kitchen door close, she entered the library and picked up the bottle of tablets. Instead of returning them to the kitchen cabinet where they kept all the medicines, she slipped them into her cardigan pocket. Running barefooted up the grand staircase she made her way to her room and like an excited child placed the tablets in the drawer of her dressing table.

Downstairs, Penny had retrieved her keys and handbag and grabbed her coat from the stand and left the house.

It was a bright sunny afternoon but the breeze that swept across the Abbey grounds gave it that chill factor still. She turned the collar up on her coat. Taking a short cut across the grounds she passed the Lady Chapel where a young couple were so engrossed in their love making, they never heard her approach. Seemingly more embarrassed than them, Penny quickened her pace and made her way towards the High Street. Passing the Pilgrim Inn and the local fortune teller's shop she took a quick glance up and down the road before turning into the narrow alleyway that ran between the book shop and the bakers.

Penny climbed the metal staircase to the flat and using the spare key, opened the door quietly and slipped inside. She placed her handbag and book on the sofa and walked across the lounge to the bedroom. The door was open a little so she peered inside. Kelvin Ward was lying on top of the bed, dressed only in pyjama bottoms.

'What kept you?' he asked with a grin on his face.

He watched Penny as she undressed and beckoned her towards him the moment she was naked. She walked around the side of the bed and stood looking down at him. Her nakedness and erect nipples had excited him. Penny knelt on the bed and her hand immediately felt his arousal. She was with Kelvin. If only for a couple of hours.

Stepping out of the shower she could hear Kelvin busy in the kitchen.

'Tea and toast OK?' he called out hearing the hair dryer.

'That sounds good to me.'

Kelvin placed the tea and toast on the small table as Penny entered the kitchen.

'When are you going to leave that idiot husband of yours?'

'Please not now. Let's just enjoy these few hours together today. I've told you. I need to get the timing right before I say anything to Michael.'

'Yeah, yeah I know.'

Penny slammed her cup down on the table.

'It's easy for you,' she shouted. 'You only have yourself to think about.'

'Why don't you make more noise? I'm sure the old girl in the bookshop will hear you one day.'

Penny's face reddened.

'I'm sorry. I'd better be on my way. I left Michael a note saying I was just popping out to the bookshop. That was some two hours ago.'

Kelvin walked around the table as Penny stood up. He pulled her towards him and kissed her on the lips.

'Promise me, you'll sort this out,' he said.

'I will. Just be patient, that's all I ask.'

4

The hustle and bustle of Fulham and the city now seemed a thousand miles away and in some ways almost a different lifetime ago.

John Wesley was sat on the low brick wall that divided the lawn from the patio area in their country garden. Wesley and Jane had now been married for over a year and had moved down to Street in the West country following his transfer from London. They found Jasmine Cottage purely by chance.

Having spent a morning looking into local estate agents windows they had travelled to Glastonbury for lunch and were discussing some of the properties they wanted to view, when the waitress who was in the process of collecting their plates interrupted.

'Excuse me. I do hope you don't think I'm being rude, but I couldn't help but overhear you talking about property for sale. You see, my auntie has just moved into an old people's home and wants to sell her cottage but she hasn't put it on the market yet. A pretty little place it is, real picture postcard, if you know what I mean. It's in Street, just a couple of miles from here.'

'Oh that sounds lovely,' said Jane. 'That's where we've just driven from. I don't suppose you know where we could obtain some details from? Or maybe how we could arrange a viewing?'

'I can do more than that. If you are able to wait until three o'clock when I finish, you can follow me there. Auntie gave me the keys only last weekend so I can keep a check on the post.'

That was nearly eighteen months ago. It was love at first sight. Jane and Wesley moved in within two months. Jasmine Cottage stood at the end of a small un adopted cul-de-sac with fields to the rear leading down to a small stream that ran through the heart of the village. The cottage was nothing like the flat that Wesley had had in Fulham or the house that Jane once owned in Kensington.

Outside, the porch entrance was surrounded by Honeysuckle and Roses, and the small front garden was enclosed by a tall thick privet hedge that gave the property an air of privacy.

Inside, the rooms were small, but cosy, with dark wood beams running across low ceilings and flagstone floors that had probably never been even. The kitchen was new, but still included a range cooker and the original open fireplace. The only change they had made to the property was to bring the outside toilet inside, adding a downstairs shower at the same time. The uneven flagstone flooring in all the downstairs rooms gave one a feeling of past history. Original sash cord windows still looked out proudly at the front of the property. In the front room, several horse shoes hung around the picture rail. An ancient custom to bring good luck to all those who lived within.

Jane was in the back garden busy planting half a dozen new small plants she'd just purchased in the village.

'They don't look very straight,' said Wesley rolling a cigarette. Crawling around on her hands and knees, Jane simply looked up and raised her eyebrows. Wesley laughed.

'I'll go and make some tea.'

'Yeah good idea. Do make yourself useful for a change,' Jane replied with a smirk on her face.

Wesley walked back into the house and filled the kettle. He plugged it in before checking his mobile which he'd left on the kitchen worktop charging. He had one new message. It was PC Philips just providing a brief update regarding some dodgy bank notes that had been circulating the local area. Laughing to himself, Wesley left the phone on charge and made the tea. Back in Fulham he would have had twenty or more texts by now. The chance to transfer down to Somerset was too good an opportunity to turn down and Wesley was beginning to feel more relaxed than he'd been in years.

'Where are we eating tonight?' Jane asked as he carried the tea out into the garden.

'What's your fancy girl?'

'I was wondering what the new Italian restaurant was like in the village. It's one of the few places we haven't tried. I hear it's quite expensive.'

'Let's give it a try then. It's your turn to pay,' Wesley replied laughing.

It was early evening and the walk into the village took them past the local church and the village hall. The last of the sun's rays were still peeking through the trees as Dorothy Hallerton was hanging bunting outside the village hall in preparation for the following day's Spring festival.

'Good evening, Mrs Wesley. Hello Inspector,' she said rather sheepishly. Dressed in a flowery frock, tights and an old pair of trainers, she looked quite a sight.

'Dorothy, it's time you called us Jane and John don't you think?'

'Oh as long as you don't mind. Your husband being a policeman and all that.' She was stood on a chair trying to reach the hook above the hall door to attach the bunting.

'Here give me that,' said Wesley reaching for the end of the cord and wrapping it over the hook. 'We can't have you falling off that chair.'

'Oh I wish I had a strapping young man like him around the place,' she said to Jane as Wesley helped her get down.

'It's the first thing he's done all day,' Jane replied winking to her.

'You're both looking very smart,' said Dorothy. Are you going somewhere nice?'

'We're going to the new Italian restaurant. Have you been there?'

'Me? No,' Dorothy replied looking somewhat embarrassed.

'The last time my Eddie took me anywhere was during the war when we had to run to the air raid shelter,' she laughed. She thanked Wesley for helping with the bunting.

Passing the local school and art college they entered the High Street and walked towards Crispin Hall. Built in the 19th century, it now provides the entrance to the new shopping centre where the Italian restaurant was located.

A young waiter greeted them and led them to a table near the window. It was hard to tell if he was Italian or whether he was a local lad with a poor Italian accent.

They ordered a bottle of Pinot Grigio Blush and Jane studied the menu whilst Wesley sat observing the other customers.

Having come to a decision about what she was going to order Jane looked across the table.

'John Wesley. You are so nosey,' she exclaimed thrusting the menu towards him.

'Sorry. I was just looking to see if I recognised anyone.'

Jane looked down her nose at him knowing too well that wasn't the case.

'You're not on duty tonight,' she whispered.

'Oh that's a shame,' he replied winking at her.

'I meant for work.'

Jane blushed as she placed her napkin over her lap.

They spent a pleasant evening eating their way through soup, pasta, steak in white wine and Dover sole, washed down with two bottles of wine and Irish coffee.

The manager had recognised Jane as he said he and his daughter had been in the bookshop a few days ago and Jane had served them. Jane couldn't remember him but thought she remembered his daughter who had been dressed like a hippy which looked so strange for someone so young.

'If we were still in London, we'd never have organised this,' said Jane as she reached across the table to take his hand.

'I know and long may the peace and tranquillity last.'

Wesley raised his glass.

'I think we should do this every weekend.'

Jane swirled the remains of her free brandy around the bottom of her glass and looked around the restaurant at the other tables. The restaurant was full and the manager was offering his apologies to a young couple who stood in the doorway who hadn't booked.

'It looks as if the whole village is in here.'

'Sure is popular,' Wesley replied rolling a cigarette.

Jane looked down her nose at him. It was a look that Wesley knew well, which meant that Jane didn't approve.

'Don't worry. I'm not going to light it in here.'

Wesley went to the bar to pay the bill as the young waiter came across to clear their table.

'So where's the waiter from?' Wesley asked as they walked back through the village.

'He's from Taunton. He's only been working there for a fortnight. Apparently there's not a lot of work in Taunton so he decided to look further afield. He's only nineteen. He's taken a room above the restaurant.'

Wesley started to laugh.

'What's wrong with you?' she asked squeezing his hand.

'You moan at me about not switching off and the next moment you're interrogating the poor waiter.'

'Of course I was. He's very fit.'

They were both still laughing when they reached home.

5

The film had been about a group of hitchhikers travelling around the US. Slowly but surely they were being murdered by an unknown assailant who was taking his revenge out on them following the death of his girlfriend who had been killed by someone who had been camping in the woods on the outskirts of his local town.

Colin had tried to keep awake but tiredness had eventually won the day. When Suzie tapped him on the shoulder he wasn't sure where he was for a moment.

He smiled as she straightened the collar of his jacket and pulled him towards her before kissing him on the cheek. Walking out of the cinema, they crossed the road heading towards the High Street.

'Did you enjoy the film?' Suzie asked with a sarcastic grin on her face.

'I'm sorry. It's been a long week. I do remember that guy getting shot in the bar.'

'He was the first one to be murdered. There were three others after that.'

'Oh was there?' he replied looking somewhat embarrassed. She squeezed his hand and kissed him again on the cheek. It was a typical Friday night in Bath and the streets were crowded with both students and tourists alike.

'Pizza or a pint?' Colin asked as light rain began to fall.

'Oh you do spoil me,' Suzie replied giggling.

They agreed the pub would be the best bet as it was already quarter past ten, so they headed for the Kings Arms in the High Street as the first two pubs they passed had queues of people outside trying to get in.

Although the pub was busy they were served quite quickly and managed to find a small table near the window. By now the rain was falling heavier and hammered against the stained glass window.

'So what do you think of my idea about us going away for a weekend?' Colin asked as he threw his jacket over the back of the chair.

'Oh Colin, I don't know. Please don't get me wrong I'd love to say yes. I'm just concerned about my parent's reaction. I've told you how protective they've been since my divorce. Peter was violent and even after the divorce he sent me threatening messages.'

'I know Suzie, but you have a life to live and your parents really need to move on from there.'

'It's easy for you to say though. They took it all so badly. You see it was Dad who first introduced me to Michael. He blames himself for everything.'

'Would you prefer it if I spoke with them?'

'Colin, I do appreciate your concerns. I really do but can we please just hold on for a while? I know it's a lot to ask, but once they get to know you, I'm sure they'll be a lot happier. Tell me you don't mind.'

'I don't mind at all. The last thing I want to do is make your life difficult but I do want to see more of you and if that means having to talk with your parents then that's fine.'

'Thank you Colin. I was scared you would tell me to forget it and say we wouldn't be seeing one another again.'

'Don't be silly,' he replied as the last bell went. 'What, when it's your turn to buy the drinks.'

He watched her as she made her way through the crowded bar. Her long blonde hair hung down below her shoulders. She was wearing a light blue V-neck jumper that showed a glimpse of her petite breasts. With long slender legs and a slim line waist that clung tightly to her short pencil skirt, Colin sat back and admired the view as she waited to be served.

A few of the younger students who stood at the far end of the bar were getting raucous and the barman who had seen it all before used his customer experience in calming them down and politely reminding them that the last bell had just rung.

Suzie had been served and stood talking to a group of friends before returning to the table.

'Who's that?' Colin asked pointing towards the crowd who were now beginning to disperse.

'Oh they're mostly people I know from school days. Actually, Brian, the youngest is still at school.'

'I thought most of them looked young.'

'Everyone looks young to you,' Suzie laughed and pulling him towards her, kissed him on the lips. They received a few wolf whistles from a group of lads seated at another table. Colin looked more embarrassed than Suzie and promptly drank from his glass.

'So where do you plan us spending a weekend?' Suzie asked reaching across the table and stroking his arm. 'Somewhere exotic?'

'I was thinking about Minehead,' he replied rather sheepishly.

'You're such a romantic,' she laughed. 'That's what I like about you.'

They were amongst the last of the crowd to leave the pub and began the half a mile walk downhill to the bus station. Although it was early May there was still a chill to the evening air but the rain had now stopped. Suzie pulled the collar up of her leather jacket and wrapped her arm around Colin's waist. She seemed relaxed as they strolled back to the bus station.

The station was a hive of activity as numerous people hung around waiting for some of the last buses to leave for the night. A commotion started at the front of one of the queues as the bus driver refused to let two young lads get on his bus as they were drunk. It was twenty minutes later before the late night bus pulled into the station. The two of them sat on one the benches whilst waiting for the replacement driver to appear.

'I don't like leaving you like this. One day I'll learn to drive. Are you sure you don't want me to order a cab?'

'I'm fine, Colin. I've been getting the bus all my life and it stops less than a quarter of a mile from home. The cab is far too expensive. Anyway I would rather you saved the money towards our weekend away.'

'So I can book it then?'

'You impatient fool. Wait for me to introduce you to Mum and Dad. As soon as they get to know you then I'll drop it into the conversation that we're going away with a group of friends for a weekend. Yes?'

'OK but please arrange it sooner rather than later. I'm not as young as I used to be,' he replied with a smirk on his face.'

Just then they heard the sound of the bus engine starting up. Putting a hand around the back of his neck, Suzie kissed him before getting on the bus.

Colin waited until the bus began to pull away before turning around and starting the long walk back to the University. He never saw the stranger board the bus as it turned out of the garage.

6

It was Saturday morning and Wesley was enjoying a lay in. Something he never experienced in all the years he worked in London. He and Jane had spent the previous evening at the new Italian restaurant and had arrived home just after midnight. He turned over to cuddle up to her just as his mobile rang.

Sighing, he checked the phone to see who the caller was before answering.

'Hello son, what's up?'

PC Adam Broad was only eighteen years of age and from the day they'd first met Wesley had treated him like a son. The young ginger haired, freckle faced lad, looked like he'd just left school and walked in the ungainly way that most teenagers do whilst they're still growing.

'Sorry to bother you, Sir, but we've just received a call at the station from a very distressed lady in Glastonbury who says she's found a dead body.'

'Found a body? Where?' He sat up in bed.

'Up on the Tor. Near the Abbey. A lady was walking her dogs. Two collies. It appears that one of them wouldn't come down the slope when she called him back. When she climbed up to get him she found him sat barking at the body. PC Philips is on his way there now.'

Having just woken, Wesley was trying to gather his thoughts.

'OK. Get the whole area cordoned off and get forensics up there. I'll meet you there in half an hour.'

'Just one thing. The Tor is a popular place. It's going to be hard to keep the public away.'

'I appreciate that,' Wesley replied slipping out of bed heading towards the bathroom.

'Go and help Martin to cordon off the road at the bottom of the hill. Apart from forensics I don't want anyone else up on the Tor today.'

He showered and dressed before telling Jane of the situation.

'Oh my God! That's awful. What on earth would someone be doing up on the Tor at that time of night? Assuming that is, that they were there last night'

'I don't know,' he sighed. 'I only hope I find the answer. What was I saying last night about peaceful weekends?'

By the time Wesley parked up, there was already a crowd of gathered along the taped off area. He threw his jacket on and turned up the collar. Being high up and exposed, The Tor was several degrees colder than the town down below. He ducked under the tape that cordoned off the crime scene, leaving PC Martin Philips facing a multitude of questions from the public.

PC Adam Broad greeted him on the slope. The young lad looked grey even in the early morning light.

'You OK son?' Wesley asked.

'Yes thank you, Sir.'

'Is this the first corpse you've seen?'

'Yes.'

Wesley nodded and patted him on the shoulder.

'Go down to the gate and help Martin. He's going to need all the help he can get in keeping those reporters at bay.'

'OK, Sir.'

'What have we got Terry?' he asked breathing heavily as he approached the forensic team half way up the Tor.

Wesley knew he was a little overweight these days and climbing the grassy slope of the Tor was hard work.

'Bloody hangover that's what I've got,' Terry Austin answered standing up. He removed his plastic gloves and shook hands.

The two men had only known one another for a year but they had already become good friends.

Terry knew that Wesley appreciated the difficult job he had. He was grateful that he was one of the coppers he worked with who didn't expect all the answers straight away.

'Young female. Early guess would be mid-twenties. Given the marks on the body I'd suggest she was probably strangled.'

'Out here?'

'Yes. Whoever killed her, committed the crime here I'd say.'

'Any idea when?'

'I thought you'd ask that. I would estimate somewhere between midnight and two o'clock this morning. I can't be more accurate at present.'

'Any signs of sexual assault?'

'Can't be sure as yet, but I don't think so. Nothing obvious in any case. There's no sign of bruising anywhere and her clothes are all intact.'

Wesley peered over Terry's shoulder to where the body lay but only the back of the victim's head was visible face down in the grass. Apart from her lower legs and feet, the rest of her body was hidden by clothing.

'Local girl too,' said Terry.

'What makes you so sure she's a local girl?'

'Bus ticket in her jeans pocket. It's the N17. Runs between here and Bath,' he said handing it over.

'Hmm. She could be a student from the University who'd just spent the night in Glastonbury,' said Wesley relighting his roll up.

'Any other form of ID?'

'Nothing I'm afraid. If she was carrying a handbag or any other items, then someone has removed them.'

'Anything else you can add right now?'

'I can't be certain. But I'd say she was strangled by someone taller than her judging by the finger indentations at the front of the neck.'

'So she may have seen her attacker?'

'It's possible. I'd guess she came up here with someone. Otherwise why would she have been on the Tor on her own in the first place? If you look at the footprints on the path, I'd say she walked up here with someone. The trouble is that last night's heavy rain has washed away most of the prints. The grass has been flattened in a few places near where the body was found so I think the poor girl put up quite a struggle.'

'Yeah, good point,' said Wesley looking down at the grassy bank and the sodden pathway.

'OK, thanks, Terry. I'll get the public moved when you're ready to take the body away.'

'Thanks. Pop over to the lab later. Hopefully I'll be able to provide you with a bit more data once I can start work on the body. What a lovely way to spend a Saturday afternoon.'

Wesley trudged back down the Tor trying to work out how to keep the press out and trying to remove any grotesque thoughts of the pathologist dissecting the poor girl's torso.

After escaping the clutches of the TV crew and sightseers, Wesley left orders for the area to be completely cordoned off before phoning Jane.

'I'm on my way to the station.' He gave Jane a quick update and said he'd call later.

The local press were already stood by his car as Wesley crossed the road. Pete Bentley was a typical press officer who could smell a story a mile away but he'd met his match in Wesley. After repeatedly explaining that he had nothing to say except that a body had been found on the Tor, Bentley walked away with his tail between his legs like a young child who had the sulks.

By the time Wesley arrived back at the station, two more press guys from Bath were already waiting for him. Having wasted more than ten minutes advising them there was no more he could tell them at this stage he walked past the reception desk and went straight into his office closing the door behind him. He made a couple of quick calls then replaced the receiver and called WPCs Mandy Tredwell and Alison Bolt into his office.

He motioned to them both to take a seat whilst he rolled a cigarette.

'OK. All we know so far is that the victim is female, around mid-twenties. There's no apparent sign of sexual assault and it looks as if she died of strangulation. Time of death is estimated between midnight and two a.m.'

'Do we know who the girl is?' Mandy asked.

'No. But it's possible she lived fairly local. Forensics found a bus ticket in her pocket.' He extracted the ticket from his coat pocket and handed it across the table.

'I'm told it's the local night bus. Runs between Bath and Glastonbury.

Mandy, you're from around these parts. Have a wander around the village then pop into town. See what the local gossip is. You know what I mean, anyone not come home yet from last night.'

'Sure thing.'

'Alison. Give the main bus garage in Bath a visit. Try and find out who the late night driver was. See if he remembers seeing the girl and whether she was with anyone.'

'I'll meet you both back here later. If there's anything urgent call me on my mobile. I'm just going to pop round to see Eddie Hallerton. There are some dodgy bank notes in circulation and I believe he knows where they originate from. There's nothing else I can do from here at the moment.'

7

Sally put the two cups of tea down on the small table and switched on the TV to listen to the news. As she raised the cup to her lips she stopped to stare at the screen. The local TV station reporter was stood outside the gates to Glastonbury Abbey just a short walk from the entrance to the Tor.

'David, come and look at this!' she shouted grabbing the remote control to turn up the volume. The reporter was asking Inspector Wesley where the corpse was found.

'The body of a young female was discovered around six-thirty this morning by a woman walking her dogs.'

'Are we looking at a murder case?' the reporter asked.

'Early signs would certainly indicate that a struggle took place but I can't confirm anything else until we get the report back from pathology and forensics.'

'So you do believe the young lady was killed on the Tor.'

'As I say, the pathology unit and forensic team will provide the answers after further examinations have taken place.'

The TV screen then reverted back to the studio.

'Oh my God. Can you believe that? Had we not decided to give the Tor a miss because of the worsening weather, we may have seen that poor girl yesterday and possibly her murderer.'

'Yeah maybe you're right. Either way it's horrible.'

'I think it will be a few days before the police allow the public on the Tor,' said Sally switching the TV off.

'I always feel sorry for the relatives and friends,' said David, returning to the bathroom.

'What would someone be doing on the Tor at that time in the morning?'

'That's a question for the police to answer. At the moment I doubt if they know if she was killed there or somewhere else.'

'Surely no one would be able to carry a dead body onto the Tor. It's far too steep,' said Sally.

'Yeah good point. I would think whoever murdered the poor girl, did so after they had both walked up but as you said just now, why would anyone want to be on the Tor that time of the morning or even overnight. It's not as if you could watch the sunset. It was so foggy and damp this morning. The visibility up there would have been poor to say the least.'

'I suppose they could have walked up there last night?' Sally replied.

'I'm sure we'll know all the answers soon. The forensic team and the pathologist will know for sure. They have such advanced techniques these days. They have the ability to find a single hair in a field of corn.'

Sally switched the television off as a shiver went down her spine.

After waiting impatiently for David to get dressed they eventually walked into the town centre deciding that an early pub lunch was what they needed. It was a fairly warm morning now and the early mist had begun to disappear. Although they both decided on wearing tee shirt and jeans they both carried jumpers. As they entered the new shopping arcade it was Sally who spotted Colin Dempster coming out of the newsagents.

'Hi Colin!' she called but he appeared not to hear.

'Hey Colin!' shouted David who letting go of Sally's hand strode across the road to grab Colin by the shoulder.

'We've been calling you, you deaf old bird,' David said as Colin turned to face him. David couldn't help but notice how down he looked.

'Hey what's up? You look like someone who won the lottery but lost their winning ticket.'

'Hi you two,' he replied just as Sally caught up with them.

'Sorry I was miles away. How are you both?'

'We're fine, but you look awful,' said Sally. 'Are you feeling OK?'

'I'm fine really. Just a bit down in the dumps. Being selfish really, I was hoping to see Suzie again today but I can't get hold of her.'

He explained how and why she took the bus home the previous evening saying she'd give him a call but he hadn't heard anything from her.

'I expect her parents gave her a bit of grief about going out,' said Sally not sure if it was the right answer to give.

'I'm sure you'll see her at University on Monday and she will explain everything.'

'We had such a lovely evening,' Colin replied looking down to the floor.

'Well, as Sally said I'm sure she'll explain her reasons,' said David. 'We're just going for a pub lunch. Would you care to join us?'

'No I'm fine but thanks. I've got some shopping to do and if I stop for a drink now I know I won't shop later. I'll see you two in the week.'

He kissed Sally on the cheek and patted David on the shoulder before walking away.

'He looks really down,' said Sally.

'Yeah. Sure is unlike him.'

Just as they turned the corner, heading away from the shopping centre, they walked straight into an agitated Pete Stanley.

'Oh, sorry. I wasn't looking where I was going,' Pete stammered.

'What on earth is up with you lately?' David asked.

'One minute you're arguing with someone in University, the next you're running down the road like a scared rabbit.'

Pete held his hands up.

'I'm sorry. I've got someone chasing me for the rent money. That was the guy you saw me talking to back in the University. He's a nasty piece of work and I'm trying to avoid him while I get the money together.'

'OK, but take care of yourself,' David replied.

'Everyone seems a bit touchy today,' Sally remarked.

Some fifteen minutes later, sitting at a table in a small café just off the High St, Colin Dempster phoned Suzie's mobile for the third time that morning but the result was the same as on the previous occasions. The phone went straight to voicemail. Damn, he said to himself. He could only guess she had gone straight to bed last night and was now having a lay in. He typed another text.

Thanks again for a lovely evening. See you in Uni. Colin x

He assumed it was probably going to be difficult for her to reply in any case, especially as her parents had such control over her.

At the same time, Wesley was pulling his car into the Rose and Crown car park in Street. He stepped out of the car just as Eddie Hallerton appeared along the country lane.

'I'd get someone to look at those scratches on your car,' said Eddie walking over and pointing to the front of the vehicle. Wesley bent down to take a look. Sure enough there were numerous small scratches under and around the front bumper.

'It's those small stones on these un adopted roads. The local garage survives on them repairs,' he laughed.

Cursing the state of his new car's body work Wesley stood up and pressed the key fob to lock the vehicle.

'Does Mrs Wesley know you're out for a quick pint?'

'Actually Eddie, I'm here on police business.'

'Oh, someone we know?'

'Yes, you. I want to talk to you about forged notes.'

The colour drained from Eddie's face.

'Let's go inside and you can buy me a coke whilst we have a little chat.' He took a seat at a small table by the window as Eddie went to the bar to order the drinks. Eddie looked the typical country gardener. Wearing his usual collarless blue and white striped shirt with the sleeves always rolled up, braces and a pair of blue cords that were too short even for Eddie's five foot seven inch frame. Eddie returned to the table, placed the drinks down and rolling up his flat cap placed it into his jacket pocket.

They had only been talking for five minutes when Wesley's mobile rang.

'Excuse me for a minute,' he said. Leaving Eddie sat at the table he walked to the far side of the lounge bar where no one could hear him.

'Wesley here.'

'Hi, Sir. It's Adam. This may or may not be connected to the murdered girl but we've just received a phone call from the guys over at Bath. A Mr Reginald

Potter phoned this morning saying that his daughter has not returned from a night out last night and they're concerned because it's so out of character.'

'I've heard that story many times,' Wesley sighed. 'Anyhow, have you got the address?'

'Yes it's a place called Ashcott. It's a small village not far from here.'

'OK get over there, and see what information you can gleam from the parents. Get a photo of the girl, recent one if you can. Hopefully there's no link to last night but you never know. I'll be back at the station just after midday so give me a call if you're going to be late.'

'Sure thing,' replied the young PC as he went in search of the station's push bike. PC Philips had already gone out in the only pool car taking two other PCs over to the Tor to keep tourists and locals away from the murder scene, so it looked as if he was going to have to start pedalling.

When Wesley returned to the table, Eddie was looking dejected.

'I wasn't to know they were dodgy,' he said looking down at the table.

'Eddie. Don't play games with me. You may act dumb at times, but I for one don't believe you would be stupid enough not to realise you'd be dealing in dodgy bank notes.'

The sweat was running down Eddie's forehead and he continually ran his hand across his brow.

'Look, right now I've got more important issues on my plate,' said Wesley. 'However, give our little conversation some thought. We'll catch up tomorrow.'

He walked away leaving Eddie staring into his beer glass.

Wesley arrived back at the station just ahead of PC Philips who pulled up alongside Wesley's car. They exchanged glances as Wesley lit a cigarette.

'Hello Martin,' said Wesley as he approached the side door to the station.

'Good hunting?'

'Not much so far.' Wesley started to laugh.

'What's funny?'

'Take a look behind you.'

PC Adam Broad was struggling up the hill with the push bike looking as if he'd just completed the Tour de France. He lent the bike up against the wall and removed his cycle clips. He walked towards them with a reddened face and ruffled hair.

'Hello,' he panted still trying to catch his breath. Wesley smirked whilst Martin had to look away laughing.

'Go and get yourself a drink and meet me in my office in ten minutes,' said Wesley. 'And lock that bike away. The kids around here will steal it if you leave it there.'

Wesley listened to the feedback from his two young PCs.

'Sorry to say there's very little gossip in the village,' said Martin.

'I think people are often frightened to speak up when something like this happens.'

'OK but let's keep our ears open.'

'What about you Adam?'

'I did phone the local cabs. They haven't come up with anything yet but they are going to supply me with a list of the late night drivers.'

Wesley nodded.

'Actually I've just got back from Mr and Mrs Potter's place in Ashcott.' He took a small 6 x 4 inch photo out of his pocket and handed it across the table.

'It's their daughter Suzie. Taken last year on the day she started University as a lecturer. According to her parents she went into Bath last night to have a drink with a girlfriend. Name of Melony Forbes. Apparently they both work at Bath University. Suzie's father explained that Suzie had a very traumatic marriage before getting divorced last year. The old man used to knock her about a bit and has threatened her since.'

'Do we have a name?' asked Wesley.

Adam retrieved his notebook and flipped over several pages.

'Yes, name of Michael Parkinson. Now believed to be living in Somerset, working at the holiday camp. Suzie was due home on the late night bus but has failed to turn up yet and has not made contact either, which according to both parents is extremely out of character. Her father says he's phoned her mobile numerous times and left several messages but she hasn't replied to any of them.'

Wesley sat back in his chair and took a deep breath, pausing to consider the options.

'OK Adam. Find Michael Parkinson and find out where he was last night and when he last spoke to Suzie.'

Wesley stopped to light a cigarette.

'Martin, drive over to Bath. Have a chat with Melony Forbes. See if she can shed some light on Suzie's movements. I'll get a few blown up photos of Suzie done and head over to the mortuary.'

'Any questions?'

'What do we say to the press? There's already half a dozen outside now,' asked Martin.

'Leave the press to me.'

'Adam, any questions?'

'Only Mr and Mrs Potter. They asked me to keep them updated. What do I tell them?'

'Nothing for the time being. Let me have their number. I'll call them after I've been to the mortuary.'

8

Michael Westbrook woke with a thumping headache. Grabbing his dressing gown, he made his way downstairs to the kitchen where he could hear someone handling cutlery.

'Good morning my dear,' said Penny glancing over her shoulder. 'Sit down, I'll make coffee.'

'God, my head is killing me. How many drinks did I have last night?'

'Just a few.'

'But I've slept for over eight hours and that's on top of sleeping most of yesterday afternoon.'

'You obviously needed the sleep,' she replied placing his coffee on the kitchen table along with his tablets.

'Where's that bloody Jenny? She should be making the coffee. That's what we pay her for?'

'Oh, Michael. It's Jenny's day off. She's probably still asleep.'

'Asleep? I'll never understand why we employed a maid who only works six days a week,' he said sipping his coffee.

'Now it's not like you to moan about anything.'

Penny stood behind him and began to massage his shoulders.

At forty-two years of age, Michael Westbrook was the owner of Abbey House which stood in the grounds surrounding Glastonbury Abbey. He had inherited the estate along with some of its debts from his father. The adjoining grounds were purchased by the National Trust with the written agreement that Michael also received ten per cent of the public admission monies. Michael and Penny now retained sole ownership of Abbey House and the adjoining Chapel that stood at the rear of the grounds, at the foot of the Tor.

He had had a hard upbringing with a father who constantly beat him and a mother who was a registered alcoholic. The long term effect was that he now lived on tranquilisers to control his own insecurities. People scared him. Often life scared him.

'I expect them damn tourists will be staring at us again today,' he remarked looking out of the kitchen window. Penny didn't answer him. She was searching through her handbag for some money.

'What are you looking for?'

'It's OK I've found it,' she replied holding up a twenty pound note.

'I'm going to walk into the town. I want to buy a book from that nice little bookshop in the High Street. Do you want me to get you anything while I'm out?'

'Something to shoot them damn tourists with.'

'OK my dear. I'll see what I can find you.' She kissed him on the forehead as she headed out to the hallway.

'Don't forget to take your tablets. I've got a front door key!' she shouted but Michael didn't reply. He was still staring out of the kitchen window.

It was just after midday and Glastonbury was already busy as a number of tourist coaches were already parked up in the main visitors car park.

Penny weaved her way in and out of the crowds and headed straight for the Speaking Tree bookshop. The doorbell tinkled as Penny closed the door behind her.

'Good afternoon, Jane. How are you? It's going to be another busy day by the looks of the number of people out there.'

Jane, just about visible behind the counter was busy ripping open a large cardboard box that contained the latest delivery of paperbacks.

'Hello Penny, yes we've not had a quiet moment all day. How are you?'

'I'm very well thanks.'

'How's Michael? I haven't seen him in town for a couple of weeks.'

'He's fine thanks Jane. He's happiest at home. He thinks all tourists should be banned and goes out of his way to avoid them but he's happy to collect their entrance money and the money they spend on brochures when they visit the Chapel,' she replied laughing.

'We've got a few new novels in this week,' said Jane reaching under the counter. 'We haven't even unboxed them yet.'

'That's OK. I'm actually looking for something from the historical section. Our housemaid Jenny keeps asking me things about the history of the Abbey and the Tor but I'm embarrassed to say I don't know the history. Michael says there used to be a whole collection of books about the Chapel in our small library at home, but I can't find them. I expect they've been put away somewhere. In any case, it's always nicer to give someone a new present rather than something second hand.'

'I think you'll find several local history books on the middle shelf over in the corner there,' said Jane pointing. 'If you can't find what you're looking for, there's always the Tourist office but their brochures can be quite basic, and I shouldn't say it, rather expensive too.'

'I really wanted something nice. It's Jenny's birthday in a couple of days, you know, our housemaid. So I want to give her something a bit more expensive. More of a present if you know what I mean.'

Jane went off in search of a book on the myths of Glastonbury for an elderly couple who had just come into the shop with their grandchildren, while Penny went to choose which book to purchase.

Some ten minutes later after wrapping the books the grandchildren had purchased, Penny handed Jane the book she'd chosen for Jenny.

'I expect your husband has his work cut out right now, what with that poor girls body being found on the Tor.'

'Yes. It's terrible isn't it? I can't understand how someone can do harm to someone else like that.'

'I know this sounds awful, Jane, and I don't mean it that way, but a murder in the town could destroy our tourist trade.'

'Penny, I do know what you mean. It's not exactly the kind of headline any town wants, especially a town like ours that relies so heavily on tourists.'

Jane finished wrapping the book and handed Penny a gift tag to sign which she then stuck to the outside.

'Do come over to our place one afternoon,' said Penny placing the book in her bag after handing the money over to Jane.

'I'd love to. Thank you.'

'Here you are.' Penny handed Jane a card with her telephone number.

'Oh thanks. That's very kind. I'll call you on one of my days off.'

'Please do. We'll have tea in the grounds if the weather is nice and I'll give you a tour of our home. We're having one of the wings refurbished. It's not been touched in years and was actually closed off a few years before I moved in. We've had to have a safety inspector in just to confirm the building's not going to collapse.'

'In that case, I'll stick to the safe parts if you don't mind.'

The two women laughed.

'The card with my number on it will also get you past the main entrance to the grounds without having to queue or pay.'

'Thank you. I look forward to seeing your lovely home.'

9

Wesley entered the mortuary. The clinical smell of chemicals always made him feel nauseous so he wanted to make his visit as brief as possible.

He found Terry Austin stood at the far end of the corridor speaking to an elderly woman who looked as if she had been crying. Wesley stood back for a few moments out of courtesy, taking the opportunity to roll a cigarette. The elderly lady eventually took her leave and gave him an acknowledged glance as she made her way out of the building. Terry shook Wesley's hand and led him into the cold steel room.

'I'll never get used to that part of the job. Her and the old man,' he said nodding in the direction of a corpse lying on a trolley up against the wall. 'Were married for over fifty years.'

'Life can be cruel my friend,' Wesley replied.

'Even more so in her case. She buried her only son just a few months ago. He died of a heart attack. She's on her own now.'

Terry pushed the corpse back into the recess making sure the door was closed.

'So, I guess you've come for an update on the girl?' he asked as he walked over to where another row of steel cabinets stood.

'Yeah, I've got a photo here of someone who's been missing since yesterday,' said Wesley.

Terry selected one of the drawers from the bottom row and pulled hard on the handle as the covered corpse rolled out towards him on a metal slab.

'She was definitely strangled. My best guess is between midnight and two a.m. this morning. The other marks on her body would suggest she put up a bit of a fight,' he said as he pulled back the sheet exposing the face and upper body.

'Oh God,' Wesley exclaimed.

'What's wrong John?'

Wesley handed him the photo he was holding in his hand. It was a match. Terry sighed.

'Local girl?'

'Yeah. Parents phoned this morning. Said she hadn't come home. They believe she went to meet a girlfriend last night for a few drinks in Bath.'

'If she'd gone to Bath, how on earth did she end up in Glastonbury?'

Wesley shook his head.

'No idea.'

'Any other information yet?' asked Terry covering the girl's face before he slid the body back into the recess.

'None other than that her parents say that Suzie's, oh, that's her name by the way, Suzie Potter. They say her ex-husband was pestering her. Apparently there's history of domestic violence.'

'So you think he could be responsible?'

'Too early to say at this stage, Terry. I've already sent one of boys out to find him though.'

'Well I can tell you that whoever murdered Suzie was wearing gloves. Almost certainly leather, but well worn, or certainly scratched.'

'Was she…?'

'Sexually assaulted? No. Whoever attacked her only had one thing in mind. That was to murder her.'

'OK thanks, Terry. I know you'll want to do more of an autopsy. I'll arrange for someone to bring her parents over later today to confirm identity so you can continue with the autopsy tomorrow. Always such a sad moment. Are you going to be around long?'

'I've got a few other things to get on with, like writing the report for one. Don't worry I'll hang about until they've seen her. I'll do the full autopsy tomorrow and fax you a copy of my report.'

'Much appreciated.'

Wesley shook hands and departed leaving Terry sliding the girl's body back into the recess.

Twenty minutes later he pulled into the police station car park. Street's police station looked just like a picture taken from Dixon of Dock Green. The blue lamp still hung outside the main entrance and the large blue wooden doors gave the appearance of entering Dr Who's TARDIS.

PCs Adam Broad and Martin Philips were sat opposite Wesley whilst he read their reports. Finally after several minutes he put the paperwork down, took a last drag on the remains of his roll up, before rubbing the remains between his thumb and forefinger. A habit that Jane pulled him up on every day.

'OK, good work guys. So our first suspect Michael Parkinson, Suzie's ex-husband is actually out of the country which rules him out.'

'Yeah he's been in France for several days and isn't due back until Wednesday,' said Adam.

'And Suzie's friend Melony Forbes says she had no arrangement to meet Suzie on Friday night, which raises the question as to who Suzie had agreed to meet,' said Martin. 'Having spoken with Melony, she did tell me that Suzie's parents had always been extremely strict with their daughter following her divorce from Michael Parkinson. Apparently she and Suzie had an agreement for some time that if Suzie ever went out on a date, she would tell her parents she'd gone out with Melony. However, she failed to tell Melony who she was actually going to meet.

I have to say, the girl was absolutely distraught. I felt it was inappropriate to question her more than necessary.'

Wesley nodded.

'Did she have anything else to add apart from what you've put in your report?'

'Not really,' replied Martin. 'Except to say that although Suzie was an outgoing character she was also very nervous. Taking into account the way her ex used to treat her it's not surprising.'

Wesley read the text message on his mobile and sat deep in thought whilst rolling another cigarette.

'Suzie's parents have just identified the body and I've arranged for WPC Audrey Harris from Bath to spend time with them today. She's very experienced at handling these situations. I'm going over to the University in the morning to talk with Melony Forbes myself. Whoever it was who killed Suzie, I want them found and quick.'

Wesley sat back in the chair and reached into his jacket pocket for his lighter.

'I don't think we can do anything else today. Martin, I want you to keep an eye on the desk in the morning. Adam, I need you to drive over to Suzie's parents and with the help of WPC Harris take a discreet look around the place, especially the girl's bedroom. See if you can find anything that may provide us with a clue as to who she was expecting to meet. See what you can find out about the girl. She may have kept a diary, anything. I want to know everything there was about Suzie Potter.'

10

It was a drizzly dull grey morning and although the drive to Bath only took Wesley just over fifteen minutes, the journey from one end of Bath High Street to the University, a distance of only four hundred yards took another ten minutes due to the sheer weight of traffic. Wesley pulled up to the barrier and held his ID up to the camera. A muffled voice asked him who he was visiting.

'I'm here to speak with Melony Forbes, one of the students. I believe she is studying Geography. Her lecturer's name is Colin Dempster.'

'OK. Proceed to Level 4 in the multi storey then take the stairs on the East Wing down to Level 2. You'll find Mr Dempster's office there, half way along the corridor. If he's not in his office, you'll find his timetable on the notice board. That will tell you where Melony should be.'

'Thanks,' Wesley replied as the barrier started to lift.

As soon as he opened the door from the car park to the corridor on Level 2 Wesley was astounded with the amount of people making their way to lecture rooms. It was almost like the tube train in London during the rush hour. He found Colin Dempster's room easy enough and knocked loudly on the door. He could hear someone cursing, shuffling books and papers on the other side of the door before it was eventually opened by someone who looked like a typical lecturer.

Dressed in a patterned tee-shirt, loose fitting beige cardigan and blue cords Colin Dempster peered over the top of his small rimmed glasses. Thirty-four years of age, going on fifty-four, he fitted Wesley's mental picture of a Geography lecturer.

'Good morning. Inspector Wesley. I assume you must be Colin Dempster,' said Wesley as they shook hands.

'Please come in. It's a bit of a mess I'm afraid. Can't find a damn thing.'

Wesley surveyed the book and paper littered room but declined to comment.

'Security told me you were on the way up. How can I help you? One of the students drunk again I expect.'

'Actually it's more serious than that. I need to speak with one of your students, a Miss Melony Forbes.'

'Melony? Don't tell me she's in trouble. She's one of the quietest people in the class.'

'It's actually about a friend of hers. A Miss Suzie Potter.'

Colin looked up as he almost dropped the wad of papers he was trying to force into his briefcase.

'Suzie?'

'Yes. Do you know her well?'

Colin hesitated for a second before answering.

'She's a young lecturer here. We've become good friends,' he stammered. Wesley closed the door and pulled up a chair, motioning for Colin to sit down.

'What's wrong?' he asked now looking very concerned.

'I have some bad news Mr Dempster. Suzie's body was found on Glastonbury Tor yesterday. She'd been strangled.'

Wesley shot out of the chair to catch Colin as he slumped towards his desk.

'Are you OK?'

Wesley helped him back into his chair.

'Yes, I'll be fine. It's just such a shock. This must be some kind of joke. Please tell me you're not serious.'

Wesley pulled up a chair and sat facing Colin.

'Sorry Mr Dempster, but I don't joke about murder. I know this is difficult but I need to ask you a few questions.'

Colin nodded.

'When did you last see Suzie?'

Colin looked up, a vacant stare on his face. When he spoke it was the voice of someone in total disbelief.

'Friday. We went to the cinema in town here.' He gulped and his eyes were misting over.

'Take your time,' said Wesley trying to comfort him.

'After the cinema, we popped into the pub for a drink just before closing time.'

'Which pub?'

'The Fox and Hounds.'

'Did you see anyone you knew?'

'There were a few people at the bar who Suzie spoke to. She said they were students from the University.'

'Did you recognise any of them?'

'No. But to be honest I didn't take much notice.'

'How long were you in the pub?'

'We left just after the last bell.'

'Then you drove her home?'

'No, I don't drive. Suzie insisted on getting the bus home on her own. Her parents thought she was out with one of her girlfriends.'

'Melony?'

'Yes. You see she'd had a rough time with her previous marriage and they were kind of being protective I guess.'

'So where did you leave her?'

'We walked to the bus garage and she caught the night bus that travels between Bath and Glastonbury.'

'Do you know what time that was?

'It would have been around half past eleven I guess. Oh God I knew something was wrong. I just knew it.'

'What makes you say that?' Wesley asked intrigued.

'The fact that Suzie never answered my calls. I just assumed she couldn't phone because of her parents,' he replied shrugging his shoulders as the tears began to flow.

Wesley walked across to the small kitchen area and after searching for a glass, poured a glass of water which he handed to Colin.

'Thanks.'

'I know this is difficult but I do need to ask just a couple more questions.'

'Sure. I understand,' Colin replied looking up through tearful eyes.

'How long had you and Suzie been seeing each other?'

'It was our first date. I know that sounds old fashioned. We'd been to bars and restaurants with other people before. You know what I mean. A crowd of us. But we'd never had an evening out before, just the two of us on our own.'

'How long have you known Suzie?'

'She joined the University last September, so about nine months.'

'Did she hang around with any of the students away from University?'

'Only Melony I believe. They've been friends for a few years. They often spent time together. They have similar interests. They're both keen photographers. Melony has a car. An old Vectra. They would often disappear at weekends photographing some place or other. This is an ideal part of the country for that kind of activity.'

'Colin, I have to ask. Can you think of anyone who might want to hurt Suzie? Apart from her ex-husband, who we already know was out of the country.'

Colin put his hands to his face and shook his head. Just then there was a knock on the door. Wesley stood up and made his way across the room. He opened the door to a tall freckle faced girl whose wavy ginger hair looked like a bird's nest that had just been plopped on her head.

'Oh hello. You must be the policeman. The guy at the front desk said he'd sent you up here as you were looking for me.'

'You must be Melony,' Wesley replied offering his hand. He stood back to let her enter the room and she immediately saw Colin sat in the chair. It was obvious he was upset.

'You OK?' Melony asked looking at Colin.

'I've just received some bad news.'

'Please, take a seat,' said Wesley.

'I'd prefer to stand.'

'I'm afraid I have some bad news Melony. It's regarding Suzie,' said Colin.

'I already know,' Melony replied. 'A police officer informed me earlier. Sorry Colin, but I didn't realise it was you that Suzie was meeting.'

Colin looked up as the tears ran down his face.

'It was a last minute decision and I know she was going to tell you.'

'What I don't understand is what she was doing on the Tor? Why was she even in Glastonbury?' she asked a minute later.

It was Colin who spoke next.

'She took the bus home on Friday night. Except she obviously never got home. You see, we had a couple of drinks in the pub before closing time. I walked Suzie back to the bus garage and sat with her until she got on the bus. That's the last time I saw her.'

There was a deafening silence in the room for a few minutes before Wesley spoke.

'I'm going to phone the station to get one of my colleagues over here. Is there anyone on the campus right now who you wish me to inform?' he asked Colin.

'Yes. David Hare. He's a good friend. You'll probably find him in the library this time of day. He does a lot of his marking there.'

After leaving Melony with Colin, Wesley made his way along the corridor to David Hare's room.

'I can't believe it,' said David shaking his head as Wesley broke the news to him of Suzie's murder. 'My God. I don't know what to say. I just feel numb.'

He stood staring into space.

'I want to go to sleep then wake up and find this has all been a bad dream. What is this all about? Why would anyone want to kill Suzie? She never hurt anyone did she?'

'Not that we're aware of,' Wesley replied.

'Didn't her ex-husband beat her up? Have the police spoken to him?'

'Yes we have. He was in France this weekend. He's not the culprit.'

Two minutes later, Wesley stood in the corridor speaking to WPC Tredwell on his mobile.

'Oh my God. Surely not another murder?'

He listened as she gave him the full details. A male this time, found on the Tor.

Leaving both Melony and Colin in the safe hands of WPC Alison Bolt, Wesley returned to the lecturer's room with David. The phone call he'd just taken caused him grave concern.

There must be a link, he said to himself.

'Mr Hare, I understand you teach history in the University.'

'Please call me David. Yes I do. Have done for several years now. How can I help?'

'As you know, Suzie's body was found up on the Tor. I'd like to know the history of the Tor. Can you help me?'

'Yes of course,' David replied. 'What's the interest in the Tor though? I don't understand.'

Wesley moved his chair close to the small table and leaned forward.

'David, can I confide in you?'

'Yes for sure. What is it Inspector?'

'I've just received a call from the station. Another body was found a short while ago. A male this time.'

'Oh my God, where?'

'Within the walls of the tower ruins at the top of the Tor. It looks like a stabbing. I won't know any more until I get over there.'

'So you think there's some connection?' David asked.

'It's too early to tell. However, I have a feeling that the more I know about the history and the geography of the Tor, the better chance I'll have of solving these murders. It would seem that someone knows their way around the place far better than I do.'

'So you think it's someone local committing these crimes?'

'I don't know.' Wesley shrugged his shoulders. 'It's just a gut feeling.'

It took Wesley almost an hour to get back over to Glastonbury where he found PC Philips standing like a sentry by the tower ruins.

Wesley knelt down to examine the corpse.

'Who found the body?'

'A tourist. A Mr Markham. Luckily his two children hadn't got this far. They were playing hide and seek. As soon as Mr Markham reached the top of the Tor and entered the ruins, he found the body slumped against the wall.'

'What time was this?'

'The call came in about two hours ago. That would make it around eight o'clock this morning.'

'Did Mr Markham see anyone else up here?'

'No, he said it was quite misty this morning and had only made his mind up at the last minute to walk to the top as his children had kept pestering him about climbing the Tor.'

'Have you searched the victims clothing?'

'No I thought it best not to touch anything.'

'Yeah quite agree. What about forensics?'

'On their way. I've also got two other PCs in the car park keeping the public away.'

'Yeah I met them at the foot of the Tor.'

'Do you want access to the Abbey grounds closed off too?'

'No Martin. There's no need, so long as we keep the public off of the Tor. Christ, we only re-opened it to the public this morning. Is there any trace of the murder weapon?'

'No, Sir. I've had a quick scan but there's nothing obvious lying around.'

'Whoever did this needed some strength,' said Wesley examining the deep cut across the neck.

'Whoever committed the crime used a long knife,' said Martin squinting at the wound.

'What makes you say that?' Wesley asked standing up to search his pockets for his tobacco.

'The wound is deep. There's a red line at the back of the neck to show that the blade has almost sliced the head off.'

'Have we any idea who the body is?' Wesley lit a roll up.

'Oh yes. Sorry I forgot to mention. His name is Kelvin Ward.'

'Has someone already identified him then?' asked Wesley, looking somewhat confused.

'Yes. Me, Sir. You see I know him. Or knew him I should say. He owned the Speaking Tree bookshop in Glastonbury.'

'The Speaking Tree?'

'Yes the bookshop down in the …'

'I know where it is son. My wife works there.'

Wesley reached for his mobile and walked away from the scene. He hit the button for Jane's mobile but it went straight to voicemail. He left a message just as a call was coming through from the station.

'Wesley speaking.'

'Hi, Sir. It's Mandy here. A Mr Hallerton is waiting for you in reception. He says you asked him to come down to the station.'

'Oh yeah I did. I'd forgotten. I'm just leaving the Tor. I expect you've heard we have a second murder on our hands.'

'Yes it's on the local radio.'

'What? Already?'

'Yes. I Don't know who leaked it but someone has.'

'OK. Tell Hallerton to wait. I'll be back in half an hour. Oh, and put the kettle on would you? I'm gasping.'

'Sure thing.'

Wesley walked back to the where PC Martin Philips was standing near the corpse. The young lad looked frozen.

'Could I ask you for a cigarette please?' he stammered as Wesley approached.

'I didn't think you smoked?'

'I don't normally but then it's not every morning you get to face someone with their head hanging off their shoulders.'

Wesley nodded and smiled.

He remembered the first couple of times he'd been called out to incidents when he was a young cadet. The first one was an old tramp who had died in the night of pneumonia outside a sweet shop but the second one had been a hit and run. By the time he arrived on the scene the forensic team were scraping the remains of a young child off the road.

He handed Martin a roll up and his lighter. The young lad took a deep drag and coughed for several seconds as his face turned blue.

'I'll send a replacement up for you shortly,' Wesley said.

'As soon as forensics have finished and taken the body away you can head back to the station. I assume you have a contact number for our witness?'

'Yes, Sir. I was going to ask him to stay until you arrived but then he had the children with him. It didn't seem appropriate.'

'No that's fine. You did the right thing. Phone Mr Markham and ask him to pop in and write a statement. If he needs transport then arrange for someone to pick him up. After you've done that, you're finished for the day. Just leave me a message to let me know when he's coming in.'

'Thanks, Sir,' he stuttered, still trying to regain his breath following his coughing fit.

11

'You asked me to come down to the station,' said a worried looking Eddie Hallerton when Wesley arrived. Wesley hung his coat on the stand and motioned for Eddie to sit down.

'I'm sorry Mr Wesley I screwed up. When this fella offered me two hundred notes for one hundred quid I thought it was easy money.'

'Hold on, slow down,' said Wesley cutting him off in mid-sentence. 'Give me a chance to sit down.'

Wesley pulled up a chair opposite and began to roll a cigarette. He lit it and took a deep drag before continuing.

'Did it not occur to you that it had to be forged money you were dealing with?'

Eddie hesitated before answering and kept toying with his cap that was resting on his lap.

'I thought it was just to keep me quiet.'

'Keep you quiet? Now I am confused, Eddie. Tell me more.'

'Well you see, the fella that gave me the money, well, he's got his hands in a lot of things, and although I don't say much to anyone, I does keep an eye out and listen to what goes on around these parts.'

Wesley raised his eyebrows.

'And what has been going on?'

'Well it's not for me to say really, Mr Wesley. There are some people around here that wouldn't take too kindly if I started telling you or anyone else some of the things I've heard.'

'If you want me to overlook the dodgy notes you used the other night in the pub, and the dodgy note you handed in at the bookies, I suggest you tell me a few snippets of local gossip,' Wesley replied.

Reluctantly Eddie began his story whilst Wesley drew on his roll up and sat back in his chair. Ten minutes later Wesley sat looking at the list of names and events that Eddie had provided him with. Looking up across the table he could see that Eddie was sweating profusely and nervously tapping his feet.

'So what happens now?' Eddie asked. 'Are you going to arrest me? My old woman is going to kill me.'

He ran his fingers through the few strands of hair left on his head.

'What about you helping me?' said Wesley rubbing the remains of his cigarette between thumb and forefinger across the top of the ash tray that already piled high with tobacco flakes and used matches.

'I don't understand Mr Wesley.'
'I'm sure you've heard about the two murders.'
'Two?'
'Yes. I'm afraid a second body was found a short while ago. A male this time but that's confidential.'
'But I had nothing to do with them,' Eddie shouted standing up.
Wesley raised his hands and beckoned for Eddie to sit down.
'I don't believe for one minute that you do. However, as you've just told me, you seem to know a lot about what's going on in the town and who's who. Why don't you start asking a few of your associates if they've heard anything? Or maybe, someone has seen something. You know what I mean? People heading for the Tor late at night. A stranger in town. Someone asking lots of questions. That kind of thing. Ask around for me, Eddie, and I just might be able to overlook one or two of the things we've discussed.'
Eddie sat biting his lip, staring across the desk. Wesley stood up and walked over to the door.
'Go home to your good lady Eddie. And remember. I want to know about anything that sounds suspicious.'
He opened the door and watched Eddie trudge down the hallway like some school boy who had just received a caning or had been caught playing truant.

12

Denise Wright didn't particularly like working in the Tourist office but it did help to pay towards her university fees. She had little interest in the history of Glastonbury and even less patience when customers came into the shop asking stupid questions about where did so and so live when they were alive, and where was so and so supposed to be buried?

She wasn't your typical university student and couldn't wait for her final exam's days to arrive. She wanted to get her qualifications and start work in London as soon as possible. She had always dreamed of walking around the streets of London, looking into shop windows filled with expensive clothing and jewellery. Going home to her Mayfair residence where the maid would take her coat from her as soon as she entered and declare that dinner would be served shortly. Where she would find her tall, dark haired, good looking husband waiting for her in the parlour pouring her a glass of champagne. Oh well, she could dream.

Denise was a plain looking girl, with short brown hair and just a little over weight. She stood just five feet tall therefore any books above the second row of shelving in the bookshop could only be reached by use of the small wooden step ladder that looked as if it had been built when the shop was, over a hundred years ago.

'Denise, can you open those boxes with the new books in them please. I don't want customers falling over them,' said Mrs Harper pointing to a large unopened box that stood near the doorway.

'Yes, Mrs Harper. I'll just finish putting the magazines out then I'll get the books unpacked.'

'Thank you, Denise. I'll make us a nice cup of tea before it gets busy.'

Denise was pushing the box away from the shop door when suddenly she jumped.

'That looks heavy,' said the visitor standing behind her. Denise looked up. She never heard the customer come into the shop.

'Oh yes. They can be a trifle heavy.'

She stood up straight and wiped her hands on her jeans.

'How can I help you?'

'Oh I'm just browsing,' the young woman replied. 'I live at Abbey House. You know. The big mansion at the back of Abbey grounds.'

'That big white building?'

'Yeah, that's the one,' she laughed. 'I've just realised that I don't know a thing about the Abbey, the estate or any of the local history.'

'Well you've come to the right place here,' said Denise pointing at the shelves of books lining every wall. 'Let me know if you need anything specific.'

'Thank you. May I ask your name?'

'Yes, it's Denise.'

The woman scanned the room and apparently made a decision as to what she was looking for and made her way across to one of shelves on the far wall. Denise studied her for a moment. She seemed younger than most of the people who came into the tourist shop. The majority were middle aged women looking for something to take home to their grandchild or so they said. But this woman seemed cool. Wearing a short light brown leather jacket, brown knee length boots and skin tight jeans, she was dressed how Denise would like to dress, if only she could lose some weight and if only she had some money.

Denise was stood on the step ladder putting the remaining books on the shelf when the woman spoke to her again.

'Well it's been nice to meet you Denise. I'll sure pop in again when I've got more time to look around,' she said heading for the door.

'I'm not here every day. I'm actually studying at Bath University,' Denise called out as the woman closed the door behind her.

'Who was that?' asked Mrs Harper returning with two cups of tea.

'I don't know her name but she seems like a nice lady.'

Denise was still looking out of the Tourist office window watching the woman walk towards the shopping centre.

Mrs Harper started talking about the weather and how it affected the number of tourists and visitors to the shop, but Denise wasn't listening. Her mind was on the woman who had just left the shop.

'Who owns Abbey House?' she asked as Mrs Harper handed her a cup of tea.

'That would be the Westbrook's. A strange couple. She's alright, Mrs Westbrook. Always says hello when passing but he's a weird one that husband of hers. He rarely ventures out of the place and when he does he always looks so angry. Personally I don't think he's very well.'

'What do you think is the matter with him?'

Mrs Harper pointed to her head. 'I think he's a bit, you know. Not quite all there.'

Denise giggled. 'Oh Mrs Harper, you are so funny when you make those faces.'

When they had finished drinking their tea Mrs Harper resumed her daily tasks of keeping the bookstore tidy. However, Denise stood staring out of the window, looking across the road towards Glastonbury Abbey, Abbey House and the Tor beyond. She was dreaming of what it must be like living in such a lovely home, with such wonderful views and having a maid to wait upon you all day.

13

Jane was busy picking weeds away from the garden path when Dorothy Hallerton appeared by the garden gate.

'Hello Jane. How are you my dear? And how's that good looking husband of yours? I do hope you're looking after him.'

'Oh of course, and we're both fine thanks,' said Jane standing up and holding her hands to her back. 'Getting too old for this gardening lark though.' They both laughed.

'I heard about the murders. It's awful isn't it? What's wrong with people these days? I was saying to Eddie that it's just not safe to go anywhere.'

'I know,' Jane replied leaning on the garden gate. 'It's horrible. I was hoping we'd escaped from that kind of thing when we moved out of London but I guess wherever we humans live there's always a chance of it happening to someone.'

'Human nature I suppose,' Dorothy replied shrugging her shoulders.

'I expect your husband will be looking for the murderer though.'

'Yes all part of the job,'

'Does he think it's someone local?'

Jane had a feeling this was going to be question time, so she tried to redirect the conversation.

'I'm sure they'll catch whoever it is. I did hear something though.'

'What was that?' asked Dorothy moving closer hoping to pick up some gossip.

'I heard your Eddie was handed some forged notes the other day.'

Dorothy's face went a crimson colour and the smile disappeared from her face.

'Oh, err ...yes. Mr Wesley did have a chat with Eddie earlier this morning. I think there was some confusion about where a few bank notes originated from,' she replied nervously. 'That's the problem being an odd-job man. People nearly always pay him in cash and you never know what they're giving you is real.'

'I suppose not.' Jane tried to hide the grin on her face.

'Oh well, best be off. I need to get to the butcher's before they close. There's so few butchers left these days. Good ones I mean.'

Jane watched Dorothy walk off and smiled.

You're a wicked person, Jane said to herself.

A short while later Jane had thrown her gardening equipment into the shed, grabbed her handbag, locked the house and found herself running to the bus stop. She'd almost forgotten that she was due to meet Penny today.

It was twenty minutes before the bus arrived. Full of school children. The journey only took fifteen minutes, even though the bus seemed to stop every few seconds to let a group of people off. Jane alighted in the High St, crossed the road and made her way towards the grounds of Glastonbury Abbey. There was a queue of several coach loads of school children near the main entrance so she had to jostle her way through the crowd. She showed her pass to the girl on the reception desk, indicating that she wasn't a tourist and that she was only visiting a friend at Abbey House. The girl looked at her pass and let her through the turnstile.

There were numerous youngsters running around the Abbey's grounds with the sound of a teacher's voice bellowing from the entrance of the grounds to the remains of the Lady Chapel, some two hundred yards away. By the time Jane reached the gates to the house and rang the buzzer she felt so exhausted she hadn't even taken in the majestic entrance.

'Jane!' Penny exclaimed as she pulled the door open. 'I'm so glad you could make it. Do come in.'

'What a beautiful home,' Jane said as Penny ushered her into the front parlour.

'Thanks Jane. We like it. I do sometimes think it's too big for Michael and me though. I mean, there are more than twenty rooms to clean.'

'Well I wish I'd had the chance to live somewhere like this.' Jane handed Penny a box of cakes.

'Oh Jane, you shouldn't have. They look too nice to eat. I'll put them on a plate. Take a seat while I get some tea organised.' Penny left Jane sitting in the parlour admiring some of the pottery and ornaments on display. Jane walked across to the fireplace to study the oriental vase that caught her eye.

'Nice isn't it?'

Jane turned to find Michael standing in the doorway.

'Oh good day. Yes it is. It's Ming isn't it?'

Michael laughed. 'I wish. Actually it's not a Ming but still pretty valuable. You must be Jane from the bookshop?' He walked over to shake her hand.

'You have a beautiful home Mr Westbrook.'

'Thank you. I just wish it was more private.'

'I'm sorry...I don't understand.'

'Just take a look at the main gates. The damn tourists stand and gawp at the house every day. It's like we're living in a zoo. During certain times of the day we have to open the gates to allow the public into the Chapel but I guess their entrance fee does go some way towards the upkeep of the property.'

'I expect it's very expensive to run a place of this size?' said Jane. At that moment, Penny reappeared with a tray of tea and cake.

'Ignore Michael please Jane. It's the only thing he has to moan about,' she said, as she placed the tray on the table. It's your pet hate isn't it dear?' She gave Michael a curt smile.

'Nice to meet you.' Michael slammed the door behind him.

'Sorry about that Jane. Michael has been on tranquillisers for a while now and the smallest thing seems to be a major event to him.'

'Oh that's alright. I know tablets can have a funny effect on people. I used to have an aunt who thought she could fly across the moors after mixing her gin and tonics with her prescription.'

The two women laughed as Penny poured the tea.

'So Jane, tell me how you and your husband came to live in this part of the world.'

'Well it's a long story. We'd both had enough of London and when John was given the opportunity to oversee a new recruitment drive for the West Country police force, it was ideal timing for us. John was constantly working a sixty to seventy hour week and there were too many memories in London. We've both been married before you see and both lost our partners. On top of that the pace of life in London, especially for John, due to the type of work he's in, was getting too much. So when the opportunity came up to move down here, it was something we couldn't turn down.'

'So are you settled here?' asked Jenny as she walked into the room.

'Oh hello my dear,' said Penny. 'Jane, let me introduce you to Jenny Stevens. Jenny is our housemaid. That's her job title in any case, but she's really part of the family here.'

'Mrs Westbrook, you're too kind,' Jenny replied blushing.

'Pleased to meet you,' said Jane shaking hands.

'So you like it down here?'

'Oh yes Jenny. It's such a lovely part of the country don't you think?'

'Yes, apart from the recent murder. Shall I refill the teapot Mrs Westbrook?'

'Yes please Jenny, and can you prepare a snack for Michael. He needs to eat before he takes his tablets.'

After spending more than two hours chatting with Penny and being given a guided tour of Abbey House and the private grounds Jane said she had to leave to get back home. They agreed they would make arrangements to meet up again.

Jane took her leave and headed back towards the High Street to purchase some groceries before the shops shut.

Retrieving her mobile from her hand bag she noticed she had a voicemail from John. She listened intently as she made her way through the grounds of Glastonbury Abbey. When the message had finished she stopped to look up towards the Tor. Suddenly she felt a shiver down her spine and she pulled the collar up on her coat.

She reached the park gates near the Tourist office and stopped to cross the road when she was sure she spotted Jenny Stevens walking in the direction of the Tor some way to her left. Jane called out as the tall blonde haired woman in the black rain coat strode up the hill but the woman appeared to be in a hurry and never responded to Jane's calling and waving.

It was twenty minutes later after purchasing a few shopping items that Jane eventually sat on a bench to give Wesley a call. The phone rang twice when Wesley answered.

'Hi Jane, you OK? Did you get my voicemail?'

'Yes I did. John, what's going on? That's two murders in two days. Do you think they're related?'

'It's too early to tell. I'm back at the crime scene now. We've got the forensics here now, they're just about finished. As soon as they remove the body I'll pop home on the way back to the station. I could murder a coffee.'

'I think you may have a visitor soon. I'm sure I just saw the Westbrook's housemaid walking towards the Tor just now.'

'Hmm. Well she won't get far because most of the area is cordoned off,' he replied. 'I'll keep a look out for her in any case.'

An hour later, Jane was unpacking the shopping when Wesley turned the key in the front door. He walked into the kitchen and threw his jacket on the back of a chair.

'I thought I would have a quieter life down here,' he said smiling as he kissed Jane on the cheek.

'Sit down for a minute,' said Jane. 'I'll make you a coffee.'

Wesley sat at the kitchen table and rolled one of his cigarettes. Jane placed a saucer on the table and gave him that it's about time you quit smoking look.

'So this second victim is a male?'

'Yeah and I think you know him,' said Wesley waiting for Jane's reaction.

'Me?' exclaimed Jane turning round to face him.

'Who is it?'

'The body has been identified as Kelvin Ward. He apparently owned the bookshop.'

'Oh my God!' She put her hand to her mouth and threw the cleaning cloth into the sink to join Wesley at the table.

'I only met him once. The first day I started in the book shop. His father left him the shop when he died but he rarely worked there, just collected the takings.'

'Any idea where he lived?'

'In the flat above the shop. But as I say he rarely came down into the shop. There's a side entrance that leads to the flat. He used that all the time.'

'Was he married or did he have a partner?'

'He wasn't married and come to think of it I've never seen anyone around,' said Jane. 'You ought to try some of the local pubs. I believe he was a bit of a drinker.'

'OK, I'll send one of the lads over to take a look around the flat and ask a few questions in the town.'

'So did you have a good afternoon with Penny?' he asked, changing the subject.

'Yes I did, she's a lovely girl. Strange husband though.'

'What makes you say that?' Wesley asked lighting his cigarette.

'Well I only met him briefly. He was complaining about the number of tourists who constantly peer at the house.'

'That's what comes with living in a mansion,' he replied shrugging his shoulders.

'I agree, and it is a beautiful place, but he seemed so angry about it. You know, really over the top.'

'Well if that's all he's got to worry about then I'm jealous.'

Wesley added another sugar in his coffee whilst Jane wasn't looking.

'It's a big house for Penny and him to manage I would imagine,' he said.

'It is but they have the housemaid there. She seems OK. I thought I saw her walking towards the Tor earlier.'

'Yeah you mentioned it. I didn't see her though.'

He took a final drag on his cigarette and rubbed the remains between his fingers over the top of the saucer, getting another disdainful look from Jane.

'I'd better get back to the station. The press are sure to be there already.'

'OK darling. Let me know if you're going to be late. I'll make sure the milkman's gone before you get back.'

Jane turned away towards the kitchen sink. A smile on her face.

'Oh and by the way. I saw Dorothy Hallerton earlier. She was asking about you and I mentioned the fact that you had spoken to Eddie about those forged notes. You should have seen her face.'

'You are wicked. I can picture poor Eddie getting a right rollicking from her when he gets home later.'

They both laughed as Wesley closed the front door.

14

'Where are my damn tablets?' Michael shouted from the top of the stairs. 'That bloody woman has moved them again.'

Penny thought about ignoring him but she knew it would only make him worse. 'Try looking on the dressing table. That's where they were last night.'

Penny returned to washing the dishes from breakfast. Jenny, their house maid had gone into town to pick up a few things so Penny busied herself around the house for a while.

'Where's that woman gone now?' Michael asked, storming into the kitchen.

'I sent her into town to collect a couple of bits,' she replied without looking up.

'Always moving my stuff. Why does she have to open all the bloody drawers just to put clothes away? The bedroom is a bloody mess.'

'I'm sure she doesn't do it on purpose. Why would she?'

Michael stared across the kitchen, an angry look on his face.

'Help me put some of this crockery away dear.' Penny handed him a tea towel. Michael took the tea towel, looked at it and threw it on the draining board.

'That's what we employ that bloody girl for,' he said and walked out of the kitchen, slamming the door behind him.

One day I'm going to kill that bastard, Penny thought to herself.

After putting the crockery away she picked up the clean clothes from the laundry room and made her way upstairs. She liked Jenny, she was good company but she was a messy person, always leaving doors and cupboards open.

She stepped into the doorway to reach for the doorknob to Jenny's bedroom door which was left open as usual when she suddenly noticed the pink bath towel lying on the floor. Picking it up it felt wet so she tucked it under her arm to put it in the wash basket. Having put the clean clothes in the airing cupboard Penny walked into the bathroom and dropped the bath towel into the basket. Turning to face the bathroom mirror she raised her hand to push back her hair when she noticed the red marks on her hand and on the side of her blouse. What on earth is that? She asked herself.

Removing her blouse she held it up to the light. The red stains felt damp. Rubbing the blouse between her fingers she suddenly tensed. No it can't be, she thought. She ran the cold water over the blouse and watched in horror as the blood flowed away in the sink.

Without Penny noticing, Michael watched from the bathroom door.

15

'Yeah I know I can't believe it either,' said David toying with the buttons on his new Kindle. Somehow he had managed to download several books but couldn't fathom how to place them into his collection folder.

He'd eventually got through to Sally who always seemed busy when he telephoned. He gave her the bad news about Suzie Potter.

'Oh my God, that's awful. How has Colin taken it?' Sally asked.

'He seems OK at the moment but I don't think the whole horror has sunk in yet.'

'Is there anything I can do? I have to stay in London until tomorrow at least but I could get the train down on Wednesday.'

'Oh Sally that would be great. I mean could you? I think Colin will appreciate our company. He's normally a bit of a loner as you know but right now he seems really lost.'

'Sure, no problem. I'll be down on Wednesday evening. I'll give you a call when I'm on the train.'

'OK Sal I appreciate it. I hope you didn't mind me asking. I know how busy you are. I don't suppose you'll be able to stay until the weekend?'

'You do push your luck,' she laughed. 'I'll see what I can do. I'll have to do some washing if I'm coming down for a few days otherwise I'll run out of clothes.'

'Oh dear, that would be a shame. I'd hate to see you running around the flat naked.'

'David Hare! We may be speaking over the phone but I can still see that lecherous look on your face.'

'You know me too well. I'll see you Wednesday.'

16

It had been a busy day. The pile of paperwork in his tray was higher now than when he'd started to tackle it. Wesley knew the press were still milling around outside the police station and the local TV crew were trying to get him to do an interview for the evening news, whilst his superior was also asking for an update. Wesley pressed the buzzer on his desk and asked for both PC Philips and PC Broad to pop into his office.

'You wanted us, Sir?'

'Yeah come in lads. Shut the door.'

Two young lads who had been brought in for questioning about a recent spate of burglaries were shouting in the corridor.

'Martin, I want you to take a drive into town,' said Wesley, handing a bunch of keys over the desk. 'Take a look at Kelvin Wards flat. It's above the Speaking Tree bookshop in Glastonbury High Street. See if you can spot anything of interest.

Mandy's already taken a quick look but see if you can spot anything. Two pairs of eyes are often better than one. Also, while you're in town pop into the shops and local watering holes and ask a few discreet questions. See if anyone knew Kelvin or knew of his activities over the past few days. Unless you come up with a lead or something you feel is urgent you can go home from there.'

'OK sure,' Martin replied.

'Adam, you've always fancied being on TV. Well now's your chance. The local TV crew are outside. All they need is a two minute question/ answer session. Just inform them that a man's body has been found on the Tor but until we get a report back from forensics and pathology we can't tell them anymore at this stage. They may already know who the victim was. Word gets around fast. As far as we know there is no next of kin.'

'Yes, Sir.' Adam looked really chuffed at the opportunity to speak with the local TV station. As they both stood to leave Wesley spoke.

'And one other thing Adam.'

'Sir?'

'Comb that bloody hair of yours before you go on TV.'

'I will,' he replied with a smile.

Wesley was about to roll a cigarette when Adam reappeared in the doorway.

'Sorry I almost forgot. Eddie Hallerton is in reception. Do you want me to bring him up?'

'No. Can you escort him to the interview room for a minute?

I don't want him to think I've just called him in for a chat. We need Eddie to sweat a bit. He works better when he's under pressure,' Wesley replied smiling.

'I get your drift. I'll take him there now.'

Wesley deliberately let Eddie wait another ten minutes before he entered the Interview room. A nervous looking Eddie sat chewing his fingernails.

'Hi Eddie. How's it going?' Wesley pulled up a chair on the opposite side of the table.

'I'm OK Mr Wesley. What have you called me in for? I've already told you what I know about the forged notes, and you asked me to keep an ear out around town which I've been doing, but I haven't heard anything of interest yet. I only…..'

Wesley raised his arm to stop Eddie in his tracks.

'I understand you have done a few odd jobs for Michael Westbrook recently.'

'Hey hold on. They're all legit. You just ask him.'

'Eddie, calm down. No one is accusing you of doing anything. Just listen to me for a moment.'

Eddie looked puzzled.

'I'm sure you're well aware by now that there have been a couple of murders on the Tor.'

'But...'

'Eddie let me finish. Michael Westbrook and his wife Penny live next to the Tor. They're property, as you know, actually overlooks most of it. I want to know what or who they've seen lately. I've got a gut feeling that Michael especially, watches who is around the Abbey grounds and Tor more than anyone else. I think there's a better chance of him or his wife Penny, passing on idol gossip to you, than of them divulging anything if I pay them a visit. I'm sure you can think of a reason for popping in. Check up on some recent work you've done or ask them if there's anything else needs doing.'

Eddie took a while to respond. He'd never trusted a copper before.

'So what's in it for me?' he eventually asked.

'As I told you before, you help me and I'll help you. Help me find out who's been seen around the Tor in the past few days. I know we have tourists in town every day but I believe the person who's been committing the murders is a local and the Westbrook's seem to know most people around here.'

Eddie seemed to weigh up the situation.

'As I said Mr Wesley, what's in it for me?'

Wesley leaned forward across the table. His face was only inches from Eddie's.

'Find out who the Westbrook's have seen and when. If you do I'll see just how much we can forget about the forged notes you handled. I'm sure you understand my meaning.'

Eddie nodded and smiled.

'I'll see what I can do Mr Wesley.'

Grabbing his cap Eddie left the room in a hurry.

Wesley made his way back to his office where he found WPC Mandy Tredwell trawling through a pile of paperwork.

'Hi, Sir. Martin's just dropped this stuff off. It's from Kelvin Ward's flat. He was certainly a bit of a hoarder. Every room in the flat has piles of books and magazines littered all over the place.'

'Anything stand out? A particular interest maybe?'

'No but what is interesting is that someone has ripped to shreds a number of books about the Abbey and the Tor.'

'Hmm. That is strange.'

'Yeah a bit scary really. It looked as if someone had systematically cut the pages into tiny pieces.'

Wesley sat back in the chair toying with his cigarette papers.

'OK. For now we'll have a look through what's there and see if we come up with anything. Split the pile in half and we'll share the load. It will make interesting bedtime reading. I've got to see forensics shortly. Actually you can come with me.'

The drive into Bath took almost an hour as they contended with the day time traffic. Terry Austin was expecting them and had arranged for them to be given clearance to the mortuary as soon as they arrived. They entered an area marked Forensic Pathology Unit and followed a security guard along a dimly lit corridor. At the end of the corridor the guard swiped his pass along the keypad opening the heavy duty door. Entering the room, directly in front of them, two aluminium dissecting stations stood side by side and fat juices had leaked into the pans below.

WPC Tredwell looked away to avoid vomiting.

'First time?' Terry asked. Wesley nodded as the young WPC made her excuses and left the room for a moment. The smell of disinfectant and human flesh along with identity tags hanging from the feet of the corpses gave the place a surreal feel. The two bodies were lying on metal trolleys in the cold windowless room. Wesley could see the uncertain look on Mandy's face when she reappeared.

'You OK?' the forensic asked.

'Yes, sorry.'

'Don't be. It's not very nice is it?'

'In all the years I've been a copper I've never got used to it,' said Wesley placing a hand on the young WPCs shoulder.

'How are things, John?' Terry Austin asked. Wearing his usual white coat and wellington boots he looked a strange sight.

They walked over to what looked like a row of white filing cabinets sunken into the wall. Terry pulled back on one of the handles and Kelvin Ward's body slid out on the supporting trolley. Except for the head the body was covered in a white sheet.

'The cause of death was a knife wound across the throat severing the main artery. However there was a high level of alcohol and drugs still in the blood system. From experience, I would say the person died where he was found and was probably unconscious when his throat was slashed.'

'Are you saying he was a drug addict?' Wesley asked.

'No. There are no signs externally or internally of repeated drug abuse. Alcohol abuse yes. I would guess whoever murdered him gave him a fix knowing it would render him defenceless.'

He pulled back the sheet to expose the gaping neck wound.

Mandy stepped back looking ashen faced. Wesley asked Terry the time of death whilst motioning to Mandy that she could step outside.

'I would estimate the time of death to be somewhere between one a.m. and three a.m. Certainly no later.'

'What about the instrument used?'

'Well, a knife obviously. Long bladed though. Whoever did this knew what they were doing.'

'Thanks Terry. Let's hope I don't see you again too soon.'

Terry smiled. 'I hope you're young WPC is OK. It's always the same reaction the first time they come here.'

'She'll be fine,' Wesley replied looking across the room to where Mandy now stood near the doorway. 'As soon as she's bought me lunch.'

The two friends shook hands and Wesley made his exit.

17

Jenny Stevens sat on her bed watching the evening news, listening to the young constable providing a brief update on Kelvin Ward. He looked rather dishy and she quite admired the way he stood there puffing out his chest as if he were giving the King's speech.

After the broadcast she switched off the TV and wandered around the bedroom picking up her dirty clothes. She wasn't the tidiest of people. Not in her own room in any case. There was several days' worth of dirty washing lying around and the bed hadn't been made for a few days. She ran down the stairs and into the laundry room where she threw everything into the washing machine, added washing powder and switched the machine on. As she turned to leave she almost ran into Michael who was stood blocking the doorway.

'Oh sorry. I never heard you come downstairs,' she said apologetically.

Michael just smiled, undressing her with his eyes. Suddenly aware that she was only wearing a tee-shirt and panties, Jenny blushed.

'I always leave my washing to the last minute.'

As she tried to squeeze past him in the doorway, his arousal brushed the side of her leg.

'Penny found one of your blouses earlier with blood on it. How did that happen?'

'Oh I wondered where that had gone. I cut myself cleaning those old floor tiles in Chapel. I'll speak to Penny about it.'

'Make sure you do,' he said removing his arm from the doorframe so she could leave. As she slid past him, he suddenly grabbed her arm.

'You've been crying.'

'Oh no. It's just hay fever,' she replied pulling herself away.

Jenny could feel his eyes burning into her as she made her way up the staircase.

Back in her room she sat on the bed and opened the book that Penny had bought her for her birthday. Turning over the pages, she began to read the in-depth history of Glastonbury Abbey and the Tor.

Towards the back of the book she also found a couple of pages dedicated to the history of Abbey House. She read how monks who were fleeing from Henry VIII's soldiers dug tunnels underneath the Tor to escape crucifixion. The tunnels supposedly led down to where the ruins of the old Abbey now stand. But what caught her eye was a page detailing the history of the Chapel that was built next to Abbey House.

Hearing footsteps outside of her bedroom door she quickly closed the book and placed it under her pillow.

By the time she would finish reading the book, it would be full of yellow stickers, with notes scribbled everywhere.

18

'Sal over here!' David shouted across the track as he stood on the opposite platform. She eventually spotted him and pointed towards the exit. He turned and made his way to the end of the platform then took the footbridge over the track.

'How do you manage to stand on the wrong platform?' she asked walking up to him. She dropped her suitcase and bag to the floor as he gave her a hug and kissed her on the lips.

'You know what my sense of direction is like,' David replied laughing. He relieved her of her luggage and they walked hand in hand out of the station.

'How was your journey?' he asked as they crossed the road to the car park.

'Not too bad. I had a seat all the way even though I travelled 2nd class. How's Colin? Where are we meeting him?'

'Taking into account everything that's happened, then Colin's bearing up well. I took him to the local last night and have to admit having a rather heavy head today.'

Sally looked down her nose at him. Heavy drinking was something he knew she disliked.

'I've said we'll pick him up and go into Street for a change. It's a little village not far from here and they've got a rather nice new Italian restaurant by all accounts.'

'That sounds good. I'm starving. Oh does that sound selfish? I didn't mean it to.'

'Colin knows how important your food is to you.'

David pulled a face.

'Oh I hate you sometimes.' She punched him on the arm.

They walked hand in hand out of the railway station and joined the throng of shoppers in the High Street until David led her in a small side road where he'd parked the car on a meter.

The drive back to his apartment took nearly half an hour as Sally insisted on stopping at the local baker's to buy some fresh baked bread, the biggest weakness to her diet. Back in the flat, Sally began to unpack whilst David phoned Colin.

'Hey old chum. You OK? Listen, Sally and I will be over at seven. I'm driving, so you and Sal can have a drink.'

'Are you sure?' Colin replied. 'I understand if you two have other things to do.'

'Just make sure you're ready. We'll see you later.'

Having ended their call David entered the bedroom to find Sally getting changed. 'Here, let me help you get out of those jeans.'

He skipped around the side of the bed as she turned to face him. A smile on her face. Wearing only a bra and with her jeans undone, he pulled her towards him as their tongues immediately probed each other. She could feel his excitement as she pulled him onto the bed.

Colin was already stood outside the University gates waiting, when David pulled the car into the kerb. Sally jumped out and for a few moments neither of them spoke as she hugged him.

'Come on you two,' said David winding down the passenger window. 'I'll get nicked for kerb crawling in a minute.'

Sally jumped in the front as Colin slid in the back. The drive to Street took them just under twenty minutes and the conversation was minimal although Colin seemed in good spirits.

The restaurant was only half full so they didn't have to wait long for their food. All three of them ate heartily and David thought it was good to watch his friend smiling for a change. He knew bringing Sally over would help Colin relax a little. They were drinking coffee when suddenly Colin asked the question, 'Are you two coming to the cremation?'

David and Sally looked at one another. Neither had given it any thought. Sally was the first to speak, 'Yes of course. If you want us there.'

'I could do with some support,' Colin replied looking down at the tablecloth. 'Apart from anything else, I think Suzie's parents are going to give me a hard time.'

David and Sally had tried to avoid talking about Suzie's murder. But they felt more comfortable discussing it when Colin raised the issue.

'Have the police come up with anything yet?' Sally asked.

'No. Well, if they have, they haven't told me.'

'I expect you've heard about the other murder?' David asked.

'Yes. Do you think they're related? The murders I mean.'

David shrugged his shoulders. 'I don't know Colin. Seems pretty strange though. Both being in the same vicinity.'

'Yeah I guess.'

Sally gave David a discreet kick under the table, noticing the tears in Colin's eyes.

'How about we settle the bill and wash this good food down with a couple of drinks back in Bath,' he said.

'Yes, why not,' Sally replied. 'Come on Colin, it's your turn to buy the drinks.

'Yes, why not. I mean, there's nothing to rush home for.'

Sally and David glanced at one another, but neither spoke.

19

Wesley reversed the car into the empty space at the back of the crematorium car park, switched off the ignition and extracted his tobacco from his jacket pocket. As usual his car was littered with empty sandwich containers, empty coke bottles and a mass of sweet wrappers.

'I think it's time you had a bit of a tidy up in here,' said Martin undoing his seatbelt.

'I think your job is to watch who attends this cremation,' Wesley replied with a smirk whilst rolling a cigarette.

They had made little progress so far in tracking down Suzie Potter's killer and Wesley knew it wouldn't be long before the national press started to hound him.

'I know it's probably not the right time to bring this up, but Kelvin Ward seems to have been a bit of a recluse,' said Martin.

'What makes you say that?'

Wesley opened his window and blew a plume of smoke into the crisp air.

'Having spoken to quite a number of people in the local pubs, the only one he frequently used was The Pilgrim which was just across the road from his flat. He would usually have a couple of pints then go on to shorts. Vodka and Tonic. Which he would consume until closing time. According to the landlord, he helped Kelvin cross the road on several occasions after closing time because he was worse for wear.'

'What about a partner? Was there a woman on the scene?'

'No. Well if there was he never took her to the pub.'

Like all crematoriums the place was busy. They watched as a throng of people started to leave the Chapel as another group stood to the side awaiting their turn to enter.

'It's like a conveyor belt,' Martin commented.

'Yeah. That's exactly what it is. The only guarantee is that you and I will end up here one day.'

Wesley flicked the ash from his cigarette out of the window.

'Thanks. That makes me feel good,' Martin replied loosening his tie.

'These things are never happy occasions. The worst ones are those involving children,' said a grim faced Wesley.

The two of them sat in silence for a few minutes until Martin pointed to the hearse that had just come through the gates and was heading slowly towards the Chapel.

'That's Colin Dempster, with David Hare.'

Martin suddenly pointed to where two men and a young woman got out of a car opposite them.

'That must be David Hare's partner or wife,' Wesley replied.

'Who's the old lady getting out of the following car?'

'That must be Suzie's mother. She's being escorted by Sharon Donnelly. She's a support officer from Bath HQ.'

'Where's Suzie's father?' Martin asked looking around.

'He's taken it real bad I'm afraid,' said Wesley. 'The doctor has advised him not to travel. They've left a nurse with him.'

'Poor guy. It must be dreadful for them both.'

'Which is what always makes me more determined to find the killer,' Wesley replied as he undid his seatbelt.

Wesley and Martin stood by the car until the congregation had followed the coffin into the crematorium. They were the last to enter and sat in the back row. Neither spoke during the short ceremony through which the vicar repeatedly expressed his sadness at the death of someone who was just starting on their life venture.

Melony Forbes spoke the final words. She told the congregation that not only had she lost a friend, but the world had lost a friend also. As she returned to her seat, piped organ music began to play and the curtain slowly closed as the coffin disappeared from view.

Once Suzie's mother had been led out of the building, Wesley and Martin waited until the rest of the congregation departed. Back outside, Martin turned to walk back to the car when Wesley nudged him, looking at the woman who was stood some way off near the car park. She was dressed in all black with a wide brimmed black hat pulled low over her face.

'I wonder who that woman is over there. She's not sat with anyone or spoke to anyone since she arrived,' said Wesley.

'I couldn't get a look at her face. Take my car keys and see if you can follow her. I want to know who she is. I'll get a lift back to the station.'

Wesley stood back from the congregation and waited whilst people passed on their condolences to Suzie's mother. He watched Colin move forward to speak to the old lady. He couldn't make out what they were saying but the old lady took his hand in both of hers before turning away. It was David Hare who spotted Wesley first as they turned to depart. They shook hands as David introduced him to Sally.

'Nice to meet you Sally. I wish it wasn't at such a sad occasion.'

By now Colin had walked over to join them.

'You OK Colin?' asked Wesley.

'Yes thank you,' he sighed. 'I didn't know what to say to her mother but she seemed to understand. If you know what I mean.'

Wesley just nodded. He was at a loss for words.

20

Jane was busy putting clothes away when the phone rang.

She managed to pick it up by the fourth ring.

'Hello Jane, its Penny here. Are you OK? You sound out of breath.'

'Hi Penny. It's me just getting too old to run down the stairs,' Jane replied laughing.

'What's up? How can I help?'

'I was just wondering if you fancied a girls night out. Jenny and I are planning an evening in Bath and wanted to know if you would be interested.'

'Oh that would be lovely. Yes I'd love to. Have you any particular date in mind?'

'I know its short notice but we were thinking about Friday. It will be a nice way to end the week.'

'I'll pencil it in the diary. I can get John to drop us over there if you wish.'

'No need darling,' Penny replied. 'Jenny doesn't drink, so she'll be using my car. She can watch us get drunk.'

'I will look forward to it. Thanks,' said Jane.

'How's Michael by the way? He was looking a bit stressed when I came over.'

'Oh he's fine Jane. Strictly between you and me he has to take a daily dose of tranquillisers to calm his nerves. I'll tell you about it when we meet. Don't worry, I'll dose him up for the night before we go out,' she replied laughing.

Deciding it was too nice a day to stay indoors, Jane changed into her gardening clothes and went out into the back garden. Although her garden in Kensington had been much larger, it could not match the peace and tranquillity of their new country garden. With nothing but open fields on either side of the garden and a small stream running across the back of the garden Jane felt she was in another world. The marigolds and dahlias she had planted were now in full bloom and provided an abundance of colour along the edge of the path. Jane first busied herself by attending to the line of daffodils that ran the full length of the garden. Having obtained a small box of elastic bands from the kitchen she proceeded to fold each individual plant in half, wrapping an elastic band around it. She always remembered watching her mother doing this. 'It will allow the goodness of the sac to run down into the bulb for next year' she would always say.

Having finished tying the bulbs she set about pruning the clematis that covered the back fence. She stopped once in a while to peer over the fence, looking down to where the ground sloped away before it gave way to the small stream that flowed down towards the village. She jumped as a kingfisher flew past before purchasing itself on a small branch that overhung the bend of the stream further down.

After tidying up and returning the gardening equipment to the shed Jane sat down on the small wooden bench that stood below the kitchen window. She breathed in the fragrance of the wisteria that clung to the back of the house.

Closing her eyes, she took in the smell of the garden, the sounds of birdsong and the soothing sound of the trickling water from the stream. It wasn't long before she drifted into a relaxed sleep.

21

Although both inquests had concluded that the victims had died where they were found, Wesley felt something was missing. He picked up the phone and dialled Colin Dempsters mobile.

'Hi Colin, its Wesley here. How are you?'

'I'm OK, Mr Wesley, how are you doing?'

'Call me John, please,' he replied searching his jacket pocket for his tobacco.

'Colin, I want to ask a favour. Actually, you and David.'

'Sure. That's fine with me and I know David would be happy to help in any way he can.'

'Thanks Colin. As I briefly mentioned before I need to know more about the history and geography of Glastonbury Abbey and the Tor.'

'I can understand the history bit but why do you need information about the geography of the place?'

'One of my PCs, a local lad, tells me that the Tor is built on a series of levels, and rumour has it that there is both a well, and underground tunnels below it that spread out across the surrounding area. I would imagine there are ordinance survey maps of the area that would confirm some of the data. If there are, I will need your expertise to explain to me what I'm looking at.'

'There is certainly a well. It's called the Chalice Well. It dates back before the time of King Arthur. I believe there used to be a lake somewhere too in the grounds that almost surrounded the Tor. In any case it's not a problem. I've arranged to meet David after lectures today for a beer. I'll tell him what information you need and we'll get back to you.'

'Thanks Colin. Obviously I would appreciate it if we kept this confidential. I believe there's someone out there who is using this knowledge to commit murder.'

22

'Mrs Hallerton is a nice lady,' said Denise as she unpacked the daily delivery of new books.

'I didn't realise you knew Dorothy,' Mrs Harper replied straightening a row of books.

'Oh is that her name? I only know her as Mrs Hallerton. We often meet on the bus or at the bus stop. She always says hello and asks me how I am, how many hours I'm working or what kind of day I've had if we're on the way home.'

'I didn't know Dorothy came into Glastonbury so much. Her husband Eddie is the maintenance guy over at Abbey House.'

'What a coincidence,' Denise replied.

'What makes you say that love?'

'I'm sure I've seen Dorothy heading for the house on a couple of occasions. She was actually asking me how much I knew about the place and if I knew Mr and Mrs Westbrook. Well, I said I'd heard of them obviously but I've never really spoken to them and to be honest Mr Westbrook frightens me. He's got a funny look about him.'

'Oh Denise. You really shouldn't say that about anyone.'

Denise looked hurt and a little shocked at Mrs Harper's response.

'But you didn't tell her anything else about them did you?'

'No. I don't know anything else,' she replied shrugging her shoulders. 'Why would I?'

'Oh I'm sorry Denise. I didn't mean to be rude. It's just that I don't like people gossiping about other people. Word gets around so quickly in a little town like ours. I'll make us a nice cup of tea while it's quiet.'

23

'There's someone ringing the bloody buzzer on the gate again,' Michael shouted from the front parlour.

'Can't you answer it?' Penny asked.

'You know I can't stand bloody salesmen,' he replied staring out of the front parlour window.

'It's Eddie Hallerton,' said Jenny as she entered the room.

'He phoned earlier to ask if we needed any more odd jobs done and asked if he could check the boiler. I'll let him in.'

She was half way along the hallway before either of them could reply.

'Sorry to be bothering you,' Eddie said folding his cap and placing it into his coat pocket.

'Just thought I'd pop in and take a look at that old boiler of yours to make sure it's not poisoning anyone.'

He entered the front parlour where Michael stood next to the window.

'Your boiler is long overdue a service, so I thought I'd take a look to see if I need to order any bits and pieces before giving it a clean-up. We don't want to spend any unnecessary money.'

'Hopefully not,' Michael answered abruptly and brushed past him heading towards the back room.

'Just ignore him,' said Penny. Take a seat for a minute,' she said pointing to the settee.

'How's Mrs Hallerton? I haven't seen her in town lately.'

'Dorothy is fine, thanks for asking. She doesn't come into Glastonbury as much as she used to. Arthritic you see. It's a shame. There was a time when she used to walk here and back from home, but not anymore.'

'Oh well, please send her my regards.'

'Thank you. I will ma'am.'

Jenny stood hovering in the doorway.

'Can you take Mr Hallerton through to the boiler room? He knows his way around from there.'

Jenny left the room without speaking, with Eddie following behind. Luckily Penny never saw the look on Jenny's face.

'I expect you get a lot of people walking by here?' Eddie asked as they entered the garden via the French doors that led out from the library.

'Oh yes. Tourists mainly, walking through the Abbey grounds.'

'Not many locals I shouldn't think,' he replied.

'No. But now you come to mention it. I did see that poor Mr Ward walking past the gate the other evening. I even called out to him but he obviously couldn't hear me because he didn't acknowledge me.'

'I guess he was just taking a stroll.'

'Yes. I thought that at first, but then I'm sure it was him who walked past again some twenty minutes later heading for the Tor.'

'When was this?'

Jenny put her hands to her mouth.

'Oh God. I think it was the evening he was murdered,' she stammered.

'Was he waiting for someone do you think?'

'I don't know. I didn't see anyone else,' she replied looking frightened.

'Did he often walk through the grounds?'

'I don't recall seeing him before but of course that doesn't mean he's never been out walking this way. I mean, he only lived in the High Street and he's lived around here for years. It's almost a certainty he knew his way around here.'

'Yeah good point.' Eddie dug his hands deep into his pockets as he struggled to think of anything else to ask. As they turned a corner Jenny pointed to the boiler room which was next to the maintenance shed.

'I don't know why I'm directing you really. I expect you know where the boiler is.'

'Yes, I've serviced it a few times before. It won't take me long to check it out ma'am.'

A short while later Jenny was sat on the bed reading when she heard the quiet knock at the door.

'Come in,' she said looking up.

Michael entered the room closing the door slowly behind him. She knew the look in his eyes.

'What do you want?' she asked looking up and closing her book.

'You know what I want.'

'But your wife is downstairs,' Jenny replied with a grin on her face.

'She's gone outside to find that silly old fool Hallerton.'

He made his way to the side of the bed. Suddenly grabbing her arm, he pulled her up towards him until she was knelt on the bed in front of him. Placing one arm around her waist he kissed her whilst his other hand reached under her skirt.

Jenny managed to grab his arm and pushed him away.

'Oh come on, let's have a bit of fun,' said Michael excitedly.

'Not now. If your wife catches you in here I'll be dismissed.'

'I can handle her.'

Releasing her grasp of his arm, Jenny leapt off the bed and opened the bedroom door.

'I think you ought to leave.'

Michael laughed.

'You don't really mean that.'
'Get out.'
Jenny pointed to the doorway. She was shaking.
Michael shrugged his shoulders and sauntered past her.
'Your loss,' he whispered.
Jenny closed the door behind him and turned the key in the lock before she sat on the edge of the bed and began to cry.

24

'So when does Inspector Wesley want to see us?' David asked placing his beer glass on the table. The pub was busy so Colin almost shouted his reply.

'He said to phone him in the morning or as soon as we have some information ready for him. He just wants as much info about the area that we can find.'

'Do you think he believes that the murderer is someone local?'

'I don't know,' Colin replied. 'He sure seems keen on getting as much data as he can about the Abbey and the Tor though.'

'I've got historical data on both,' said David.

'That's cool. I've already dug out some old ordinance survey maps of the Tor. There's certainly some discrepancy between them and the current geographical printouts that you find in the brochures.'

'Hmm, that could be interesting. Come on let's finish our beer. Sally has prepared some dinner for us. Before you object, it was her idea.'

'So the police believe that the murderer is a local person?' Sally asked as they sat down to eat.

'Well Inspector Wesley seems to think so.'

'How do you feel about helping the Inspector?'

'I'm more than happy to,' said Colin. 'As long as it helps to catch the bastard who killed Suzie.'

David glanced at Sally as they both noticed the way Colin clenched his knife and fork. Sally put her hand on his shoulder.

'I'm sure the police will catch whoever was responsible.'

'And we're going to help them aren't we?' said David.

Colin nodded and sat there picking at his dinner.

25

Denise Wright was pleased that the day was nearly at an end. Although she quite enjoyed working in the Tourist office there were some days that simply dragged and today had been one of those.

'You look tired today my dear,' said Mrs Harper who had spent the day stock taking. She carried yet another pile of books into the front of the office and placed them next to the counter.

'I've had a couple of late nights,' Denise replied. 'My final exams are in four weeks and I find it difficult to remember so much information.'

'I'm sure you'll be fine my dear. It's remarkable just how much information we store in our brains without realising it.'

Mrs Harper winked and placed a reassuring hand on Denise's shoulder.

'I remember when I was a young girl. I would get home from school and do my homework straight away. If I didn't, mother wouldn't let me go out with my friends. Oh like all youngsters, I used to hate her for it but as I got older I realised how right she'd been, She was doing it for me and I used to give her such a hard time.'

'Oh look,' exclaimed Denise suddenly pointing out of the window. 'Isn't that the lady who came in the other day? The one who lives in Abbey House.'

'Yes I think it is.' They watched the tall figure walk around the base of the Tor heading down the hill.

'Where are your glasses?' Mrs Harper asked. 'You screw your face up so much when you can't see properly. I do wonder sometimes how you manage to find the shelves to put the books on.'

Denise didn't answer. She was still watching the woman who had now changed direction and was heading towards the Tor. There was something strange about how the woman kept looking up and down the road. Who was she looking for?

26

Colin pinned the map on the wall and spread out a number of smaller drawings on the table. It was the first time in years he'd tidied up his room in the University. Wesley put his mobile back in his pocket just as David entered the room with a pile of books under his arm.

'Good morning gentlemen. Wow, that's an impressive looking map.'

'Morning,' said Wesley. 'I'm just waiting for Colin to explain to me what it is I'm looking at.'

'It's an ordinance survey map of the Tor,' Colin answered.

'The lines I've coloured in over the top and the few I've added elsewhere represent what is believed to be underground tunnels and waterways.'

Wesley raised his eyebrows.

'I thought that would interest you,' said Colin looking at the raised eyebrows.

Having placed his own books on the floor, David stood in front of the map observing and tracing, some of the lines with his hand. Colin had moved across to the small kitchen area and set about making them tea.

'I always work better with a cuppa in my hand.'

'There's certainly a lot of history to the place,' Wesley remarked still trying to understand what he was looking at. Colin handed out the teas as the three of them studied the map for a few minutes in silence.

It was David who first spoke, sounding as if he was giving one of his well- rehearsed lectures to his students.

'The captivating appearance of the Tor and its history still brings thousands of people every year to the site where the vast majority want to climb the open staircase to the church tower. There are wonderful views from the top. From up there you can see the shape of the old peninsula on which the town of Glastonbury stands and Glastonbury's ruined Abbey below. Privileged pilgrims would have stayed in the Abbey itself and excavations have disclosed a special apartment at the south end of the Abbot's House, erected for a visit from the English King, Henry VIII. This is now known as Abbey House where the Westbrook family now live.' He pointed to the location on the map.

'The Tor itself though is a powerful natural phenomenon, visible from many miles away, yet imperceptible from nearby. It rises 500 feet above the Somerset levels and has inspired many spiritual guides. St Michael's church sits at the top of the Tor, unfortunately, as we all know, nowadays it's mostly a ruin. The lower levels of the Tor here,' he said pointing, 'are really drained marshland.'

'You've given this presentation several times before I would guess,' Wesley remarked.

'Yeah. Sorry, I probably have.'

Wesley stood up and pointed to the map.

'So are you saying there is an apartment within Abbey House that leads to the Tor?'

'I don't know that one actually exists today but there are many unconfirmed reports that one did exist sometime in the past.'

'If I may interrupt for a second,' said Colin. He walked over to where David stood next to the map and pointed at a specific area just to the right of the Tor.

'These wavy blues lines do show a significant density here which increases the possibility of there being underground excavations or natural underground springs. If you follow this strong line here,' he said pointing, 'it leads directly back to Abbey House.'

'So in your view there's a strong possibility of a passage of some sorts linking the house to the Tor?'

'In my opinion, yes' Colin replied 'but I don't think it's the only underground link. There is a similar pattern running between the old Abbey and the Tor. But that's quite a steep decline.'

'I've walked the Abbey grounds a few times but never seen anything obvious,' said David.

'Legend says that treasure still exists in underground rooms but several surveys, including the last one back in the nineties found nothing,' Colin stated pulling up a chair. 'The spot near the well is supposed to conceal the Holy Chalice. Hence the name the Chalice Well.'

'Well, I don't hold out much hope of finding the Holy Chalice but it would be nice to confirm whether or not the Tor is accessible from underground,' Wesley remarked.

'One thing's for sure,' said David. 'If my equations are correct, there is a two hundred foot drop from the centre of the Chalice Well to the riverbed below. I for one certainly wouldn't fancy being down there.'

Another ten minutes of discussions followed before Wesley announced that he to go as he had a meeting with the council.

He thanked them both for their time and suggested they all get together again in a day or two.

An hour later, Wesley walked out of the council offices feeling frustrated. All he had asked for was permission to explore the grounds of Glastonbury Abbey at some point when it was closed to the public. However, the council didn't seem too keen, although they did agree they would give him their full support in finding the person responsible for the murders.

He was advised that the ruins of Glastonbury Abbey were still of historical interest and some parts were in such poor condition that even minor exploration could destroy centuries of historical data.

Sitting on the low wall outside the council building he extracted his tobacco pouch from his jacket pocket and pulled out one of his pre-rolled cigarettes. He sat overlooking the square, taking a long drag, before deciding what his next move would be.

'Hello Mr Wesley,' said a voice from behind him. 'You don't know me do you? My name is Denise. I work in the Tourist office. I've seen your face in the paper from when you gave the local press an interview regarding that nasty murder business.'

'Hello Denise. Pleased to meet you,' Wesley replied almost blushing although he wasn't sure why.

'Where are you off to?' she asked. 'Oh I didn't mean to be rude. Just wondered where you were going. You looked lost for a moment.'

Wesley smiled.

'Actually I was Denise, lost in thought, but don't tell anyone.' She laughed and put her hand on his arm.

'Don't worry Mr Wesley, your secret is safe with me,' she said as she walked off down the road.

Wesley wandered off in the direction of the High Street and was still unsure of his next move until he realised he was standing opposite the tea rooms. Ah, he thought to himself. That would seem the most appropriate option. The little doorbell tinkled as he closed the door behind him. The little shop was crowded. It seemed like the whole village had stopped for tea. He eventually found a spare chair at the back of the shop but had to share the table with three women who were halfway through their cream teas.

'Oh do please join us,' said a rather plump woman who was wearing a rose patterned dress and a small hat on the side of her head with matching design.

'I'm Pamela Armstrong, this is Ruby Carlisle and the lady next to you is Annie Parsons,' she said excitedly. 'We already know who you are,' she prompted wiping some of the potted cream away from her mouth.

'You're quite famous around here Mr Wesley.'

'Am I?' Wesley replied looking rather embarrassed.

'Oh yes,' she continued. 'It's not every day a little town like Glastonbury has a double murder on its doorstep now is it?'

'I suppose not.'

'I was only telling Ruby yesterday that I bet that Eddie Hallerton is involved. Wasn't I Ruby?'

'Yes you did my dear, although I have to say he's behaved himself of late.'

'Ladies I'm afraid you're one step ahead of me,' said Wesley as his tea arrived. 'What makes you think Eddie Hallerton has anything to do with the murders?'

'Well. It's obvious Mr Wesley,' said Pamela Armstrong.

'Eddie's plans for a new Tourist office where the old bookshop still stands were turned down by Kelvin Ward just a few years back. Everyone knows how they argued. If I remember rightly Eddie said he'd get even with him one day.'

'When was this?' he asked sipping the hot tea. 'I've spoken to Eddie regarding several matters in the past few days but he's never once mentioned anything to me about knowing Mr Ward.'

'Oh he wouldn't,' Ruby Carlisle interjected.

'But why? I don't understand. What's the secret?'

'Well, I'm not one to gossip Inspector, but at the time Eddie was told by the police to keep away from Kelvin after the threats he made. You see there was already bad blood between them. Kelvin worked for the council in those days. Only part-time mind you, but he had enough influence to lose Eddie a couple of tenders he submitted for other jobs in town.'

Wesley put the cup down on the table and sat back in the chair.

'Ladies, you have helped me enormously,' he said and left a ten pound note on the table before standing up to leave.

'Please tell the waitress to put the change towards your bill. Have a good day ladies.'

'I've always said he was a lovely man,' he could hear Pamela Armstrong saying to her friends as he closed the door behind him.

'What have you been saying to the police?' Michael asked Penny as he strode into the front parlour wearing his usual angry face.

'The police? What are you talking about?'

'You must know. Someone called Wesley. Some Inspector chap. He just phoned to say he would like to have a chat with me and could he call round this afternoon.'

'I don't know anything about it,' Penny replied without looking up from her newspaper.

'Damn inconvenient,' he said more to himself than anyone else and stormed out of the room. Penny waited until she heard his bedroom door slam shut, then folding the newspaper she reached into her jeans for her mobile phone.

'Hi Jenny its Pen. Would you do me a favour? While you're in town could you pick up my clothes from the laundry?'

'Yes, of course. You must have shares in that place. I mean, you take stuff there to be cleaned nearly every day.'

'Only because it's an excuse to get me out of the house. I'd wait forever if I had to wait for you to clean everything.'

The two women laughed.

'Oh by the way. Inspector Wesley's wife Jane has said she would be delighted to join us on Friday night.'

'Oh that's good. The more the merrier. Hopefully there'll be some young talent on show.'

'Jenny Stevens, you're a wicked girl but hopefully yes.'

27

Wesley hung his jacket on the coat stand and was searching the pockets for his tobacco and cigarette papers when PC Philips knocked on the door.

'Hi, Sir. Have you got a minute?'

'Sure, come in son. What have you got for me?'

'I just saw Mrs Wesley in town. She said to remind you that you're supposed to be quitting smoking.'

Wesley looked across the desk as he rolled his next cigarette.

'I'm sure that's not what you wanted to see me about,' Wesley replied looking down his nose at the young lad.

Philips' face went crimson. 'Err, no. I spoke with Harry Fenton. He runs the men's outfitters in Glastonbury. He says that Kelvin Ward purchased a new suit a couple of weeks back and he was apparently excited about someone he was going to meet.'

'Is that anything unusual?' Wesley asked.

'For Kelvin Ward, yes. According to Harry, it's the first new item of clothing the man had bought for years. In addition to that he had a reputation for being a bit of a recluse.'

'So are you assuming this is a female friend he had planned to see?'

'Can't be sure,' PC Philips replied his face reddening for the second time in a few minutes.

'You see Kelvin Ward was kind of...'

'Yeah I get the idea,' Wesley interrupted saving him from further embarrassment.

'Oh, I forgot to mention. The woman you asked me to follow the other day, when we left Suzie's funeral. That was Penny Westbrook.'

Wesley looked up and stared in thought for a moment before answering.

'Oh, OK. Thanks son.'

'Is that all, Sir?'

'Just one more thing. Ask Adam to pop over to Bath for me. I've just had a call from Colin Dempster at the University. He's got another drawing of the Abbey grounds he says I may be interested in. I'd like to take a look at what he's found.'

After the young PC had left room, Wesley sat thinking about Kelvin Ward. The more he found out about the man, the less he liked him. Even his funeral was strange. There were just a few local people and the vicar. It would seem that no one actually got to know the man.

Wesley decided he needed to clear his head, so after making a couple of quick calls he grabbed his car keys and headed towards Glastonbury.

Sitting at the top of the Tor next to the old Abbey ruins, Wesley looked down towards the northern side of the town, and Magdalene Street, where Abbey House stood. From where he was positioned he had a complete view of the entrance to the Abbey grounds and the access areas to the Tor. It was easy to imagine that numerous underground passageways led from the grounds of the Abbey to the Tor. The one thing that kept nagging him was that the murderer, or murderers, must have known that their victims would have easily been found, but must also have known where and when to enter the Tor without initially being seen.

He searched his pockets for his tobacco and cursed as he realised he'd left it on his desk.

There were two ways to gain access to Abbey House. One through the Abbey grounds which led to the main gates at the front of the property and another to the rear, via Silver Street which was the tradesmen's entrance. Both had gated entrances that required for someone in the house to let the visitor in. Deciding to walk through the grounds, he descended the Tor to Magdalene Street and crossed the road to the Ticket office. At the turnstile entrance he showed his ID to Mrs White. That was the name on her badge.

'I have an appointment at Abbey House,' said Wesley 'but I just want to have a wander through the grounds on my way. Is that OK?'

'Of course it is,' she replied fiddling with the brooch on her dress.

'Just give me a shout if you need any information about anything. I know most things about the Abbey and the grounds. My names Margaret. Margaret White.'

'Thanks Margaret.'

'Oh do take this,' she called out and handed him one of the tourist maps. Wesley nodded and smiled again.

Wesley's route led him towards the Lady Chapel where several visitors were already standing listening to one of the local guides.

'It was here in 1191 the monks dug to find the remains of King Arthur and his Queen Guinevere. At Easter in 1278, with great pomp and ceremony, their bones were reinterred in a black marble tomb in the presence of King Edward I. However, the tomb has since been lost, believed stolen by King Arthur's knights.'

They followed the guide for another ten minutes before she turned and pointed to the remains of the Abbey high above them on the Tor.

'Due to its holiness and stature, the Abbey we see at the top of Tor was the last to be closed by Henry VIII at the time of the Abbey's dissolution in 1539. Legend has it that several escape routes were built under the Abbey leading down from the Tor to the Abbey where we now stand. These were used as escape routes by the monks who were in danger of being executed by Henry VIII's henchmen.'

'Was the Abbey very wealthy?' asked one of the tourists.

'Yes, extremely so. By Tudor times Glastonbury Abbey was second only to Westminster Abbey in its wealth and influence. It's no wonder that history tells us there are so many precious artefacts buried within the grounds.'

Wesley moved on as soon as the guide stopped talking whilst some of the visitors started to take photos. Taking a left turn he passed King Arthur's tomb and King Edgar's Chapel before reaching the gates to Abbey House which was open to the public today. Crossing the gravel entrance he ascended the stone steps to the front entrance and pressed the bell. He could hear someone shouting inside the building, a man's voice, long before he heard footsteps approaching the door. The door was eventually opened by a young dark haired woman wearing a white blouse and dark blue pleated skirt.

'Good afternoon. How may I help you?'

'Good afternoon. I'm Inspector Wesley from Street police. I'm here to speak with Michael Westbrook.'

He showed her his ID.

'Please step this way,' replied Jenny standing aside to let him in.

'Excuse me for asking, but weren't you at Kelvin Wards funeral the other day?'

'Yes I was.' Jenny stared at him with a quizzical look on her face.

'What a lovely house,' Wesley exclaimed changing the subject and looking around the enormous hallway.

'Yes. It is a nice place. If you would like to wait in the sitting room I'll tell Mr Westbrook you're here,' she said leading the way. Wesley took in the décor and tried to envisage what the property would have looked like over two centuries ago.

He was still deep in thought when Michael Westbrook strode into the room looking rather agitated.

'Hello Inspector,' said Michael carrying a book under his arm. Wesley stood up to shake hands.

'Thanks for allowing me some of your time,' said Wesley. 'Hopefully I'll not keep you long.'

'No worries Inspector. I don't have any immediate plans.'

'Please call me John,' said Wesley after being offered a seat.

'I was just saying what a lovely place you have here.'

'Thank you. We are fortunate to live in these wonderful surroundings I know. However it does get somewhat tedious having the public traipse in and out most days.'

'I'm sure they help with the financial upkeep of the place,' Wesley replied smiling and waiting for a reaction.

'Yes I suppose so. They congregate in the damn Chapel every day. Anyhow how can I help you?'

Wesley could tell it was a sore subject so decided to move on. 'Living so close to the Tor and having so many visitors each day, I was wondering if you or your good wife had seen anything suspicious recently. I'm sure you're aware there have been two people murdered on the Tor in the past week.'

'I don't see how that has anything to do with us,' said Michael standing up and walking towards the French doors.

'I mean, it's a police affair is it not?'

Wesley stood and followed Michael across the room. 'Nice grounds. Three to four acres I guess?'

'Four acres in all,' replied Michael lighting a cigarette.

Wesley regretted he'd left his tobacco in the office. 'Is that a Fortingale Yew?'

'Yes. One of my prized possessions. Are you much of a gardener Inspector?'

'Given the time and a bigger garden, I would be. However, very few of the plants I buy ever last very long.'

Michael pushed open the French doors. 'Ah, fresh air and no bloody tourists on this side. Follow me, I'll show you around.'

They walked in silence until they reached a range of trees and shrubs including a fully grown, healthy Elm. They sat on one of the wooden benches looking down the slope where two bee hives were located.

Anticipating Wesley's next question, Michael pointed just ahead.

'The two bee hives over there are new to the estate. My wife has visions of us producing our own honey.'

'That's sounds good to me,' Wesley replied. 'I'm sure my wife will purchase some.'

Michael stood up again and led the way across the landscaped garden.

'Can I ask what security you have here?'

Michael gave him a glance before answering.

'At the back of the house we have security cameras placed on all boundary walls and an infra- red beam that runs zigzag across the lawn. Partly for our own security and partly to protect the badger set that we have located further up the slope. Why do you ask?'

'In the strictest of confidence, I believe whoever carried out the recent murders is a local person. Someone who knows how to get in and around both the Abbey grounds and the Tor. I'm just trying to tick off all the boxes.'

'I don't think it's one of us Inspector,' Michael replied and turned back in the direction of the house.

'I'm sure it's not,' Wesley replied.

They shook hands by the front door.

'Thanks for your time Michael. Much appreciated.'

Michael Westbrook smiled and began to close the door.

'Oh just one last question,' said Wesley.

'Legend says there is an underground passageway leading from the Chapel to the Tor. Do you know if such a thing exists?'

'Not to my knowledge Inspector. If there's nothing else?'

He closed the door. Half way down the drive Wesley could hear raised voices back in the house.

28

'You don't really think there are underground tunnels running from the grounds of the Abbey to the Tor do you?' David asked.

'Well I know historically there is a lot of myth surrounding the idea but it is possible,' Colin replied.

'There have been several surveys on the Tor in the past few years. Surely they would have found something by now.'

David gathered a collection of books for his next lecture.

'May be, maybe not. I guess it depends where one searches.'

'What's that you're studying now?' David asked peering over Colin's shoulder as his friend spread a map out across the table.

'I've managed to get hold of an old map, dated 1962, which shows the water table surrounding the whole area. The interesting thing is that the water level in the lake that's located in the grounds is on the same level as that of the water table that is in the Well.'

'Which proves what?'

'From a geographical perspective, it proves there is a high probability that the two are linked. Now taking into account the vast volume of water in both the lake and the Well, one can safely assume that there is not only an underground stream, but also an underground passageway. This would have been used in ancient times to ensure the free flow of water to the Abbey.'

'And the only way to do that, would have been for the monks to follow that water flow underground then pump it up to the Abbey?' asked David.

'Exactly. You see, the limestone in the White Spring here,' he said pointing to the map, 'is geological evidence of tunnels existing under the Tor.'

'It's possible that some of the Abbey's original assets may have found their way into these tunnels, and may even still be there,' Colin replied rubbing his hand on his chin.

'I think Inspector Wesley might find this information useful.'

'You don't believe that someone still has the knowledge and access to the passageway today do you?'

Colin shrugged his shoulders.

'I've no idea but if it exists, which I'm pretty sure it does then it's certainly a possibility. One of Wesley's boys is coming over to pick this up in a while. He can take a look and see what he thinks for himself.'

'I've got the map you asked for,' said PC Phillips as he laid it on the table.

'Something else you might find interesting too about our Mr Ward.'

'Something you found at his flat?' asked Wesley. He pulled up a chair and sat down. He was tired and hungry. It had been a long day.

'The place is squeaky clean. Almost as if someone went through it before we did. The only thing I found was these.' He held up a pair of theatre tickets.

'Oh where were they for?'

'Bath Theatre. The interesting thing is that the tickets are for a play that was showing on the night the victim died.'

'So Mr Ward spent the early part of the evening in the theatre?'

'No. Take a look. The tickets haven't been split. They were never used.'

Wesley licked the edge of his tobacco paper.

'Hmm that is interesting. So someone, or something, changed his mind. And who was he intending on taking?'

'Well, I drove over to the theatre,' said Philips. 'Having provided them with the ticket reference numbers they were able to tell me that the tickets were purchased by credit card. You'll like this one. The name on the card is Penny Westbrook.'

'What?'

'Yeah, and what's more, it would seem the same card has been used several times before. Interesting eh?'

'Yes it is,' Wesley replied grabbing the phone.

'Let's give the young lady a ring shall we? I'm sure she'd like to visit the station tonight for a little chat.'

PC Adam Broad limped into the police station. Having spent the whole day cycling around Glastonbury, he was both exhausted and sore.

'You alright there son?' Wesley asked as he came out into the reception area to put some post into the out tray.

'Yeah fine thanks,' Adam grimaced. Wesley smiled.

'Come into the office and sit down.'

'So what little snippets of local gossip have you obtained today?'

Wesley placed a cup of tea in front of him.

'Thanks.' Adam took two sips of the hot tea before replying.

'The only piece of information that may be some use is that Brian Williams who runs the fish stall in the market, says that his father always told him a story about there being ghosts on the Tor.'

Wesley raised his eyebrows.

'Hold on, let me finish. What his father used to say was, that you could occasionally see someone standing on the Tor, then a few seconds later they would be walking around the grounds of the Abbey or even down the High Street.'

He could see Wesley's confused look.

'It took me a moment of two to work it out. Don't you see?' said Adam leaning forward. 'If someone could be seen in two different places only minutes apart, then, if they weren't visible the whole time, they had to be out of sight. Presumably underground.'

Wesley leant back in his chair and lifted his chin, a characteristic when he was deep in thought.

'What are you thinking?'

'I'm beginning to believe there may be some truth in the matter,' Wesley replied. 'The map I've just received from Colin Dempster seems to suggest exactly the same thing.'

29

Eddie Hallerton was sitting at home having a relaxing afternoon watching the horse racing on TV. He'd backed four horses today and already lost out on the first three, so was eagerly awaiting the start of the four o'clock race, itching to get his money back. He had his money on Morning Star which was two lengths in front with just four hurdles left to jump when the phone rang. Damn he thought. He knew Dorothy was out so he reluctantly got out of the chair. Kicking the footstall away, he made his way out into the hall. Eddie didn't like change so the old telephone stood on the table by the front door in the same place as it had for the past twenty years.

'Hello,' he shouted down the phone. For some reason he always struggled to hear anything on the damn thing.

'Is that Mr Hallerton?' asked a female voice.

'Yeah who's calling?'

'It's Penny Westbrook. You know, from Abbey House.'

'Sorry who is it?' Eddie asked. He was desperately trying to listen to the TV that was in the backroom at the same time.

'It's Penny Westbrook,' she shouted.

'Oh hello,' he replied sticking his finger in his other ear.

'How can I help you?'

'Michael has asked me to give you a call. He is having some new mature shrubs delivered tomorrow and wandered if you would be so kind as to plant them.'

'Yes that's no problem. What time do you need me over there?'

'Michael said they are due to be delivered in the morning, that's all I know,' said Penny apologetically.

'OK no worries. I'll be over about 10:00am. I'll need to do some digging before they arrive. Ask him to let me know where they're to be planted. Do you know what they are?'

'No sorry.'

'OK no problem.'

'Thanks Mr Hallerton. I'll tell Michael to expect you in the morning.'

'Right O.' He hung up and went back to watch the television.

The TV commentator was just reading out the result of the race.

1st King & Country at 10 -1, 2nd Summer Dream at 6-1 and 3rd Morning Star 4-1.

'Jesus Christ!' Eddie shouted to himself. Only at the last minute had he changed his mind from an each way bet to backing Morning Star to win. He was relying on winning some money today.

He tore up the betting slips and threw them in the waste bin before Dorothy came home. He then made his way upstairs where he searched through all his clothes, looking for any spare money he could use to place more bets the following morning.

30

It was early evening when Penny Westbrook sat in the reception area of Street police station. It was the first time she had ever been called in by the police.

Wesley watched her through the glass petition that looked out onto the reception area. She kept fiddling with her mobile phone and checking the contents of her handbag. She looked nervous. He knew from experience that it didn't hurt to keep the person waiting for a while.

'Hello Penny,' he said when he finally walked out into the reception area. Penny jumped.

'Oh Mr Wesley. Good evening.'

'Follow me Penny if you will.'

Wesley led her along a dimly lit corridor, passing two other interview rooms. When he opened the door to the next room Penny looked around the two tone green walled interview room. It felt cold, making her shiver.

'Take a seat. I just want to ask you a couple of questions. It won't take long.'

Wesley took a seat at the table opposite her.

Penny placed her hands in her lap looking apprehensive.

'Thanks for coming down to the station Penny. There are a couple of things that have come to light in the past twenty-four hours that I'd like to talk to you about.'

'Oh OK,' she replied hesitantly.

'Can I get you a tea or coffee before we start?'

'Err, no I'm fine thanks.'

Wesley decided the direct approach would get her talking.

'Penny. What can you tell me about Kelvin Ward?'

'Kelvin Ward? The man who was recently murdered?'

'Yes.'

'Very little I'm afraid. Obviously I knew him but I think everyone in town will tell you he was a bit of a recluse. Kept himself to himself.'

'So you weren't friends?'

'Friends? No but we spoke occasionally.'

'So how would you describe your relationship?'

Penny looked somewhat confused.

'As I said Mr Wesley, we spoke a few times but that was about it.'

'Can I ask you then, why we found a pair of theatre tickets in Kelvin

Ward's flat that were purchased on your credit card?'

Penny's faced turned a crimson colour.

'I'd had completely forgotten about that,' she replied twisting the straps of her handbag.

'Kelvin...I mean Mr Ward approached me one afternoon several months ago as I was just leaving the bookshop. He was coming down the staircase from his flat above the shop when he called out. He looked harassed, so I asked him what the matter was. We had spoken a couple of times before but only in passing. He said he wanted to take a friend to the theatre but when he phoned the theatre they wouldn't accept his credit card as they only took visa. So to help him out I offered to use my card so long as he gave me the cash, which he did.'

'Did he say who he was planning to take?'

'No he just said it was to be a surprise.'

'So were the tickets delivered to you?'

'No, I had to speak with the theatre to confirm my address and details but ask them to deliver the tickets to Mr Ward. Inspector, have I done something wrong?'

'No Penny you haven't. I just needed to clear that up. I was hoping to find out who he had planned on taking to the theatre. You see the last tickets purchased were dated for the evening he was murdered.'

Penny put her hands to her mouth and looked as if she was about to be sick. Wesley walked around the table and put his hand on her shoulder.

'Let me go and get you that cup of tea.'

Half an hour later Penny left the station. She was clearly shaken and appeared to have no knowledge of who the other ticket was for. His grabbed his mobile and rang Colin Dempster.

An hour later Wesley met Colin and David at the entrance to the Chalice Well.

'Good evening gentlemen. Sorry I couldn't get here any earlier but it's been one of those days.'

'Fully understand,' said Colin. 'We've only just arrived ourselves.'

'I wanted you to take a look at a theory I have,' said David.

They were stood on the slope of Glastonbury Tor.

'The Chalice Well is a holy well,' he said pointing to the floor just in front of them.

'This wooden well-cover with wrought-iron decoration was made quite recently in the early nineteen hundreds. However, archaeological evidence suggests that the Well has been in almost constant use for at least two thousand years.'

All three of them looked through the small grill where running water could be heard.

It was Colin who spoke next, 'The water feeds from the Chalice Well Spring which has an outflow of 25,000 gallons per day. That would require an underground passage of some considerable size.'

'Enough for someone to walk through?' Wesley asked.

'I would say so,' Colin replied extracting two maps from his pocket which he laid on the ground.

'Now this first map is a simple ordinance survey map of the area produced by the local water authority. You can see here on the map that the tunnel runs from the Chalice Well here where we're standing right now, across to the Abbey, then up towards the Chapel.'

'The Chapel in Abbey House?' asked David.

'I do believe so. In any case if you lay this tracing of an ancient map of the Tor over the top, you can see the bore holes were apparently drilled down from the Tor into the tunnel at three different points, on two different levels. I know this is dated c.500 – 1000 AD but I can't find anything that had been produced since to show they no longer exist.'

'These bore holes would have presumably have been used to hoist water to the upper levels of the Tor?' commented Wesley.

'Exactly, and possibly used as a means of escape by the monks trying to escape the murderous Henry VIII's guards.'

David extracted yet another piece of tracing paper from his pocket.

'Now, if you then lay this over the top, this drawing dates to around the time the top of the Tor was levelled to build the church. You can see another bore hole running from where the church originally stood directly down to the second level into the tunnel.'

'So let me get this straight,' said Wesley standing up to relieve his backache. 'What you're suggesting is that these bore holes, along with the tunnel, are still accessible. Accessible enough for someone to travel from one point to another?'

'Yes, theoretically it's possible,' Colin replied. 'Legend also supports our theory, saying there is an ancient ritual labyrinth or maze running under the Tor. You see, the Tor is an aquifer and is supported by water-bearing beds of stone, shale and heavy clay, which are all kept replenished by rainfall. When it rains, the water doesn't run off the Tor, it soaks into the ground. Some of it runs into the Chalice Well but some emerges into other springs, such as the Ashwell Spring at the foot of the Tor.

Unlike the water in the Chalice Well, the water at the lower part of the Tor moves so slowly it's likely that it remains there for hundreds of years but the whole area fluctuates according to rainfall.'

He could see the confused look on Wesley's face.

'What I'm trying to say is, that at certain times of the year, like summer, when the weather is dryer, some parts of the Well may be accessible for a short period of time as the water level drops.'

'Hmm. I think this is something I'm going to have to explore further,' Wesley replied.

After the short drive back to Street, Wesley placed the key in the lock of his front door. As soon as he entered the house he could smell his favourite dinner. The aroma of mince and onions wafted from the kitchen where he found Jane.

'Come and sit down.' She kissed him on the cheek.

'Your dinner is ready.'

'Why only one plate? Aren't you eating?'

'John Wesley. You've proved that you never listen to me. I'm going out tonight with Penny Westbrook and her housemaid Jenny. We're eating in Bath later.'

'OK, so I forgot. I saw Penny earlier but she didn't say anything.'

'You saw her? Where?'

'I actually called her into the station.'

Jane nearly dropped the full frying pan on the floor and looked horrified.

'It's nothing to worry about. I just needed to clear up an issue regarding some theatre tickets.' He briefly explained what had been said.

'I thought for a minute you were going to say you suspected her of something.'

'What time are you meeting her?' he asked changing the subject.

'Oh, Jenny is driving. She should be here in about fifteen minutes. Hence your early dinner.'

Jane spent the next five minutes explaining how Dorothy Hallerton had stood talking to her by the front gate, complaining about her husband Eddie, who had spent his previous day's wages betting on the horses.

Wesley tucked into the mince and onions with mashed potato as if he hadn't eaten for days. When he'd finished he placed the plate in the sink to wash up later and headed upstairs to where Jane was getting ready to go out. She was stood naked except for a pair of panties when he walked into the bedroom.

'Are you sure you want to go out?'

'Can't think of anything better to do,' she replied laughing.

He grabbed her around the waist and pulled her close. They were still kissing when Penny tooted the car horn.

'Another time big boy,' she said slipping the dress over her head. 'I'll give you a call if we're going to be late.'

Jane slipped on her shoes and grabbed the small handbag from the dressing table.

'I've got money. I raided the money in your wallet.' She blew him a kiss and ran down the stairs.

Wesley watched as Jane got into the car. Jenny was at the steering wheel and Penny Westbrook was sat in the back.

Wesley spent the early part of the evening watching CCTV footage from the Abbey's security cameras from the two evenings in question. The camera angles made it difficult to see anyone walking across the grounds as the two cameras pointed at the Visitor's Car Park and the main entrance just along from the Tourist office.

After replaying the footage several times he decided there was nothing there of any relevance but something was bugging him. Something wasn't right. After pouring himself a large brandy he replayed the footage one more time from the night that Suzie was murdered.

At first there was nothing of interest. Then he saw what he'd been missing. The shadows of two people who must have been walking directly below the car park cam. He stopped the tape, rewound it and played it back again in slow motion. There was no doubt that two people walked through the car park sticking close to the boundary fence heading up the hill in the direction of the Tor. He checked the time on the camera. It read 00:38. That meant that assuming they hadn't driven there and there was no vehicle in the car park to support that idea, then they would have had to have walked from the High Street.

Wesley grabbed his mobile and rang the station.

WPC Alison Bolt was on the late shift. He gave her the date and time of the footage and asked her to contact the security company who monitor all the CCTV cameras in town.

'I want copies of all CCTV footage from Glastonbury High Street on the nights of the two murders.'

'Sure thing. I'll call them now.'

'Thanks Alison. If I could have the tapes on my desk by the morning that would be good.'

31

The Dolphin Inn in Bath was busy as usual as Penny, Jane and Jenny tackled their way to the bar.

'This is the first time I've been in here,' said Jane admiring the décor.

'I have to admit that Jenny and I have been here once or twice,' Penny replied laughing.

'I think we have shares in place,' Jenny remarked.

After being served a round of drinks they headed to the back of the building where the restaurant was located. They were soon seated at a table in the middle of the room.

Prawn cocktails were soon dispatched and the girls ate hungrily.

'It's so nice just to go out for the evening,' said Jane who was now busy dissecting her steak.

'Yes it makes a change from boring Glastonbury,' Jenny replied eyeing one of the young men who stood at the bar.

'Hmm. Not many sights like that in Glastonbury,' Penny mumbled with a mouthful of fish.

'I don't know that I can eat much more.' Jane sat back holding her hands to her belly.

'I could eat plenty of him,' Jenny replied still staring at the guy by the bar.

'Behave yourself.' Penny took a sip from her wine glass and took the opportunity to glance in that direction.

'I'm glad it's Saturday tomorrow. I fancy a lazy day. The tourist guides help out at the weekends escorting visitors around the Chapel so I have a free day. By the way Jenny, don't forget that Eddie Hallerton is coming over to plant the new shrubs.'

'Ugh!' Jenny replied as she wiped the remains of her dinner from her mouth.

'That man gives me the creeps.'

'Why do you say that?' Jane asked.

'He's always staring at me. I feel like he's mentally undressing me all the time.'

'That's just wishful thinking,' said Penny laughing.

'Ugh!' Jenny repeated. 'Disgusting little man.'

'You ought to wear something sexy. You know a little see through top and mini skirt. That'll give him a heart attack,' said Jane.

'Hopefully,' Jenny replied stern faced.

'Are we going on to the Wine Vaults from here?' asked Penny.

'They've got a live band there tonight.'

'Are you trying to get me drunk?' Jane drank the remains of her wine.

'I'll drop you two there if you wish,' Jenny said. 'I have a bit of a headache and I'm real tired. It's been a long week. Don't worry Pen I won't damage your car.'

Penny gave her a discerning look but didn't reply.

Once they had finished their meals and paid the bill, Jenny duly dropped them outside the Wine Vaults. It was a wine bar and club. The live band could be heard playing somewhere at the back of the vast dome shaped building that stood under the railway arches. Penny couldn't help but look at the amazed look on Jane's face.

'Don't worry they're not all eighteen years of age. There's always a couple of younger one's for you and me.'

That really broke the ice for Jane. She couldn't stop laughing.

Carrying a large glass each, they jostled their way through the crowd. It was the first time Jane had danced in years.

By the time they were dancing to the third song, Jenny had returned home. Slipped into bed and put her arms around Michael.

'She won't be home for another two hours,' she whispered.

32

'Hello,' said Denise just as she was about to shut the door.

'I'm afraid we're just closing for the day.'

'Oh that's OK. I'm on my way home actually. Are you walking to the station? If so, I'll wait while you lock up.'

'Yes I am. I'll just be a moment.'

Denise ran back into the shop, checked the till was locked, slipped her trainers on and grabbed her coat. Once she'd locked the front door they walked away towards the town centre.

'I do dislike Friday nights. I know it's the end of the week for some people but it's the late night finish for the Tourist office. By the time I get out its dark. I do so hate being out in the dark on my own,' said Denise.

'Yes I think we all do. We're far happier when we can see everything around us. God would have given us cat's eyes if we supposed to be walking around in the dark.'

Denise raised the collar of her jacket and wrapped it tightly around her neck as the bitter wind swirled down the street.

'Have you had a busy day today?'

'I wasn't too bad actually. Quite often Fridays are quieter for some reason.' Denise shivered as the rain became more persistent.

'Shall we take the short cut through Abbot's Walk? We might just make it in time for the bus.'

'Oh yes. If you think it's quicker,' Denise quickened her pace to keep up.

33

I'm glad someone made a start, Eddie Hallerton thought to himself as he surveyed the dug up area. There were ten large shrubs and two small Yew trees lying on the grass waiting to be planted.

He walked back to the machinery room where the industrial digger, petrol driven lawnmowers and a whole array of gardening equipment was housed. He opened the key box to grab the ignition key for digger but it was missing. After sifting through all the keys and searching the drawers of the old wooden bench that stood at the back of the building, he checked the digger. Sure enough, the keys were still in the ignition.

Eddie thought that was strange as he was usually very careful about putting keys away but shrugged his shoulders, climbed on board and powered the machine up. He adjusted the seat and pressed the pedal. Suddenly the machine jumped forward and stalled. Not only had someone moved the seat forward but they had also left the digger in gear.

Just over an hour later he was planting the last of the shrubs when Penny came out of the house.

'Hello, Mr Hallerton. How's it going? Oh they do look nice don't they? Those trees especially. They will provide us with just a touch more privacy.'

'I hope you like them, ma'am.'

'The two trees there will need a lot of watering this year to fully establish themselves but they'll be fine. There's enough light for them here and they're protected from the wind.'

'I'm sure you will look after them for us. You ought to bring Mrs Hallerton over here one afternoon and show her the gardens. I mean, they're nearly all your own work.'

'I thank you, ma'am. I surely will. She'll enjoy that,' he said, tipping his cloth cap.

Penny left him to tidy up and went back into the house. The last thing Eddie did that day was to lock the door to the garden machinery. Something was bugging him but he couldn't put his finger on it.

34

Wesley was making Jane a strong coffee. It had been a long time since she'd partied late into the night.

'Oh my head,' she said as he placed the steaming cup of coffee in front of her.

'You're getting too old for all that clubbing lark,' Wesley joked ruffling her hair.

'Clubbing? All I did was dance to a live band.'

At that moment the phone rang.

'I'll get it,' said Wesley and walked out into the hall.

'John Wesley speaking.'

'Morning, Sir, I'm sorry to disturb you. It's Adam.'

'What's up son?'

'I've just had an extremely anxious mother on the phone saying that her daughter never came home last and hasn't turned up yet.'

'Oh no. Not another one. I assume you got the address?'

'Yes. The girl lives just half a mile out of Glastonbury.'

'OK. Phone the team over at Bath. Find out which WPC is on shift and arrange to meet her at the house asap. If you have any problems just give my name and ask them to phone me for confirmation. Call me with an update after you've spoken with the mother. I'll be on my mobile.'

'Certainly.'

'Oh and one other thing. If the girl is still missing when you get over there, try to get a recent photo but be discreet. There's no need to cause further upset to the mother.'

'Sure thing.'

When Wesley re-entered the kitchen Jane was fast asleep. He refilled the kettle, placed Jane's empty coffee cup in the sink and closed the door behind him.

Having showered, he slung on tee-shirt and jeans before phoning the station from his mobile. PC Martin Philips answered.

'Hi, Sir. How's Mrs Wesley this morning?'

'A bit hung over. What made you ask?'

He could hear Martin's muffled giggling even though he obviously had his hand over the phone.

'Some of the lads from Bath saw Mrs Wesley in the wine bar last night. She was strutting her stuff to one of the bands.'

'Did they now? That would help to explain the way she looks this morning.'

He couldn't help but laugh.

'Martin, can you try to contact someone at the council offices. I appreciate it's the weekend but I need to find out who has the keys to the Chalice Well. I assume the council have access to the Well. You can ask them also who maintains the Well. Is it the council or do they contract the work out? If they do, I want names and addresses of the businesses.'

'How soon do you want to gain access?'

'As soon as possible. If you do manage to speak to someone, please stress that the request is to be held in the strictest confidence as it's related to the recent murders. If you need a name ask for Councillor Jacobs. He owes me a favour.'

'I understand. I'll call you back in a while.'

35

'Don't keep moaning about it all day,' said Dorothy. 'Go and tell Mr Wesley what Penny told you. If she saw Kelvin Ward on the Tor the night he died then Mr Wesley ought to know.'
'But he's going to ask me why I haven't mentioned it before.'
'Why didn't you?'
'You know why,' Eddie replied raising his voice. 'If she saw Kelvin Ward she must have seen me too. Even if she didn't say as much.'

Wesley replaced the receiver. There was still no sign of the missing girl. He looked across the desk to where Eddie was sat toying with his cloth cap. He wasn't really in the mood to listen to the man.
'Why on earth didn't you tell me that Penny Westbrook told you she saw Kelvin Ward on the Tor the night he was killed?'
'I only just remembered,' Eddie answered apologetically.
'Rubbish! I don't believe it's something you would easily forget. Come on Eddie, you can do better than that.'
Eddie looked dejected. He knew there was no way out. He would have to come clean.
'I didn't mention it because I was on the Tor myself. I saw him too.'
'What! Oh this gets better and better.'
Wesley leaned back on his chair, took his tobacco and cigarette papers from his jacket pocket and began rolling the first of several roll ups.
'OK, in your own time Eddie, and let's have the whole story this time.'
'When I first saw Kelvin Ward at the foot of the Tor he was looking towards Abbey House.'
'What time was this?'
'Must have been about nine o'clock in the evening. It had been dark for about an hour.'
'Did you speak to him?'
'No. I did wave to him but he didn't acknowledge me.'
'Where were you?'
Eddie hesitated before answering.
'I was on the Tor walking past the railings to the Abbey grounds, heading towards the back of the house.'
'On your own?'
'Yes.'

'What were you doing there, especially at that time of night?'

Eddie watched Wesley lining up his roll ups. All expertly made.

'They don't need the stuff, they throw it all away. It's not really stealing,' Eddie stammered.

Wesley shrugged his shoulders in despair.

'What are you talking about?'

'The lead, from the old Chapel roof.'

'Explain.'

'The Westbrook's have just had the roof repaired on the Chapel. All the old bits of lead that are for scrap had been left at the back of the house. No one wanted it, so I thought I could sell it.'

'So you stole it?'

Using a matchstick Wesley carefully prodded the ends of each of the roll ups pushing the tobacco contents in.

'Yes, Mr Wesley,' Eddie replied looking down on the table.

'Dorothy made me tell you. I knew you wouldn't see it my way.'

'Stealing someone else's property is theft,' said Wesley placing his carefully rolled cigarettes into his tobacco pouch.

Eddie looked downcast like someone awaiting sentencing.

'So did you see Kelvin Ward after that?'

'I ran past the edge of the grounds heading across the Tor as quick as I could but the few bits of lead I was carrying were heavy. I'd just reached the roadside when I heard a shout.'

'From someone on the Tor?'

'Yes.'

'A man's voice or a woman.'

'I couldn't be sure Mr Wesley but I think it was a man's voice.'

'Was it a shout or a scream?'

'I'm not sure Mr Wesley. It spooked me a bit so I turned and ran off. What sentence will I get?'

'What?'

'I mean for stealing the lead. What sentence will I get?'

'As no one has reported anything being stolen, then I guess the answer is none. Do me a favour Eddie. Go home and look after Dorothy.'

Eddie shot up from the chair.

'Oh, thank you Mr Wesley. Thank you,' he said making his way to the door.

'Eddie, one more thing.'

'Yes Mr Wesley?'

'Where did you take the lead?'

'I left it in the back of my van. The van was parked around the back of our local. I often leave it there overnight, especially if I've one or two too many. If you know what I mean?'

'So you left the van open for someone else to take the lead way?'

'Yes.'

'And who might that be?'

'He's not from the village. You won't know him.'

'I don't want to particularly know him Eddie. I just want his name.'

'They call him Matt. I don't know if that's his real name. He lives on the caravan site on the Bath road just outside of Wells.'

'When are you going to see him next?'

Eddie wiped the sweat from his brow.

'Come on Eddie. I haven't got time to waste.'

'He's, err, due in the local tonight.'

'How much?'

'Sorry Inspector?'

'How much is he paying you for the lead?'

'Eighty pounds for the slates I got him.'

'Hmm. I'd say he was ripping you off Eddie. In any case I'll tell you what. Pay the eighty pounds into the local hospital fund. I'll want to see the receipt.'

A dejected Eddie Hallerton nodded his head.

'One last thing. From now on, if you hear or see anything that I might be remotely interested in, tell me.'

'Yes, Mr Wesley. I certainly will,' he replied closing the door behind him.

Wesley opened his tobacco pouch. Extracted a roll up. Lit it and exhaled deeply, blowing the blue smoke upwards watching it spiral towards the single naked bulb.

36

It was late Saturday afternoon and Wesley was still sat in his office, now listening to the information that Adam had managed to gleam from a distraught Mrs Wright.

'So Denise finished work at eight o'clock last night?'

'That's correct.'

'Who else works in the Tourist office?'

'According to Denise's mother there is just one other lady, a Mrs Harper. She runs the place. Works there seven days a week apparently.'

'OK. Ask Martin to go and have a chat with her. Do we know if Denise was planning on meeting anyone last night?'

'I did ask that question and got a short reply from Mrs Wright. She says her daughter doesn't have a boyfriend and keeps herself to herself.'

'Oh one of them eh? They're usually the worst cases when the parents deny their daughter does anything other than go straight home every night. Did you manage to get a recent photograph?'

Adam extracted two passport photos from his pocket.

'These were taken earlier this year,' he said passing them across the desk.

'How old is she?'

'Eighteen.' Wesley sighed and rubbed his hands across his face.

'You OK, Sir? You look tired,' Adam remarked.

'Yeah I'm fine. Tired too. Tired at seeing photos of missing kids. Get these blown up please Adam and pass them around. Find out who's on the beat today and make sure they take them with them and ask around. What have you said to the girl's mother?'

'I told her we would look for her daughter but asked for her to phone should her daughter turn up or get in contact. I said if we didn't hear from her by teatime we would give her a call.'

'OK, that's fine. I'll speak with her later if the girl hasn't turned up. I don't want the press involved at this stage. I don't need them pestering us all day drawing up all sorts of incorrect assumptions.'

'OK, Sir.' Adam stood up to leave the room.

'Oh by the way Adam. Good work son.'

Adam walked out into the corridor pleased with himself and the praise he'd received.

'You missed a good night,' said Penny reaching for the nurofen.

'Looks like it,' Jenny smirked.

'Oh I've always got a hangover. It doesn't matter if I have one glass of wine or ten.'

'So how many did you have?'

'Probably closer to ten.' Penny screwed up her nose.

'I would have stayed with you but to be honest I was shattered. What with looking after the place all week, having to be up early every day to make sure the Chapel is clean and tidy before the daily hoard of visitors turn up. I just couldn't stay awake,' she said pouring cornflakes into a bowl.

'Good morning ladies.' Michael waltzed into the kitchen.

'How are my lovely ladies today?'

Penny noticed Jenny's face redden.

'You were snoring most of the night,' Penny said.

'And you my dear were quite drunk if I remember right,' he replied with a sickly grin. Penny ignored him and spoke to Jenny.

'What are you doing today Jenny?'

'I'm walking into town this morning. I need some fresh air. The weather forecast is for rain this afternoon so I want to make the most of the morning.'

'What about you Penny?'

'I was thinking about moving some stuff about upstairs. The plan as you know is to open the east wing to the public next year but before we do that, the whole place needs tidying up. If anyone wants me, that's where I'll be.'

She refilled her glass of water and walked out of the kitchen glancing at Michael who returned her stare.

Waiting until he was sure she was out of earshot, Michael crossed the kitchen to where Jenny stood by the fridge eating cornflakes. He stood in front of her and ran his hands over her buttocks.

'Nice silk pyjamas.'

'I thought you had a pair of your own,' she laughed.

Michael pulled her close and tried to kiss her but she pulled away.

'What's wrong?'

'Michael. For God sake. You're wife has just walked out of the room. If she catches us you'll be in for a divorce.'

'She doesn't care what I do.'

'I'm sure you will find that she does and what's more, I don't want to be implicated.'

'You should have thought about that,' he sneered.

37

'I'm sure there's no need to worry'. PC Martin Philips was trying to console Mrs Harper after asking if she had seen Denise since Friday night.

'You know what these young girls are like. Denise has probably stayed at a friend's and forgotten to tell her mother that she was staying over.'

'Oh do you think so?' she replied tearfully. 'She's such a lovely girl. I do hope she's OK. I don't think she's the kind of girl who would stay at friends. I mean, she never mentions any friends. She's quite a loner really.'

Mrs Harper directed Martin to a seat in the kitchen at the back of the shop where she began to fill the kettle.

'Can you confirm what time you last saw her?'

'Last night. We close up late on a Friday, at eight. Denise usually leaves just before me as she gets the quarter past the hour bus from the High Street. She locked up last night as she insisted on staying behind for a while to finish putting all the new books on display.'

She retrieved two cups from a small cupboard above the sink.

Do you take sugar?'

'Just one please. Does Denise always go home by herself?' he asked accepting the tea.

'Yes. I've never seen anyone waiting for her, if that is what you mean.'

'Hmm, no boyfriend?'

'I don't think Denise is into boys. I mean, she's never mentioned anyone. The only person she talks about is her mother.'

'Has there been anyone hanging around the shop lately. You know, suspicious like?'

'I don't think so,' she replied looking nervous.

'I'm sorry Mrs Harper. I didn't intend to frighten you. We just need to ask these questions.'

He took a sip of tea before continuing.

'Has Denise got a locker or anywhere she keeps her stuff?'

'Not really. We only have this small room and the toilet next door. There is a coat hook by the toilet door. I'll show you.'

There were only two coats hanging up.

'This black one is mine. The duffel coat is Denise's.'

Martin checked the pockets. Feeling inside the right hand pocket he pulled out Denise's University card.

'May I keep this?'

'Yes of course.'

Seeing that she was becoming upset again he decided to end the questions about Denise for the time being.

'So how long have you worked in the shop?' he asked changing the approach.

'About six years. I started part-time at first, just after my husband passed away but I suppose I've gradually extended the hours over the years. The council, who own the premises, now allows me to virtually run the place.'

'Well, it looks like you're doing a good job.'

He placed the remains of his tea on the table. After making a note of what Denise had been wearing the day she disappeared, he put his notebook away.

'I'll leave you with my contact details,' he said standing up and handing his card to her. 'I know Denise is not expected in work today but if you hear from her please give us a call and ask her to phone the station.'

'Yes of course,' she replied blowing her nose.

38

Denise woke with a thumping headache. She tried to move when to her horror she realised that both her hands and legs were tied. Her initial instinct was to scream but the tape that covered her mouth prevented her from doing so. She tried to take in her surroundings as her eyes slowly became accustomed to the dull grey light.

Feeling nauseous and somewhat disorientated she managed to shuffle backwards on her bottom until she rested her back on the wall. She was desperately trying to control her nerves and ignore the pain running through her head.

It soon became obvious to her that she was in a small windowless room. The only air getting into the room was from a small grill high up on the far wall. She was sat on a dirt floor. There was a door to her left. She tried desperately to remember what had happened and had a vague recollection of sitting on one of the benches in the grounds of the Abbey. She had been talking to someone but she couldn't remember who.

They'd had a drink of something or other. Possibly cider? That would at least explain the headache.

But after that everything was a blur.

39

Michael Westbrook was surprised to hear Inspector Wesley's voice when he answered the buzzer.

'This is a surprise Inspector,' he said as he opened the front door. 'Do come in.'

'Thanks.' Wesley took off his wet jacket.

'British summer eh?' Michael laughed. 'Here let me take that from you. I'll hang it in the kitchen. It'll dry quicker in there.'

'Much appreciated,' said Wesley handing it over.

'Take a seat in the back room. I'll fetch some tea.'

Wesley was looking out of the French doors when Michael reappeared with a tray of tea and biscuits.

'That's a nice new array of shrubs out there,' remarked Wesley pointing towards the edge of the back lawn. Michaels face turned almost crimson with rage.

'Who on earth asked for them to be planted. I didn't order them.'

'Well someone obviously did and those two young Yew trees must have cost a fortune.'

Wesley took the tray from him, setting it down on the table.

'Well, yes. Sorry Inspector. I do hate it when people organise things without even speaking to me about it.'

'I'm sure Mrs Westbrook was going to mention it.'

Michael looked at Wesley without replying.

'Shall I pour?'

'Here let me do that,' said Michael. 'So what brings you over here?'

'I want to take a look at the Chalice Well and I believe you have one of the sets of keys.'

Michael's complexion changed from red to ashen grey in seconds.

'May I ask why you want to enter the Well?'

'Just part of our investigations.'

'I don't believe anyone has opened the Well since my father was alive,' Michael replied handing Wesley his tea.

'Let me see if I can find the keys.'

He left Wesley sat in the back room. Just as he was helping himself to a biscuit, Penny entered through the French doors.

'Oh, Mr Wesley. You made me jump. I didn't know anyone was here.'

She was soaked to the skin, wearing a thick brown jumper and denim jeans which were covered in mud. A pair of muddy wellington boots under her arm.

'Oh, I just stopped by to pick up some keys.'

'Keys?'

'Yes. I want to take a look at the Chalice Well and I was told that your husband has a set of keys.'

'May I ask why you want to enter the Well? It seems a strange request.'

'Just part of our investigations Mrs Westbrook, nothing to worry about.'

'Have you any idea who the murderer is?'

'Not yet. But we're pursuing a number of enquiries.'

'Well if you'll excuse me I need to change out of these wet things.'

'Yes of course.' Wesley stood up as Penny left the room.

As he sat down again to finish his tea he could hear Penny and Michael arguing in the hallway.

'Where the hell have you been? Look at the damn mess you're making. God give me strength,' Michael shouted.

'Go to hell,' Penny replied.

Wesley heard a door slam somewhere off the hallway. He pretended to be checking his mobile for messages when Michael reappeared in the back room.

'Sorry I took so long Inspector. I thought the keys were in the kitchen where we usually keep all the estate keys in the wall safe. Someone must have taken them out for some reason and not put them back. I found them in the draw under the kitchen table in the end.'

'That's OK,' said Wesley taking them from Michael.

'I only need them for a few hours. I'll drop them back later.'

He stood to leave.

'Thanks for the tea. Sorry I can't stop to have a chat, but murder enquiries just won't wait.'

'I understand. Let me get your coat for you. You'll need something warm if you're going into the Well. I would imagine its damn cold down there, especially with all that running water.'

It was pouring with rain as Wesley left Abbey House. He phoned the station and asked for an update on Denise Wright. She was still missing. He jotted down her mother's address and said he was headed there now.

Wesley spent the next hour using his vast experience to comfort Denise's mother, assuring her he was doing everything he could to locate her daughter. After refusing several offers of more tea he left her in the capable hands of WPC Lucy Clarke who was well experienced in handling these types of situation.

When he eventually arrived home he felt exhausted. Jane took his coat from him and told him to go and sit in the lounge, where she would bring him his dinner shortly. Ten minutes later, Jane carried the dinner tray through to their back room only to find Wesley sound asleep in the chair. She put his dinner in the microwave and left him a note on the kitchen worktop before locking the front door and turning the downstairs lights off.

40

Wesley dialled the number and began rolling a cigarette while waiting for an answer. It only took three rings before the receiver was picked up.

'Good morning Colin. Its Inspector Wesley speaking. I appreciate its short notice but I was wondering if you had anything planned for today?' he asked whilst searching for his tobacco that Jane had probably hidden.

'Not really Inspector, why do you ask?'

'I've managed to obtain the keys to the Chalice Well and I would appreciate your expertise about the Well's layout.'

'Sure not a problem. I'll need to dig out my old hiking gear and walking boots if you plan on going into the Well. I'm sure it's going to be wet and cold down there.'

'That would be great if we could. Look, its ten o'clock now. Can you meet me there at two this afternoon?'

'I shall look forward to it.'

Wesley lit a cigarette and pondered about the prospect of crawling through underground tunnels. It wasn't something that particularly enthralled him. He was claustrophobic and hated being stuck in confined spaces.

By the time Wesley and Colin arrived at the Chalice Well they were already wet. For once the weather forecast was right and the heavy rain arrived exactly on time. The grassy slope of the Tor was slippery at the best of times but the heavy rain had made it quite treacherous.

'Thanks for coming over,' said Wesley shaking his hand.

'You could have picked a nicer day,' Colin replied laughing.

'You look as if we're about to go mountaineering with all that gear.' Wesley pointed to the belt and array of attachments that Colin had fitted around his waist.

'This is a guide rope,' said Colin opening another bag. 'It's nylon and is commonly used by potholers.' He unravelled the thirty foot length of rope, which had a belt and clips on each end. He dressed himself first wearing one belt then fitted the other on Wesley.

'This way we won't get lost.'

'Don't lose the chief down there,' said PC Martin Philips laughing as he came up the slope.

'Martin. I need you to keep an eye on the entrance here whilst Colin and I take a look down the Well,' said Wesley.

'Quite seriously, it's going to be dark down there and slippery,' said Colin. 'If one of us slips or falls, the other simply tugs the rope to let the other person know.'

'Sounds good to me,' said Wesley.

He knelt down to where the Chalice Well cover lay and unlocked the padlock before placing the key back in his pocket. He pulled back the grill cover to expose the dark void below.

'Looks a bit grim down there,' said Martin.

'No wetter than it will be up here while you're waiting for us to return,' Wesley replied grinning at Colin. Colin stepped forward handing Wesley a Maglite torch.

'I'll go first.' Colin sat down by the entrance with his feet dangling into the void. Keeping his hands planted firmly on the ground he lowered himself until he found the first step that was sunk into the concrete wall.

'If the map is accurate, this is a straight drop of about twenty feet.'

Both Wesley and Martin peered down into the void and watched as Colin slowly descended. The light from his torch was eventually the only sign that anyone was down there.

'OK. Your turn,' Colin called up.

'Good luck,' said Martin with a smirk on his face.

'You'd better pray that I return son. No other bugger is going to sign off your overtime.'

Wesley made the slow descent, trying hard to overcome his fear of enclosed spaces. A minute later he nearly jumped out of his skin when Colin tapped him on the back.

'You're down. You OK?'

'Yeah thanks. Which way now?' He sighed as his eyes slowly grew accustomed to the dark.

'We're going to take a left turn.' Colin raised his voice a little to be heard in their cold subterranean world.

'This will take us from the third level where we started down to the second level then first level and eventually to the Wells core. It's downhill from now on. I'll take the lead. Dependent on the level of water, let's see how far we get.'

'OK, let's do it.'

Colin could sense the tenseness in Wesley's voice.

The ledge they were standing on was no more than two feet wide and they both had to bend down to avoid hitting their heads on the roof of the tunnel. There was a similar ledge on the other side of the tunnel. In between, lay a four foot wide expanse of water.

'Do we know how deep the water is here?' Wesley asked.

'It's difficult to tell but I would estimate around four to six feet.' Their progress was slow because of the slippery floor and the fact that both men were continually bent in half.

'I get the feeling we're going in circles.'

'That's exactly what we're doing. The Well circles the Tor, gradually descending each level until we reach the bottom.'

'Where does the bottom come out?'

'That's a good question. The maps are inconclusive. The Well is fed from underground streams that cover half of Somerset and is replenished by rainfall some miles from here. The two maps I've managed to obtain show the Well bottom being somewhere near King Arthur's tomb but if you line them up together I'm more inclined to think the actual bottom is nearer to Abbey House. There was some work carried out on the Well just over hundred years ago which appears to have sunken the Well deeper.'

'How far have we travelled? My back is killing me,' said Wesley.

'Just ahead we should level out before we drop to the next level. I think we'll be able to stand up straight there.'

Wesley shivered as the dampness started to get to his skin.

Colin moved forward whilst Wesley waited for him to tug on the rope.

'OK I'm there!' Colin shouted just a minute later. I'll keep the rope taught, just keep walking towards me.'

Wesley was delighted to be able to stand upright and leant back against the wall to rest for a second.

'This is harder than I imagined,' he said taking deep breaths.

'Yes, but obviously not that difficult.' Colin pointed to the opposite wall.

'Look at the ledge.'

At first Wesley wasn't sure what he was looking at. Then he spotted them. Footprints. He kept the torch aimed at the far ledge. It was obvious that someone else had been in the Well quite recently.

'Now that is interesting.'

'Yes, but almost impossible to tell whether male or female from here,' Colin replied.

'Let's move on. I'm getting cold,' Wesley said turning up his coat collar.

They had walked for a further two minutes when suddenly Colin called out. 'Have you noticed the walls? The tiles are different size. I think this is the newest part of the Well.'

'How far underground are we?'

'I'd guess about a hundred feet but not for much longer. The ledge is level here and we're about to start ascending the Well.'

'Thank God for that,' Wesley cried out.

A minute later Wesley could feel the rope start to slack.

'You OK up there?' he shouted.

'Sure am. Come and take a look.'

When he reached Colin he found himself standing upright in a circular vault. A metal ladder was embedded into both sides of the wall and some ten feet above them, an open metal grill let in a faint glow of daylight.

'I wonder where that leads to.'

'I'm not sure but we're going to find out,' Colin replied as he started to climb. The grill was unlocked and he managed to slide it away from the opening. Hoisting himself up, he sat on the mosaic floor and whistled to himself as he observed his surroundings.

'You might want to see this.'

Wesley followed and eventually stood at the top of the ladder where he could look over the top of the vault. He stared in amazement.

'Where the hell are we?'

'This is the old basement level of Abbey House,' Colin replied.

'Better known today as the Chapel.'

Wesley walked past the font and the lectern towards the large oak door that provided entrance to the Chapel from the outside.

It was locked, which was a good thing as Wesley would have had to explain what they were doing there. Both men sat on the floor with their backs to the wall resting while they gathered their thoughts. It was Colin who spoke first.

'I don't know if you noticed but the grill cover wasn't locked, and looking at where it sits in the floor, I would say it's been lifted before quite recently.'

'I would have to agree with you,' Wesley replied looking at the marks around the edge of the grill cover. 'The question is, why?'

'Who has access to the Chapel?' asked Colin.

'Michael Westbrook and his wife Penny have access, as I assume does the vicar, although I'll need to confirm that. The only other key owners are the council.'

Colin couldn't help but laugh.

'What's funny? Wesley asked.

'I just had this vision of the vicar talking to the congregation and saying please carry on with the next psalm. I'm just popping down the Well.'

'Yeah, put like that it is rather amusing. I don't see any reason for the vicar wanting to go down there though. I think I need to talk to Michael and Penny.'

Wesley cursed as he stood up. His back was killing him.

'I think we will have to go back the way we came,' he said trying to stretch his painful legs.

'Yeah we will as the door to the Chapel is locked. I'll lead the way again,' said Colin. 'Watch your fingers when you slide the grill cover across. It's damn heavy.'

It took them over thirty minutes to reach the other end of the tunnel. Colin grabbed Wesley's arm as he hoisted him out onto the Tor and back into the fresh air.

'Thanks Colin,' he panted. 'Definitely getting too old for this kind of thing.'

'Well I'm heading for the pub,' said Colin laughing as he started getting out of his hiking gear.

'If I weren't on duty I'd join you.' Wesley was searching for his tobacco.

Martin coughed politely. He had been standing in the background. Having been stood patiently waiting for the men to return for over an hour he was drenched.

'Martin. I think you ought to go home and get changed,' said Wesley. 'I don't need you any more today. By the way those trousers of yours looked creased. Make sure they are ironed before you come into the station tomorrow.'

'Yes, Sir,' he answered. Looking dejected, he turned to walk away.

'Oh, another thing,' Wesley called out.

'Yes, Sir?'

'I owe you a pint.'

'Thanks,' Martin replied. A smile spreading across his face.

41

'Sal! Breakfast is ready,' David shouted from the bottom of the stairs.
'Just coming.'
Sally walked into the kitchen and was immediately greeted by the aroma of eggs and bacon.
'Hmm, sure smells good,' she said sitting at the table.
'I'm so glad you could make it this weekend.'
David placed the plate down in front of her. 'I love it when we spend time together.'
'So do I. Especially when you cook breakfast too. What are we going to do today?'
'I was thinking perhaps we could go back to bed after breakfast,' he replied with a grin on his face.
'Think again Casanova.' She aimed the tomato sauce bottle at him.
'It's Mum's birthday next week. I'd like to go into town to see if there's anything I can buy her.'
'Sure OK Sal, only if we can have a pub lunch somewhere afterwards.'
'That's a deal. I accept your offer of lunch.'
After breakfast, having decided they would wash up when they got back, David grabbed his keys and they headed to the shops.
'Have you heard anything from Colin for the past few days?' she asked as they strolled along with the other Sunday shoppers.
'No I haven't spoken to him for a couple of days. I did try to phone him but he didn't answer and he hasn't returned my call yet. To be honest he seems a bit remote right now.'
'What do you mean?'
'I can't explain it really Sal. He just seems quiet. Almost as if he just wants to be left alone.'
'I guess that's understandable. Maybe it's just his way of handling things. She grabbed his arm. Oh David, look at that jewellery. Isn't that pretty,' she said dragging him into the shop.

Eddie was cleaning the gardening equipment when Michael entered the machinery room at the back of the house.
'What are you doing here today? It's Sunday for Christ's sake,' Michael asked quite abruptly.
'Cleaning some of the equipment. The digger needs to be washed down

and the petrol mower needs to be ready for collection as it's going away for servicing tomorrow.'

'Oh right. You can clean them dirty wellington boots too while you're here. And by the way, who ordered those new shrubs and trees?'

'I assumed you had.'

'Well it wasn't me.'

Michael and Eddie walked off in the direction of the car garage.

'Who's moved the bloody car seat forward?'

Eddie could hear Michael ranting and raving to himself but chose not to get involved in a dispute. He pulled down the wellington boots from the shelf and noticed the wet rim around the toes as if someone had been standing in water. That didn't seem so strange but what caught his eye was the dried clay that was stuck to the top of the boots. The only place that could have come from was the gardens where he had just planted the new Yew trees.

Why would someone walk in the clay? Eddie thought to himself. He stood looking around the place. There was something going on. It was beginning to worry him. Someone other than Michael asking for trees to be planted. Clay on the wellington boots and machinery left in gear. He began cleaning the boots. Not sure that he was doing the right thing.

42

Wesley had just walked out of the shower when his mobile rang.

'Hi Wesley speaking.'

'Hello Mr Wesley. It's Eddie Hallerton here. I hope you don't mind me calling you. You did say to give you a ring if there was anything I thought you ought to know.'

'Sure Eddie, go ahead,' Wesley replied drying his hair with the towel.

'Well, it may be nothing Mr Wesley, but when I was over at Abbey House this morning to get the industrial lawn mower ready for collection. You see it's going in for servicing. Well, I noticed a pair of muddy wellington boots.'

Wesley put the towel down and sat on the bed.

'Muddy wellington boots? I don't understand.'

'Well you see. The boots were wet, as if someone had been standing in the rain, and they were covered in clay.'

Wesley rubbed his hand across his face and yawned.

'Eddie. Please get to the point.'

'It's the clay that struck me as odd. You see, the only clay area on the estate is where the new Yew trees have been planted. Now, apart from when I planted the trees, why would anyone else want to dig up the grounds or go walking through the clay? That's what I've been asking myself.'

'So are you telling me that someone else had already been digging in the grounds of the estate where the trees were going to be planted before you started work there?'

'Yes, Mr Wesley. That's exactly it. In the time I've been working for the Westbrook's neither of them have ever done anything on the estate apart from walk round it.'

'Hmm, I see what you're getting at. OK thanks Eddie I appreciate it. I'll have a word with Michael and Penny. Maybe they know something about it.'

As Wesley was getting dressed he remembered seeing Penny walk through the French doors carrying wellington boots. He entered a reminder on his mobile to speak with her later then continued dressing as Jane called from downstairs to say that dinner was ready.

43

It was a typical Monday morning. Dull, cold and wet. The kind of day you wish the weather forecasters had got their predictions wrong. Wesley was searching his coat pockets for his tobacco when Adam entered with a cup of tea.

'Morning, Sir. Did you have a good weekend?'
'Pot holing,' said Wesley without looking up.
'Sorry?'
'Don't worry. Ask Martin, he'll explain. Ah there it is.' He extracted his tobacco and cigarette papers from the top drawer in his desk.
'What are you smirking at?' asked Wesley looking at the young PC.
'Mrs Wesley still hiding your tobacco at home?'
Wesley gave him a knowing look.
'Have you got nothing else to do today?'
Adam turned to leave.
'Oh Adam, I'm going over to see Denise Wright's mother this morning. When Martin arrives, tell him I want him to meet two PCs in Glastonbury High Street, near the car park. They're expecting him at ten o'clock. I want Denise's photo shoved under everyone's nose in Glastonbury today. Someone must have seen her leave the Tourist office on Friday night.'
'OK. Anything else?'
'Yeah. I'd like you and one of the female WPCs from Bath to go over to the University. I want to know what Denise's timetable should be for this week. See if you can find anyone who knows her. Maybe someone who's been her friend.'
Wesley stood up, finished his tea and retrieved his jacket.
I'm on my mobile if anyone needs me.'
'Sure thing,' Adam replied closing the door.

Jenny stood looking out of her bedroom window when there was a knock on the door.
'Come in,' she called putting the curtain back.
Her face dropped when Penny entered the room.
'You look as if you were expecting someone else.'
Jenny looked embarrassed for a second.
'Oh no. Sorry I was miles away really.'
'Dreaming of what my dear?'

'Far away shores. A sunny beach and a large cocktail,' said Jenny smiling as she regained her composure.

'I was just wondering if you wanted to come into town with me this morning. I need to do some shopping.'

'Thanks but I really need to get on with the housework. We have a group of visitors coming down from London today who have specifically asked to see the Chapel and have paid to have a guided tour of the grounds. They will be here around two o'clock and I need to ensure everything is clean and where it should be.'

'OK, if you're sure,' Penny replied. 'I'll catch you later.'

She walked along the landing and down the first flight of stairs then passed hers and Michael's bedroom and the bathroom, before descending down to the hall. She was halfway across the hall when she heard the click of their bedroom door as it was slowly opened from within.

She smiled to herself and carried on walking. She expected Michael to be in Jenny's room as soon as she left she house. She knew the time would come when she would have to confront the two of them.

44

'Oh David it's beautiful. I'm lost for words.'
'I was praying you'd say yes,' he replied. His hands were still shaking.
'You silly thing. My answer was always going to be yes. I love you.'
Sally stared in amazement at the engagement ring on her finger.
'David can I phone my mother? She's going to be thrilled.'
'Do you think she'll want to come to the wedding?' he asked jokingly.
'You try and stop her.' Sally gave him a huge hug and ran into the lounge and picked up the phone to call her mother as David dialled Colin's number on his mobile. Colin answered almost immediately.
'Hi Colin, its David. How are you?'
'I'm good, you OK?'
'Yes thanks. I just wanted you to be one of the first to know that Sally and I have got engaged.'
David was expecting an immediate response but for a few seconds there was silence.
'Oh, congratulations.'
'Colin, are you OK?'
'What? Oh sorry. Yes, it's just that I'm late for a class and I can't find some bloody charts.'
'Oh OK. Don't worry I'll give you a call tonight. I'm on leave today. Sally and I are going out to celebrate.'
'Sure. Catch you later,' Colin replied and hung up.
David stood looking at his mobile for a moment. He was staggered at the lack of interest in Colin's response.
'Who was that?' Sally asked as she breezed back into the bedroom.
'It was Colin. I told him about us getting married. I thought he would be excited but he didn't seem interested.'
'I'm sure it's because of recent events.'
'I'll have a chat with him later. I think he's just trying to keep himself occupied.'
'Maybe you're right.'

45

Denise Wright's mother entered the front room of their small terraced house. She was carrying two cups of tea and some biscuits on a wooden tray that looked as if it was only used on special occasions.

'Do you take sugar Inspector?' She placed the tray on the table.

'Just the one please. My wife tells me I should cut it out altogether but then if she had her way I wouldn't take sugar, smoke or have the occasional pint,' he laughed.

'A little bit of what you fancy does you good. That's what my mother used to say to me. She should know she had six kids.' She handed Wesley his tea and sat down in the armchair opposite him. He noticed that she was shaking.

'May I ask if there is a Mr Wright?'

'I'm afraid my Harold passed away three years ago. He had cancer.' She was silent for a moment, lost in thought.

'I'm sorry to hear that. I had to ask. So you and Denise live here alone?'

'Yes. She's been so good to me since Harold died. I don't know what I would do without her.'

She placed her cup on the table and reached for the handkerchief that was tucked inside her sleeve of her cardigan. Wesley never spoke for a few moments but watched her quietly sob, unable to hold back the tears.

'Mrs Wright. I know you have already told me that Denise didn't have a boyfriend, but is there anyone that you can think of who she might have gone to stay with?'

The old lady wiped her nose and replaced the handkerchief into the sleeve of her cardigan. 'There's no one Inspector. I've racked my brain but I don't know anyone that Denise knew well enough to stay with. You see, she is a very quiet girl. Very reserved. She's always found it hard to mix with people. I don't even know of anyone at the University who she might have been friends with. She never talks about anyone or mentions any names come to think of it.'

'What is Denise studying?'

'She's doing a Travel and Tourism course. You see, there's little work around this area unless you are actually qualified in something specific. I've always told her that the tourism industry is important around here and that's where she could make her money. She says she wants to make her mark here and then set up her own company in London.'

'Mrs Wright, has Denise ever stayed away from home before?'

'No, never Inspector. Not even when she was at school. Oh they had the usual school trips to places but we could never afford them and Denise never showed any interest in being away from home.'

'I assume you've checked her bedroom out?'

'Yes. One of your PCs has already taken a look also.'

'Do you mind if I take a look? You can lead the way.'

Wesley followed her upstairs to the back bedroom. The room looked tidy enough. Almost too tidy. 'Is there anything obvious missing?' he asked as he looked through the dressing table.

'Not that I can see Inspector. Denise is a very tidy girl. She never leaves anything lying around.'

Wesley decided there was nothing to be gained by causing more distress, so he led the way out of the room. Back downstairs he grabbed his tea and sat himself on the settee. He drank the cup almost in one go.

'How long has she been working at the Tourist office?' Wesley placed the cup back down on the table.

'She started there just a couple of months ago at the start of the Tourist season. She was so excited when she got the job. It's only a couple of days a week but it's something that interests her. She loves Mrs Harper too. Says that what Mrs Harper doesn't know about Glastonbury isn't worth knowing about.'

'She's probably right.'

He stood up to leave.

'My team are in Glastonbury right now and other officers are at the University. As soon as I get any news I'll give you a call.'

Denise's mother stood up slowly. The rheumatism in her back prevented her from doing anything quickly. She walked around the table and took hold of Wesley by the arms. 'Please find my little girl,' she begged, as the tears began to flow again.

Wesley sat in the car outside for a few minutes. Before he drove away he phoned WPC Lucy Clarke and asked her to pay another visit to see Denise's mother later in the day. He'd only driven half a mile when his mobile rang so he pulled over and switched off the ignition.

'Wesley here.'

'Hi, it's Adam. I'm over at the University. I think we found something.'

'What is it?' Wesley asked, as he lit a cigarette.

'There's a guy here, name of Ian Hemming. He's a student studying Art. It appears he shared a locker with Denise. The part-time students don't have individual lockers they have to share with other students. Mr Hemming heard we were in the building asking about Denise so came over to inform us there was a letter for her in the locker. He says it's been there for a week or so but he left it as he thought she would pick it up. It's still unopened. What do you want me to do with it?'

'Wait there Adam. I'm just leaving Denise's mothers. I'll be there in about fifty minutes. I'll take a look at the letter and I want to have a chat with Mr Hemming.'

There was a throng of students swarming all over the University campus and Wesley had to push and shove his way through the labyrinth of corridors. He found Adam sat with the young student in the library. After introductions had been made Wesley examined the envelope. Denise's name was handwritten on the front.

'Have you any idea when this was placed in the locker?'

'No, Sir.'

'Who else has a key to the locker?'

'No one apart from Denise and myself. Maybe the janitor has a master key?'

'Would it be possible to slip the envelope inside the locker without opening it?'

'Yes I suppose so,' he replied fidgeting in his chair.

'Has something happened to Denise?' Ian asked looking nervous.

Wesley looked across the room at the young spectacled lad and remembered just how nervous he'd been when he'd first spoken to a policeman as a teenager after his friend's push bike had been stolen.

'That's what we're trying to find out. When was the last time you saw Denise?'

'Probably a couple of weeks ago. We were never in the same class but occasionally we would see one another when we needed something from the locker. I'm only here three days a week and I think Denise is only here two days a week.'

'I see. Do you know if she has any friends at the University?'

'I doubt it,' Ian replied with a smirk on his face.

'What makes you say that?'

'I mean she was always so quiet. I can't imagine her speaking with many people.'

'Hmm OK. Thanks for letting us know about the letter. If you should hear or see anything of Denise please give me a call. Wesley handed him his ID and shook the lad's hand. He decided there was nothing to gain by keeping the lad sitting around.

'So what's next?' asked Adam.

'Continue with the search around the campus Adam. Leave a few photos of Denise around the place. Oh, and while you're here, ask the janitor if he carries a master key to the lockers. We know there's nothing else in the locker now but I want to know who else may have had access. I'm going back to the station. Report to me there at four.'

'Hello Penny,' said Jane. 'Fancy seeing you here.'

The small grocery store was busy as usual with a mixture of locals and tourists taking their pick of the locally produced items.

'Hi Jane. I just popped in with a grocery list. Jenny usually does the shopping but the girl misses half of the things out. I didn't realise the place would be so busy,' she said looking at the queue. 'I've got so much to do today I didn't want to spend half an hour queuing here. I've got an appointment to have my hair done later too.'

'Leave the list with me,' Jane replied looking at the piece of paper in Penny's hand. 'I'm in no rush. I'll leave Mr Tompkins your list and you can pick the items up on the way home.'

'Oh Jane would you mind. That's awfully kind. Penny handed the grocery list over to Jane.

'What no nurofen?' Jane asked as she read down the list of items.

'Did you have a hangover too?'

'Only for two days.'

'We will have to arrange another evening out. It was fun, even though I've suffered for it.'

'Give me at least a week's notice before the next one. I'll then have the chance to prepare this old body for some punishment.'

The two of them stood laughing until someone politely reminded them that the queue had moved.

Knowing he had time for a quick lunch Wesley decided to drive home before returning to the station. He pulled into the drive just as Jane turned the corner of the road carrying the shopping. 'Here let me take those bags,' he said jumping out of the car.

Jane kissed him on the cheek. 'What a nice surprise to see you at this time of day.'

'I'm afraid it's a quick sandwich. I've got to pop over to Abbey House and be back at the station before four.' He carried the shopping into the kitchen as Jane put the kettle on and set about making some food. He was eating his sandwich when he remembered the letter in his pocket. He tore open the envelope and took out the paper inside. There was just one written line on a piece of A4 paper.

Meet me after work one night and I'll show you the real Glastonbury.

'What have you got there?' asked Jane as she reappeared with a bundle of washing in her arms.

'It's a note that was left for Denise Wright, the girl missing from the Tourist office.' Wesley handed Jane the note while he finished his lunch. She wiped her hands on the tea towel before reading the contents. Wesley noticed the way Jane stared at the piece of paper.

'What's wrong Jane?'

She looked at him and then back at the note before answering. 'I know the hand writing.'

'What? Are you sure?'

'I'm absolutely positive.' She handed him the sheet of paper back. 'I saw the same hand writing on a grocery list just this morning.'

46

Wesley walked through the main gates of Abbey House and followed the pathway towards the front entrance. There was a queue of people to his right waiting for the Chapel to open. Wesley had seen the coach in the car park which had obviously come down from London. The giveaway being Acton Coach Hire W3 emblazoned all over it. However most of the students appeared to be speaking French.

He pressed the buzzer to the front door for the second time when suddenly the door burst open.

'Can't you read the damn sign? The Chapel is next door.' Wesley didn't answer but simply stared at the enraged face of Michael Westbrook.

Realising his mistake Michael stopped his verbal assault.

'Sorry Inspector. I thought it was those bloody tourists again. Half of them can't read English and listening to the cackle from that lot most of them can't speak it either. Please come inside.'

Wesley nodded and stepped into the hallway, removing his overcoat.

'This is an unexpected visit. How can I help you?' Michael asked regaining some of his composure.

'I actually wanted to have a chat with you and your good wife.' Wesley watched Michael's reaction.

'Well do come in.' Michael pointed the way to the front parlour.

'Please take a seat, while I look for Penny. I'm sure she's around somewhere.'

Wesley sat looking at the opulent surroundings. On the outside Michael and Penny seemed to have so much but he doubted they were happy. There was always an air of caution between them.

Less than a minute later, as Wesley was looking through a pile of magazines that were lying on the top of a small nestle of tables, Penny appeared with Michael behind her. She looked flushed as if she had been arguing or crying.

'Inspector. It's good to see you. Please, don't get up. I've asked Jenny to make us some tea.'

'Michael tells me that you want to speak with both of us. Is that right?'

'Yes Mrs Westbrook.'

'Oh, please call me Penny. You make me feel like we're strangers and we both know that's not true.'

'OK, Penny it is.'

Wesley noticed that they never sat next to one another. Jenny sat in the armchair opposite Wesley but Michael selected the leather wing backed chair just to his left. It was Wesley who started the conversation.

'Yesterday, having used the keys that Michael kindly lent to me, I managed to take a look inside the Chalice Well.'

'You mean you crawled inside?' asked Penny screwing her face up. 'Why on earth would you want to climb down into that hole?'

'That sounds like the voice of experience,' said Wesley.

'Oh no. You'd never get me down there. I'm claustrophobic in town when there are too many people about,' she replied pretending to shiver.

'So what was your interest in the Well?' Michael asked looking at Penny in distaste.

'I wanted to ascertain if it were possible to enter the Well on the Tor and exit it somewhere else nearby.'

'And can you?'

'Yes.'

Penny and Michael looked at one another.

'So where did you magically arrive?' asked Michael putting on a sarcastic looking face.

'It took me to the Chapel next door.'

Wesley watched their reactions.

'The Chapel? But I thought the only way in and out was by King Arthur's tomb out there in the grounds.'

'That exit would appear to be grated off.'

'So where is this magic entrance? I've never seen it,' Penny remarked.

'The grated entrance is at the far end of the Chapel. Immediately behind the Altar and behind the curtain that separates the back of the Chapel from public view.'

Wesley noticed again the brief glimpse between them.

'So what does that prove?' Michael shrugged his shoulders. 'Perhaps you think Penny and I are smugglers now.'

Wesley ignored Michael's sarcasm and continued.

'So can I assume from your reactions that neither of you have been down into the Well recently?'

'I can assure you that neither of us has ever been down the bloody Well, or have any intentions of doing so,' Michael replied indignantly.

'Then, as the keepers of the only set of keys, can you explain why there are recent footprints down there and why the grill cover in the Chapel has recently been lifted and put back?'

Penny and Michael looked at each other again. For the first time since he'd known him, Wesley saw Michael's guard drop a little.

'I have absolutely no idea Inspector.'

'What about you Penny? I can't imagine you going down there for a second.'

'I can't answer you either Inspector. I didn't even know we had the key to the Well and certainly didn't know there was access to it from the Chapel.'

'What about the council?' Michael asked. 'They must have access surely? I mean, they're the people responsible for ensuring the whole place doesn't bloody flood.'

'Their records show that twice a year they lower a device into the Well from the entrance on the Tor which simply measures the level of water. They don't physically enter the Well, which rules out them leaving footprints.'

'Must be King Arthur himself going for a stroll!'

Wesley ignored Michael's remark and continued with his questioning.

'Who else apart from you two has access to the Chapel?'

'Well Jenny has a key to the Chapel as she's responsible for ensuring its open and properly cleaned for when the public view it. Also the vicar. He has a key, as he often rehearses in there with the small choir we have.'

'Do you have a contact number for him?'

'Yes. I'll write it down for you,' said Penny and walked across to a small dark wood bureau to obtain a pen and paper. She jotted down the details and handed it across to Wesley before returning to her seat.

'Is there anything else we can help you with?' asked Michael rather impatiently.

'I'd just like a word in private with Penny if I may,' Wesley replied.

'Oh. OK.' Michael looked at Penny who shrugged her shoulders.

'Can I ask one final question?' Michael asked as he stood to leave.

'Sure fire away.' Wesley slipped the piece of paper into his pocket.

'Can I assume that the reasons for your questions are because Penny and I are suspects?'

Wesley sat back in the chair and met Michael's stare with his own.

'Right now everyone in this town is a suspect Mr Westbrook.'

Michael looked at Penny then turned and left the room.

'Do excuse my husband,' Penny said after he had closed the door.

'He thinks the world is watching him half the time.'

Wesley nodded to acknowledge her comment.

'So you wanted to speak with me in private?'

'Yes.' He extracted the envelope from his pocket.

'Can you tell me what this is all about?'

Penny took it and stared at it in disbelief.

'Where did you find this?' she asked.

'It is your hand writing is it not?'

'Yes. But where did you find the letter?'

'It was found in Denise Wright's locker at the University. Can you explain how it got there?'

'Why would you be looking in her locker?'

'Denise has been reported missing.'

Penny stared open mouthed, and looked as if she were about to have a heart attack.

'I have everyone possible, looking for her right now.'

123

'Can I have one of your cigarettes please Inspector?'

Penny fidgeted in the chair as she tried to compose herself. Wesley handed her one of his pre rolled cigarettes. Lit it for her then lit one for himself. Penny inhaled deeply then coughed and exhaled at the same time.

'Sorry they take some getting used to.'

Penny stood up and looked out of the window.

'I placed the note in Denise's locker,' she said still facing the window.

She then turned to around to look at Wesley. There were tears in her eyes. She took another drag on the cigarette then placed the remains in the ashtray before sitting down opposite him.

'I have written to Denise several times in the past couple of years. The older she got the more I wanted to get to know her better.' Penny could see the confused look on Wesley's face.

'You see Mr Wesley. Denise is my daughter.'

Wesley sat up straight, staring at Penny.

'I thought that would surprise you.'

'I don't think surprise is quite the word, Penny. Astonished, yes.'

'Oh, it's a long story. I got myself pregnant when I was fifteen. I was living in Somerset then. Anyhow, I had the baby but immediately had to give her up for adoption. You see, I was in a care home. There was no way they would let me keep the child. There were problems during the birth and I was told that I would never be able to have children again. Michael knows none of this. He thinks the reason we haven't got kids is his fault.'

'Carry on,' said Wesley.

'About two years ago I went into the town to get some bits and pieces and ended up in the newsagents. I went to pay for my purchases when this girl served me. There are some things a mother never forgets, even at fifteen years of age,' said Penny.

'When the girl handed me my change I noticed her hand straight away.'

'Her hand?' he interrupted.

'Denise was born with two shortened fingers. It's a hereditary thing.' She held up her right hand where the forefinger and second finger stopped at the knuckle.

'You can imagine my excitement. I was about to say hello to my daughter who I thought I would never see again. In any case, I didn't have the nerve to say anything to her in the shop so I waited until she finished work then followed her home. I wrote to her a couple of times sending the letters to her home address. For the first six months I got no reply then one day out of the blue I received a phone call from someone who said hello Mum.'

Penny put her hands to her face and began to sob. Reaching into his pocket Wesley extracted a handkerchief and passed it to her.

'You see Denise had no idea she had been fostered. After receiving my first letter, she spoke with Mrs Wright her adopted mother, who at first refused to admit anything. After my second letter confirmed a few things, I believe she reluctantly admitted to Denise that she was adopted. I visited them a few months ago when we agreed that Denise should stay with Mrs Wright although I wanted to help out financially.'

'Mrs Wright never told me any of this,' said Wesley.

'She swore to secrecy.'

'The letter you found, I posted in Denise's locker at University a week ago. I stopped sending her letters to the house as Mrs Wright always gets upset. I had previously told Denise that I would never put any pressure on her but if she ever needed me I would be there.'

She picked the note up from the table and held it in her hand.

'I told her I would show her around Glastonbury. My intention was to show her Abbey House. You see my plan is to leave the property to her. Please don't look so shocked. You see Michael has a terminal illness Mr Wesley. His life expectancy gives him another five years at the most.'

'I'm sorry to hear that.'

Penny looked down at the table then up at Wesley. There were tears running down her face.

'Please don't tell Michael about this. I'll tell him in my own time. I only ask you one thing,' she said. 'Find Denise. I lost her once. I couldn't bear to lose her again.'

47

Colin Dempster had tried to keep himself occupied since Suzie's death. It was his way of trying to get over the ordeal. He'd shut himself off from friends and family for the past week occupying his time sifting through a pile of old geographical maps of the Tor and the grounds surrounding Glastonbury Abbey. He was deep in thought when someone rapped on the door.

'I'm busy,' he shouted. 'If it's a parcel leave it downstairs. If it's personal then email me.'

'It's Pete Stanley. I need to speak with you.'

'Can't it wait?' answered Colin getting agitated.

'No. It's important.'

Colin placed a small book at the bottom corner of the map he was studying to stop it rolling up and walked across the room to open the door.

'What do you want?' he asked the Chief Librarian who was stood in the hallway.

'Colin, you have several books outstanding that other students are waiting to borrow. Normally I wouldn't bother you but you have over a dozen or more.'

'I'll be finished with them by the end of the week.'

He started to close the door but Pete stepped forward and placed his foot in the doorway to prevent Colin from closing it.

'Colin, are you OK? No one has seen you for several days and I can't ignore the fact that you have got half of the library sitting in your room right now.'

'Look Pete. Thanks for the concern but I'm fine. I just have something to finish right now. Give me a day, two at the most and I'll return all the stuff I've borrowed.'

'OK. As long as you're alright,' Pete replied and walked away.

Colin closed the door and leant back against it. He was tired but he knew he was close to finding the truth.

Sally walked into the lounge still looking for her handbag.

'So are you going to be out with your Mum all day?' asked David looking up from his newspaper.

'Probably, but only if I can find my handbag that is. You know what she's like. She'll want a coffee, then want to stop for lunch somewhere and I know she's just going to pester me all day about the wedding.'

'Tell her we got married yesterday in a registry office as we have no money.'

'Oh my word. Can you imagine the look on her face?'

'Go on. I dare you,' he replied.

'You're wicked David Hare.' She put her arms around his shoulders and gave him a kiss.

'And you're sexy. Let's go back to bed.'

She pushed him away laughing.

'You're terrible. But I love you. Now where is my handbag?'

'Have you tried the settee? That's where it normally is,' he called out hearing Sally in the bedroom. She reappeared a few minutes later clutching her handbag looking embarrassed.

'You must have moved it last night,' she said smirking.

'I'll phone you when I'm on the way home. Love you.'

David picked up the huge pile of history assignments. He was two days behind in marking the 2nd year students' work.

He sifted through the pile until he came to Debbie Harris's submission. He thought he would start with hers as her work was usually detailed and interesting. He left the boring ones until last. Her essay was about the history of a number of well-known family names in Glastonbury. In particular, the Westbrook family. Having lived around the same area for most of his life he thought he knew as much as there was to know about the Westbrook's because of where they lived. Not many families live in such an historic location. He scribbled down a couple of notes to himself and decided he would investigate further.

Good old Debbie Harris he thought. She always came up with something different in her essays. Always managed to find something out that most other people couldn't.

48

'It's nice just to sit down for a while,' said Jane as she studied the menu. Jane and Wesley had decided to visit the Ancient Raj Indian restaurant in Glastonbury. One of the few things they missed from London was the abundance of Indian restaurants to choose from. They would often go for an Indian after they had been to the theatre. Korma's in Soho was one of their favourites where the proprietor would always offer them a drink on the house when they had finished their meal.

'You've nearly finished that bottle of Cobra already.'

'Yes I know. And what's more is that I'm about to have another,' Wesley replied.

The waiter promptly returned with Wesley's drink and refilled Jane's glass with from the chilled wine bottle before replacing it in the ice bucket. It had been a long day and they were both starving. An hour later they had devoured their chicken tikka masala and chicken korma.

'That was just the job. Just what the doctor ordered.'

Wesley leant back in the chair with his hands on his belly.

'Look at you,' said Jane, 'your belly's bulging and half of your dinner is down your shirt.'

They both looked up as two more people entered the restaurant. They soon recognised the voice.

'I don't know why you wanted to come here. You know I don't like foreign food,' the man said closing the door.

'Hello Eddie,' said Wesley.

'Oh, hello Inspector, and Mrs Wesley,' he replied taking off his cap.

'Hello Dorothy,' Jane said as she turned around in her chair.

'I didn't know you and Eddie ate out. I always imagined you cooking your own food from your garden.'

'I just fancied a change my dear,' Dorothy replied. 'It's only taken me twenty years to get him out.'

Eddie could be heard talking to one of the waiters.

'What do you mean you don't sell stout and mild?'

'I'd better go and rescue the poor waiter,' she sighed. 'Have a lovely evening.'

Jane looked at Wesley and burst into laughter.

The waiter had just served Wesley with an Irish coffee when Jane raised the issue of Denise Wright.

'So poor Penny has just found her daughter, and now she's gone missing. How awful. She must be in a right state.'

'Yes she is. And so is Mrs Wright. I'm more worried about her, because she's on her own and looks so frail to start with.'

'Is there anything I can do?'

'I guess you can keep an eye on Penny. What she has told me is in confidence though, so I wouldn't want her to think that we've spoken about her daughter.'

'Oh no, of course not. I'll leave it for a couple of days then invite her out for drink or something to eat.'

'Be sure to check we've got some nurofen,' Wesley replied with a grin.

'I told you I'm not keen on this stuff. What's wrong with homemade pie and mash every night?'

'Nothing. Except you don't have to spend all day cooking it.'

Jane sniggered into her glass and Wesley discreetly watched amused as Eddie and Dorothy started arguing at the corner table.

'Shall we ask for the bill? The entertainments too much for me,' said Jane.

The waiter opened the door for Jane and Wesley just as two other people were about to enter the restaurant.

'Oh good evening,' said Michael Westbrook. The person with him simply nodded her head and walked on looking for a table.

Wesley took Jane's hand as they strolled towards the car park.

'Did you see who that was who was with Michael Westbrook?'

'Yes. Jenny Stevens. The housemaid,' Wesley replied with a grim look on his face.

The following morning Wesley sat on the edge of his desk as the rest of his team drew up chairs at the back of his office.

'OK, thanks everyone for being on time. I appreciate we're all busy. I just thought it was a good time for a quick get together to assess what we currently know about the two Tor murders.'

He pointed to the wipe board where Adam had already placed the photos of the two victims. He pointed first to the photo of Suzie Potter.

'Suzie was a University student studying at Bath. Twenty-four years of age. She was found strangled on the Tor. Her body was located here.' He pointed to a photo of the Tor alongside.

'The second level here is approximately three hundred yards from the main road. I don't believe anyone carried her there. My view is the same as the pathologists in that she died where we found her.' He pointed to the next photo.

'Kelvin Ward. Owned the bookshop in Glastonbury. Thirty- seven years of age. He was found at the very summit of the Tor, inside the ruins of the tower. His neck had been sliced clean through. Again, it's both mine and the pathologist's view that he died where he was found. Any questions so far?'

'Isn't there another girl missing?' asked one of the young PCs that had just driven over from Bath.

'Yes. I'll come to her in a second,' Wesley replied nodding.

'We know that Kelvin Ward was quite a recluse and his social life was pretty dull by all accounts, and for some reason he made few friends. However, we do know that he recently purchased new clothes, along with tickets to go to the theatre. Someone had entered his life and I want to know who that someone was.'

He coughed to clear his throat.

'As for Suzie. A totally different character. She was divorced after having been the subject of domestic violence. However we have already confirmed that her ex-husband was out of the country the night she was murdered. We know she met Colin Dempster, a University Lecturer at Bath University the night she died. They parted company when she got on the bus to go home around midnight. Her body was found the next morning on the Tor. I want to know where she disembarked the bus and who with. As with Kelvin, she must have gone to the Tor with someone she knew or trusted. But why the Tor? The killer would know that the victim would be found.' He paused for a moment.

'We need to find the killer. Any questions anyone?'

For a moment there was silence in the room.

'I think it's someone with local knowledge,' said Martin.

'Go on,' Wesley replied encouraging the young PC to speak up.

'Well, it's just that we have two murders, both on the Tor, yet there are no obvious indications that anyone was parked near the Tor either time. This makes me believe that both victims had walked through the town before entering the Tor. There's no sign either of anyone walking across from the adjacent farm, which by the way has already been thoroughly searched.'

'Yeah good call. Initial checks on CCTV footage in and around the High Street have yet to provide us with anything concrete to go on. Anyone else?'

There was silence in the room.

'OK, that brings me to Denise Wright. Denise is a local girl, eighteen years of age. She's a part time student at Bath University studying Tourism and Leisure. When she's not in University she works in the Tourist office in Glastonbury. Has done so for about two months. She's been missing now for three days. I want to know who her friends are. Who she socialised with and where she hung out. Let's study all available CCTV around town. Show her photo everywhere and talk to shopkeepers, publicans and tourists alike. The girl simply can't vanish into thin air. Time is running out and we need to find her.'

Wesley stood up from his desk and looked around the room at the determined faces of the team at his command.

'Between you all there is a fountain of local knowledge. I beg you to use it. Someone or some persons out there know what happened to Suzie and

Kelvin. Someone out there knows where Denise is. Find out who's responsible for the murders and find me Denise Wright. I do believe all three are linked. Thank you.'

Wesley watched and listened as everyone started shuffling out of the room, a few muttering amongst themselves.

'Oh Martin, a quick word before you leave.'

'Yes, Sir?'

'Look after the station for the next hour will you. I want to pay the Hallerton household a visit this morning.'

'Surething, no problem.'

'That's a good lad. I'll have one sugar in mine when you've made the tea. I need a cuppa before I speak with them.'

The early morning torrent had turned into a fine drizzle. That annoying type of rain which you can't clear from your windscreen. As Wesley pulled up outside the Hallerton's cottage he was sure someone had just closed the curtain.

'Good morning Dorothy,' said Wesley as she opened the front door.

'Hello Mr Wesley.' She wiped her hands on her pinafore and beckoned him.

'What a horrible morning. Let's hope it brightens up later.'

'Yes, it would make a nice change.'

'What brings you over Inspector?'

'I've actually popped round to speak with Eddie. Is he at home?'

'No he's not. Actually, you've only just missed him. He got a call this morning from those people over at Abbey House. Oh what's their name?'

'Mr and Mrs Westbrook.'

'Yes it must have been one of them. Anyhow, he put the phone down and said he had to run over there for some urgent thing or other they needed doing.'

'Oh that's a shame. Never mind I was going to pop over there in any case. I'll probably catch up with him.'

'He's not in any trouble is he?'

'No nothing like that. I just wanted to ask him about some trees he planted recently.'

'Please wait a second before you go,' said Dorothy. 'You can take something with you.'

Wesley stood by the front door and she wandered off into the kitchen. Within a minute Dorothy reappeared with a bag of rock cakes.

'There are four rock cakes in there,' she said, handing Wesley the bag. 'Careful now they're hot. Let them cool down a bit before anyone eats them.'

'That's very kind Dorothy. Thank you. I'll eat a couple of these before I go back to the station. They smell too good to share.'

'If you do see Eddie please remind him that I'm going to my sisters this afternoon will you?'

'I certainly will, and thanks again.'

Holding his belly, wishing he'd not eaten two warm rock cakes so quickly, Wesley walked up the drive towards Abbey House. He could see a flock of people coming out of the Chapel at the time when the midday service was due to start. He thought it was strange, but shrugged his shoulders and continued towards the house. Just as he approached the front door he heard someone call his name. Turning round he saw Robin Pettigrew the local vicar running towards him.

'Good morning,' said Wesley looking a little surprised.

Robin was still relatively young at forty three years of age but extremely unfit as his size elaborated.

'Inspector. Just the person -' he panted, placing a hand on Wesley's shoulder.

'What's wrong?'

Wesley could see the distraught look on the vicar's face.

'There's been a terrible accident. Please, come with me. I can't believe this.'

He grabbed Wesley's sleeve and urged him to follow.

About thirty people were stood on the lawn area outside the Chapel muttering to themselves. Wesley followed Robin into the Chapel where the young vicar headed straight to the far end of the building, past the font, and onto the flagstone floor where the entrance to the Chalice Well was. Wesley immediately noticed that the grill cover had been removed and was in fact leaning on the back of the font. Robin stopped several feet in front of the Well.

'He's in there Mr Wesley,' he pointed.

'Who are you talking about?' He pushed the vicar aside and knelt down next to the Well peering down into the black void.

'Here use this,' said Robin handing Wesley a torch.

Wesley switched the torch on and pointed the beam of light into the Well. Twenty feet below, lying headfirst with his head half submerged in the water was the unmistakable body of Eddie Hallerton.

'Oh, good God no,' Wesley exclaimed. He sat down on the ledge with his legs hanging over the side and extracted his mobile phone. 'Adam. It's Wesley here. I'm in the Chapel next to Abbey House. Get Martin and two other PCs over here now along with an ambulance and some rescue equipment to pull a corpse out of the Well.'

'Did you say a corpse?' Adam asked stunned.

'Yes, that's correct. I also need forensics over here. Tell Martin I need the whole area cordoned off and quick.'

Wesley ended the call, and stood up to walk across to the front pew, where the ashen faced vicar was now sat.

'You OK Robin?' The plump vicar was sweating and breathing heavily. Wesley had seen the signs many times before and quickly escorted the man out of the Chapel and into the fresh air where he immediately vomited against the side wall.

'Mr Wesley, what on earth is going on?' cried Penny as she hurried across the gravelled drive.

'I'm afraid there's been an incident in the Chapel. Do me a favour Penny.'

He pointed to the crowd of visitors who were still stood on the far lawn.

'Get them back on the coach, but tell the driver that I don't want him driving off until someone has spoken to them.'

'But what's happened?'

'It's Eddie Hallerton. He's dead.'

49

PC Martin Philips had sealed off the entrance to the Chapel and Penny was stood next to her husband Michael who had come outside to see what was going on. It was clear that Penny was badly shaken.

'This is bad for publicity Inspector,' Michael said. 'Can't we simply close the Chapel doors and send those bloody visitors home.'

'I apologise for any inconvenience,' Wesley replied walking towards Michael with a fearsome look on his face. 'But I'm sure you will appreciate that we have to remove the body and the forensic team have a job to do right now. I'm absolutely positive that you could make yourself more useful other than standing there moaning about bad publicity.'

Wesley stood menacingly in Michael's face, until Michael turned to Penny to say he was going indoors because he was getting cold.

'I'm sorry Inspector,' she said. 'I can only put Michael's behaviour down to his prescription. I'll go and speak with him.'

'Good idea. Keep him out of my way.'

Wesley found a bench to sit on and phoned Jane to tell her what had happened.

'Do you think there is any chance it was an accident?' she asked.

'I'd like to think so but after recent events I'm not so sure. Jane, I need to ask a favour. If I send one of the female WPCs over to pick you up, would you break the news to Dorothy? I understand if that's an unfair request. She may have already left to go to her sister's.'

'It's OK John. I'll head over there now and tell her. She's going to take this hard but it's probably better if someone she knows is with her. I'll call you if I need to.'

'Thanks Jane. I appreciate it. I'll head over there when I'm finished here.'

PC Philips came running across the drive.

'Hi, Sir,' he panted. 'It seems as if one of the individuals in the group of sightseers called the press. There's a whole string of cars pulling into the car park.'

'That's all we need. OK, I'll deal with them now but get Adam on the phone and ask him to send two more PCs over here asap. Let's close off all access to the grounds. If Michael Westbrook gives you any grief then point him in my direction. I'm just in the mood to sort him out this morning.'

Jenny had been looking out of her bedroom window after hearing the voices of the crowd of people outside.

'What's going on?' she asked as she came down the stairs.

'Why are all those people standing back by the main gate?'

'There's been another bloody murder,' Michael shouted passing her as he made his way upstairs.

'We don't know that yet,' said Penny. She put her arm around Jenny and led her into the kitchen.

'Come and sit down,' she said pointing to a chair next to the kitchen table. 'I have some bad news I'm afraid. Eddie Hallerton the maintenance man who looks after the house and grounds for us. He was found in the Chapel at the bottom of the Well.'

'Oh my God! When was this?' Jenny asked putting her hands to her mouth.

'This morning. About an hour ago. He was found by the vicar who had just opened the Chapel prior to the scheduled visit this morning of a group of tourists from London.'

'Michael says he was murdered,' said Jenny looking terrified.

'Just ignore Michael.' Penny handed Jenny a cup of coffee.

'He jumps to conclusions. It could have been an accident. The police are already here and a team of guys are trying to get the body up from the Well.'

'I didn't know you could access the Well from the Chapel,' said Jenny clutching the hot cup.

'Yes there is a grill cover that leads down into the Well but it's only ever used for maintenance according to the Inspector,' Penny replied.

'This is awful.' Jenny was shaking.

'Yes I know.' Penny stood looking out of the kitchen window as two ambulance crew walked towards the Chapel carrying a stretcher.

50

Denise woke from her slumber. The cold walls were bare and damp, and the old stonework was crumbling in places. The room was still devoid of any sunlight or fresh air. A rat appeared out of nowhere, hesitated and sniffed the air before running up the far wall from where she was sat before disappearing through a small hole in the stone work. Denise sat motionless. Her mind completely numb. She had lost count of the number of hours or days she had been held captive. Although her legs had been untied, she was no longer able to stand. Her hands were still tied and she was extremely weak.

Knowing she had soiled herself more than once, she felt dirty and embarrassed. Unsure whether it was day or night, she tried to call out for the millionth time but she knew it was in vain. Wherever her captor had left her, was obviously remote and away from anyone else. The bread that had been left was now curled and hard and she expected that the rats had taken bites from it. The empty glass of water, she had accidentally knocked over soon after it had been placed there, now had a layer of dust over it. Denise leaned back on the cold wall and began to sob. She knew deep inside that she needed to continue to believe that she would get out alive but as the time passed her will and expectation grew less and less.

Unsure how long she had slept, she suddenly became aware of someone or something moving above her. For a few seconds the sound seemed to stop then she heard the sound of the door scraping across the wooden floor.

Denise hardly had the strength to look up. All she could see was a pair of legs dressed in jeans and a pair of dirty boots.

The masking tape was removed from her mouth.

'There's fresh water and food there.'

A china jug filled with cold water and a plain looking sandwich was set down beside her.

'How long are you going to keep me like this?' Denise groaned.

Her captor didn't reply and the door was immediately slammed shut.

'You can't just leave me here!' she shouted. 'What is it you want from me? What have I done?'

Denise tried to fight back the tears but the frustration and anger she felt overwhelmed her and the flood gates opened as the tears ran down her face. She coughed as she took a sip of water. Her throat was burning and her lips had cracked. She managed just two mouthfuls of sandwich before she leant back against the wall.

It must have been the water she thought to herself. The strange tangy taste. It must have been drugged.

Denise tried hard to concentrate but her world was becoming blurred. The last thing she remembered was trying to lift her harms to prevent herself from hitting her head as she slumped forward.

She was unconscious long before the masking tape was reapplied.

51

There had been no answer from the front door so Jane stuck her head around the side of the house. She saw Dorothy at the bottom of the garden working on the vegetable patch. Jane gave a polite cough which made Dorothy look up.

'Oh hello Jane,' she called out the smile on her face disappearing from the moment she saw a female WPC standing in the back ground.

Once inside, Jane led Dorothy to the back room whilst WPC Alison Bolt went straight to the kitchen to make tea.

'What's all this about, Jane?' Dorothy asked.

Jane took a deep breath before replying.

'I have some bad news concerning Eddie.'

'Don't tell me he's in trouble again. That man will never change. All the years we've been married he's flaunted with the law. I don't know how many times I've told...'

'Dorothy,' said Jane interrupting her in mid-sentence as WPC Bolt placed three teas on the table.

'There has been an incident over at Abbey House. I'm sorry but Eddie is dead.'

At first Jane wasn't sure if Dorothy heard what she said as there was no response.

'Dorothy, are you OK?' Jane moved around the table and sat next to her, placing her arm over the woman's shoulder. Dorothy's head bowed and she leant against Jane sobbing. WPC Bolt left the room to make a phone call to the number Jane had just given her.

'I can't believe this,' Dorothy said sitting up. She looked at Jane with unseeing eyes. 'He said he would be home early today as I was cooking his favourite pie.' She wiped the tears from her eyes and pushed her hair away from her face. Jane handed her the cup and urged her to drink her tea.

'What happened?' she asked placing the cup down on the table.

Jane didn't want to tell her how or where exactly Eddie was found but didn't want to lie to her either.

'Eddie was found in the Chapel. That's all I know. Do you know why he was over there?'

'Someone phoned him earlier and said there were some chores to do. He's been the maintenance guy over there for years,' replied Dorothy as she yawned.

The tablet WPC Bolt had put in Dorothy's tea was beginning to work.

Five minutes later she entered the back room with Doctor Evans, the local GP. Dorothy was already dosing on the settee and Jane was placing a blanket over her.

The doctor checked Dorothy's pulse and temperature. Once he was satisfied she was comfortable he extracted a handful of tablets from his case and handed them to Jane.

'These will keep her sedated for a while. I'll pop back this evening to see how she is. If you need me before that just give the surgery a call.'

After the doctor had left Jane text Wesley to say she would stay with Dorothy for a while.

WPC Bolt sat in the kitchen writing some notes whilst Jane went back out into the garden to put Dorothy's gardening tools in the shed. Having put everything away she locked the shed door and turned to walk back up the garden path.

The aromatic smell from the small herb garden seemed to hang like a cloud, attracting Jane's senses. She looked down at the abundance of herbs and spices that were growing in the middle of the vegetable plot. Jane thought it was strange. It looked as if they were deliberately being hidden from view. Jane retrieved her mobile phone and after spending a minute trying to work out how to take a photo, she took two snaps of the small herb garden to show to Wesley.

She wasn't really sure why but something about it bugged her.

52

Colin Dempster had started to fold away the pile of maps that now cluttered the desk in his room when he saw the envelope slip under the door. He dropped the map he was holding into the small chair by the window and retrieved the envelope from the floor. His name had been hand written on the front. He tore open the envelope and extracted the sheet of A4 paper. There were just two lines of text.

> Under the Tor a corpse doth lay
> Do not disturb or you will pay

It took him a few moments to digest the threat. He sprang to open the door and looked up and down the corridor but there was no one around.

He went back inside and dialled the University's gate house and reception. The phone was answered almost immediately.

'Hi, it's Colin Dempster here. I'm in Room 301. Has anyone been asking for me?'

'Not that I'm aware of,' the security guard answered, 'although I only started my shift ten minutes ago. I'll check the log to see if we have let any visitors in. Hold on.'

Colin could hear the rustle of pages being flipped over.

'The last visitor was signed in over two hours ago. That was a delivery for Jacob Welling.'

'OK thanks.' Colin replaced the receiver before picking it up again to dial Wesley's mobile.

After speaking with the press Wesley drove back to the station. He was sat deep in thought when his mobile rang.

'Wesley speaking.'

'Hi Mr Wesley, its Colin Dempster. How are you?'

'Hello Colin. I'm fine thanks. Just about recovered from our pot holing expedition. What about you?'

'I was fine until a few minutes ago when someone slipped a warning note under my door.'

Wesley stood up as he lit his cigarette balancing the phone between his shoulder and his ear.

'A warning note? How do you mean?'

'It's just a couple of lines of text. Hand written. It infers I could be a corpse under the Tor if I interfere.'

Wesley raised his eyebrows as he blew a plume of smoke into the air.

'Sounds like someone saw us on the Tor the other day. We're obviously treading on someone's toes. Did you see or hear anyone when the note arrived?'

'No. As soon as I saw the note slipped under the door, I opened it then took a look outside but there was no one in the hallway. I checked with security too but they say there have been no visitors asking for me at the University. The trouble is that people can just walk in and out of the University pretty much.'

'OK. Can you drop the note into the station? I'll get our guys to take a look. See if they can match the handwriting against anything we may have on record.'

'Sure thing Mr Wesley. I was going to pop over in any case. I borrowed all the maps of the Tor and the Abbey that I could find from our extensive library here at the University and I think I've come up with a solution as to how someone could get around without being seen.'

'Really!' exclaimed Wesley rubbing away the remains of his cigarette between his thumb and forefinger. 'Now that is interesting. Can you meet me here at the station tomorrow morning, say at eight thirty? I have to leave the station right now. There's been another incident. I'll bring you up to speed when you come over.'

'OK, Mr Wesley. I'll see you in the morning.'

Having worked his way through a pile of paperwork, Wesley left the station and drove to the Hallertons'.

'How's Dorothy doing?' Wesley asked as Jane let him in.

'Sleeping like a log at the moment.' She led the way into the kitchen. 'WPC Bolt is in the back room keeping a watch over her. Go and say hello while I make some tea.'

Wesley entered the back room and gave a polite cough. WPC Bolt immediately sat upright.

'Oh, good afternoon Inspector,' she said straightening her uniform and standing up.

'Hello Alison. Please don't get up. Jane's just making some tea.'

'Mrs Hallerton has been sleeping like a log. The doctor said he'll call in later to check her over.'

'OK, that's fine. I'm going to take a look around while she's asleep. You stay there and drink your tea. Jane makes a lovely cuppa,' he said smiling.

There was nothing of interest in the front parlour of the old cottage so Wesley made his way upstairs. The first door led to a small bathroom and toilet and the second door led to the back bedroom which apart from a single bed and a small dressing table was empty. The stale atmosphere told him that Eddie and Dorothy had rarely used the room.

He opened the door to the front bedroom and was astonished to find the bed littered with paperwork. There were old receipts for petrol and building materials and hand written invoices from Eddie to other people.

Wesley sat on the edge of the bed and started to collect the papers together. He took the empty bag that was lining the waste bin and shoved everything in. There was little to be found in the dressing table or the wardrobe, so he concentrated on the bedside tables.

What was obviously Dorothy's, was crammed full of birthday cards and anniversary cards and little else.

Eddie's, contained a few personal items along with a small bundle of what Wesley guessed would prove to be forged notes. He placed these in the bag too. He felt it was unnecessary to burden Dorothy with that worry right now. What caught his eye was a birthday card lying at the bottom of the drawer. From its appearance he guessed it was only a year or two old. The front of the card read 'Happy Birthday Dad.'

Wesley opened the card and immediately recognised the writing.

When he returned downstairs, Alison was talking to Dorothy who had woken and was sitting up on the settee.

'Hello Dorothy,' said Wesley, sitting beside her and taking her hand. She stared at him with a blank expression as if she wasn't sure where she was or what had happened.

'I want you to get plenty of rest. Alison is going to be here so you won't be on your own. You have Jane's phone number and my mobile number, so all you have to do is call us if you need anything.'

Alison was impressed at the way that Wesley was handling the situation. He seemed so sincere.

Jane entered the room and sat the other side of Dorothy holding a cup of tea for her.

'I think you would be better off lying on the bed.'

Dorothy looked at Jane and simply nodded as her eyes closed for a second. Wesley waited in the kitchen while Jane and the young WPC put Dorothy to bed. He phoned the station to get any update from PC Philips.

'Hi, Sir. I've just got back to the station. Adam's in charge of things over at Abbey House. I've left instructions to say the Chapel will remain closed until you give the OK for it to re-open. But just to give you the thumbs up so to speak, Michael Westbrook is on the warpath. He wants to know why it can't be re-opened straight away. He says he's losing revenue.'

'He'll lose the ability to speak very soon,' Wesley replied.

'Don't worry I'll deal with him. Have we any updates?'

'Yes, Sir. One other thing. Terry Austin from pathology has just this minute phoned to say that Eddie Hallerton had a broken neck and it's highly likely this was caused by him falling backwards onto the edge of the marble floor and the entrance to the Well. In which case, we're looking possible manslaughter.'

'It looks that way.'

'OK. I'm going to head back to Abbey House later. I have to take Mrs Wesley home first. She's been staying here with Dorothy Hallerton. I've asked WPC Bolt to stay here. Can you arrange for someone to take over from her at six?'

'Will do.'

'Call me on my mobile if anything else comes to light. Oh by the way. Good work,' said Wesley and hung up.

PC Martin Philips puffed out his chest and began to tidy his desk.

53

'Jenny, where the hell are you?' Michael shouted from the foot of the staircase. 'I don't know where that bloody girl has got to,' he cried redirecting his comment at Penny who was just coming out of one of the back sitting rooms.

'Really? That is a surprise. I thought you two always knew where each other were,' she replied sarcastically and walked past Michael to ascend the stairs.

'What the hell is that supposed to mean?'

'Have I called at the wrong time?' Wesley interrupted, just seconds later. 'Sorry but the front door was open.'

'When can we open the bloody Chapel?' asked Michael. 'I can't see why it has to remain closed all day just because of some bloody accident.'

'It will remain closed until forensics have finished their work and I'm completely satisfied that we haven't missed any valuable evidence.'

'Valuable evidence? What because of some accident?'

'No, Mr Westbrook, because it's possible someone was murdered.'

There was the sound of someone dropping something onto the floor from upstairs.

'Are you telling me that Eddie Hallerton was murdered?' asked Michael now sounding not quite so confident.

'The pathologist tells me that it's a possibility. I'm going across to the Chapel now to see how things are going.' He turned to leave as Michael Westbrook began to ascend the stairs.

'Oh, by the way,' said Wesley as he grabbed the front door handle. 'Please ask Mrs Westbrook to join me in the Chapel. I need to ask her one or two things.'

Wesley was stood peering down into the Well listening to the forensic team talking amongst themselves, when Penny approached. It was obvious she'd been crying.

'Why didn't you tell me that Eddie was your father?' Wesley asked quietly without looking up.

'We, that is, Dad and I, had agreed that it was best if no one else knew. How did you find out?'

Wesley extracted the birthday card from his pocket and handed it to her.

'No one else has seen it. I suggest you keep it.'

'Thanks.' Penny read the card and slipped it into her jeans pocket.

Wesley walked away from the Well and sat in the front pew motioning for Penny to join him.

'So why all the secrecy?' he asked.

'It's a long story. Dad had an affair just after he had met Dorothy. When the woman became pregnant they agreed that she would have the child but the child would be adopted.'

'That child being you I guess.'

'Yes.'

'And Dorothy never knew?'

'No. Eddie was already in love with Dorothy and didn't want her to know.'

'What happened to you?'

'Dad arranged for me to be looked after in a foster home. He knew the lady who had organised everything so he managed to keep in touch. It was our little secret. He knew he would get into trouble if the authorities found out that we were corresponding several times a year.'

Penny was silent for a minute before continuing.

'Although I moved house twice with my foster parents, I always managed to tell Dad where I was. At sixteen I moved back into Somerset and into rented accommodation. That's when I had Denise.'

'Did he know about Denise?'

'Yes he provided for her even though I had to give her up.'

'I assume Dorothy knew nothing about the child either?'

'I don't think he told her anything,' Penny replied blowing her nose.

'Tell me honestly, Penny. Why would someone want to murder your father?'

Penny wiped the tears from her eyes and pushed her hair behind her ears.

'I don't know Inspector. Dad was always a bit of a wheeler dealer and he's upset a few people in his time but not to the extent that they would want to kill him.'

Wesley turned sideways to look her in the eye.

'Penny, I need you to tell me everything you know about Eddie. If the pathologist team are right and I've not known them to be wrong so far, then your Dad was possibly murdered. His death may have been no accident.'

Penny leant forward. Her elbows on her legs. She covered her face and began to sob.

'Let it all out.' Wesley put his arm on her shoulder as her whole body racked with emotion.

Wesley arrived back at the station and made his first priority a cup of tea and a roll up. He then set about searching through the list of invoices and receipts that he'd found in Eddie's bedroom. He'd just tipped the contents of the plastic bag over his desk when PC Martin Philips entered the room. The result being that the wind blew most of the papers on to the floor. Wesley and

Martin were both crawling around the floor when PC Adam Broad entered Wesley's office.

'Oh sorry. Hope I'm not disturbing you two,' he said.

'If you don't wipe that smirk off your face you'll be walking the beat for the next six months,' replied Wesley from under the table. 'What do you want?'

'You said you wanted me to organise something for tomorrow morning,' Adam replied looking a little embarrassed.

'Oh yeah. Call a meeting for eight a.m. in the briefing room. I want everyone there.'

'OK, happy hunting.' Adam quickly closed the door and left the room.

Wesley seated himself back at the desk once all the papers had been retrieved.

'So, Martin. You must have come in to the office for a reason?'

'Yes. We've had a phone call from a Mrs Weston who's a hotel receptionist in Bath. She's only just seen the photo of Kelvin Ward in the local paper and recognises him as someone who has used the hotel a few times in the past couple of months.'

'I thought our Mr Ward never went anywhere?'

'Maybe as Kelvin Ward he didn't but according to Mrs Weston he stayed at the hotel under the name of Holloway. Just as interesting is that he always stayed with a young lady.'

'Really? Well he is proving a dark horse.'

Wesley stood up from his desk and retrieved his tobacco and papers from his jacket that was hung on the coat stand.

'After the briefing tomorrow, I want you to go over to Bath and meet this Mrs Weston. See what other information you can gleam from her. Perhaps they have CCTV which backs up her claim. Make a note of all the dates that Kelvin Ward supposedly stayed there. Find out how he paid the bill, credit card or cash. I'm going to see Colin Dempster in the morning after the team brief so we'll meet back here later in the day.'

'OK. Is there anything else?'

'No. You go home Martin. It's been a long day.'

'Thanks, Sir. Appreciate it.'

'Just remember it's your turn to buy next time we're in the pub,' Wesley shouted, as Martin closed the door.

An hour later he dialled Jane's mobile number as he walked towards his car.

'Hi. I was just going to call you,' answered Jane almost immediately. 'I'm going to pick up a take away on the way home. Are you hungry or have you eaten?'

Wesley laughed.

'What's so funny?'

'I phoned to ask you the same thing. Yes I'm hungry and anything will do. I'm just leaving the station. How's Dorothy?'

'She's fine for the time being. Alison has just handed over to WPC Mandy Tredwell. Mandy is going to stay with Dorothy overnight.'

'Oh OK that's fine. Thanks Jane. You've really been a great help today.'

'That's not a problem. It's going to cost you,' she replied laughing. 'I'll pick up the curry. You can pick up the wine.'

54

'So when are you going to leave Penny?' Jenny asked, entering Michael's bedroom.

'It's not as simple as just telling her is it? I have to plan things properly.' He looked up from his dressing table.

'And what about me? I just sit and wait do I?'

'You just need to be patient.'

'Oh go to hell. You've got one month to sort this out otherwise it's over between us.'

Jenny walked out of the bedroom door and started to descend the stairs.

'Where are you going?' he called out.

'Just out,' she replied without looking back.

To Wesley's surprise the whole team had already arrived at the station when he walked in the following morning.

'Good morning everyone. I am impressed to see so many eager faces this early in the morning.'

'We always make an effort for you,' said young Adam with a smirk on his face.

'I'm pleased to hear of it.' Wesley patted him on the shoulder. 'In that case you'd have no objection in making the teas young man.' Everyone in the room laughed at Adam's expense. Once teas and coffees had been handed out Wesley got down to the business of the day.

'OK. Our top priority of the day is another complete sweep of Glastonbury and the nearby villages.' He pointed to the local map on the wall.

'Denise Wright has been missing for several days now. We need to find her or at least get some sort of lead as to her whereabouts. She can't simply leave work and disappear.'

'Martin, I want you to take three officers with you and comb the area south and west of Glastonbury. Organise their routes and get them to report back to you every couple of hours. While they are doing that I want you to visit the hotel in Bath and get as much information from the receptionist regarding Kelvin Ward. Understood?'

'Yes, Sir,' Martin replied taking notes of the area to be covered by his team.

'Alison, you're a local girl. I want you to gather a couple of recruits over from Bath and scour the north and east side of the town, including all the shops and premises in Glastonbury. I know we've already done it once but I can't believe that no one has seen this girl.' Alison nodded acknowledging Wesley's orders.

'What about the Tor?' Adam asked.

'Good question son. I have a meeting scheduled with Colin Dempster later. He's one of the lecturers from Bath University. Colin has some theories about access to the Tor, so I'll be going there myself with him later this morning. Subject to anything else cropping up, I may ask you to come with us Adam.'

'Thanks, Sir,' he replied aware of everyone's eyes on him.

'If any of you hear or see anything you think I may be interested in then call me on my mobile. Otherwise we'll meet again at the same time tomorrow.'

Wesley turned to grab his jacket as he wanted to pop outside for a cigarette before his meeting with Colin Dempster.

'Oh by the way, Alison' he called out just as she was gathering her paperwork for the day.

'Can you give Mandy a phone call when you get back to your desk? I'd like to know how Dorothy is this morning. You may need to send someone else round to stay with her for a while.'

'OK. I'll ring her now. Assume Dorothy is OK unless you hear from me.'

'Thanks Alison. You did a great job round at Dorothy's yesterday.'

Wesley didn't see Alison blush.

Colin Dempster was sat in the police station reception area when Wesley re-entered the building.

'Good morning Colin. Sorry to keep you waiting. I'd actually nipped around the back for a cigarette.'

'Good morning Mr Wesley. I trust you're keeping well.'

'Yeah I'm OK. I've only just about recovered from our pot-holing expedition,' he replied laughing as he led the way towards his office. Wesley made some space on the far wall so Colin could pin the maps up on the board.

'I've been reading maps all my life but these have proved to be a bit of a puzzle,' Colin said. Wesley sat back in the chair as Colin started to explain.

'This first map details the underground spring running across the Tor. This area here,' he said pointing to the map. 'This is what is currently known as the Chalice Well. This map is over a thousand years old. What I'm going to do now is place my tracings over the top. These are taken from newer maps that have been produced over time.' He pinned the first tracing over the ancient map.

'You can see quite clearly from this, that excavation work was carried out some three hundred years ago, which made the Well far deeper at its central point. The left hand entrance is where you and I climbed down at the weekend. But on the other side of the map we can see that the exit is clearly marked next to King Arthur's tomb.' Colin turned away from the map for a second to face Wesley.

'However, it is my opinion that the direction of the Well was altered when King Arthur's final resting place was supposedly moved to another part of the Abbey grounds.'

'Supposedly?'

'There's no concrete proof that King Arthur is buried in Glastonbury.'

'Are you saying it's all a myth?'

Colin smiled.

'All I'm saying is that the actual tomb has never been found.'

He then pinned the next tracing over the top and stood back to examine it before speaking.

'Now, this is a tracing of the most recent map I could find. This is dated 1987.' He turned to look at Wesley to see his reaction.

'I thought that would raise an eyebrow.'

Wesley stood up and walked across to the wall and pointed at the new line that ran from the bottom of the Chalice Well up towards the Chapel.

'What's that?' he asked.

'I thought that would interest you. That is the route that you and I followed when we found ourselves in the Chapel the other morning.'

'So this section is relatively new then?'

'Yes. It was built just over twenty years ago,' Colin replied extracting a bundle of Somerset Council building application approval documents. He quickly flipped through a few pages before coming to the one he wanted.

'Ah here it is. You'll find this interesting,' he said passing it over.

Wesley read the first paragraph and looked astonished.

'So planning application from Michael Westbrook was approved in 1987 to allow access to the Chalice Well, in order to be able to pump water into the Chapel for the purposes of selling the Holy Water to the public.'

'That's correct,' Colin replied handing Wesley another sheet of paper. 'And look who was commissioned to do the work.'

'Eddie Hallerton. You old devil.' Wesley scratched his head.

'But there's more.' He retrieved a final tracing from the desk and pinned it over the top of the others.

He waited for Wesley to respond.

'Sorry Colin. I'm confused. What am I supposed to be looking at?'

'Look at the red dotted line that runs from the lowest part of the Well up towards Abbey House on the other side to where the Chapel is located.'

'Oh yeah I see it. But what is it?'

Colin held an old piece of parchment in his hand and read from it.

'In 1697 excavations disclosed a special compartment at the south side of Abbey House. This was erected prior to a visit by King Henry who demanded that all monasteries and associated building be demolished. It was used to hide the monks who were in danger of being slaughtered by the Kings troops. The monks are believed to have used an escape passage from the hidden compartment via the Chalice Well and out across the Tor.'

'Let me get this right,' said Wesley rubbing his hand across his chin.

'You're suggesting this co called compartment still exists and not only that, it could still provide access to the Well and the Tor?'

Colin Dempster shrugged his shoulders.

'Yes I believe I am. I can't find anything in the archives either at the Council offices or the University that disproves my theory that both the compartment in Abbey House and the access to the Well still exist.'

'If your right, this could be the clue we've been looking for. Not only that but surely the Westbrook's must know of it?'

55

David was getting impatient waiting outside the shop whilst Sally was trying on the fifth dress in the past hour. A woman entered the shop and acknowledged him with a smile. David waited another fifteen minutes and was about to drag Sally from the shop when she appeared in the door holding a collection of shopping bags.

'It looks as if you've bought the shop,' he exclaimed.

'Now, now. I'm only going to buy one dress but I want Mum's advice first before I choose one of these,' Sally replied holding up all the bags.

David shook his head in disbelief.

'Did you see that girl who entered the shop just now? The one with the shoulder length, jet black hair.'

'I did as a matter of fact, and why would you be so interested?'

'I'm not,' David replied angrily. 'I'm only asking if you saw her. I recognise her face from somewhere.'

'You wish,' said Sally. 'Come on grumps. I'll buy you lunch.'

They had ordered lunch and were sat by the window in their favourite pizza restaurant when David spotted the girl again on the other side of the road. This time she was talking to a gentleman.

David nudged Sally and discreetly nodded in their direction. It was soon obvious that the couple were having an argument as the girl started waving her arms at the guy and gesticulating in an aggressive manner.

'I think I know her from somewhere,' said Sally.

'See, I told you so,' David replied.

The couple continued to argue until the guy turned away from the girl and crossed the street in their direction. David and Sally only got a quick glimpse of him as he strode away. The girl remained where she was for a few seconds still shouting and waving at him before she turned and walked off in the opposite direction.

'I do know who she is,' said Sally. 'That was definitely Michael Westbrook. You know the guy who lives at Abbey House. Where the body was found yesterday in the Chapel. Don't you remember we watched him being interviewed on local TV last night?'

'Yeah I remember now, but what about the girl?'

'She was stood in the background,' Sally muttered with a mouthful of pizza. 'She's the housemaid at Abbey House.'

'Yeah got it now. She was standing just behind him on the steps outside the house listening to the interview. Well she certainly seemed angry about something,' David replied trying in vain to slice his pizza.

'What's interesting is that for someone who I guess doesn't earn a fortune being a housemaid, she just spent over four hundred pounds in the clothes shop,' Sally remarked.

'Don't look now,' David muttered. 'He's running back this way.'

They both watched as Michael Westbrook sprinted down the High Street in the direction that Jenny had just taken.

Before leaving the station, Colin handed Wesley the warning note that had been stuck under his door in the University. Wesley read the one line threat but didn't recognise the hand writing.

'I'll get someone to check the handwriting for any matches we may have. Obviously if you receive anything else or someone threatens you in any other way then contact me immediately.'

He handed Colin his contact details.

'Thanks Mr Wesley. Sure will.'

After thanking Colin for the information he'd provided about the Chalice Well, Wesley waited until he had left the building before picking up the office phone to dial Bath CID. He was told that the search warrant to search Abbey House would be with him by tea time.

An hour later Wesley pulled up outside Dorothy's. Jane opened the door for him even before he knocked.

'Hello,' she said quietly and kissed him on the cheek.

'Dorothy has just gone back to bed. I came over as soon as WPC Tredwell phoned to say she was going off duty. She'd been here all night.'

'Thanks Jane. I do appreciate your help and I know Dorothy will once she gets herself back to normal.'

'If there will ever be such a thing as normal for her now.'

Jane closed the front door and followed Wesley inside.

'I had a long chat with her this morning. Eddie did just about everything for her. He's provided the only income into the house since they married some forty odd years ago.'

'Well I know one area he was certainly busy in,' Wesley replied and brought Jane up to date with his earlier meeting with Colin Dempster.

'Eddie must have worked with someone else whilst digging underground. He couldn't have excavated tons of earth or carried materials up and down into the Well on his own.'

'That's a good point.'

'I don't know. I thought you were the policeman,' she laughed.

'So what's the plan of action?'

'Well I can't just go marching into Abbey House demanding to look around the place, so I've put in a request for a search warrant which I should sometime later today.'

'That's going to ruffle Michael Westbrook's feathers for sure,' Jane replied.

'Hmm. Penny's too I believe. I think there's a lot more to learn about their home and her relationship with Michael.'

'Do you think there's something going on between Michael and Jenny then?' she asked. 'It had crossed my mind. I mean, we did see them in the restaurant didn't we?'

'Yes, but that alone doesn't mean they're having an affair,' he replied sipping his tea.

'Oh you men can be so short sighted at the best of times. Don't you remember when I spent the evening with Penny and Jenny last week that I told you Jenny disappeared half way through the evening?'

'Yes, but you said she'd commented on how tired she was.'

'She's half my age John. Why on earth would a girl of her age be tired at nine o'clock in the evening?'

They were still sat in Dorothy's kitchen deciding what the best plan would be for over the next few days when his mobile rang.

'Wesley speaking.'

'Hi, it's Martin. I've just come away from the hotel. I've managed to obtain a couple of cassettes of CCTV footage and the receptionist has already confirmed that it was Kelvin Ward who had been using the hotel. The other piece of information you'll find interesting, is that the description of the girl he always met matches Jenny Stevens to a tee.'

'Great work Martin. Bring the tapes back. We'll run through those this evening. Before that, Adam and I are paying a visit to Michael and Penny Westbrook at Abbey House. I'll explain when I meet you back at the station.'

Wesley had decided against waiting for the search warrant to arrive and called Adam into the office.

'You wanted to see me?'

'Yes. I want you to come over to Abbey House with me. Although we don't have a search warrant yet, it's something we can keep up our sleeve. Assuming that both Michael and Penny Westbrook will be there, as soon as we arrive I want you to interview Michael whilst I interview Penny at the same time in another room. You OK with that?'

'Certainly. Is there anything specific you want to find out from Michael?'

'Just tell him that we are continuing with our investigations and there are a couple of points we need to clear up. He may get defensive but I think he'll speak up. Ask him where he was when he first heard about Eddie's incident in the Chapel and who told him. Ask him if he has any ideas as to why someone would have wanted to murder Eddie and ask him if he knows why Eddie was in the Chapel to start with.'

'Sure thing. Anything else?'

'No not at this stage. I've got a feeling we will push him further when the search warrant arrives. That's going to be our ace card.'

'Are you going to be asking Penny the same questions?'

'Yeah in a roundabout way. I have a few other questions to put to Penny and some information that may affect the way she responds to my probing. Let's have a pot of tea then we'll take a drive over there. You put the kettle on while I go for a fag. I'll meet you in the mess room in ten minutes.'

It was nearly three o'clock in the afternoon when Adam pulled the car into Silver Street car park. After crossing the road they made their way through the grounds passing the Abbey ruins. They were met at the entrance to Abbey House by several news reporters who were still waiting for scraps of information. However they were left disappointed as Wesley refused to make any further comments, except to say there would be an update of the enquiries with local television in the morning. It was Jenny Stevens who opened the door.

'Oh good afternoon Inspector,' she said after viewing Wesley's ID. 'Please, come in.'

Jenny directed Wesley and Adam into the front parlour.

'I'll tell Mr & Mrs Westbrook that you're here.' She disappeared towards the library.

'Sure is a nice place,' Adam remarked as he looked around the room. 'Some of this furniture must be worth a fortune.'

'Yeah I expect it is.'

Wesley casually rolled a cigarette for later. He was too old in life to be overwhelmed by someone else's property.

'I expect it takes a fortune just to run this place.'

Wesley looked up but before he could comment Michael and Penny walked into the room.

'I assume you're here to tell me we can open the Chapel again,' said Michael as he slumped himself into one of the brown leather wing backed chairs without inviting his visitors to sit down.

'Oh Michael don't be so rude and abrupt,' Penny intervened.

'Please gentlemen. Take a seat.' She pointed to a large leather settee that took centre stage in the room.

'Thanks,' Wesley replied, 'but I would like a word with you in private please Mrs Westbrook, while PC Broad has a chat with your husband.'

'Have you got nothing better to do?' asked Michael standing up.

'While we're sat here having nice little chats, Penny and I are losing money because we can't let visitors into the Chapel.'

'We won't keep you long,' Wesley replied looking at Penny rather than Michael. 'Perhaps we could find another room?' he suggested.

Penny quickly glanced at Michael before replying.

'Yes of course, Inspector. Follow me.' Penny led the way across the hall and into the library.

'Take a seat, please.' She closed the door behind her.

'What a lovely room,' Wesley exclaimed looking at the vast array of books that lined the shelves on all four walls.

'Yes I like it. I come here to read and relax.'

'You do that often?'

'Most days. It's nice to get away from Michael for an hour or so. He can be so demanding.'

'He does come across that way.'

'So how can I be of assistance?' Penny asked.

'I've been going through Eddie's paperwork. Do you have any idea why he was so heavily in debt?'

'In debt? Surely there must be a mistake Inspector. I know he never made a fortune in life but I see no reason why he would owe anyone money.'

'If I tell you that he'd extracted three hundred pounds in cash, every week from his bank account, for quite a period of time, whatever income he received. Would that surprise you?'

'Yes of course,' Penny replied sitting up straight.

'Would it also surprise you to know that when he died, Eddie was over four thousand pounds in debt?'

'Oh my God! Does Dorothy know about this?' she exclaimed.

'I doubt it for one minute.'

'So just how long had he been withdrawing that kind of money?' Penny asked looking concerned. 'He could have always asked me for money. I would have made sure he was OK.'

Wesley extracted his note book and flipped over the pages.

'We know he started extracting the money regularly just over six months ago. Penny, I need to know if you have any idea what this money was for or to whom he was paying it.'

'I've no idea Inspector. Eddie never travelled far that I know of. He used to like a beer and a flutter on the horses but I don't believe he ever spent vast sums of money on either.'

'We've run a quick check on the local betting shops and drawn a blank so far,' said Wesley.

He watched Penny for a few moments as she sat staring into space as if she were on her own. Thinking this was the right time to change the subject for a moment he put his hand into his jacket pocket and extracted a silver object.

'I think you ought to have this.' Wesley opened his fist over Penny's hand and dropped the silver pendant into her palm.

'What is it?' she asked.

'Open it,' he replied sitting back in the chair.

Penny pressed the side of the locket to view the inside. When it opened, she took one look and began to sob. Wesley sat in silence while Penny sat clutching the pendant to her chest as her whole body racked with her sobbing. He took a handkerchief from his pocket and handed it to her.

'Where did you find this?' she muttered.

'It was found in the waistcoat he was wearing when he died. The little girl in the photo is you, isn't it?'

'Yes.' Penny put her head into her lap and sobbed.

'So, Mr Westbrook. Where were you when you first heard about the incident in the Chapel?' asked PC Adam Broad.

'What do you mean? Where was I? Here of course.'

'So someone must have informed you as to what had happened.'

'Err yes. Err no. I mean, I looked out of the window and saw people standing outside the Chapel and a few others running out.'

'So you went outside to see what was happening?'

'Yes. One of the visitors said there had been an accident in the Chapel. The next thing I knew was Eddie Hallerton had fallen down the bloody Well.'

'What was he doing in the Chapel?' Adam asked taking notes.

'How should I know? Penny is the one you need to talk to. She schedules most of the work done around here.'

'So you don't know what he was working on that particular morning?'

'No idea,' Michael replied sternly.

'Is that the only access to the Well from the house?'

Michael shrugged his shoulders.

'As far as I know. So can we re-open to the public now?'

'I'm afraid not Mr Westbrook. The forensic team have been asked to go over the area again.'

'Whatever for?' asked Michael raising his voice. 'Just because the old man had an accident. We need to get some revenue in.'

'I'm afraid it may not have been an accident,' Adam replied standing up.

'Eddie Hallerton may have been murdered.'

56

Jenny knew she had taken a risk when she had made a copy of Kelvin Wards door key. Having stolen it from Penny's handbag one morning she had run into town to get a copy cut and had only just replaced it when Penny burst into the library saying she had mislaid her handbag. Having followed Penny on several occasions into town, she was sure that Penny and Kelvin were having an affair. She had seen Penny turn into the alley next to the bookshop and mount the back stairs to Kelvin's flat on several occasions.

Making sure no one was around Jenny turned the key in the lock and closed the door behind her. Having made a discreet enquiry with Jane in the bookshop as to what was happening with the flat since Kelvin's death, she found out that the flat was to be sold in the coming weeks.

However, as yet it had not been put on the market as the estate agents were waiting for the police to empty it of any further personal belongings. Jenny slipped the key into her jeans' pocket and started to look around the flat.

The first thing she noticed was how tidy it was. Maybe too tidy. She had the feeling that someone had already been in before her. The small sideboard in the lounge was full of glass and china and there was a small amount of food in the kitchen but nothing else of any value or interest. She opened the door to the bedroom that was located at the back of the flat and stood looking at the destruction. The mattress was lying on the floor, cut to pieces. A painting and a mirror were both smashed, also lying on the floor. Every drawer had been taken out of the bedside table and emptied out. Whoever had been in the flat before her was certainly looking for something specific.

Jenny closed the bedroom door quietly so as not to be over heard in the bookshop downstairs. She was halfway down the outside staircase when her mobile rang. It made her jump and she realised she was sweating. She let it ring until the caller gave up. Checking the screen she saw that it was Michael who was trying to contact her. Waiting until she had left the shopping area Jenny sat on a bench near the main entrance to Glastonbury Abbey before returning Michael's call.

'Where the hell are you?' he shouted.

'That's a lovely welcome,' Jenny snapped.

'Well, where are you? The bloody police have been here again.'

'So what's that got to do with me?' she asked flippantly.

'They were asking questions about Eddie Hallerton.'

She could hear the strain in Michael's voice.

'Oh, the maintenance guy who had an accident in the Chapel?'

'Yes the bloody maintenance guy but the police are saying it was no accident.'

There was silence between them for a minute.

'Are you listening to me?' he shouted. 'The police are saying that the old boy was probably murdered!'

'I'll be home in a few minutes' Jenny replied calmly and hung up.

57

WPC Lucy Clarke was sat having a cup of tea with Patricia Wright. The poor woman had been on tranquilizers since the day Denise had been reported missing. Lucy watched her as she used both hands to raise the cup to her lips. It was obvious that in just a matter of days she had lost weight and was looking frail.

Lucy was trained especially for this type of situation and had been to the house every day to spend time with Patricia.

'So was Denise born here in the house?' Lucy asked. 'I know it was more common then.' She observed Patricia's response to the question as the woman drew her cup to her lips to take another sip of tea.

'I was born at home you know. We lived in Somerton Road in those days. That's when my parents were both working at the biscuit factory.'

'She's not mine.'

'I beg your pardon?' Lucy placed her cup down on the table.

'Sorry, Patricia. I didn't quite catch your reply.'

'She's not mine. Denise is not my child.' Patricia put her hands to face and began to sob.

Lucy walked around the table and put her hand on her shoulder.

'It's OK. Let it all out,' she said. Lucy handed her a handkerchief and sat beside her whilst Patricia told her story.

A short while later Lucy walked into the kitchen and closed the door behind her. Tapping in a number on her phone she asked to be put straight through to Inspector Wesley.

58

Denise was sleeping when her captor entered the room. After untying her hands and feet and removing the masking tape from her mouth, her captor then dropped a carrier bag of clothes by the door for Denise to change into. Food provisions consisting of two plain rolls and a jug of water were also placed on the floor.

'Eat and get changed. You have to move elsewhere.'

Denise consumed one of the dry stale rolls and drank the jug of water in gulps. Slowly changing her clothes, she was embarrassed at being momentarily naked in front of her captor and of having soiled herself. Her legs were beginning to shake due to the fact she hadn't stood for several days.

'Where are you taking me?' Denise asked her voice trembling with fear.

'You'll see.'

'Why can't I just go home?' she sobbed.

'Hurry up. I don't have time to waste,' her captor replied. 'It will be dark soon. We need to move now.'

Once outside of the room, they appeared to be standing in an old corridor. The walls were made of stone but the floor was mainly earth. They had only taken a few steps when her captor pointed to a hole in the floor just in front of them.

'Down there. Come on, move.'

Although she was shivering, Denise could feel the sweat running down her face. A sharp push in the back and she found herself slumped against the wall with her feet dangling into the hole. She gingerly reached down, her feet searching for a secure footing. Once she had found the first step carved out of the side of the interior wall, she soon found the others and within a minute both of them had reached the bottom and were stood in a tunnel. Denise felt the excruciating pain and cramp in her legs that was the result of having so little exercise. She could hear running water somewhere up ahead. Her captor lit a torch and pointed the way. They were walking on a concrete ledge no more than two feet wide. In the middle was a trench some six feet across with a trickle of water running in the direction they were headed. In places, both of them had to bend low to avoid hitting their heads on the concrete roof.

They had been walking for two minutes when they came to a sharp bend as the tunnel started to slope uphill to their right. Directly in front of them was a huge void, a black chasm, where the water was pouring into. Denise suddenly felt a hand on her shoulder as her captor motioned for her to stop. Without warning, her captor quickly retied her hands and covered her eyes and mouth with masking tape.

'Stand still,' her captor said.

'What are you going to do with me?' Denise mumbled as the fear began to rise in her tummy.

Her captor never replied but guided her away from the chasm. By the strain on her legs she could tell the gradient had changed and they were now steadily rising away from the chasm.

A minute later they stopped again and Denise was told to stand still. She was now shaking with fear and the cold when she heard the sound of a lock being opened.

Almost immediately two hands grabbed her by the shoulder and marched her forward. They had only taken half a dozen steps when they halted and Denise was forcibly turned to the right.

'Right in front of you are a set of steps. There are only eight. Move on.' Extending her tied hands in front of her to make sure she didn't walk into something, Denise walked forward and after making sure she had a foot hold slowly mounted the steps.

At the top of the steps she had to crawl on hands and knees into the open space. She was immediately aware that the air had changed. The surroundings now were less claustrophobic. For a few seconds she stood in silence before her captor pushed her forward until they reached the far wall where Denise was made to sit.

She could feel her legs being tied again and tried to call out but it was impossible. The masking tape that her captor had just applied only allowed a muted muffled moan. When the masking tape was eventually removed from her eyes, for what seemed like an eternity, she could only hear her captor moving around somewhere in front of her as her eyes slowly adjusted to the greyish light.

The expectancy that she was going to murdered at any time suddenly arose and she felt the urge to vomit. Her captor must have been watching her as without warning the masking tape was removed.

Denise immediately vomited on the floor and began to sob.

When she couldn't be sick any more she leant back against the wall and closed her eyes for a moment.

'Why are you doing this? I have no money. I haven't hurt anyone. Why can't you let me go?' she pleaded.

Her captor almost stood over her facing the other way. Denise tried in vain to see what it was that her captor was extracting from the duffel bag on the floor. When her captor turned around,

Denise looked aghast as she felt the needle prick her arm.

Staring, open mouthed in protest, she instantly felt the room begin to spin as she slumped forward.

59

'Come and sit down, dinner is ready,' said Jane and pushed him out of the kitchen towards the lounge. Wesley sat down and put his feet up on the foot stool as Jane placed the dinner tray on his lap.

'Thanks my dear.'

Jane sat next to him on the settee.

He waited until they had both consumed dinner before asking about Dorothy.

'So Dorothy has agreed to go away for a couple of days eh?'

'Yes. She has a sister in Minehead who is coming to pick her up. It's only until the funeral. My understanding is that she hasn't seen much of her sister for the past few years, since her own husband passed away following a sudden illness. However, when I phoned her, she sounded keen to get Dorothy away for a few days.'

'That should do her the world of good.' Wesley tucked into homemade steak and kidney pie. Half of which was already down the front of his shirt.

'Just look at you,' said Jane. 'I ought to buy you a bib for your birthday.'

'Have either you or the two WPCs been able to get anything out of Dorothy at all?' he asked.

'Not really. I know you said that Eddie was in debt. I obviously didn't mention that to Dorothy but I did ask if she was going to cope financially. She seems to think that Eddie had a life insurance that would see her OK.'

'Hmm. I hope he did but I wouldn't bank on it.' Wesley tried to rub the gravy off of his shirt.

'Leave that stain alone,' said Jane taking the dinner tray from him. 'I'll put some stuff on it before putting it in the washing machine.' She hurried off to the kitchen and returned with two bowls of apple pie and custard.

'Blimey you are spoiling me tonight.'

'Just eat,' Jane replied laughing. They were both silent until pudding was over.

'So what was Penny's reaction to Eddie's murder?' she asked as she started to gather the plates.

'She was obviously startled and very upset. She says she has no idea why anyone would want to have murdered him, although she did agree that her father was a bit of a wheeler dealer.'

'Oh poor love. I'll give her a phone this evening to make sure she's OK. Oh by the way I forgot to tell you. PC Philips dropped an envelope in for you. Said to give him a call if you need him. I left it by the phone in the hall.'

Wesley got out of the chair and stretched before making his way out into the hall. The envelope contained the search warrant for Abbey House.

I think we'll be using this in the morning, he said to himself carrying it upstairs.

60

'Did you see that Dempster guy walking around the Tor with all those bloody maps?' Michael ranted as Jenny entered the house.

'I saw someone,' she replied nonchalantly. 'Why what's he doing?'

'Being bloody nosy. He's been there over an hour and keeps walking backwards and forward past the house,' he replied still irritated. 'I asked him what he was doing but he just looked at me and ignored me. He's on my bloody land.'

'Since when do you own the Tor?' She stroked Michael's hair and whispered in his ear. Her hand brushed his groin as she walked past.

'I'm going to take a shower before I start preparing dinner.'

Michael watched her ascend the staircase with a mixed feeling of anger and passion. He made his way upstairs and walked into his own bedroom as Penny was getting dressed. She was standing by the dressing table wrapped only in a towel. It had been some time since he and his wife made love.

'What are you staring at?' she asked as she searched for a tee-shirt. Michael didn't answer. He walked across the bedroom floor and grabbing her waist turned her around so she was facing him. His tongue probed her mouth as his hand went straight to her breast. His urgency caught Penny by surprise. In a matter of seconds he pulled her towards the bed and began kissing her neck and shoulders before sliding himself down onto his knees. She knew instantly that there was no way back. All of her current worries vanished for a few minutes as her body arched against the probing of his tongue. Unbeknown to them, Jenny stood in the doorway watching, as they pleasured themselves before she silently made her way downstairs to the kitchen. She removed the carving knife from the drawer and in one swift movement buried it deep into the chopping board.

It was only mid-morning but Wesley was tired already. He'd just held a press conference with local TV and answered questions to a few concerned members of the general public who had congregated outside the station.

He was sat at his desk deep in thought when the office phone rang.

'Hi Wesley speaking.'

'Hi John, how are you keeping?' It was Terry Austin from the pathology lab.

I'm OK. What have you got for me?'

'Well I'm ready to release Eddie Hallertons body now. There's no further evidence I can give you except to say that Mr Hallerton had scraping of silver under his nails.'

'Silver? How do you mean?' Wesley asked somewhat confused.

'Well it's my guess that unless Eddie had actually been engraving something just before he died, then he had certainly been carrying or holding something silver. The strange thing is that this type of silver is no longer used, hasn't been for donkey's years.'

'So are you saying that whatever the object was, it was worn or old?'

'I don't know what the object was but I can assure you that it's antique. Almost certainly something ancient.'

'Hmm that's very interesting but also very confusing. We know Eddie Hallerton used to be a bit of a wheeler dealer but I can't imagine him having anything of considerable value. It just wasn't his style.'

'Well, style or not John, the type of silver we found under his nails was used back in medieval times. I'm talking about hundreds years ago.'

'OK. What else have you got for me?'

'Only confirmation that Eddie died from a blow to the back of the head. The damage to the back of his skull indicates that he snapped his neck when he fell backwards. Whether he slipped or was pushed though I can't tell.'

'Thanks Terry.'

Wesley hung up and pressed the intercom buzzer.

'Gather everyone in the briefing room would you Martin. I'll be there in five minutes.'

The team brief lasted more than an hour. Although the local house to house searches and the patrols around the shopping centre had proved fruitless and no one had seen Denise since the day she went missing. Two pieces of information had come to light from CCTV footage in the High Street taken from the night Denise disappeared. PC Adam Broad wound the tape forward to 21:15 then pressed the play button. Within a couple of seconds Denise could be seen heading towards the bus station. She appeared to be on her own. However, he then wound the tape back to 21:08 and ran the tape again. This time to everyone's surprise Eddie Hallerton appeared on the screen as he exited the alleyway next to the shop and walked across the road towards the Abbey. At that point he went out of shot as he turned right into Chilkwell Street.

'Can you replay the shot of Eddie Hallerton again?' Wesley asked.

When the footage finished, Wesley nodded for the lights to be turned on.

'I think there are two interesting pieces of information here,' he said rolling a cigarette.

'Firstly, I know I'm an old fogey compared to some of you but I'm sure that Mandy and Alison will confirm that Denise didn't look as if she was dressed to go straight out for the evening. Am I right?'

'I agree,' Mandy replied. 'It was a Friday night. If Denise was going out somewhere I would have thought she would have changed out of her daytime clothes.'

'Thank you.' Wesley smiled across the table.

'I didn't realise you were a bit of a connoisseur of women's evening clothes,' Adam commented.

'We'll ignore that remark Adam, unless of course you don't want to be the only one of the team on late shift next week.'

Everyone in the room laughed.

'Secondly, I don't know of anyone else noticed but Eddie Hallerton seemed to be in an awful hurry. In fact I never saw him walk that fast.'

'Another interesting point is that Eddie was wearing an overcoat,' Adam commented.

'What's strange about that?' asked Alison.

'It's not even cold at nine in the evening. Certainly not cold enough to wear an overcoat.'

'Unless of course you wanted to conceal something,' Adam replied.

'Good point,' said Wesley. He paused for a few moments before continuing.

'OK. Mandy, can you check on Dorothy this morning. She's going to stay at her sister's for a few days. Just make sure everything is alright. Adam, run through the CCTV footage of Denise again. Make a note of what she's wearing and let me have the list. See if you can get the guys over at Bath to blow up a good shot of her from the footage we have. I then want a poster put up around town but show me first.'

'Sure thing,' Adam replied.

'As for Alison and Martin, between you, can you please decide who is going to make the tea before the three of us pay a visit to Abbey House? I have the search warrant now so it will be interesting to see their reaction.'

Everyone left the room except for Adam who was playing with the controls on the video recorder.

At the same time Jenny and Michael were having an argument.

'Where are you going?' he asked as Jenny entered the library looking for something. 'You're all dressed to go out.'

'That's where I'm going. Out!'

Michael put the newspaper down, stood up and walked across the room.

'Have I done something wrong?' He grabbed her by the waist.

'Get your hands off me.' Jenny pushed him away and strode back out into the hall. She didn't look back to see the astounded expression on Michaels face.

61

David replaced the telephone back into its cradle as Sally entered the room still towel drying her hair.

'Who was that?' she asked.

'Inspector Wesley. I phoned him to tell him that we saw Michael running after Jenny the other night and then saw her again at the cinema wearing muddy shoes. I'm not sure whether he thought I was an idiot but I said it may or may not be important and just thought he ought to be made aware.'

'So what was his response?' Sally asked trying to get a knot out of her hair.

'He just thanked me for the information and said to let him know if we see anything else that we think may be of interest to him.'

'Well we've done our bit for the police force.'

Sally continued tugging at the knots in her hair.

'Come on Sal. We're going to be late,' David shouted from the other room. 'The film starts in an hour.'

Sally came down the stairs wearing a loose top and a pair of jeans that clung to her body.

'Hmm lovely,' said David rubbing his hands.

'Stop it you. I thought you said we were late. What film are we seeing?'

'I've told you twice,' he replied putting his jacket on. 'It's a bit of a thriller. Some psycho who starts killing prostitutes.'

'Oh that sounds nice,' she replied sarcastically. 'There's nothing better than a comedy.'

David noticed how quiet Sally was throughout the film. She was usually so full of chatter they missed half of what they were watching. Sally didn't want to admit that she had really quite liked the film.

Colin Dempster didn't hear the click of the lock. He had a habit of having the radio on loud when he was busy marking exam papers.

The caller turned the knob handle and peered into the room. Colin was sat at the small bureau that stood underneath the window with his back to the door. He never knew who his assailant was. The first blow to the back of his skull threw his head forward so that he head butted the bureau. The second blow killed him, as his skull caved in. Blood spurted out across the desk and the wall below the window.

62

Wesley, along with WPC Bolt and PC Philips, were approaching the main gates at the front of Abbey House, when Jenny strode past with a stern look on her face. She failed to acknowledge Wesley's gesture of hello and completely ignored Alison's apology as she quickly moved aside to allow Jenny to pass.

'My, that is one angry lady,' said Martin.

'Angry and rude,' Alison replied.

It was Penny Westbrook who opened the front door.

'Hello Inspector. This is a surprise,' she said looking between him and the two constables. 'I didn't know you were coming over. Please come in.'

Everyone entered the hall. This was the constables' first visit to Abbey House and they looked impressed as they took in the grandeur. The tall, floor-standing, grandfather clock chimed eleven o'clock before anyone spoke. Penny looked somewhat edgy.

'I'd like to take a look around the Chapel and the house,' said Wesley smiling as he tried to relieve a bit of the tension.

'Of course you can take a look around the Chapel but why the house?'

'I'll come straight to the point.' He extracted one of the tracings that Colin Dempster had produced. 'I'm led to believe there may be a way to access the Chalice Well other than by the floor grating in the Chapel. I have an old drawing here that shows that some three hundred years ago, excavations found a special compartment leading from the house to the Well from the East Wing of the building.'

'The East Wing? But that's been closed off ever since I've lived here and many years before that I believe. It's in dire need of repair and the outside wall is cracked so I'm told.'

'And it's bloody well out of bounds,' shouted Michael as he came down the staircase. 'You can look around the damn Chapel as long as you like but I'm not having people traipsing around my home.'

'It's part of our investigations into the recent murders,' Wesley said taking a step forward.

'Rubbish,' he retorted. 'I'm sick to death with people either gawping through the windows or wanting to pry inside. I'm simply not having it.'

Wesley extracted the search warrant and handed it to Michael.

'What's this?' he asked without unfolding the piece of paper.

'It's a search warrant, Mr Westbrook. I was hoping I wouldn't need it.'

Michael Westbrook unfolded the piece of paper and read the contents before handing it to Penny.

'See how the police treat us. I told you we shouldn't encourage their visits. You know how I hate people in the house.'

Penny looked embarrassed at her husband's outburst and her face reddened. She read the description of the search warrant, folded the paper and handed it back to Wesley.

'Please give me one second,' she said directly to Wesley. 'I will obtain the key to the door to the East Wing. It's always remained locked. Excuse me for a moment.'

Penny walked off towards the kitchen leaving a flabbergasted Michael Westbrook stood in front of Wesley and his colleagues.

'I think it's a damn liberty. I don't see any reason why you and your colleagues need to start rummaging about in the East Wing. The damn place is unsafe. That's why it's not used,' Michael retorted.

'Hopefully we won't be in there long,' Wesley replied placing the search warrant back into his jacket pocket. Penny reappeared in the hallway clutching a set of keys.

'That's it. Show everyone the damn place, why don't you,' Michael shouted at her and stormed off, slamming every door in his way.

'Please, follow me,' said Penny rather meekly and led the way down the corridor towards the back of the house. On a couple of occasions Martin and Alison who were behind Wesley, nudged one another to look at some of the paintings and furniture that adorned the wall and the recesses. At the end of the hall they took a right turn and followed the corridor to the far end where a cream coloured door stood imposingly in their way.

'Is this the only entrance to the East Wing?' Wesley asked.

'Yes, to my knowledge in any case.'

She tried to open the lock twice before finding the correct key.

Upon opening the door she searched for a light switch but found none.

'It doesn't look like there is any electricity in this side of the house,' said Wesley lighting a match and running his hand along the side of the wall. They all stood in the doorway for a minute whilst their eyes grew accustomed to the light.

'There looks to be a small window at the far end of the room,' said Penny pointing ahead. 'Let me open the curtain to let in some light.'

As she made her way across the room Martin tapped Wesley on the shoulder and pointed towards the floor away from where Penny had trodden. There were unmistakable footprints on the wooden flooring, leading across the room, identifiable because of the dust that the footprints had disturbed. It was obvious the room hadn't been cleaned for quite some time. Possibly centuries. Wesley nodded his acknowledgement and waited for Penny to open the curtains.

The natural daylight gave the room an eerie look and made the visitors feel as if they were imposing on a past history that wanted to be left alone.

White sheets covered most of the furniture and a previous tenant had left an empty wine glass on the table that was now covered in cobwebs.

Martin and Alison followed closely behind Wesley as he walked towards the far end of the room. Suddenly Alison shrieked, as a mouse ran along the skirting board, and disappeared behind a sideboard. For a brief second she held Martin's hand, then realised to her embarrassment what she had done as her face went a crimson colour. She pulled her hand away and readjusted her uniform. Martin smiled before she gave him a discreet kick in the shin.

'Where does that lead to?' Wesley asked pointing to another door next to the sideboard.

'To the kitchen area and the back staircase.'

'Back staircase? But I thought you said this was the only entrance?'

'The staircase is blocked off. I believe our predecessors had it blocked off before Michael's father bought the house.'

'So Michael owned the house when you first met?' asked Alison.

'Yes, he's lived here all of his life.'

'Shall we go up? I'll lead the way if you wish,' said Wesley.

'But it's a dead end,' Penny exclaimed.

'Just a quick look.'

The old staircase creaked and groaned as they ascended the stairs. When they reached the landing they faced a solid wall in front of them and a small wooden door to their right. Wesley tried the handle but it was locked.

'I told you Inspector. The other side is completely sealed off. The doorway no longer exists on the other side.'

'In which case there must be a gap between this door and the other side,' commented Martin.

'Very good point,' said Wesley. 'Can I borrow your keys for a second?' he asked Penny. He was about to concede defeat when the final key turned in the lock. Turning the handle he pulled the door towards him and opened it wide enough for all to see what was on the inside.

About two feet in front was the interior wall. Penny was right it had been bricked up. To the right was a wall divide that was made of breezeblock that had obviously been put in when the door had been blocked up. However to the left there was a narrow gap just wide enough for someone to enter.

'Can you fetch me a torch from somewhere?'

They waited in silence until Penny returned carrying a small square shaped torch.

'Sorry this was all I could find. It works though.' She handed it over to Wesley who shone the torch into the void. A narrow wooden staircase came into view. After a dozen steps down, the staircase turned left and down again.

Wesley was the first to notice that the steps were no longer wooden. They were now descending concrete steps and the wall either side was no longer brickwork, it was solid stone. After another dozen or so steps the floor evened out and became a mixture of stone flagging and dirt.

There was another door to their left a few yards ahead and what appeared to be a hole in the ground just beyond that where the passageway ended. They took a few steps forward as Wesley shone the light over the hole. Martin bent down to take a closer look inside as Wesley handed him the torch.

'There are steps cut into the side of the hole here. Do you want me to have a look? I can see the bottom. It's no more than eight to ten feet down.'

'Yeah might as well while we're here. You're a bit thinner than me.' Wesley noticed the smirk on Alison's face.

They watched whilst Martin lowered himself down and all stood peering into the hole as the light from the torch started to diminish.

'It's OK, I've reached the bottom,' Martin called out some twenty seconds later.

'What's down there?' asked Penny.

'Hold on,' came the reply. They waited for almost a minute before they could hear Martin ascending the steps. Once back on top Wesley gave him a few seconds to get his breath back.

'So what's down there?' asked Alison getting impatient.

'I can't say for certain because I didn't go far enough but I'd take a guess that the concrete tunnel down there leads to the Chalice Well. It's certainly heading in that direction and I can hear running water.'

Wesley helped Martin to stand up in the confined space around the edge of the hole.

'Good work son. We'll get some of the boys down here with the proper equipment.'

As Wesley turned around he noticed that Penny was missing. They suddenly became aware of her sobbing. The wooden door in the recess behind them was open. Wesley stepped inside followed by Alison and then Martin who was still brushing himself down.

Penny was sat on the floor clutching a cardigan. Next to her was a plate with a half-eaten bread roll almost green in colour and an empty water jug.

She looked up at Wesley as the tears ran down her face.

'This is Denise's,' she said clutching the cardigan. 'I bought this for her birthday only two weeks ago.'

Wesley turned to Alison.

'Get the forensic team down here asap. I want the area sealed off to anyone other than them or us.'

Once back in the main building, Alison led Penny to a seat in the library whilst Martin poured her some water from the cut glass water jug. Wesley was about to phone the station for additional support when Michael strode into the room.

'Where the hell have you been?' he asked directing his question directly at Penny. Wesley placed his phone on the sideboard and crossed the room in about three strides.

'Mr Westbrook I need to speak with you,' said Wesley extending his hands forward.

'I was asking my wife a question,' replied an irate Michael.

Wesley placed his hands on Michael's shoulders and looked him straight in the eye.

'We'll talk elsewhere.'

Years of expertise in handling delicate situations and forcibly removing people from conflict came in handy. Wesley grabbed his phone and marched Michael out of the library, across the hall and into the front parlour, closing the door behind him.

'Take a seat Mr Westbrook. Give me one minute. I need to make a quick phone call then I'll update you on things.'

Michael sat impatiently on the arm of the sofa as Wesley walked over to the window and phoned the station. He spoke with Adam who had just returned from getting some photos of Denise made up.

'Giving Adam a quick update on the situation he asked for a support team to be sent over to Abbey House. I want the whole area cordoned off. They'll need pot holing equipment and I want forensics here asap.'

'Can you just confirm pot holing equipment?' Adam asked.

'Confirmed,' Wesley replied and hung up.

'What's going on?' Michael asked and stood up as soon as he saw Wesley come off the phone.

'Mr Westbrook, you told me that no one has ever used the East Wing because it is in need of repair.'

'That's correct. I was informed that that side of the building is unsafe.'

'Then can you explain how we managed to find recent footprints in the back room as you enter the damn place and more importantly, how we managed to find evidence that Denise Wright has been held captive there?'

Michaels face turned ashen grey and he put his hands to his mouth.

'Oh my God. Are you serious?' he gulped.

'I never joke about kidnapping. Do you know if any relationship exists between Denise and Mrs Westbrook?' He wanted to know if Michael did actually know anything about Penny's daughter.

'Relationship? I don't understand,' Michael replied looking confused.

'It's OK. I just wondered if they knew one another.'

It was obvious that Penny had never told Michael about her daughter.

Half an hour later and the whole estate had been cordoned off by the support team. The forensic boys and the backup team were led to the entrance to the East Wing.

Wesley asked for fingerprints to be taken from that point onwards. He explained that he expected them to identify his, Penny Westbrook's, Martin's and Alison's but wanted to be informed of any others immediately. He led a member of the forensic team and the leader of the backup team to the room where Denise's cardigan was found and pointed out the entrance that was expected to lead to the Well. Wesley explained what was expected from both teams and leaving them to organise things he went in search of his two officers who were looking after Michael and Penny Westbrook.

63

Edith Brown was running late. She closed the dormitory door and collecting her mop, bucket and other cleaning utensils and walked along the corridor to the next room. She liked Mr Dempster. He was always polite and would thank her for cleaning his room whenever they met up.

She knocked on the door twice as was her custom before using the master key. There was no reply, so she put the broom and bucket to one side and extracted the bunch of keys from her apron pocket.

Edith unlocked the door and pushed it open a little, then picked up her utensils before using her shoulder to push the door open enough to gain entry.

Her scream echoed around the old University halls. In a few seconds a small crowd of students were stood in the doorway. Colin Dempster was sat in his chair slumped over the desk. A dark pool of blood had spread across the table and was now dripping onto the wooden floor.

Pete Stanley the Chief Librarian, who had the room next door pushed his way through the crowd, took one look at the scene and immediately dialled 999. Another student, Jamie Harris escorted Edith out of the room and into the corridor, whilst his girlfriend and part time student Rose Appleby went running off to get someone from the medical team.

Wesley was sat with WPC Bolt who was sitting alongside a sedated Penny Westbrook when the call came through.

Alison could see the look on Wesley's face even before he hung up.

'What's wrong? More bad news?'

'Yes.'

He motioned for her to follow him across the room to the French doors.

'It's Colin Dempster. It would seem that he's been murdered in his room at the University.'

Alison put her hand to her mouth.

'When did this happen?' she asked trying to compose herself.

'I'm not sure. A woman cleaner found him slumped over his desk. It's thought that he was hit over the head with a heavy object.'

He telephoned Jane as soon as he got back to the station and filled her in on the latest events.

'Yeah, I don't know where all this is leading right now. I've just provided Bath CID with an update, and now I'm heading over to the University. It will take me forty minutes to get there this time of day.'

He listened whilst Jane gave him an update about Dorothy who was now staying at her sisters just outside Bath.

'Jane, can I ask a favour? It's just that I can't be everywhere at the same time.'

'Yes of course. What is it? You know it's going to cost you,' she joked.

'I know. I know. I guess you still have the spare key to Dorothy's place.'

'Yes it's in my purse.'

'Could you pop over there for me? Take a close look around the place. I'm sure we've missed something. I don't know what. It's just a hunch that there's something in the house that may spread a bit more light about the Hallertons' background.'

'You don't think Dorothy was involved in any wrong doings do you?' Jane asked sounding surprised.

'No I don't. Certainly not knowingly, in any case.'

'OK, I'll pop over a bit later. Call me when you're on the way home. Perhaps you can pick me up from there.'

'That sounds like a good plan. See you later this evening.' Wesley hung up.

Love you too, she said to herself and replaced the receiver.

He was walking back to his car when his mobile rang. He recognised the voice immediately.

'Hello Superintendent.'

'Inspector Wesley, how are things? I hope you and your good lady have settled down to life in the West country.'

'We certainly have. I don't think either of us would return to London for any price.'

'Ah that's good to hear. I hope you have more good news for me too.'

Wesley knew this was the reason for the call.

'I wish I had but we've still no trace of the missing girl, apart from the clothing found in Abbey House. We've covered all possible leads and spoken to just about every person in Glastonbury. We have another problem too. Colin Dempster has just been found, murdered in his office.'

'I'm sure you have but you must appreciate that the powers here are jumping up and down for a conclusion to this affair. You've got two more days before we go national.'

Wesley shook his head in despair. He knew from experience that kidnappers often panic as soon as the story hits the TV screens. The result, usually being bad news for the victims.

'I understand, Sir. We have every available person working on the all the cases. I'm confident we'll make a breakthrough very soon.'

'Indeed. Well, two days Wesley. I'll be in touch.'

The line went dead.

Wesley replaced the receiver in its cradle. He'd known of Superintendent

Richard Adams for several years before he transferred to the West country and they had met on a couple of occasions during Wesley's career. Richard was a hard man but fair, and Wesley knew he was under pressure to get results.

64

Harvey White was sat in his conservatory that overlooked the Somerset Moors. That's what he'd always known them as, although the new breed of local inhabitant now referred to them as the Somerset Levels. His father had built the bungalow back in the 1968 and when he passed away it was handed over to Harvey. Harvey's mother had died during childbirth and his father Henry never remarried.

Having opted out of college some six years ago Harvey lived at home and nursed his father until his death last year. He was reading the local obituary column when he spotted Kelvin Ward's name. He read the details more than once before turning the page where he suddenly came across Kelvin's photo.

It took several minutes for him to comprehend that his best friend from his college days had been murdered. The story line was hard enough to accept without the final line that said that Kelvin Ward left no next of kin.

Harvey laid the newspaper on the chair and reached over to grab his walking stick. He was diagnosed with polio at the age of six and although it was treated then, it left him with a permanent limp. He walked through the kitchen diner and into the front lounge where the telephone stood. He dialled directory enquiries and asked to be put through to Street Police where he asked to speak with Inspector John Wesley.

The receptionist took his details and said that Mr Wesley would return his call asap. Some ten minutes later he was stood in the kitchen making a coffee when the telephone rang. It took him four rings to get to the phone.

'Harvey White speaking.'

Wesley listened to the rasping voice on the line as Harvey tried to catch his breath.

'Good afternoon. This is Inspector Wesley. I'm informed that you wished to speak with me Mr White.'

'Ah Inspector. Thank you for returning my call. It's about the article in the local newspaper pertaining to the death of Kelvin Ward. I believe I may have some interesting information for you?'

'And what would that be may I ask?'

'The article states that Kelvin left no next of kin. Well unless she died at an early age, then that fact is incorrect Inspector. Kelvin Ward had, or should I say has a daughter, who would be around seventeen or eighteen years of age by now.'

This took Wesley by complete surprise and he took a while to answer.

'Are you still there Inspector?'

'Err yes. Mr White. I think you and I need to have a little chat. When would it be convenient for me to pop over?'

The two men agreed a date and time before they both hung up.

65

PC Martin Philips and WPC Alison Bolt stood by the open front door to the building. Abbey House was currently like a fortress with police guarding the whole of the estate.

They had left Michael and Penny Westbrook in the library. They obviously had a lot to discuss. The local doctor had insisted that a nurse stayed with Penny at all times as she was in a state of shock and insisted that Penny wasn't to be left completely alone.

Michael was sat next to her on the settee and took her hand. Something he'd not really done for a long time.

'I don't know where to begin,' Penny muttered smiling meekly.

She squeezed Michael's hand with both of hers.

'You see, I gave birth to a daughter. Eighteen years ago. Long before we ever met.' She looked at Michael waiting for a reaction but he didn't flinch.

'I was not in a position to look after her so I gave her up for adoption. I don't want to go into all the details right now but about three years ago I found out she was living just outside of Glastonbury. I don't expect you to understand but I had to see her. I had to get to know her.'

Michael simply nodded.

'As you've probably guessed. Her name is Denise. Denise Wright. She's the girl who has been missing for the past week.' At this point Penny started to sob uncontrollably. The nurse walked over and tapped Michael on the shoulder motioning that Penny ought to rest.

Michael left the library and walked out through the front door towards the gravel drive before turning left to go around the back of the house and the private grounds. PC Philips and WPC Bolt both noticed he was crying.

By the time Wesley reached Bath University, the forensic team were already on site along with Terry Austin, the local pathologist.

'What have we got this time?' Wesley asked poking his head around the door of Colin Dempster's room.

'The deceased was hit on the back of the head twice, with a heavy instrument. Wooden object, I would say, going by a couple of splinters in the back of the head.'

'Time of death?'

'I would estimate somewhere between one o'clock and three o'clock. I'll be able to tell you more once we get the body back to the lab.'

Wesley felt that nauseous feeling coming on just thinking about the role that Terry had.

'OK, thanks, Terry. Mind if I have a look around?'

'So long as you don't touch anything,' said one of the forensic team who was on his hands and knees crawling around the floor.

Wesley was mostly interested in what Colin had been looking at when he was murdered and was trying hard not to look at the corpse but it was difficult to ignore the dark congealed pool of blood next to the head.

'Looks like a map of some sort,' said Terry leaning over Wesley's shoulder. 'Any idea what he was working on?'

'In confidence, he did help us to find some ancient routes under the Tor,' replied Wesley looking around the room to make sure no one was listening. Terry acknowledged with a glance towards the door. Once out in the hall he pulled Wesley to one side.

'As soon as the body is removed I'll slip the map into my bag. Drop in tomorrow morning and you can pick it up. I should be able to provide you with some information about his death too by then.'

'That's great. Thanks,' said Wesley and patting Terry on the shoulder walked away searching his jacket pockets for his tobacco.

He found Pete Stanley downstairs in the student's hall arguing with one of the students about the fine imposed when losing a book belonging to the University. The young student was pleading his innocence but Pete was explaining the cost of replacing the lost book.

'Ah Inspector.' They shook hands as Pete led Wesley to a small table away from everyone else.

'What's going on Inspector? How many more murders are there going to be around here?'

'What makes you think that Colin was murdered?'

'I was the person who put the call in. I saw his head smashed in.'

Pete Stanley had the face of a rabbit caught staring into in a car's headlights.

'Oh I see. Forgive me I didn't know who put the call in. Can you please tell me what happened?'

'I was busy in my room. It's the one next to Colin's by the way. I was in the process of grabbing some dirty washing to take to the onsite launderette when I heard old Edith scream.'

'Edith? I assume you mean the woman who cleans the rooms?'

'Yes. Anyhow, I heard her scream and rushed out to see what was happening. As I looked down the corridor I saw her backing out of Colin's room. She was still screaming at that point.'

Wesley nodded as Pete continued.

'I asked her what was wrong and she just pointed into the room. That's when I saw him. I've never seen so much blood.'

Wesley could see that the man was shaking.

'It's OK Pete. In your own time.'

'Luckily I always carry my mobile with me so I phoned the police straight away. By this time there was a crowd of people in the doorway. Some of the girls were crying. I got someone to take Edith to the medical block and closed the door so no one else could get in. The janitor stood on the other side until the ambulance people got here.'

'You did a great job Pete. However I still need to ask you a couple of questions. Are you OK to carry on?'

'Sure.'

'Do you know if Colin had any visitors today?'

'You'd need to check with security Inspector but not to my knowledge. Of course it's possible that one of the students may have visited his room. I mean, Colin was one of those lecturers who made himself available 24 x 7 to anyone who needed his help.'

'Do you know of anyone who may have had a disagreement with him or anyone who he may have argued with?'

'No. I've never known Colin to argue with anyone. He would always debate something that he studied but never argue. He was like a walking encyclopaedia. I will say though, I think everyone you talk to will tell you that Colin was stressed lately. I think he was working on something that was puzzling him. Something that was obviously important to him for sure.'

'What makes you say that?'

'He'd borrowed just about every book we have in the library that relates to the Tor and Glastonbury Abbey. I only spoke to him a couple of days ago asking him to return some of them. A couple of the books are well overdue.'

'Did he say what he was working on?'

Pete shook his head.

'No, but whatever it was, he seemed obsessed by it.'

'Can you provide me with a list of the books he'd borrowed from the library?'

'Sure thing Inspector.'

Wesley didn't see the need to explain the reason why Colin had borrowed the books.

'Pete, one last question. Do you know anyone who might have wanted to hurt Colin?'

'I don't know anyone who disliked him Inspector. He was one of the most liked lecturers here.'

'OK thanks. I'm going to be around for a while talking to security and speaking with one or two of the students who were outside his room after he was found.'

Wesley handed him his card. 'If you do think of anything just give me a call. Anytime.'

'Thanks Inspector.'

66

When Denise awoke, it took her several minutes to remember that she had been moved. She sat almost trance like for several minutes without blinking as the effect of the drug started to wear off.

There was a pain in her arm where the injection had been administered and her neck was stiff and sore from where she had been slumped against the wall. Although her hands and feet were still tied and her mouth was taped over, the blindfold had been removed.

Slowly her eyes became accustomed to the dull grey light and she began to observe the room and her surroundings. It was obviously an old kitchen. Octagonal in shape, with four vast arched fireplaces. In each corner the room had a vaulted roof that lead up to a circular outlet. Denise could view two recesses high up in the roof where windows had once been. These were now boarded up with planks of wood as were three others around the room. A huge oak door appeared to be the only exit.

Leaning to one side so she could rest her hands on the floor, Denise twisted round so that she ended up on all fours. Slowly and painfully she crawled across the wooden floor where she found a trap door in the floor. This is where she and her captor must have entered, she thought to herself.

After several tugs on the black iron handle it was obvious that the door was locked from below floor level, leading Denise to assume that her captor had made their exit that way too. It took her nearly two minutes to drag herself across the floor to the nearest fireplace where she rested her weary torso against the rounded recess.

A cold stream of air was coming from the void in the roof sending a shiver down her spine. She sat listening to the mournful sound of the wind as it whipped around the outside of the building. There was a stale smell in the room like rotting vegetables. Denise tried to block it from her mind. A minute later she began to doze again as exhaustion set in.

Denise woke with a start. Her mind was trying to register what the sound was. She listened as the sound grew louder. Then her brain registered what the sound was. What she could hear was muffled conversation. She tried to call out but the tape over her mouth was preventing anything other than mumble. The muffled conversations grew louder and it was obvious that a group of people were passing somewhere near the building.

Denise's cries were in vain so she turned herself round to where she could the kick her feet against the brickwork of the old bread oven but to no avail. As voices started to recede Denise began to panic and thoughts of no one ever rescuing her raced through her mind. Her legs were now tired and her feet sore from kicking the brickwork.

    Denise lay back exhausted. Tears ran down her face as she cried herself to sleep. The small group of tourists had passed the derelict building of the Abbots Kitchen totally oblivious to the plight of the poor girl within.

67

Wesley opened the door to his office to find PC Broad toying with the volume controls of the tape machine he'd borrowed from the CCTV room.

'Having fun?' asked Wesley.

'Actually I think I've found something from the CCTV footage we have that links the High Street and the corner of the building next to the Tourist office.'

He continued to twiddle the dials on the machine whilst Wesley sat back rolling another cigarette.

'OK. Ready. You may want to listen in. I've enhanced the sound on the film.'

Wesley sat forward as Adam hit the play button. There was a sharp hissing noise as the High Street came into view, followed by a crackling sound as if someone was walking on glass.

'Let me try to adjust the sound a little more,' said Adam moving the dial.

'There that's better.'

'When was this?' Wesley asked.

'The footage is from the actual night that Denise Wright disappeared.'

Several people could be seen in the distance walking along the High Street and a man walking a dog passed from behind the camera to the other side of the road before turning left towards the Tor. Adam watched the counter on the machine for a moment and then hit pause.

'This is now just after nine o'clock in the evening,' he said, turning to face Wesley.

'Watch and listen.'

'Yes teacher,' Wesley replied grinning.

Above the crackling noise, the sound of a door closing could be heard. A few seconds later Denise came into view from below the camera and could be seen walking towards the town with her back to the camera. They watched the video footage until Denise took a right turn into the High Street and disappeared from view.

Adam stopped the tape again and began to rewind.

'Now let me replay the tape from the same moment but this time with the help of the sound box I borrowed from the security company.'

Again, they heard a door close somewhere behind the camera, presumably the door to the Tourist office. At this point Adam slowed the tape down and increased the volume on the sound box. This time they could just make out voices, at least two. Although the voices were muffled they were able to pick out a few words here and there.

Wesley was straining his ears to listen as Adam passed him a piece of paper across the desk.

'I've already written down what I could make out,' he whispered.

A voice crackled on the tape.

'Why did you move the artefacts? They will get damaged.'

A different voice replied.

'You worry too much.'

Adam stopped the tape.

'After that bit it's impossible to decipher anything.'

'But watch the tape again.' He pressed play and pointed to the shadow that appears just before Denise enters the frame. He stopped the tape again, rewound and replayed it.

'Did you notice that Denise's shadow turns around just before she appears into view? I believe she overheard these people but more importantly, they must have seen her.'

'And you think that's why she was abducted?'

'It's certainly a possibility.'

'The two voices. One male one female?'

'Sounds like it. Can't say for sure, but I'd put my money on it.'

Adam replayed the whole scene several times until they both felt there was nothing else to gain from it.

'OK, good work Adam. I want everyone in the station to view the tape. The more of us who can see this, the better. What's the betting that one of these people was actually in the Tourist office just before they closed for the night?'

'Where the hell have you been?'

Jenny knew it was impractical to ignore Michael, so she turned away from the house and walked across the lawn to where he was standing.

'I asked you a question,' he said sternly as she approached. Jenny noticed he had been crying.

'What's wrong now for God's sake? I only went into town for a while. I went to the cinema. I got fed up being cooped up in the house with all the police about.'

'They've found clothes belonging to Penny's daughter,' he muttered.

'Penny's daughter? What are you talking about? What clothes? I didn't know Penny had a daughter. Michael, what are you talking about?'

He took a deep breath, trying to control his nerves.

'Penny has just told me that she had a daughter several years back, long before she and I met.'

He stopped for a moment as if trying to put things in order in his mind.

'The police have gained access to the East Wing,' he continued, and pointed back to the house. 'They have apparently found clothing belonging to the missing girl. You know, Denise something or other.'

'Denise Wright?'

'Yeah that's the one.'

He took hold of Jenny's arm.

'Denise Wright is Penny's daughter.'

Jenny pulled her arm away and took a few steps backwards, not believing what she was hearing.

'Denise Wright is Penny's daughter? Are you sure?'

'That's what everyone says. Penny, the police. I also heard them saying they have found another access to the Well too. Somewhere in the East Wing.'

Michael wiped the tears from his eyes and looked up. Jenny was already halfway across the lawn heading towards the house.

He called out to her but she just kept walking.

Entering the library she found a nurse sat with Penny, who was asleep on the settee. Jenny introduced herself and asked if there was anything she could do.

'Mrs Westbrook is fine. She's been asleep for half an hour. The sleep will do her good,' said Nurse Connelly.

'I'll bring you in some tea shortly,' Jenny replied. 'Just ring the buzzer by the light switch if you need me for anything.'

As she made her way back out into the main hall she passed the front door which was still open where she could hear WPC Bolt and PC Phillips conversing outside.

Running up the staircase two steps at a time Jenny made her way to her bedroom where she scribbled a note and left it on the dressing table. Retrieving a small sports bag from her wardrobe she started to fill it with a selection of clothes. Having extracted her credit card and the spare cash she had stored in the top drawer of her dressing table, she slipped it into her jeans' pocket. After changing into a pair of old trainers and locating her zip up fleece, she grabbed her sports bag and left the room, closing the door quietly behind her.

At the top of the staircase Jenny paused to listen for any sounds in the house. It was all quiet. She descended the stairs and slipped into the kitchen without being seen. Opening the key safe she extracted the keys to Michaels Land Rover and exited the back door. The garage doors were already open and within minutes she was driving away from the estate.

68

Jane turned the key in the lock and closed the door quietly behind her. She felt guilty about entering Dorothy's home when it was empty. She walked into the kitchen and placed her handbag on the table.

Dorothy was extremely house proud. There was nothing lying around on the worktops. In fact, everything had been put away in a drawer or cupboard. Having convinced herself there was nothing to be found either in the kitchen or the living room, Jane made her way upstairs. The search proved fruitless. There was nothing to be found.

Jane was exhausted. She made her way across to the window seat that looked out on the back of the property. She looked down at the well-kept garden which had obviously been their pride and joy. At the end of the lawn there was a vegetable patch and beyond that a small wooden shed that appeared to lean to one side. The garden backed on to open fields whose only occupants were two horses standing side by side both eating from nose bags.

She made her way back downstairs and into the kitchen where the back door led to the garden. For some unknown reason the garden shed had attracted her attention and she wanted to pay a closer look.

Surprisingly, the shed door wasn't locked and opened easily as Jane pulled on the handle. She knew Eddie had been a handyman all his life so she wasn't surprised at the vast array of tools that lined all three benches. Under the far bench a small cupboard had been built. The door was padlocked. Jane searched around for something to prize the lock off. A long handled screwdriver seemed a good option. Slipping the top of the screwdriver between the lock and the door catch and gripping the handle of the screwdriver with both hands, she yanked the device upwards. The locked failed to open but the door splintered from where the catch had been screwed in. One more yank and the whole unit came away as the door swung open.

Jane knelt down to peer inside. The cupboard was half full of clothes, women's clothes, and certainly not Dorothy's. After finding a pair of gardening gloves and a black sack, Jane placed the contents into the bag.

Closing the shed door behind her she leant against the side of the shed to phone Wesley from her mobile. He answered almost immediately.

'Hi John. I'm over at Dorothy's. I've found a whole pile of clothing in the garden shed which I think you might find interesting. They're women's clothes and I'm sure they're not Dorothy's.'

'Really? In the garden shed? Jane that's brilliant. What a clever girl. We'll make a detective out of you yet.'

'Cut out the compliments and get someone over here to pick it up. Oh and by the way. That's another night out you owe me.'

'You drive such a hard bargain,' said Wesley. 'Give me half an hour and I'll pick you up myself. I'm nearly finished here. I just have one more call to make.'

69

David Hare was just placing the key in the lock to his room when the telephone rang.

'Hi, David speaking.'

'David. Hi, it's Inspector Wesley. How are you?'

'Oh hello. I'm fine thanks. What do I owe the pleasure for?'

'David, I have some bad news I'm afraid. There's no easy way to tell you but Colin Dempster was found murdered earlier today.'

'What? Oh my God no. Why? How? I mean, I can't believe it.

We only saw him first thing this morning. When did it happen?'

David threw his keys on the table and slumped into the small wing backed chair.

'I can't give you the exact time yet, but assumptions are around between one o'clock and three o'clock. He was murdered in his room.'

'Have you any idea who did this?' David asked in a state of shock.

'No we don't. But I'm pretty sure it's related to what Colin was working on.'

'I assume you mean the maps. He seemed excited this morning about something he'd found and said he was going to call you.'

'Hopefully the maps might provide a clue,' said Wesley. 'The forensic team have cordoned the place off at present but hopefully I can get access to all Colin's personal stuff later today or early tomorrow.'

'I'm sorry, but I can't believe this,' said David motioning for Sally to join him by the phone. 'Is there anything Sally and I can do Inspector?'

Sally walked over to stand next to David, concern etched on her face.

'Not for now David but we'll stay in touch. I don't want to frighten you or Sally, but I think you ought to keep a low profile at present. Whoever is carrying out these atrocities is a dangerous person who appears to have no qualms about killing people who seem a threat. If they trace any link between what he was looking at and yourself then, well you know what I mean.'

'I understand Inspector. Of course we'll be careful. We will contact you the moment anything dubious occurs. What happens with Colin now?'

'Once the forensic team have finished in here, the body will be taken to pathology for examination.'

'It's hard to take this all in,' David replied.

'I understand. I know it's no consolation but I would think Colin died almost instantly.'

'You're right Inspector. It doesn't make me feel any better.'

David replaced the receiver and gave Sally a big hug before informing her of Colin's murder. For the next few minutes the two of them sat in silence trying to come to grips with the news.

It was Sally who spoke first.

'What was it that Colin had found?'

'I'm not sure,' David replied running his hands over his face.

'Whatever it was though, someone didn't like it.'

'Oh my God. You don't think whoever killed Colin thinks we're involved as well do you?'

David shook his head. 'There's no link to us Sal. Of course everyone who knows us will know that we were Colin's friends but so were half of the people here at University.'

'Oh David I'm frightened. This is all too much.' Sally put her hands to her face and burst into tears. He placed his arm around her shoulder and tried to console her.

'Don't worry Sal. Inspector Wesley will find out who did this. You mark my words. He'll sort it out.'

Having collected Jane from Dorothy's place and dropped the bag of clothes at the station to be sent on to forensics, Wesley stopped off at the Chinese takeaway to purchase their evening meal.

'So, what made you think of looking in the garden shed?' he asked as he slipped the car into gear.

'A woman's instinct,' Jane replied laughing. 'No seriously, I don't know. I just felt attracted to it for some reason. I'd searched the house and then thought that the shed was the only other building where no one had looked.'

'Well I have to admit it was a clever piece of detection. Of course, I was going to suggest you look there.'

He glanced across at Jane before they both started to laugh.

'I've got to make a phone call before I eat,' he said as he pulled the car into the drive.

'OK. I'll dish up and leave yours in the microwave. That way I get to choose the largest prawns,' she joked trying to cheer him up. She led the way into the house.

'There must be a connection to all these murders.'

'I think you're right, but I'm under pressure to find out exactly what the connection is.' Wesley threw his jacket on the kitchen table.

She leant forward and kissed him on the cheek.

'You'll work it out John. You always do.'

An hour later after having eaten dinner Wesley was fast asleep in the armchair. Jane smiled as she looked across at him.

They had been through a lot together over the past two years and he hadn't aged one single bit except for a small streak of grey hair above his right ear. She knew he would get the case solved but couldn't help wishing they could spend more time together. Just then the phone rang. Jane went out into the hall to take the call, closing the lounge door behind her. To her surprise and delight the caller was David O'Hara. David had become a friend of the family since his working days as a private investigator but these days he was living in France working as a car mechanic.

David and his wife Clare had got back together and were now settled in Marseille along with their daughter Libby. The change of air had done wonders for their young daughter who almost lost her life twice through asthma. As part of the deal in getting back together Clare had insisted that David retire from being a private investigator. Too often away from home and facing too many dangers was how Clare had described it.

Jane and David chatted for over half an hour as she gave him an update on their move to Street and a brief line regarding the murders that Wesley was currently investigating. They agreed that once Wesley could get time off, he and Jane would visit David and his family. By the time she'd said goodbye and replaced the receiver Jane already felt happier and was looking forward to their proposed visit to France.

70

A minute after pressing the doorbell, Wesley was greeted by Harvey White opening the front door to his bungalow. He was nothing like the person that Wesley had envisaged. For a man still in his fifties he looked closer to sixty.

'Good morning, Inspector. Do come in.'

'Thank you, Mr White.' The two men shook hands.

'Please make your way through to the lounge at the far end of the corridor. I'll catch you up. Unfortunately I can't get around very quickly.' He motioned to the walking stick he was leaning on.

The dark brown patterned carpet was threadbare in places and Wesley noticed several areas along the hallway where the wallpaper was beginning to peel away. Passing two bedrooms, a bathroom and kitchen, the hallway opened up into a wide lounge that spread the width of the bungalow.

'Carry on through to the conservatory,' said Harvey pointing the way. 'It's a much more pleasant area to converse.'

Wesley stepped through the patio doors and into the conservatory which was by far the biggest room in the bungalow and had magnificent views over the Somerset Moors.

'What an amazing view,' Wesley exclaimed trying to take in the vast area of moorland he could survey down the valley.

'That hill in far the distance must be the Tor,' said Wesley pointing.

'It certainly is. My father originally purchased the bungalow purely because of its location and the elevated view it allows of the Moors and in fact most of Somerset.'

'Well he made a good choice I would say.'

'Please take a seat Inspector. Can I offer you tea or coffee?'

'Tea would be lovely. Thanks.'

Wesley was admiring the collection of books that lined every ledge around the conservatory when Harvey appeared with two cups in his hand. Wesley took them from him and placed them on the small glass table.

'So, I seem to have surprised you regarding Kelvin Ward having a daughter,' said Harvey as he manoeuvred himself into the small wing backed chair opposite Wesley.

'Yes you certainly have, Mr White.'

'Oh please call me Harvey. It's far more informal and I think names are so important, don't you?'

'Yes I suppose they are,' Wesley agreed. 'So Harvey, you believe that Kelvin had a daughter some eighteen years ago.'

'I not only believe Inspector, I can go one better than that,' he said extracting a small black and white photograph from his shirt pocket.

'Since we last spoke I managed to find this.'

He passed Wesley the photograph.

'This is the young girl when she was about three years old.'

Wesley studied the photo of a little girl with bundles of curly black hair sitting on top of a garden gate.

'May I keep this?'

'Yes of course if it helps to trace the poor child.'

'I don't think the girl will inherit a fortune but she has a right to know her father is dead,' Wesley replied looking solemn.

'When did you last see Kelvin Ward?' he asked reaching across the table to pick up his cup of tea.

'I have been Secretary to the Committee of the Somerset Levels and Moors Preservation Group for the past five or six years. Trying desperately to preserve the view you see outside my window. Unfortunately there are people in this world who have no interest or respect for our countryside. All they want to do is to continue developing new housing estates and building new roads. Digging up the place looking for things that don't exist. Destroying our heritage.'

'So was Kelvin Ward part of your committee?'

Harvey White gave a short rasping laugh.

'No, unfortunately not. He was in fact trying to persuade the local council to agree to new excavations six miles or so away from Glastonbury Abbey, on the pretext there were historical artefacts to be found dating back to the time of King Arthur. Can you imagine the disruption and destruction that would have caused to the village of Havering where these things are supposed to be? The village would have been destroyed in a matter of days by the arrival of the local and national press, TV crews and God knows who else.'

'So I guess the Committee along with local council support rejected any planning application?'

'Absolutely,' Harvey replied quite sternly.

Wesley could tell he had hit on a delicate subject.

'So when was this?'

'About four years ago. Kelvin hadn't changed much in appearance since his college days. We were best friends then. He used to help me get around the campus. Some days my polio caused me more problems than others and Kelvin would either carry my stuff or borrow a wheelchair from somewhere and push me around all day.'

He paused for a few seconds as his mind reminisced about the past. Wesley gave a polite cough.

'Oh sorry Inspector. Kelvin insisted that he knew for certain where ancient artefacts could be found but although he needed both local council and committee permission to start excavation, he insisted that anything found would be his property. Well, the short story is that neither of the requests was upheld and the unanimous decision was to reject any excavation work in the village.'

'So, was that the last time you saw him?'

Harvey took a deep sigh as he replaced his cup on the table.

'Unfortunately yes. I think the decision made to reject Kelvin's request that day cost me our friendship. You see, Kelvin thought I could sway the verdict, but the truth of the matter was that firstly I couldn't, and secondly, I had no intention of doing so. I didn't agree with his request. You see Inspector, tourism is one thing. Sustainable tourism is something else. What you see out of the window here isn't something that just appeared. It's a land that has been nurtured, cultivated and painstakingly looked after by people who care about the land we live in.'

Wesley nodded his head.

'I understand Harvey. For what it's worth, I actually agree with you.'

'Thank you,' Harvey replied smiling for the first time since they'd sat down. 'You sound very genuine.'

'I was. And I am.'

Wesley drank his tea as he watched Harvey take a small silver snuff box from his waistcoat pocket. He lifted the lid and pinched a sliver of snuff between his thumb and forefinger. He then dropped it onto the back of his other hand before sniffing it up.

'What's so interesting?' Harvey asked.

'I used to watch my father do the very same, many years ago. It brought back memories.'

'Happy ones' I hope?'

Wesley smiled and placed his cup on the table.

'Yes. Yes they are. I was very fortunate to have a happy childhood. We lived in Wimbledon then. My father used to take me to Wimbledon Common every weekend. We played football, ate ice cream and generally mucked about. Mother always worked on Saturdays in a local shop. Oh, we didn't need the money, father had a good income, but mother said it was her day out so to speak. The rest of the week she was at home.'

'Childhoods. They shape the rest of our lives,' said Harvey.

Wesley sighed.

'Oh well. My priority now is to find Kelvin's daughter and break the news to her of her father. I don't suppose you have any idea where I should begin to look?' Wesley asked.

'I know he didn't marry Inspector and I'm sure that he continued living alone after the child was born but where she grew up and who with I have no idea.'

'Was he living in Glastonbury at that time?'

'No. He was living in a bedsit in Street. I believe he fell out with his father around the time the baby was born. His father ran the book shop in Glastonbury. In fact, I believe he purchased both the shop and the upstairs flat.'

'Hmm. He was living above the bookshop when he died,' Wesley replied.

'On his own?' asked Harvey as he reached for his tea cup.

'As far as we can tell, yes. People say he was a bit of a loner but the picture we're starting to compile throws up a few doubts in my mind.'

'He always was a bit of a dark horse,' Harvey laughed.

'What makes you say that?'

'There were rumours sometime before the baby was born that Kelvin was already a father. However, I was never able to substantiate that.'

'I think it's time I did some research,' Wesley replied standing up. 'I do appreciate everything you've told me. I'm sure we'll be able to trace his daughter. Thanks for your time Harvey. Don't worry I'll see myself out.'

'If you do find her. Please let me know,' Harvey replied.

'I would like to have the opportunity to tell the girl something about her father.'

'Of course. I'll be in touch.' Wesley closed the front door and left Harvey again reminiscing of the past.

'How do I look?' Wesley asked as he stood in front of the bedroom mirror.

'You're going to a funeral not a fashion parade,' Jane replied.

'Actually the shirt and tie are fine but you can take that grubby tobacco stained jacket off and wear the black jacket that goes with the trousers.'

'But it's a bit tight,' he complained.

'Then lose weight but you are wearing it to the funeral, so hurry up otherwise we'll be late.'

Jane and Wesley were amongst the last to arrive. As they got out of the car PC Adam Broad walked across the car park to meet them.

'Hi, Sir. Hi, Mrs Wesley. Most people have gone into the church already.'

'Let's go in shall we,' said Wesley taking the lead.

The small village church was full to the rafters and they only just managed to find a seat in the back row. Adam placed his police helmet on the floor by his feet and extracted a white handkerchief from within. Wesley gave him a sideways glance.

'Sorry,' he whispered. 'I always get emotional on such occasions.'

Wesley smiled and patted the young lad on the shoulder.

Jane pointed to where Dorothy was stood. She was supported either side by her sister and WPC Alison Bolt who was dressed in a white blouse and black skirt. From a recess somewhere at the back of the church, organ music began to play as Leonard Smalling, Street's parish vicar, walked forwards to begin his sermon.

There was a hush as the vicar began to tell the congregation Eddie's life history. Wesley cast his eyes around the church studying people's body language, which was a particular trait of his. He recognised a couple of faces, including some of Eddies drinking partners.

After the singing of two hymns and a reading from the Bible given by a friend of the family, the vicar gave the nod for the coffin to be carried out to the cemetery. As the congregation gathered around the grave, the vicar gave one final reading and the coffin was lowered into the ground. As the tears flowed Dorothy had to be supported by Alison. Leonard Smalling spoke quietly to Dorothy before making his way back to the church as the congregation began to disperse.

Jane and Wesley stood back whilst Adam assisted some of the elderly in navigating their way amongst the headstones back towards the car park.

They were about to depart when a woman dressed in a black suit and black hat that covered most of her face walked towards them. Wesley had seen her in the church but hadn't recognised the face below the brim of the hat. She stood directly in front of them before looking up.

'Inspector Wesley. I'd like to have a quiet word in private with Dorothy if I may. I need to tell her that Eddie was my father and that she's not alone.'

Wesley took Penny's hand and smiled.

'Of course. I'll speak with Alison. We'll wait by the church for you both.'

Wesley left Jane at Dorothy's house and drove on to the police station. As soon as he walked into the reception area he was greeted by PC Martin Philips.

'Hi, Sir. There have been three calls for you. The forensics team have said there is no DNA match on the clothes found in Eddie Hallerton's shed.'

'OK. What else son?'

'Terry Austin telephoned from the pathology lab. He said could you pay him a visit when you're next in the area. He sounded quite excited about something. The other caller was Michael Westbrook. He wants to know and I quote.' "When are all these bloody people going to leave my house?"

'Does he now? OK, I'll give him a call from my office. You won't want to hear my response.'

Wesley walked away but stopped just as he reached the doorway to the corridor.

'Oh by the way Martin. Do me a favour, I'm gasping.'

'Will do. I'll see if I can find some biscuits too,' he replied with a smile on his face.

Wesley slammed the phone back in its cradle just as Martin appeared with the tea and biscuits.

'If I get done for murder, it will be because I've torn Michael Westbrook's head off his bloody shoulders,' said Wesley extracting the tobacco pouch from his jacket pocket.

'His wife's just lost her father, who was found murdered in the Chapel, an item of clothing belonging to her missing daughter has just been found in a basement below his damn house and all he cares about is losing revenue! The man's insane.'

'Do you think there's more to it than that?' Martin asked.

'What do you mean?' Wesley motioned for Martin to take a seat.

'Well, I've only met Mr Westbrook a couple of times and spoken to him on the telephone, but his only line is about money. Maybe the guy's in financial trouble. I mean, his continual reaction is quite excessive, don't you reckon?'

'You may have a good point there son. I think it's time we did a bit of digging into Michael Westbrook's financial status. Get on to the bank and see what you can find.'

'Certainly, I'll do it straight away.'

'Oh, and good work son. A good bit of thinking there.'

'Thanks,' said Martin closing the door and blushing.

71

Michael closed the bedroom door and walked across to the dressing table. He saw the envelope with his name on immediately.

He'd entered Jenny's bedroom for different reasons and although he was disappointed not to find her there, he was glad he had spotted the envelope before Penny might have stumbled upon it. He tore open the back of the envelope and unfolded the note inside.

Michael,

I know things have been difficult lately, what with all these gruesome deaths and the police combing the house but I feel that there's something else bothering you also. You're so distant lately. That's why I've decided to go away for a few days. I need time to clear my head and think about our relationship. Don't be mad at me. I do love you.

Jenny x

He read the letter twice before folding it and putting it in his trouser pocket. He ripped up the envelope and threw the shreds of paper into the wastebasket. Closing the bedroom door quietly he tiptoed along the passageway before descending the staircase.

He never saw Penny standing in their bedroom doorway.

Once she could no longer hear his footsteps Penny turned the lock to close the bedroom door. She had just returned from the funeral and anticipating that Michael would be in one of his moods, had decided to go straight to her room. She had heard him in Jenny's room and laughed quietly to herself until her emotions overtook her and she sobbed into her pillow.

72

Wesley was about to grab his coat and leave the office when his office phone rang.

'Wesley speaking.'

'Jane's in reception, Sir. Do you want her to wait here or shall I send her through?' Adam asked.

'Oh, send her through please Adam.'

Wesley replaced the receiver. He'd forgotten that Jane had said she would meet him when she finished work. He opened the door just as Jane was about to knock.

'Hi,' she said handing him the shopping bags.

'Oh, thanks.' He gestured for her to enter.

'How has your day been?

'Very frustrating. There's no DNA match on the clothes you found. What about your day?'

'Quite fruitful I think.'

'What have you done now?' Wesley asked as he sat on the edge of the desk.

'It's not what I've done but what I've found.'

She rummaged through her handbag and extracted a hardback book.

'What's that?'

'Shift over a bit.' She pulled up a chair and laid the book on the table, turning it around so that Wesley could read the cover.

Arthurian Legends – The Isle of Avalon

'Open the book to page twenty-six.'

Wesley looked puzzled but the excited look on Jane's face told him she thought she had found something important.

'Now read what it says,' she said as he reached the page in question.

Wesley read out loud.

'Two thousand years ago the sea washed right to the foot of Glastonbury Tor, nearly encircling the cluster of hills. The sea was gradually succeeded by a vast lake. An old name for it is Ynys-witrin, or the Island of Glass. It was called an island because it would have looked like one to anyone approaching by sea.

Ancient myth has it that Avalon, where the sea met the land, was the meeting place of the dead. For the living, it was a threshold to a doorway that led through into another realm of existence. The Tor was the home of Gwynn ap Nudd, the Lord of the Underworld and a place where the fairy folk lived.

In Arthurian legend, Avalon is the home of Morgan le Fay, who was an ancient British Goddess or Fairy Queen, though in most legends she is simply King Arthur's sister. Her name has somehow travelled as far as Italy, where she is known as Fata Morgana and as Morgain le Fee in France. Fata Morgana lived beneath the waters of a lake; suggesting some connection perhaps to the legend of the Lady of the Lake.'

Wesley looked up.

'I have to admit I'm confused now,' he said. 'What am I supposed to be looking at?'

'The story says that Fata Morgana lived below the lake,' said Jane.

'But that's impossible.'

'Not if the lake had been drained.'

'What? Now you've lost me.' Wesley stood up and walked around his desk and retrieved his tobacco pouch from the top drawer. Jane gave him a disdainful look before continuing.

'Don't you see John? The Island of Glass is situated where the small lake now exists, in the Abbey grounds. History tells us that the lake has been drained several times in order to divert the flow of water around the Tor and the surrounding countryside. Even in those days, there were several underground passageways that lead away from the lake towards the Tor, covering the grounds of the Abbey. This is where Fata Morgan may have lived for a time.'

'I think you've lost the plot,' Wesley replied scratching his head.

'Oh listen.' The frustration sounding in her voice.

'Look at the picture at the bottom of the page where the Goddess is sitting with one of her maids. In front of them, placed on a large carpet is a whole collection of artefacts. Artefacts that have been missing for hundreds of years.'

'But surely this is all myth.'

'John Wesley,' said an exasperated Jane. 'Look at the artefacts. Those two pieces in particular.' She pointed to the page.

Wesley stepped forward to take a closer look and rested his hands on Jane's shoulders as he leant over.

'What's so special about them? I don't understand,' he replied shrugging his shoulders.

'You must walk around blindfolded, John Wesley. Both of those pieces are currently standing on the mantle shelf, in the drawing room over at Abbey House.'

'What? Are you sure?'

'I'm absolutely positive.'

'But you just said that all of these artefacts have been missing for hundreds of years.' Wesley sat back in his chair looking bewildered.

'That's what the book says, but I'm telling you that at least two of them are currently in the possession of Michael Westbrook.'

'If that's the case.....'

'If that's the case,' said Jane interrupting, 'then the artefacts were no myth and were found and removed when the lake was last drained.'

'But when, and by who?'

'Well, it would be my guess that Eddie Hallerton was involved,' said Jane as she closed the book and pushed it across the desk to Wesley. 'Come on, let's go home. You can read the rest of the book while I prepare dinner.'

The following morning Wesley woke with a heavy head although he had slept quite well considering his mind was going round in circles. He reached out for the alarm clock but only managed to knock it onto the floor. Cursing, he pushed back the bed cover and sat on the side of the bed. Leaning down he retrieved the clock along with the plastic cover that had separated in the fall. Switching off the alarm he laid both parts on the bedside cabinet and walked across the bedroom to grab his dressing gown that hung on the back of the bedroom door.

Jane was already in the kitchen in the process of making breakfast.

He had just sat down when the doorbell rang.

'I'll go,' said Jane as she placed a cup of tea in front of him.

'Good morning,' said PC Adam Broad as he strolled into the kitchen. 'Wow. I like the dressing gown. Superman eh?'

He pointed to the different sketches of superman that were emblazoned all over Wesley's dressing gown.

'If I hear one snippet of superman in the office, you'll be on late shift for the rest of the month.'

'Sure thing,' Adam replied laughing.

'Would you like a cup of tea, Adam?' Jane asked trying to keep a straight face.

'Yes please ma'am. That would be lovely.' Adam pulled up a chair at the far end of the table.

'What news have you got for me,' Wesley asked.

'The forensic boys are still examining the whole of the East Wing over at Abbey House. However, the support team haven't been able to make much progress in the tunnel under the property. They believe it may well lead to the Chalice Well but unfortunately due to the amount of rain we've had lately, the tunnel is completely flooded just a hundred metres down from the entrance. All they can do is to wait for the water level to drop.'

Wesley puffed out his cheeks.

'OK. So here's the plan for today?'

Wesley placed his cup down on the table.

'Firstly, I want you to drive me over to see Terry Austin to pick up a map he's got; I'll only be a minute. Then we're going for a drive over to Bath. David Hare has a meeting later today with the Historical Society. I've asked him to take a look at the map that Terry is going to provide. If anyone can identify what the map is all about, then surely someone in the Historical Society can.'

Terry Austin met Wesley in the reception area outside of the mortuary. His white coat was splattered with blood and smear stains from some the remains of some poor soul's corpse.
'Come and take a look at this.'
Wesley followed him across the room to where a small book table stood. Terry unravelled the piece of paper in his hand and laid it on the table.
'This is the sheet of paper that was lying on Colin Dempster's desk when he was killed. Excuse the blood marks. I couldn't wash them off.'
Wesley looked at Terry uncertain as to whether the man was being serious or not. Wesley studied the drawing before shrugging his shoulders.
'What are we looking at? Any idea?'
'I was hoping you could tell me,' Terry answered. 'It looks like some kind of symbol. What's strange is that it's been drawn on some form of tracing paper.'
'It looks like a giant maze.'
'Maybe that's exactly what it is. Anyhow, I'll leave it with you to figure out,' said Terry. 'I've got three corpses in today that need my attention.'
As soon as Wesley stood outside the building he took a deep breath of fresh air. The clinical smell of the place had already started to make him feel nauseous.
The drive to Bath didn't do anything to ease his queasy feeling. The traffic was heavier than usual as they crawled towards the city centre. Wesley had been studying the drawing but his eyes were beginning to ache so he carefully rolled it up and placed it in the recess under the dashboard. As the car turned into King Street, Wesley placed his right hand on Adam's shoulder and pointed across to the other side of the road.
'That looks like Dorothy Hallerton.'
He pointed at the back view of a woman entering the History Museum.
'Hmm does a bit,' Adam replied, 'but I thought she was back at her sisters?'
'So did I.'
Wesley strained his head around as the car drove slowly past the entrance to the arcade.
Adam parked up and stayed in the vehicle whilst Wesley went in search of David Hare. David had just finished his first lecture of the day when Wesley entered the classroom.
'Good morning Inspector. I hope you are keeping well,' he said shaking Wesley's hand.
'I'm fine thanks, David. I hope you and your good lady are OK.'
'Yeah we're fine. Sally's actually gone back to London for a couple of days to spend some time with her parents. The project she's been working on has come to a halt for the time being so she's got a bit of free time and apart

from that, being away from here will do her good. Like everyone right now she's a little stressed.'

'I understand.'

David held out his hand.

'So what have you got for me?'

Wesley handed him the rolled piece of tracing paper.

'I don't pretend to know what it is. All I can tell you and in the strictest confidence, is that this is what Colin had on his desk when he was murdered.'

'Do you mean these are blood stains?' David looked ashen faced at the tracing paper.

'I'm afraid so.'

David carefully placed a couple of books, a pencil case and a stapler on each of the four corners to stop the paper from continually rolling up.

Wesley stood back to let David study the drawing for a few moments.

'Well, any ideas?'

David stood up straight and ran his hand through his hair.

'I could be wrong Inspector, but it's my guess that this is an ancient magical pattern.'

'An ancient magical pattern? Representing what?'

'That's what we need to find out. Was there anything else on Colin's desk when you found this?'

'Actually yes. I think it was a map of the Abbey grounds.'

'Hmm, OK. Can you leave it with me for a day or so? I'm meeting the Historical Society tonight. I'd like to show this to a couple of colleagues if I may. They don't need to know where it came from.'

'I'd be grateful. Oh by the way,' said Wesley as he reached the door to leave. 'I don't suppose you know a woman named Dorothy Hallerton?'

David looked up in surprise.

'Dorothy, why yes. She's been the secretary of the Historical Society for the past few years. Why do you ask?'

Wesley tried to conceal his excitement.

'Oh no real reason. I just wandered if you had heard of her. It's just that her name keeps cropping up. Nothing to worry about.'

Wesley filled Adam in on a few details when he got back to the car.

'It seems that Dorothy Hallerton is a bit of a dark horse,' said Adam.

'Yeah. I'm beginning to think Dorothy and I need to have a little chat.' Wesley rolled a cigarette as Adam put the car in gear.

73

'So where do we go from here?' asked Michael.

'What do you mean?' Penny sat looking into the whisky glass.

'Am I supposed to carry on as if nothing has happened? For Christ sake woman, you've just told me you have a daughter I knew nothing about. Doesn't that kind of affect our relationship?'

'No more than you having an affair with Jenny,' Penny snapped.

'What on earth are you talking about? An affair with Jenny? You are losing the plot my dear.'

'Don't patronise me,' she replied standing up. 'You two must think I'm blind, the way you tiptoe around just so that you can slip away for a quick shag every five minutes. Do I look like a mug?'

'I've never laid a hand on Jenny!'

Penny stepped forward and slapped him hard across the face.

'You make me sick,' she shouted and barged past him.

Havering is a small village on the outskirts of Glastonbury and only ten minutes away by car. Jenny parked the car at the end of lane where the tarmac gave way to a narrow un adopted road that eventually led down to Briars Farm.

Grabbing her overnight bag from the back seat, she closed the door and walked away without locking the car. She knew it would be safe. No one came down the lane unless they lived there and there were only three other cottages along the half mile stretch.

The garden gate hung limply from its remaining hinge, so Jenny squeezed past and stepped down into the front garden. It was overgrown now and wild rose bushes had claimed most of the space to the extent of almost obstructing the front door. Being careful not to catch her clothes on the thorns, Jenny turned the key in the lock.

She had to use all her strength to push the door open, as a few weeks-worth of junk mail and bills were lying on the floor inside. Placing the door key back in her handbag, she threw the bag on the small table that stood underneath the window. It was the first time she had been in the house and she felt a cold shiver run down her spine. Fear or excitement, she wasn't sure. Either way she was shaking.

Jenny had had a copy made of the key just after Kelvin was murdered. Having followed Kelvin and Penny to the cottage on two previous occasions, it was easy to find even though it was now dusk and the light had begun to fade. The problem with old country lanes is that many of them still had no street lighting. Jenny didn't really know what she was looking for but she was intrigued as to why Kelvin and Penny had come here. It wasn't as if they had needed anywhere to be alone. They could have used his flat for that purpose. In any case she didn't believe for one moment there had been an affair going on between Penny and Kelvin so if it was purely a platonic relationship, why all the secrecy?

The living room was sparsely furnished with a small two-seater settee, a foldaway table and an old leather wing backed chair being the only inhabitants. The faded patterned wallpaper had seen better days and the painting that hung over the fireplace looked to have been ruined by someone scrawling over the artwork.

Only when she entered the scullery did Jenny switch the light on. It was obvious that the room had never been decorated or any of the original items replaced. The cream coloured Stoves gas cooker stood alone on the far wall. On her left stood a small oval dining table and two chairs. The Twyford sink stood under the window with one single cold water tap hanging over the top as if suspended in mid-air.

Jenny pulled back the curtain to the larder which was bare except for a few tins of baked beans and an assortment of out of date biscuits in an old cake tin.

She switched off the light and made her way back into the living room where the carpet less wooden staircase stood against the side wall. As she ascended the stairs each step seemed to moan and groan as she made her way up to the bedrooms. At the top of the stairs, the only option was to turn left or right into one of the two bedrooms.

Jenny took the left bedroom first. There was no carpet on the floor and the only contents were a standalone wardrobe and a single bed. Jenny looked in the wardrobe but it was empty. She then crossed the stairs and entered the opposite bedroom.

A rug took centre stage and covered two thirds of the floor but what attracted her attention was the selection of shovels, picks and chisels that lay on the floor underneath the window.

Jenny bent down to examine the collection of tools when suddenly she heard the latch of the front door being opened. Grabbing hold of a small pick axe she hurried across to the wall cupboard and quietly stepped inside, pulling the door closed. She held her breath.

'Just bag anything that looks interesting, then we'll get out of here. I'll start in here while you look upstairs.'

Jenny heard the footsteps on the stairs. The cupboard was located in the corner of the bedroom over the staircase. Keeping as still as she could she listened as someone entered the other bedroom. She could hear the wardrobe being opened and doors being banged.

'You finished up there? Come on hurry up.'

It was a young teenager's voice that was shouting from downstairs.

'Hold on. I just want a quick look in the other bedroom,' was the reply from across the landing. Jenny listened as someone entered the bedroom and started handling the tools. She could just about view the person through the cracks in the old wooden door. He wore a black hoody so it was difficult to see his face. His jeans were ripped at the knees which was the fashion for teenagers.

'Come on, let's get out of here,' his partner shouted from near the front door.

'The police keep an eye on this place as its empty.'

'Yeah OK I'm coming. All that's up here is a collection of tools. Far too heavy to carry out.'

Jenny's heart stopped as he turned to face the cupboard.

'For Christ sake, hurry up. There's a car coming down the track.'

The person downstairs was impatient.

'OK I'm coming.' The young lad turned and ran out of the room and within seconds Jenny heard the front door slam. She sighed deeply and waited for a full two minutes before slipping out of the cupboard. Her heart felt as if it was about to burst through her chest. There was no sound of a car pulling away so she guessed the young lads were on foot.

Jenny crept to the window and peered through the old lace curtains. She noticed her hands were shaking. A car had parked further back along the road and its lights were still on although she couldn't see anyone. Having convinced herself that the two young lads were gone, she made her way back downstairs and locked the front door from the inside. She glanced around the front room and made her way to the scullery. A few cooking utensils littered the floor. Jenny sat herself at the small kitchen table and tried to gather her thoughts.

What had Kelvin been using the house for?

74

Wesley arrived home exhausted, slumped himself in the chair and within minutes he was asleep. It had been a long day which had ended with Superintendent Richard Adams advising him that both the murders and the kidnapping had gone to national press.

Although Wesley had expressed his concerns he had been advised that the decision was not his to make. It made him wonder sometimes how people in power actually got their jobs.

An hour later he was still snoring when Jane touched him on the shoulder.
'Hello sleepy head,' she said and kissed him on the forehead.
'Hello my dear. I didn't hear you come in,' he replied yawning.
'I've been home for twenty minutes.'
'No way!'
Jane started to laugh.
'No not really. I've just got back from the shops. I've bought a few things for a little picnic. I thought we could drive over to the Tor now that it's open to the public again and it's such a lovely evening.'
'Hmm, that sounds a good idea,' said Wesley standing up and stretching. 'Let me have a quick wash and change and we'll head over there. There are still another couple of hours of daylight left yet.'
When they reached the small car park at the foot of the Tor it was obvious they weren't the only people who shared the same idea. Wesley drove around for a few minutes before an elderly couple returned to their car creating a space for them to park.

He grabbed the food hamper from the back seat whilst Jane retrieved the blanket from the boot.

The usual ten minute walk to the top, took an extra five minutes as they repeatedly had to stand aside to let others descending the Tor.

It was beautiful warm cloudless evening with just a small breeze that blew away the cobwebs and the tiredness of the day. It was the first evening for almost a week that it wasn't raining and the suns evening rays were a warm welcome.

Jane laid the tablecloth on the edge of the grassy slope then set about unloading the hamper whilst Wesley poured two glasses of wine.

They sat facing West, towards the old Abbey. Just to their left the ruins of Glastonbury Abbey lay down in the dip. The sun was just starting to disappear behind the trees, leaving the vast majority of the Abbey grounds in shade. It was Jane who broke the silence.

'This is such a beautiful spot isn't it? I mean, look down the slope in any direction and all you can see are green fields, valleys, hillsides and a few villages dotted around that look like something from a picture postcard. And yet…..'

Wesley looked at Jane as she paused. For a moment she was lost in thought before she returned his stare.

'And yet what Jane?'

'I was going to say… and yet people still don't live in peace. Either up here or down there, there's murder, conflict, hate, jealousy. All things evil.'

'I'm afraid it's the same the world over,' he replied putting his arm around her shoulders.

'Take the Abbey household for example,' said Jane. 'The Westbrook's have a lovely home, they're good looking people, healthy, wealthy and yet they're still not happy.'

'I don't think everything is a clear cut as it seems in that family.'

'What makes you say that?'

'Penny has already informed me that Michael has a terminal illness and says that's the reason for his temperament. We also now know that Denise is Penny's daughter and that Eddie Hallerton had been her father. I have the Historical Society looking at some maps of the house and the grounds and following your recent observations, also looking into artefacts and their value. Added to all that, I have major doubts as to their financial status. I think Michael may be in debt but as yet that's to be confirmed. A real spider's web, as Agatha Christie would say.'

David Hare sat listening to one of the Historical Society speakers. A bald headed guy named Alan Rodgers, who tended to look over his spectacles rather than through them.

He began by explaining that the inside of the Tor is an aquifer, with water-bearing beds of stone, shale and heavy clay, which is constantly kept replenished by rainfall. He went on to explain why the water doesn't run off the Tor and just soaks into the ground. How some of it runs into the Chalice Well but some emerges into other springs, such as the Ashwell spring at the foot of the Tor and how unlike the water in the Chalice Well, the water at the lower part of the Tor moves so slowly it's likely that it remains there for hundreds of years. The whole area fluctuates according to the amount of rainfall.

He finished his brief speech then handed over the chair to Lady Margaret Smythe Jones. A tall, fierce looking woman, with wispy blue tinted hair that was combed straight back from her forehead. David guessed she must be in her late sixties or early seventies. She stood erect and held an authoritative pose whilst she spoke. She began by thanking David for attending the meeting and for bringing along the drawing.

Extracting what she described as the oldest known ordinance map, she laid it out flat on the table. She then placed David's tracing over the top.

The effect stunned everyone around the table.

'What is it?' David asked as the pattern that was now clearly displayed was unlike anything he had seen before.

It was Dorothy Hallerton who was the first to speak.

'What we are looking at here is the Vesica Piscis which is the ancient sacred symbol of two interlocking circles.'

'But what is it showing us?' he asked looking confused.

'For centuries historians have believed there to be ancient pathways under the Tor, separate to the known passageways created when the Chalice Well was built. This tracing, if authentic, confirms that belief.'

Dorothy pointed to the map as she continued.

'Around the sides of the Tor is a strange system of terracing. Much weathered and eroded, but still well-defined, it has been interpreted as a maze following an ancient magical pattern. Now, as you can see, the tracing has linked the maze with the two circles.'

'Do we know the exact location these refer to?'

'Virtually, yes. The two circles encompass the Tor and one can now clearly see how they are linked to the maze.'

'Let me get this right,' said David.

'So what you're saying is that we're looking at a pattern of underground passageways under the Tor that are separate from those of the Chalice Well.'

'I think that is a very good description,' Dorothy replied.

75

There was another hour of daylight remaining when PC Martin Philips called everyone together. The group of uniformed officers and local volunteers were stood in the car park at the bottom of the Tor.

'Right. Thanks everyone for getting here on time. What I'd like to do is for us to split up into two teams. Adam, here,' he said pointing to PC Adam Broad, 'will lead one of the teams and search the Abbey grounds. The rest of you will be with me, searching the Tor and the surrounding area. Mandy can you please go with Adam's team, and Alison will come with me. I suggest both teams meet up, in an hour from now at the far end of the High Street. If there's no questions let's go.'

'What are we looking for?' asked one of the volunteers.

'Anything unusual. Maybe someone's personal belongings, a scrap of paper. Anything you feel that's worth looking at. I appreciate that people have been allowed back on the Tor today but we may still find something that will help.'

'How come you get the flat ground and I get to walk up the Tor?' Mandy asked Alison. The two WPCs shared a private female joke before departing.

There were considerable moans and groans for the next hour along with the occasional swear word, as individuals either slipped on grassy slopes, or tripped over buried stones. The task of finding anything gradually becoming more and more difficult as the light began to fade.

'I don't know why the search wasn't carried out in the daylight?' said one of the volunteers, having just picked himself up from the grassy bank of the Tor for the second time.

'The first one was,' Martin replied from the middle of the group.

'The trouble during the day is that we can't keep all the tourists away indefinitely. The whole town relies on tourists.'

'That's correct,' Wesley interrupted, as he and Jane descended the slope.

'Oh, hello, Sir. I didn't know you and Jane were helping out with the search.'

'We're not. We're off home to our warm comfy bed. We've finished our cheese and wine and will probably stop off on the way home to pick up another bottle.'

He patted Martin on the shoulder laughing.

'Just ignore him,' said Jane. 'You're doing a marvellous job.'

'Thanks ma'am. Goodnight.'

'You're cruel John Wesley,' said Jane as they reached the bottom of the Tor. He could only smirk as he helped her get over the stile.

'I'm sure young Martin will get his own back.'

'The poor lad never has any time off to enjoy himself,' Jane replied as they crossed the road toward the car park.

'Unfortunately, as you well know, that's down to the nature of the job we do,' Wesley answered as he unlocked the car.

76

Jenny had decided there was nothing else to be found in the house and had decided to leave.

As she opened the front door, the moonlight shone into the room catching the painting over the fireplace. For a second, Jenny stared at the painting. She hadn't paid much attention to it when she'd first entered but for some reason she now felt drawn to it.

Closing the door again she walked back across the room and stared at the painting. It looked like a garden scene with crazy paving leading into the distance, partially covered by overgrown bushes and wild gorse. Jenny lifted the frame from its hook and carried it over to the window where there was more light. She tried to decipher the scribbling that someone had written in the top corner. At first she thought it might be a signature and a date but then people usually signed their work at the bottom. She reread the letters and numbers to herself a few times before she suddenly realised what she was looking at. They were directions to somewhere, or something. Jenny reached inside her handbag searching for her mobile phone. She unlocked the phone and keyed the letters and numbers in. Southwest80mtrssoutheast50down2.

Making sure she had copied them in correctly she saved the details, before replacing the painting on the wall. She then used her mobile to take a snap of the painting. Realising that she couldn't stay in the house overnight, as there were no provisions or hot water, Jenny decided she would drive to the nearest town, heading away from Glastonbury to find a hotel.

There was no point in attempting to walk across the moorland in the dark.

Looking up and down the lane she closed the front door quietly behind her and made her way back to her car. Slipping the car into gear she headed back to the main road. She felt a shiver down her spine and a sense of excitement that this could be the start of an adventure that would lead her to hidden treasures.

77

Michael Westbrook had been sat in the interview room in Street police station for half an hour. The dishwater looking cup of tea he'd been given was now cold. He'd read the posters and notices on the walls describing prisoner's rights and officers regulations whilst dealing with the public.

He couldn't understand how anyone could work in a place where the paint was flaking off the walls and the furniture, what little there was, had actually been screwed to the floor. Above all that, he was angry at being called into the station and angrier that he'd been left waiting for so long.

Wesley stood outside the interview room observing Michael through the one way mirror.

'He looks a bit edgy doesn't he,' commented PC Martin Philips as he peered over Wesley's shoulder.

'Yup. That'll teach him for winding me up,' Wesley replied with a grin.

Ten minutes later Wesley entered the room with Martin directly behind him.

'About bloody time,' Michael exclaimed. 'Do you know that I've been sat here for over half an hour?'

'Sorry to have kept you so long.' Wesley never even looked up. He threw a folder on the table and sat opposite. Martin remained stood by the door.

'So what's this all about? I hope you're going to tell me we can open the bloody Chapel now. God knows how much money I've lost in the past few days.'

'Actually I do want to talk about money, Mr Westbrook. To answer any questions regarding the re-opening of the Chapel, I'm afraid that will remain shut for another day at least.'

'That's outrageous!' Michael shouted standing up.

'Please sit down, Mr Westbrook,' said Martin authoritatively.

Michael hesitated for a moment before slumping back in the chair.

'Can we make this quick. I've got better things to do than sit around this dump all day.'

Wesley took a deep breath to control his sudden urge to punch Michael on the nose.

'Mr Westbrook. Can you tell me how long you have lived in Abbey House?'

'What? What the hell has that got to do with you?'

'Just answer the question.'

'I was born there.'

'So I take it that you've lived there all your life?'

'Obviously.'

'And you inherited the estate from your father I believe.'

'You tell me. You seem to have been prying into my background.'

Michael started drumming his fingers on the table.

'Did your father leave you well looked after? Financially I mean?'

'That's none of your business.'

'So I can assume from that remark that you don't rely on the income gained from the public looking around the estate?'

'Assume whatever you like. The public are a pain in the ass. I wish I could shut them all out and just put my fingers up to them.'

'But you can't, can you?'

Wesley stared at him across the table, looking for a reaction but Michael remained silent.

'You actually need that income. Far more than I expect your wife realises.'

'What the hell do you mean by that?'

Wesley considered his next question for a few seconds.

'I would think a property like Abbey House must be very costly to run. I mean, there is no form of income other than from the public. Am I right?'

'That's none of your business.'

'Just answer the question.'

'My financial situation is a private matter Inspector. I don't intend discussing it with you and your sidekick here.'

He looked across the room to Martin.

Wesley stood up and walked around the room whilst searching his pockets for his tobacco and lighter. Wesley deliberately took his time in rolling a cigarette, watching Michael's reaction.

'I know my rights,' Michael suddenly blurted out. 'You can't keep me here unless you're going to arrest me for something I haven't done.'

'No, I can't, Mr Westbrook,' Wesley replied as he lit his cigarette.

'However, bearing in mind someone has just been murdered on your property, what I can do, is to ask the bank to provide me with your financial details as part of our on-going investigations.'

Unbeknown to Michael, Wesley had already done this.

'Well, I suggest you do that. Can I go now?' Michael Westbrook stood up.

'Please see the gentleman out,' said Wesley.

'By the way,' he said just as PC Philips opened the door.

'I would suggest you have a chat with your wife about your financial status, sooner rather than later. I would hate for there to be some discrepancies when we talk again. You see, I may want another word with you over the next day or two. Both of you.'

Martin returned to the interview room after escorting Michael Westbrook out of the station.

'You should have seen the look on his face. Oh, if looks could kill.'

Wesley was back at his desk reading through a number of files when the phone rang. He could see that it was an external caller.

'Inspector Wesley speaking.'

'Ah, Inspector. It's Harvey White here.'

'Harvey, how are you?' He remembered how Harvey White preferred to be addressed by his Christian name.

'I'm very well, thank you. I hope I haven't called at an inconvenient moment.'

'Certainly not. How can I help you?' Wesley searched for his tobacco.

'Following your recent visit, I decided it was time I had a bit of a clear out. As you know I've been a bit of a hoarder over the years and as a result I've collected boxes of paraphernalia. Sorry, I'm rambling on. What I'm trying to say is that I've found an old Pathe News reel taken of Glastonbury Abbey and Abbey House.'

Wesley could sense the excitement in Harvey's voice.

'So what have you found that's interesting?'

'Well, that's it. I'm not really sure. If my memory serves me right, only the top of the Lady Chapel remains visible today, simply because part of the roof collapsed some years ago and the whole area is now an impenetrable tangle of bushes and overgrown forna. However, the footage which only dates back to 1958 clearly shows a gated opening to what appears to be a crypt.'

'I don't understand,' stated Wesley. 'What's so special about an old crypt? It would have just been a shell after years of pillaging and destruction.'

'It very possibly is but according to local legend, it also served as an entrance to a secret passage used by the monks to escape the clutches of Henry VIII's soldiers. I was just wondering if it was somewhere a person could be hidden?'

'Harvey, you may have a point there,' Wesley replied sitting up straight in the chair. 'It's certainly worth a look.'

'Would you mind if I came over to take a look with you? I do know something about the area in question and to be honest I'm just fascinated.'

'Harvey, that sounds good to me. Can you meet me at the entrance to the Abbey grounds at around midday tomorrow? I'll have to arrange for someone from the council to meet us there.'

'Sure thing. I'll bring the news reel with me. Your boys are welcome to take a look.'

'Thanks Harvey. Appreciate it. See you over tomorrow.'

Wesley replaced the receiver, walked around his desk and opened the door to his office and called out to PC Broad who was on the reception desk.

'Adam, get on to the council for me. I want one of their people to meet you and me at the entrance to the Abbey grounds tomorrow lunchtime.'

'Sure thing.'

'Oh, and one other thing, make sure they bring some gardening equipment. They may need to do some weeding.'

Adam stuck his head around the door and stared across the room, a confused look on his face.

'Hello Dorothy,' Jane called out as she approached the garden gate.

'Oh good morning Jane,' Dorothy replied looking up. She was on her hands and knees pulling up old plants along the garden path.

'How are you keeping?' Jane asked.

'I'm doing fine.' Dorothy stood up and wiped her dirty hands on the old pinafore she was wearing. 'Thanks to you,' she said as she walked towards the gate.

'Don't be silly,' Jane replied.

'I couldn't have got over the past week or two without the support from you and your husband. I'm very grateful for everything you've done for me.' She kissed Jane on the cheek.

'That's what neighbours are for,' Jane remarked looking somewhat embarrassed.

'I'm just walking to the local shop. Do you need anything?'

'No, I don't think so. Thanks for asking though.'

'John tells me you're actually a member of the local Historian Society.'

Dorothy seemed to hesitate before replying.

'I joined the society many years ago as a hobby. You know something to do while Eddie was either working or down the local with his mates. Anyhow, before I knew it, they asked me to be their Secretary. I don't mind, it passes the time and it can be interesting.'

'I'm sure it is. Ah well, must press on,' said Jane noticing the sudden change in Dorothy's tone.

'Give me a shout if you need me for anything.'

She patted Dorothy on the shoulder and strode off towards the village.

78

'Where have you been? I was beginning to wonder where you'd gone to. What did Inspector Wesley want to see you for?'

Penny watched Michael as he stormed into the house. It was obvious he'd been drinking.

'None of your bloody business,' he replied and walked straight past her into the front parlour where he poured himself a large brandy.

'So, you spent an hour in the police station talking about nothing then?'

'Nothing that's of any interest to you.'

Michael emptied the glass in one swig then poured himself another large measure. Penny closed the door and walked into the kitchen. Experience told her that he would stay there and slowly get drunk and even more abusive that he generally was. If that was at all possible.

She was busy making pastry, something she enjoyed doing, when her mobile phone vibrated on the kitchen worktop. She didn't recognise the phone number but decided to answer the caller anyway.

'Hello. Penny Westbrook here. Can I help you?'

'Penny my dear. It's Dorothy Hallerton. I'm sorry, I didn't disturb you did I?'

'No of course not. How are you?'

Penny hadn't spoken to Dorothy since Eddie's funeral. After explaining to Dorothy that Eddie had been her father she had decided to let Dorothy make the first move. She'd been through enough without Penny adding more stress to her life.

'I'm bearing up thank you. It's strange being on my own after all these years, but I guess it's something I've got to get used to.'

'Knowing you, I'm sure you're keeping yourself busy,' Penny replied unsure what to say. 'Anyhow, how can I help you?'

'This may be a silly question my dear, but did Eddie leave any of his tools at the house? I've been tidying up the shed and I'm sure there are some things missing.'

'To be honest Dorothy, I wouldn't know. I rarely go out to the maintenance block. That was always Eddie's territory. I don't think Michael would know either. The best thing would be to come over and take a look yourself. Why don't you pop over tomorrow? Come over for lunch and I'll show you around our home.'

'Oh that's awfully kind. I don't want to be a nuisance.'

'Dorothy, you'll never be a nuisance.'
'Well if you don't mind. It's very kind of you.'
'See you tomorrow then,' said Penny and hung up.

As she placed her mobile back down on the worktop she couldn't help but wonder why Dorothy would have any interest in Eddie's tools, apart from maybe selling them. Anyway, it would be nice to see the woman.

Jenny sat on the hotel bed with her legs tucked underneath her. She was tired. It had been a stressful day and yet the discovery of the coded message that she'd found scribbled on the painting had kept her awake.

Reaching for the glass on the bedside table, she noticed it was empty. Somehow she had managed to drink a whole bottle of wine before briefly slipping into a restless slumber.

What could the code Southwest80mtrssoutheast50down2 mean?

They had to be directions but where to and where from?

Suddenly she sat upright. Oh you idiot, she said to herself.

Of course. The answer was in the painting. Someone had painted the access to the moor at the end of the lane, just yards from the house. It wasn't crazy paving she was looking at. It was the rocky pathway that led down toward the woodland that separated the village from the edge of the Tor.

79

Having just faced the press, Wesley entered the briefing room where his team were all sat awaiting the day's instructions.

'My God, there are some tired looking faces today.'

'I'm afraid a few of us are still recovering from last night's walk on the Tor,' Alison replied rubbing the tops of her legs.

There was a ripple of laughter around the room.

'OK, I understand. Back to serious business.'

There was a shuffling of chairs as everyone sat up to pay attention.

'The reports I've received from Martin and Adam, tell me that we've drawn a blank so far. Two thorough searches of the Tor and the Abbey grounds have proved fruitless. So, let's start interviewing people in the town again. It's a fair assumption that neither of the victims entered the area by themselves. In which case, we need to be asking the public if they saw two people together. Maybe they were arguing or one of them looked upset.' Wesley paused to search for his tobacco pouch.

'Another thing. Neither of the victims was dressed as if they were going for a hike. Someone out there must have seen something. I can understand nobody recognising Suzie, she didn't live in the town, but someone could have spotted Kelvin. I know he was supposed to be a bit of a recluse but I can't believe someone who has lived in the town all his life, not a quarter of a mile from the Tor, can walk over there without being recognised. Martin, I'll leave you to organise the troops. Adam, you come with me. We're going on a little search of our own.'

As usual Glastonbury was awash with tourists sightseeing and locals going about their daily routines. Having taken an early breakfast in the café Wesley headed for the newsagents and almost bumped in to Harvey White who was making his way towards the Abbey entrance.

'Oops, sorry Harvey. Nearly sent you flying then,' said Wesley placing a hand on Harvey's shoulder. Wesley noticed just how much the man struggled to get around.

'I'm sorry Harvey,' he said. 'I should have arranged for one of the lads to pick you up.'

'That's OK. I enjoyed the bus ride. It's not very often I get out these days. It's just the walk from the bus station. I can't manage it as quickly as I'd like to.'

'Well it's good of you to come over. I'll make sure you get a lift home. Do you want me to carry anything?' Wesley could see Harvey was struggling, a walking stick in one hand and an oversized shopping bag in the other.

'Thank you. If you'd be so kind,' Harvey replied handing Wesley the bag.

'I brought the news reel over. That's why the bag is so heavy.'

Harvey waited patiently outside the newsagent whilst Wesley purchased tobacco and cigarette papers.

As they approached the entrance to the Abbey ruins they met up with PC Adam Broad who stood talking to Gary Knowles from the council. Gary introduced himself as being the gardener responsible for the upkeep of the grounds along with ensuring the safety of the ruins.

Following the introductions, Gary led the way towards the Lady Chapel. The weather had gradually worsened since the early morning drizzle and they had to endure a heavy downpour as they trudged across the grounds.

When they reached the Lady Chapel, Gary led them to what remained of the internal wall where they could at least gain some respite from the driving rain.

'So where do we think the entrance to the crypt is?' Wesley shouted trying to be heard.

Harvey pointed to a bank of grass that had overgrown against the East Wing. What appeared to be tombstones were stuck out at different angles amongst the foliage and overgrown weeds. 'We're not disturbing the dead here are we?' Wesley asked.

'These aren't tombstones,' said Gary almost pre-empting the question.

'What you see here are the remains of the two support columns that collapsed around the turn of the Century.'

Wesley nodded, to say he understood.

'Where do you suggest we start digging?' Gary asked Harvey.

All four of them huddled close as Harvey tried to explain. Extracting a photograph of the Lady Chapel from his bag, he pointed to wall of the East Wing.

'There, see where the brickwork appears to be out of line, I believe the entrance to the crypt is below there.'

'Are you OK with that?' Wesley asked Gary as they looked across to where the remains of the wall still stood.

'Sure. I may need a hand at some point though.'

Wesley looked towards Adam who shrugged his shoulders in submission.

'You don't expect an old man like me to start digging, do you?' Wesley grinned as Harvey laughed.

'I knew there must have been a reason for inviting me over here this morning,' Adam replied.

Wesley and Harvey sat by the adjacent wall whilst the other two began the job of excavating.

80

Denise had completely lost track of time or what day it was. Although she was no longer blindfolded, masking tape still covered her mouth and her hands and feet remained tied, so any kind of movement was slow and painful. It had taken her what seemed like an eternity, to move thirty feet from one recess to another. Her hands and knees were sore and she felt drained of energy.

Having recently been provided with two blankets and another change of clothes, she was a little more comfortable.

There were four huge recesses in the octagonal shaped room which Denise now recognised as being the old bakery that served the Abbey in days gone by.

Although the room was now quite bare, she tried to picture it as it would have been in those days, with all four bread ovens baking bread twenty-four hours a day and people milling around at the troughs and tables, making all sorts of pies and pastries. The smoke from the burning wood under each of the ovens must have made the workplace a death trap and the air would have been almost un-breathable.

She could imagine a queue of servants waiting with their wooden baker's trays to take bread and pies up to the church tower to serve the Abbot. There would be queues of beggars standing outside the Abbot's kitchen hoping to be thrown a morsel of bread or pastry. It was hard to imagine though that just a few centuries ago the room was in use seven days a week and virtually twenty-fours a day.

She almost laughed to herself. It was a death trap now, for her.

A sliver of light came from the roof void at the centre of the room during daylight hours but that was her only respite from continual darkness. Since her capture, Denise had spent hours trying to understand what it was that her captor wanted from her or expected to get out of the situation. She had nothing to offer so there was no point in someone holding her for ransom.

She wondered how her mother was coping and whether the police were still looking for her.

High up in the centre of the roof, Denise could hear the flutter of wings and the night sound of bats. There was a time when bats used to scare her but now they were her only company and she no longer feared them.

Oh you lucky things she thought. At least you can escape from time to time. At least you're free.

81

Jenny was sat at the dining table having just devoured a full English breakfast. Although she'd had a restless night, she had woken up with an appetite. The young, olive skinned waiter had given her the eye a few times whilst serving breakfasts and Jenny had been tempted to return the interest but she had more important things to attend to this morning.

Having settled her bill in cash, she walked out of the hotel. Crossing the street, she made the five minute walk to where she'd parked the car the previous evening. Jenny had registered under a false name and had deliberately parked her car away from the hotel so that it wouldn't be picked up by the hotel's security cameras.

The drive back to Havering took thirty minutes. Jenny again parked the car a couple of streets away and casually walked down the lane passing the house once, before doubling back to ensure no one was around. Once inside, Jenny grabbed gardening gloves, a spade and a small pick axe and made her exit by the back door.

Assuming the back garden led onto open fields, Jenny surveyed the back of the property, listening out for neighbours although the nearest cottage was some distance away. She threw the tools over the back fence and using a small water butt as a stepping stone, Jenny climbed over. Unlocking her mobile, she searched the notes file to find the code she'd stored. Southwest80mtrssoutheast50down2.

She knew that by turning left and walking down the slope she would be heading in a south westerly direction, back towards Glastonbury. The bank of trees and density of the woods obscured any glimpse of the Tor which Jenny knew would soon come into view. She still didn't understand the code. It had to represent an area near the house, but where?

After stumbling through the course grass and woodland, she eventually came to an opening where the ground sloped away sharply, descending into a densely wooded valley below. Halfway down the slope the gradient was such that she had to slide down the root ridden bank on her backside.

At the foot of the valley, Jenny wiped the sweat from her forehead and dirt from her clothes. She had no idea where this was leading to and doubts started to creep in to her mind. The steep sides of the banks made the small valley she found herself in seem so secluded. Standing up straight as the ground had now levelled out, Jenny moved gingerly forward. She had only taken a few steps when she almost tripped.

At first glance she thought she had caught her foot on a rock or root protruding from the ground but upon closer inspection, Jenny stood back in horror. What on earth! She brushed away the weed and debris with her hand and stood staring at a headstone. Within a few minutes, Jenny discovered half a dozen more headstones dotted around the area. Slowly, reality began to dawn on her. She had stumbled upon an old graveyard. Although remote and overgrown, the graveyard was peaceful, as if time had forgotten it was there. Secluded from the outside world, with its tombstones barely visible because of age or damage, Jenny felt a shiver down her spine.

Suddenly felt she was imposing and stood listening to the eerie silence. Even the birdsong had stopped.

82

Dorothy rapped the knocker twice and stood back from the front door. Abbey House seemed large and imposing on this dull grey morning. A shiver ran down her spine as she waited for someone to answer. She was dressed in her grey raincoat and wore a plastic rain hat as the rain had persisted since early morning.

A few seconds after rapping the knocker for a second time, she heard footsteps approaching from inside. A bleary eyed Michael Westbrook pulled the door open and seemed to assess her before speaking.

'The visitor's entrance is around the side. That's where you'll find the Chapel,' he said and started to close the door.

'Oh, sorry I should have introduced myself,' a nervous Dorothy replied. 'I'm Dorothy Hallerton. Eddie's wife. Your good lady Penny said it was OK if I popped round.'

Michael didn't get a chance to reply as Penny suddenly appeared from one of the rooms leading off the vast hallway and pulled the door open.

'Dorothy!' she called out, 'please do come in.'

Completely ignoring Michael, who stared at Dorothy in distain, Penny led her by the arm into the house, leaving Michael to close the door.

'You must be cold. Please let me take that wet coat from you. The weather is awful for this time of year, don't you think?'

'I think the rain refreshes things,' Dorothy replied removing her rain hat and handing Penny her coat. 'We always need a drop of rain.'

'You're right, of course you are. It does affect our tourist industry though. I'm afraid our daily attendance of visitors reduces when the weather is so inclement. Anyhow, let's put the kettle on. I'm sure a cup of tea will soon warm you up.'

Penny hung Dorothy's coat in the hallway and led the way towards the kitchen. Dorothy glanced back at Michael who was still staring at her from the front door.

Entering the kitchen Penny pulled a chair up for Dorothy.

'Tea or coffee?'

'Tea please,' Dorothy replied whilst searching through her shopping bag. 'Oh, here they are.'

She extracted a biscuit tin and placing it on the table, removed the lid to expose a dozen freshly baked rock cakes.

'Oh they smell good,' said Penny. 'Did you make these?'

'Yes. They used to be Eddie's favourites. Of course I don't make so many of them now, but people like them and I enjoy cooking so I still make a few.'

As Penny made the tea Dorothy sat observing the kitchen.

'Do you know, I think your kitchen is bigger than the whole of my house.'

'Sometimes I think it's too large.' Penny carried two cups of tea over. 'I can never find a damn thing.'

Penny was the first to break the silence after tea had been drunk and two rock cakes devoured.

'So what tools of Eddie's are you particularly looking for?'

'I'll be honest,' Dorothy replied wiping crumbs away from her mouth. 'I'm not sure what I'm looking for. It's just that I know Eddie had more tools than I could find in our shed. I want to get our garden ready for the winter but Eddie's fork and shears are not there and I'm sure he used to leave some of his tools here.'

With tea having been drunk Penny placed the two empty cups in the sink.

'Well, I have no idea what tools of Eddie's, if any, we have here. However, let's take a look shall we?'

Leading the way, Penny retrieved the keys to the garden storage block and with Dorothy close behind, they exit the back of the building via the kitchen.

'What beautiful grounds,' Dorothy exclaimed looking across the expanse of lawn towards where the new trees had been planted.

'Yes, all Eddie's work,' said Penny. She put a hand on Dorothy's shoulder as tears appeared in the woman's eyes.

'There are around four acres of garden here, most of which Eddie looked after by himself, although during the summer months we often have a couple of helpers too.'

Penny went to unlock the swing doors to where the gardening equipment was stored, but the padlock was missing and the doors unlocked. She pulled them apart. Both women stood looking at the destruction.

'Oh my God,' Penny exclaimed putting her hands to her face.

'What the hell has been going on?'

Every drawer along the workbenches that ran the full length of both sides of the room had been pulled out. Their contents thrown on the floor.

'It looks as if someone was searching for something specific,' said Dorothy. 'Why else would anyone leave such a mess?'

Penny stared in total disbelief.

'I think you ought to phone the police,' said Dorothy. 'This is definitely an insurance job. Look at the damage to the place.'

Penny sighed. She felt numb. What else could possibly happen?'

It was Dorothy's turn to comfort Penny. She put an arm around her shoulder as Penny tried to take in the scene in front of her.

83

Wesley and Harvey stood back to watch Gary Knowles and PC Adam Broad start to carefully dig away at the mound of grass and overgrown foliage that laid in front of the wall exactly where Harvey had pinpointed. The weather hampered their efforts as they continually had to hide their faces from the wind and driving rain. Their spades continually hit loose stone and the outer wall. They had been digging for five minutes or more when suddenly Adam shouted that he'd hit something different.

'Be careful. Originally, there would have been steps leading down to the crypt,' Harvey called out.

Gary Knowles helped the young PC shovel away more debris until the first step began to appear. Harvey, aided by Wesley walked across to take a closer view.

'If I'm correct, the steps run down the side of the wall into the crypt,' Harvey exclaimed getting excited.

It took the two lads another ten minutes to dig enough earth away to find the next two steps. It was then that Adam noticed the change in the supporting wall.

'Look here,' he said pointing to the bottom four inches of exposed wall. 'It looks like the wall has been bricked up here.'

'I think this is probably the top of the original entrance to the crypt,' Harvey White answered.

A short while later and after having removed numerous shovels of earth, they had uncovered another four steps. It was now very apparent they had found the entrance to the crypt. However, to their dismay the whole of the entrance had been bricked up.

'I can't wait for us to break through.' Harvey rubbed his hands together, hardly able to contain his excitement.

'I don't want to be scrooge here,' said Gary Knowles, as he sat on one of the steps, 'but before we start breaking through the wall, we need to make the area safe and ensure we support the excavation.'

'Reluctantly, I think you're right son,' said Wesley. 'Do you have the equipment at the council or do you want me to organise additional gear?'

'I think we can do it, Mr Wesley, but it's going to take some time. We can't be sure how safe the site is right now, especially with all this rain now getting into the supporting soil. I'll get on to the office now and we'll fence the area off to make sure the public or any trespassers don't come to grief.

Also, I need a certificate from the council hierarchy before I start knocking these bricks out.'

'OK, I understand. That sounds like a plan to me. Let me know if you have any problem with permissions to continue. Unless I hear from you can we agree to continue with the excavation tomorrow?'

'Sure, no problem as long as we have approval,' Gary replied.

A disappointed Harvey White didn't make comment and walked away looking dejected.

'Is Mr White OK?' Adam asked Wesley as they stood at the top of the steps whilst Gary talked to his superiors at the Council offices via his mobile.

'He'll be fine son. He's just impatient.'

Wesley watched Harvey struggling across the grounds. His walking stick in one hand and umbrella in the other.

'Just what is Harvey's interest in all this?' Adam asked.

'He's a local historian son and appears to have a genuine interest in what's behind that wall.'

'You look worried, Sir.'

'I'm not so much worried but just concerned we're spending time on some wild goose chase or the whim of a local historian.'

84

Jenny sat down and rested against the steep bank, trying to collect her thoughts. She retrieved her mobile phone from her jeans pocket and looked at the coded message again. Southwest80mtrssoutheast50down2 What did it mean? There had to be a link to where she was but where should she start looking? Aware of the darkening clouds in the distance and the scent of more rain in the air, she knew she had to move quickly. Although she couldn't see far in any direction, she knew that if she faced Glastonbury, which was directly in front of where she was sat, she was facing south west. Jenny estimated that the graveyard was oblong in shape although it did appear to slope slightly in one corner. Looking at her surroundings she took the decision to start from the north left hand corner of the graveyard and walk in a south westerly direction, down the slope.

She tried to count her steps but soon forgot what number she had counted to, so she retraced her steps back to the corner of the graveyard. This time before starting again, she broke the remains of an old branch into pieces. Then every ten paces she prodded a piece of twig into the ground. Taking the assumption that each stride was approximately one meter in length, she stopped after eighty strides, where she turned to her right towards the west. With some difficulty she eventually covered the next fifty strides and stood surveying her surroundings.

This can't be right, she said to herself.

She was standing in a clearing on the edge of the graveyard. Running her hands through her hair she tried to think. A light drizzle had started, forcing Jenny into action.

Deciding to start again from the opposite corner of the graveyard she began counting her footsteps. Straight away this looked more favourable. As soon as she turned towards a south easterly direction she began to move towards the middle of the graveyard. Jenny stopped after fifty paces.

What did two down mean? To her left was a broken headstone with its top half leaning against the remains of the bottom piece. The details of the deceased were almost indecipherable. The only thing Jenny could read was the date of birth, 1932. To her right stood the remains of a watering hole with a metal pipe protruding from the ground. Alongside it, the remains of a watering can. Jenny turned back to face the way she'd been walking. In front of her stood the remains of a headstone. The name Frederick Smalling, born 1841, being readable but the rest of the wording virtually obliterated. Jenny took a couple of steps forward. Directly behind Frederick Smallings grave, the remains of a small tombstone lay almost hidden due to the overgrown foliage that had almost consumed it over time.

Jenny knelt down by the side of the grave and pulled back the foliage to expose the marble stonework to daylight probably for the first time in centuries. The grave was smaller than most of the others that surrounded it and Jenny was about to find out why. Brushing the remains of dirt away from the inscription, she leaned forward to read. Alfred Westbrook – Born 18th August 1955 – Died 8th October 1959. Jenny's mind was racing. Was this a relative of the Westbrook's? A four year old boy but what's the importance?

Using her mobile phone, Jenny photographed the grave as the threatened rain began to fall.

85

David Hare was walking towards the bus stop when his mobile rang. He didn't recognise the number but thought it best to answer the call in case it was one of his students in need of advice. They all knew he was a soft touch when it came to helping them find information about their studies.

'Hello. Who's calling?'

'What do you mean? Who's calling? It's me Sally. Who were you expecting?'

'Hi, Sal. Sorry I didn't recognise the number.'

'Oh, yeah sorry. I'm using the company phone. Where are you? I thought you said you would be in the flat all day.'

'Sal, I think I've made an amazing discovery about the possibility of other passageways under the Tor. Sal, are you still there?'

'Yeah. Sorry what did you say? The line is real bad.'

'I said, I think I've discovered a link to new passageways under the Tor.'

'Oh that's good. You are a clever boy. Have you shown them to anyone?'

'No. I'm on my way to meet Mr Wesley now. I can't wait to see his face.'

'It will be a surprise for him.'

'Are you OK Sal? You don't sound too enthralled at my discovery.'

'It's just that I've got a lot on my mind at the moment. Things aren't going well on either of the projects I'm leading.'

'That job of yours is going to get you down. You know that, don't you,' said David waving down the oncoming bus.

'Look, I'm just about to jump on the bus, so we might lose connection. Give me a call tonight if you can, otherwise I'll see you at the weekend. Love you Sal.'

After ending the call, Sally placed her mobile on the sideboard and went into the kitchen to retrieve the train timetable. For a few minutes she studied two of the pages before coming to a decision. Grabbing her jacket and keys, she quickly made her way downstairs and out of the building.

Wesley had been home to get a change of clothes before returning to the office. Walking into reception he was met by David Hare.

'Good afternoon Inspector,' said David standing up when he saw Wesley.

'Hello David. How are you? I wasn't expecting to see you here.'

'Yeah, apologies, I should have made an appointment, but as I was passing I thought I'd pop in.' He held up a small briefcase. 'There's something I would like you to take a look at.'

'OK, sure. Come on through.'

David followed Wesley through a security door that led into a narrow, dimly lit corridor. At the top of a small flight of stairs they reached Wesley's office, Wesley beckoned him in first.

'Take a seat David. I'll get some tea ordered.'

'Oh right. Thanks.'

Wesley returned to find that David had spread a map and some form of drawing across the desk. Hanging his jacket on the coat stand, Wesley extracted his tobacco and papers and rolled a cigarette.

'So what have we got here?' he asked after lighting up.

'Well, we already know, there are said to be several passageways under the Tor, apart from the Chalice Well. Some of these accessible and some not. However, this tracing that Colin was working on, seems to confirm the myth.' He laid the tracing over the top of the ancient map of the Tor.

'What we are looking at here is the Vesica Piscis which is the ancient sacred symbol of two interlocking circles.'

Wesley scratched the side of his head looking completely confused.

'But what does it show us?' Wesley asked resting his elbows on the table.

'There is a system of terracing around the Tor here,' he said pointing. 'You'll notice that where the circles interlock, they merge with the Chalice Well.'

'I've been down the Well and I never saw any routes leading off the main Well.'

'Maybe not, but you weren't really looking for them were you? At that point I think Colin concentrated on reaching the only known outlet.'

'Yeah maybe. Do we know the exact locations where the circles cross?'

'Virtually, yes. Given the scale of the map, I think we can be quite precise. I do believe we can locate exactly where the underground tunnels are.' He pointed to a place on the map where he had marked a cross.

'That's a bit of a coincidence,' said Wesley. 'I've just returned from the Abbey ruins. Almost from the same place as you've marked here.'

'Oh really?'

'Yeah. I don't want to say too much at this point David. As you can well understand there are things I need to keep to myself as they're possibly linked with the recent kidnapping, but it certainly does look interesting. I currently need to get permission from the council to carry out excavation work within the Abbey ruins and will need the same before we carry out any tests on the Tor. We can't just start digging holes everywhere. Can I keep this? I'll need to take it to the council chambers.'

'Sure thing Mr Wesley. I do hope they allow us to check this out. I feel certain we're onto something here. If these passageways still exist, then there's always the possibility that someone with local knowledge already knows how to access them.'

'Or hide someone,' Wesley replied lighting one of his roll ups.

86

'Oh Dorothy! Look at the mess. Do you really think we ought to call the police?'

'I'm not sure they could do anything,' Dorothy replied surveying the scene. 'I guess you're insured?'

'I believe so. I mean, Michael looks after that side of things.'

'Come on. Let's start tidying up a bit, shall we?'

'I don't know where to begin.' Penny looked bewildered.

'Let's put all the drawers back first then we can start replacing the tools,' said Dorothy. It took them more than twenty minutes just to put the drawers back and pick the tools up from the floor. They laid all the tools on the top of the workbench before stopping to take a break.

'Thanks Dorothy. I couldn't have done all that on my own.'

'That's alright my dear. Why on earth would anyone want to do this though? That's the question. It's not as if anything looks broken which makes me think someone knew what they were looking for.'

'Yes, but what?' Penny asked. 'There's nothing kept out here except decorating tools, gardening and general maintenance equipment.'

'A thief wouldn't necessarily know that,' Dorothy replied shrugging her shoulders.

'I know, but as you just said, someone appears to have been looking for something specific.'

'Hopefully your security cameras will have picked up the culprit,' said Dorothy.

'I'm afraid not. To be honest, they're switched off during the day, another one of Michael's cost saving exercises,' Penny replied.

'Well I think you ought to tell Mr Westbrook just in case there is something missing that we don't know about.'

Penny took a deep sigh and Dorothy could sense the uncertainty.

It was a while before Penny spoke.

'Dorothy, can I ask a favour? Please don't mention this to Michael. He has a very nervous disposition and something like this would upset him greatly.'

Dorothy's gut feeling was that someone ought to tell Michael, but she decided it wasn't really her decision.

'Of course I won't, not if you don't want him to know but I would certainly check to make sure nothing valuable has been taken. Here, let me help you put some of these tools in the drawers and back on their hooks then we can close up. I have no idea if anything in here was Eddie's.'

'Well, you can always borrow anything you need,' Penny replied.

'Thanks, but the first thing you need to do is to get the lock repaired otherwise the whole place is easy picking.'

Penny examined what remained of the padlock. Someone has used cutters to simply snap it away from the door. She threw the remains of the lock onto the workbench and pulled the door close. A shiver went down her spine as if someone had just walked over her grave.

Michael was getting anxious as he paced up and down the library. Jenny had left almost thirty-six hours ago. Having watched Penny and Dorothy walk out towards the garden he made his way upstairs and headed straight for Jenny's room. He had looked in her wardrobe and was still sat at the dressing table looking at the contents of the drawers when the bedroom door opened and Jenny entered.

'Where the hell have you been?' Michael asked looking startled. 'I was worried that something had happened to you.'

'More importantly, what are you doing going through my dressing table?' Jenny asked closing the door behind her.

'It's my damn house,' he replied defensively. 'I was worried about you.'

'Bullshit,' she almost spat the word out. 'The only thing you worry about is the income you receive from this bloody place. You don't give a damn about me or anyone else. It's no wonder, there's no love lost between you and your wife. You're as cold as the grave.' There were tears in her eyes but she was trying hard not to let him see her upset in this way.

'What's got in to you? What gives you the right to tell me what I think or don't think? You don't do too badly from me.'

'Oh, so I should suddenly be so grateful should I? The master of the house ordains to look after me.'

'Don't talk to me like that or I'll…'

'Or you'll what? Tell your wife. Throw me out. I don't think so. I know more about your schemes and your little secrets than you know. Don't make the mistake of thinking I'm stupid,' Jenny sneered. 'I want a share of this place and I intend to get it.'

She turned and slammed the door behind her.

87

Gary Knowles and two other council workers were already standing by the site when Wesley and PC Adam Broad arrived the following morning. It had stopped raining but there was a cold chill to the air. Adam had just provided Wesley with an update from the team who had tried to follow the tunnel under Abbey House. It wasn't the news Wesley was hoping for. Not only was the tunnel still flooded but part of the roof had also collapsed and he was told it could be days or even weeks before any progress could be made. Wesley knew he couldn't wait that long.

'Good morning gentlemen,' said Wesley as they approached.

Gary made the introductions and explained how they were going to reinforce the wall and surrounding area before attempting to knock through.

'It will take about an hour or more to secure the area before we start on the wall,' said Gary.

'OK. I have a couple a things to do whilst you're doing that,' Wesley replied. He gave Gary his mobile number.

'Give me a call when you're ready to start and I'll be back.'

'Where are we off to?' Adam asked as they crossed the lawn back towards the entrance to the Abbey grounds.

'We're heading for the High Street son. There's a little café where you can buy me breakfast.'

The café was busy and Wesley had time to make a couple of quick phone calls while Adam ordered breakfast. As soon as two platefuls of egg, bacon, sausage and beans were placed in front of them, they ate in silence. Adam was the first to speak just as a group of tourists entered and squeezed themselves around the table next to them.

'What do you think we're going to find once we break through to the supposed crypt?'

Wesley shrugged his shoulders as he took a sip of tea.

'I have no idea; I don't think Harvey White has either. The fact that the entrance has been bricked up though, makes me feel that whatever we find isn't going to help us find Denise.'

'I still don't understand why this Harvey White guy so interested?' Adam commented as he dipped his bread into the remains of his egg.

'Harvey is your typical historian. He's excited by the fact that we may find 'something'. I'm happy to go along with the excavation simply to rule out anything related to the recent murders and Denise's disappearance.'

'Hmm,' Adam replied with a mouthful of food, 'but even if there is something there, whoever is hiding Denise certainly didn't gain entrance from there. The whole area is overgrown and any entrance, even if there is one, is totally sealed up.'

'Yeah I know that Adam. Also I think Harvey expected it too but when I spoke to him yesterday, he seemed almost convinced that if an entrance still existed, it would be from within the Tor.'

'Do you mean all the way down the slope? Surely that would cross the Chalice Well?'

Wesley began poking strands of tobacco into the end of a cigarette with a matchstick.

'I know son. I know.'

Penny grabbed the mail from the post box that was built into the wall next to the front door and quickly sifted through the envelopes. Two bills, a mail order catalogue invoice addressed to Jenny and junk mail advertising cruises addressed to Michael. What attracted her attention though was a white envelope addressed to her. The post mark was Glastonbury. Penny carried the mail into the kitchen and sat herself at the table. Using her thumb she ripped the envelope open, removed the sheet of paper and read the typed message.

Denise will be returned unharmed but only when the King's items are returned and I receive my share of the estate. You will shortly receive details of the expected transaction. Do not make the mistake of involving the police. I will be watching.

Penny read the message several times as the reality of the situation began to sink in. She was being held to ransom. Walking into the hallway trying to compose herself, she walked straight into Jenny who had just come down the stairs.

'I'm sorry, I wasn't looking,' said Penny.

'Are you OK?' Jenny asked. 'You look strange, like you've seen a ghost or something.'

'I'm OK. Thanks though,' Penny replied trying to force a smile.

Jenny watched her as she slowly walked in the direction of the library before closing the door behind her.

What a strange family, Jenny thought to herself as she slipped out of the front door. Striding across the Abbey grounds, Jenny headed for the local records office of births, deaths, and marriages.

88

Although WPC Mandy Tredwell was off duty she couldn't help her basic instincts and had to follow Patricia Wright as the woman headed into the shopping village in Street.

Mandy had decided to spend her day off doing some therapeutic shopping. Her income from the police force meant that she didn't have a fortune to spend on clothes so she tended to shop around at the smaller retail stores. She'd chosen the new shopping village in Street this morning as the weather forecast predicted more rain and she only had a short walk from home to the High Street.

She first saw Patricia as the woman exited the bus station. The woman seemed agitated and kept stopping to look behind her, as if she thought she was being followed. Mandy stayed well back, observing from a shop doorway as Patricia made her way slowly towards the shopping centre.

She followed the woman into the pedestrianized area where Patricia took a seat on one of the benches in front of the food hall and started rummaging in her shopping bag that she'd placed on her lap.

At first Mandy thought she may simply be stopping for something to eat as the woman extracted a small Sainsbury's bag. However, after making sure that no one was looking, Patricia simply placed the bag into the waste bin next to the bench. She immediately then closed her shopping bag, looked around again, stood up and walked briskly away.

Mandy decided not to follow but to wait and see what happened next. She didn't have to wait long. A young hoody cycled up next to the waste bin, extracted the Sainsbury's bag and slipped it under his clothing before speeding off. Mandy turned to follow without looking and ran straight into a pushchair, bruising her leg almost immediately. By the time she'd apologised to the young couple, the cyclist was nowhere in sight. Exiting the shopping centre she ran towards the High Street.

She looked up and down the road and crossed over to the green where most of the youngsters congregated by the open air swimming pool. Several teenagers appeared to be wearing a similar hooded top but there was no sight of the bike or a Sainsbury's bag and Mandy had no idea whether the cyclist was male or female.

Using her private mobile she texted Wesley a message asking him to phone her.

89

Shortly after receiving the call from Gary Knowles saying they were ready to start knocking through the wall to the crypt, Wesley and Adam re-entered the grounds of the Abbey just as Harvey White was getting out of a car by the entrance.

'Good morning, Harvey,' Wesley said as he helped him through the entrance.

'Good morning, Inspector. Thank you and thanks for arranging one of your team to pick me up. That was very kind. It will have certainly got the neighbours gossiping. I think most of the neighbourhood watched me get into the police car.'

Wesley couldn't help but grin.

'My pleasure. They can talk some more when you get dropped home later.'

Wesley updated him on progress as they made their way across the Abbey grounds.

A harsh, cold, driving wind now blew across the grounds and Wesley turned up the collar of his jacket. When they arrived at the entrance to the crypt they were surprised to see just how much progress had been made. A gap of about three feet by two had already been made in the wall, about a foot from ground level.

'It's quite a slow process,' Gary Knowles shouted looking up from where he sat in front of the entrance. 'We're cutting out a piece at a time. The old brickwork underneath is quite unstable, and the concrete that has been plastered over the top appears to be holding the whole thing up.'

'OK be careful son,' said Wesley. 'Can you see inside from where you are?'

'Yeah a little but its pitch black. I'm pretty sure there are more steps leading down. We'll find out soon.'

Wesley, Harvey and PC Broad watched patiently as the grinder slowly cut away at the concrete face for a minute at a time before Gary then attacked the brickwork with a hammer and chisel. Dust hung around the area like a rain cloud waiting to unload its contents on the labourers. It was an hour later before Gary stood up and dusted himself down.

'Do you want to take a look?' he called out to Wesley who was now sat on the grass on the far wall of the Lady Chapel. The hole was now just about wide enough for Wesley to fit through. Gary handed him a torch but asked him not to touch the wall.

Wesley shone the torch into the void and peered inside. The musty smell of air that had been trapped for decades and the dampness of the walls hit his nostrils immediately.

'Watch your step,' said Gary. 'There appears to be about seven or eight steps down before a dead end.'

Carefully stepping into the void, Wesley shone the torch downwards and negotiated one step at a time. Gary had also entered the void and now stood behind him. They had descended all the steps. In front of them was a solid concrete wall, the same to their left but when Wesley shone the torch to the right, they stood facing a grilled entrance. On the other side of the bars he could see that the ground sloped away quite sharply and less than ten feet ahead the tunnel turned left, preventing him from viewing any further.

'Can you hear that?' Gary asked straining his ears.

Wesley nodded. There was a distinct sound of running water.'

'There's no lock on this at all,' said Gary examining the grating. 'Whoever had this installed certainly didn't want the place disturbed again. It's totally sealed.'

'I have to agree with you,' Wesley replied looking through the bars into the eerie darkness. 'Do you think we can break through?'

'We'll need different cutting gear,' Gary replied. 'I'll send the lads back to the depot. We're going to need someone to stay on site though. There would be a crowd of local press outside in minutes if anyone caught wind of this.'

Wesley and Adam were sat by the Lady Chapel interior wall discussing the weekend's football results with Adam being an ardent Bath City supporter, when Wesley received the text from Mandy asking him to phone her.

'Hi Mandy. I got your message. I hope you're enjoying your day off.'

Mandy explained that she had decided to spend the morning shopping in Street when she spotted Patricia Smith.

'It all sounds a bit fishy to me,' said Wesley after Mandy had briefed him of the events that followed.' What made you decide to follow Patricia in the first place?'

'Just instinct really. In this job you learn to read peoples body language and their actions and I just got the impression that she thought she was being watched.'

'It sounds as if she probably was.'

'Do you want me to have a chat with her to find out what it was all about?' Mandy asked.

'No, you're on a well-earned break. Leave it with me. I'll pop in and see Patricia later today. Did you get a look at the person who collected the bag?'

'Not really, just someone, wearing a hoody. I couldn't even be sure if was a male or female. A teenager I would guess, but that's about all.'

'OK. Good work Mandy. Leave it with me. Enjoy the rest of your day.'
'Thanks. I'll see you tomorrow.'
'Take care.'
Wesley hung up and provided Adam with the details of the conversation.
'Hmm. Does sound a bit dodgy, has this Patricia Smith got any history?'
'Good point son. I'll get a check done before I pop round.'

'Looks like you have a visitor,' Adam replied nodding towards the far side of the Lady Chapel where the remains of the outside wall only just obscured the entrance to the Abbey grounds.

David Hare was striding across the manicured lawn that encompassed the Lady Chapel and the majority of the Abbey grounds.

'Mr Wesley,' he said breathing heavily, 'I phoned the station and they said you were over here.'

'David, good afternoon,' Wesley replied shaking hands.

David was sweating profusely. He was wearing an overcoat, jumper and jeans, and although it was still drizzling, the air was humid and warm.

'I visited the Tourist office this morning, as it had been brought to my attention that they used to hold a number of local historical books in their archives. More specifically, books relating to the Tor. In any case, apparently only a couple of years ago they had to have a lot of old archive stock destroyed because they ran out of space. Although most of it had been copied to microfiche, numerous copies have apparently disappeared over the years. Anyhow, when the lady in shop, Mrs Harper asked me what it was I was looking for, she immediately replied that no one knows the Tor better than her.'

'I gather she's quite an expert on the area,' Wesley replied.

'More than an expert, quite a historian. I explained to her that I was looking for anything relating to the Vesica Piscis when she said, oh you mean where the crypt and the Well interlock.'

Wesley raised an eyebrow.

'I'm sorry for being ignorant but what is the Vesica Piscis?' Adam asked.

'It's an ancient sacred symbol from early Christian times. When we recently placed an old tracing of the Abbey grounds and Tor over an ancient map of the same location, we discovered the two interlocking circles which represent the Vesica Piscis.'

'Mrs Harper reckons that there's a link between the crypt and the Well?'

'Yes,' David replied his eyes seeming to question what Wesley and Adam were already doing on the Abbey grounds.

'Let me show you something,' said Wesley taking him by the arm.

'Stay here for a second Adam. I don't want anyone else near this place except for Harvey White. He'll be back in a few minutes. He's gone to find a toilet.'

David followed Wesley across the inner sanctum of the Lady Chapel towards where the excavation work had started.

'We have identified possible access to the crypt and started excavation work this morning. The council guys have currently gone to get some cutting gear. There's a grated entrance at the bottom of the steps,' he said pointing down into the void. 'It could lead to nowhere but I've got a feeling it was sealed up for a reason.'

'Oh my word!' David replied unable to conceal his excitement.

'This is almost the same spot where the two circles interlock! This is amazing Inspector. We could be on to something that has been lost for centuries.'

'I understand your enthusiasm and excitement but I would be even happier if it led us to Denise Wright,' replied Wesley.

90

The tall red bricked building that housed the Registry office for births, deaths and marriages had stood in Glastonbury High Street since 1759 but the records it holds date back to the 12th century.

Having paid a small fee to look at historical records, Jenny made her way to the top floor of the three storey building. An elderly grey haired woman, whose spectacles were perched precariously on the edge of her nose, greeted Jenny as she reached the top of the stairs. She directed Jenny to a set of small tables in the middle of the room.

Having obtained from Jenny the range of dates that she said she was interested in, she walked across the room to one of the two walls that were covered from floor to ceiling in shelving that supported thousands of books and retrieved a large leather bound volume dated 1900 – 1999.

'You will find that all entries are in date order, my dear,' said Ada Chapman. 'If you need any help, just ask.'

'Thanks,' Jenny replied.

It took her less than a minute to find the first entry she was looking for.

Entry 192 – Alfred Westbrook, Born 18th August 1955. Father - William Thomas Westbrook, Farm Labourer, aged 39. Mother – Mary Westbrook, formerly Thomas, Housewife, aged 36.

The second entry of interest consisted of just two lines:

Entry 404 – Alfred Westbrook, Died 8th October 1959. Cause of death – polio. Location of deceased – Abbey House, Glastonbury.

'Are you OK my dear?'

Jenny had been lost in thought and hadn't see Ada Chapman walk up.

'What? I mean, pardon? Oh sorry. I was miles away,' Jenny replied apologetically.

'You were talking to yourself so I just wondered if you were OK.'

'Was I? It's a habit I'm afraid,' said Jenny.

'Oh don't worry about that my dear. My Alf says I whistle when I'm thinking. I answer him by saying that's why he never whistles. He doesn't think about anything other than what he's got for his dinner. A typical man.' She laughed as she walked back to her desk where another woman was stood waiting to hand some books in.

Jenny was trying to understand why a coded message, scribbled on a painting, in a house that Kelvin Ward had been renting, had directed her to a derelict, overgrown, forgotten graveyard. In particular, to a grave where a young child of the Westbrook family was buried.

An hour later, Jane was rearranging the display in the bookshop window when she noticed Jenny walk past. Curiosity got the better of her and she poked her head outside of the shop doorway to watch where Jenny was heading for but there was no sign of her. She had mysteriously disappeared.

It was only when Jane turned around to step back into the shop did she hear a door closing. Peering down the alleyway at the side of the shop, Jane suddenly became suspicious. The only door nearby was at the top of the staircase, the entrance to the flat above the shop. Kelvin Ward's flat.

Why on earth would Jenny want to visit the flat? It was empty, Jane thought. How did Jenny manage to obtain a key? And why? For a moment, Jane stood in the shop doorway listening until two young tourists broke her train of thought as they brushed past her entering the shop. They were two Americans visiting Glastonbury for the day. Jane exchanged polite conversation as they gesticulated how quant the whole area was and how they envied the English who had so much history to explore.

After wrapping their purchases and directing them towards the Abbey, Jane stood quietly behind the shop counter listening for sounds from the flat above. For a few minutes there was silence and she guessed that Jenny must have already left. Then suddenly she became aware of a scraping sound almost directly above where she stood. It was hard to decipher whether a piece of furniture was being dragged across the floor or if the floorboards were being taken up. Jane strained her ears to listen. Silence followed for a few minutes. The next sound was either something being knocked over or someone dropping a heavy object onto the floor. A small scraping sound followed for what seemed like ages until Jane jumped with fright.

'Oh I'm sorry. Did I make you jump?'

A young lad stood just inside the doorway. His wet clothes dripping onto the carpet.

'Sorry, I really came into the shop to get out of the rain. It's pouring,' he said pointing outside.

'Oh that's OK,' Jane replied. 'Do come in. I didn't realise it had started to rain. Would you like a cup of coffee? It might warm you up.'

'Well, yes, I suppose so. I mean. That would be very nice. Thank you. I don't want to put you out though.''

'It's no trouble. I was going to make myself one in any case. I'll be back in a second.'

Jane went into the back room to put the kettle on. As she reached up to retrieve two cups from the shelf next to the sink, she saw a fleeting shadow go past the back window. She pulled the curtain back just in time to watch Jenny striding across the empty waste ground behind the shops, carrying a parcel under her arm. It looked too big to be a book. Whatever it was, had been crudely wrapped in newspaper.

91

Michael walked into the library to find Penny asleep in the wing backed chair, her arm draped over the side. Noticing the piece of paper lying on the floor below Penny's arm, he walked across the room to pick it up. Being inquisitive, he decided to read what was written. For a moment he stood deep in thought, before folding the paper and quietly placing it on Penny's lap. He needed time to think.

By the time Gary Knowles and the council workers returned with the cutting equipment, Harvey White and David Hare had been introduced to one another by Wesley.

'The whole place smells damp, even from up here,' Harvey exclaimed grimacing.

'That could be just the result of being closed up for so long,' Gary replied as he squeezed past with a blow torch and other cutting equipment. 'I've tested the oxygen levels and we're OK to light the cutting gear. There's no trace of any other gases.'

'That's good,' Wesley replied. 'We'll stand at the top of the steps out of your way.'

David laid the ancient map on the grass and explained to Harvey White what they were looking at as he placed the tracing paper over the top, effectively joining the two circles.

'Oh my word, that's amazing,' Harvey exclaimed. 'I'd heard of the Vesica Piscis but never dreamt that I would ever see it or have the knowledge to understand it. Did you notice, that's where the circles overlap at the bottom here,' he said pointing.

'It's directly in line where we're now trying to access the crypt under the Lady Chapel.'

'Yes you're right,' David grinned.

Wesley stood to one side to roll a cigarette, leaving David and Harvey drooling over the map. He needed to clear his head.

'Well, we're soon going to find out what's down there. Gary tells me he's only got two more bars to cut through,' said Wesley, some thirty minutes later. He withdrew his tobacco and papers from his jacket pocket and sat on the grass while Harvey rested his heavy frame on a foldaway cloth stool that he brought with him.

Suddenly there was the sound of a crash from within the tunnel, followed by a cloud of dust emitting from the entrance. Seconds later Gary Knowles appeared at the steps to the crypt covered in a chalky dust.

'We're through, Mr Wesley. Want to take a look?' he said wiping his face with a handkerchief.

'Need a hand up?' Adam asked with a smirk as Wesley stood up.

'Very amusing. Stay here for a moment with Harvey and David whilst I take a quick look.'

'Sure thing, Sir.'

With all the bars removed, there was now enough space to squeeze through into the void. After being provided with a power torch, Wesley went first followed by Gary Knowles.

The entrance to the tunnel was approximately five feet wide and the same in height. Although both men had to crouch there was sufficient space to move forward quite easily. Ten feet in where the tunnel turned sharp left they met more steps descending to a lower level.

'Be careful, the steps are damp and quite slippery,' Wesley shouted over his shoulder.

They had taken no more than a dozen steps when they reached a solid wall ahead.

'It looks like another dead end,' Wesley sighed, 'but it can't be. I mean, why install the iron grating back there if there's nothing to hide?'

'Good point Mr Wesley. Let's have a look, shall we?' Gary replied kneeling down to examine the surface of the wall. He extracted a small pick axe from his bag and began to scratch at the surface. The plaster came away quite easily, identifying a series of small stone slabs underneath.

'It should be quite simple to knock through,' said Gary. 'We might need to reinforce the roof though. You can never be sure with these things.'

'How long do you think it will take to make safe?'

'Difficult to say really. If I had to take a guess, I'd say about an hour.'

'Can we continue today? The sooner we find out what's here, and close the entrance off again, the better,' said Wesley.

'Let's get back outside and I'll make a quick phone call. It should be OK. I'll send the lads back to the depot to get some wood to make a support for the roof.'

92

Penny woke after a restless sleep. Her head was pounding and she needed a couple of paracetamol. The letter fell onto the floor as she stood up from the chair. As she retrieved it the room began to spin. She held onto the back of the chair for a moment before walking out of the library and across the hall into the kitchen. She took two tablets with a glass of water and although still unsteady on her feet, made her way back across the hall and up the stairs.

Finding her handbag on the bed, Penny extracted her mobile phone and was about to call Wesley when a voice from the doorway startled her.

'You know I'll help you. That is if you want me to?' said Michael.

Penny tried to gather her thoughts.

'What are you talking about?'

He motioned to the piece of paper that Penny was clutching.

'You've read the note?'

'Yes. Sorry, but you'd dropped it on the floor.

'Why would you want to help me?'

Michael looked ashen faced as if he couldn't believe her reply.

'Because I'm your husband. Because I love you,' he stammered.

'You? Love me? I suppose that's why you've been shagging Jenny under my nose. In our home!'

'Penny,' he replied walking towards her. 'There's nothing going on between me and Jenny.'

'Stay away from me,' she shouted raising her hands to her head. 'Just go away. You don't care about me or my daughter. All you're worried about is the money that comes into this place and whether you have enough to cover the cost of your drug abuse.'

'Drug abuse? What are you talking about?' he replied with a nervous grin on his face.

'Oh Michael, don't keep up the pretence. I know you've been taking drugs for months now. Who supplies you with them? Is it Jenny?'

Michael stood open mouthed, as if speaking, except that no words came out.

'Well? Come on. Explain yourself.'

'Jenny does not supply me with drugs. I don't take drugs.'

'If she doesn't, then explain to me why she deals with a drug dealer in the town at least two days a week.'

'Penny, I can assure you I had no idea,' he replied shrugging his shoulders. 'If Jenny is buying drugs, they're not for me. I'm clean.'

Penny took a deep breath as if trying to control her temper and patience.

'Michael, just go away. Go and find your lover and leave me to deal with my daughter's ransom note. I don't need you interfering.'

'Interfering? But I'm your husband for God's sake!'

'Husband? You don't know the meaning of the word. Now leave me alone while I telephone Inspector Wesley.'

'But…' Michael ran his hands through his hair and stood looking bewildered.

'Just get out!' screamed Penny and slammed the door in his face. She leant back on the door and listened to his footsteps as he walked down the stairs. Wrapping her arms around her waist she burst into tears and slumped to the floor. Her sobbing racking her whole body.

93

'It would be nice for this rain to ease off,' said Wesley drawing on his cigarette. He was sat leaning against the interior wall of the Lady Chapel. Adam had been into town to get them some refreshments and was soaked to the skin.

'Yeah. Some summer we've had,' Adam replied trying to peel the wrapper off of his sandwiches.

David Hare was sat next to Harvey White, discussing the practicalities and feasibilities of underground streams and passageways being under the Tor. Wesley rubbed the remains of his cigarette between his thumb and forefinger as he listened to Harvey, who seemed to be in his element conversing with someone else who seemed to share the same historical and archaeological interests.

The council lads had returned about an hour ago with materials to support the tunnel entrance and banging and drilling noises could be heard from underground.

'What do you think we'll find?' Adam asked with a mouthful of sandwich and crisps.

'That's the thousand dollar question,' Wesley replied. 'My main concern is that we may unearth some unknown tunnel or even lost artefacts but without getting any closer, or wiser, to finding Denise.'

'Hmm. I agree with you. We've pretty much scoured the town and surrounding villages without even a trace of the girl. If she is being held somewhere on the Tor or out here in the Abbey grounds, I only hope that whoever has kidnapped her hasn't just left her somewhere to die. I mean, left alone in a room in a house, she could survive for some time, but left in a damp dark tunnel. Well, she just wouldn't survive so long. Would she?'

'I'm inclined to agree,' Wesley replied. 'Assuming the girl is still alive, wherever she's being held, we need to find her soon.'

'Do you know, what bugs me is that if the girl is being held around here, why haven't we seen anyone? I mean, the Abbey grounds and the Tor are both being patrolled and yet no one suspicious has been seen.'

'Yeah, that worries me too,' Wesley replied extracting his mobile phone as it started to vibrate. He pressed the green button and listened to Penny's scared voice as she read out the note, all in one breath. Wesley got to his feet.

'OK. Penny, listen to me. I'm tied up for a couple of hours but WPC Alison Bolt will be with you as soon as possible.'

'Someone's holding my little girl,' she cried.

'Penny, listen to me. What you've just told me suggests that Denise is very much alive and whoever is holding her knows who you are and where you live.'

He could hear her sobbing and felt her pain.

'Penny, is anyone with you right now?'

'Michael is in the house,' she sniffed, 'but he can't help.'

Wesley could sense the mixture of anxiety and anger in her voice.

'Look Penny. Alison will be with you within the next thirty minutes and she'll stay with you. Do you hear me?'

'Yes,' she cried. 'Yes, but please ask her to hurry. I'm so frightened.'

Wesley did his best to reassure her before hanging up and immediately dialled the station where he knew he would find WPC Bolt and within minutes the young WPC was on her way to Abbey House.

Wesley made another phone call before giving Adam a brief of the situation.

'As you say, Sir. The one positive thing is that it sounds as if Denise is still alive.'

'Yeah, and we need to cling to that hope, just as Penny needs to,' Wesley replied.

Jenny had entered Abbey House through the back entrance next to the maintenance building and made her way quietly up to her room. She threw her handbag on the dressing table and sat down on the bed to unwrap the parcel she'd carried from Kelvin's flat. She removed the sketch from the pillow case she'd taken from the flat to wrap it in and laid it out on the bed.

Having found the sketch laying behind the dressing table, Jenny was intrigued by the black and white impression of Abbey House. Why would Kelvin keep an artist's sketch of Abbey House hidden behind his dressing table she asked herself? There was no date or signature on the sketch and although Jenny was no expert, she didn't think it was very old. The only thing that seemed strange was the three dotted lines that had been drawn across the page with arrows leading to and from the house. She wondered what these meant. They didn't appear to represent anything she could visualise around the grounds.

She studied the sketch for another few minutes before putting it back in the pillow case for safe keeping. Grabbing a wooden chair, she placed it in front of the wardrobe. By standing on the chair she managed to hide the sketch out of view.

94

Dorothy had spent the afternoon sorting through Eddie's clothes and personal belongings. It was something she'd continually put off since his death, but somehow she summoned the courage to carry out the task.

Eddie's side of the wardrobe was sparse. He'd never been someone who spent a lot of money on clothes. Dorothy carefully folded his two suits, neither of which had been worn and placed them in plastic bags to take to the charity shop. His old shirts and working trousers she had bagged separately for burning in the garden.

She was halfway down the stairs laden with bags when there was a knock on the front door. Opening the door just a fraction, she peered outside.

'Hello, my dear,' said Jane. 'I hope I haven't knocked at an inconvenient time.'

'Of course not,' Dorothy replied. 'Do come in. I'll make some tea. I could do with putting my feet up.'

'What have you been doing? Having a clear out?' Jane asked seeing the plastic bags in the hall as she closed the door behind her and followed Dorothy into the kitchen.

'I've been sorting out Eddie's things. To be perfectly honest, it's something I've been dreading. I guess it's the final release really. With Eddie's things still in the house, I've always felt that he was still here. Silly I suppose.'

'No, it's not silly. It's perfectly understandable,' said Jane. 'I mean, you were together for a long time.'

Jane decided to change the conversation as she could see the tears welling up in Dorothy's eyes.

'So what events have we got scheduled down at the village hall this coming month? Not them male strippers again eh?'

Dorothy managed a smile.

'We should be so lucky. Apart from the weekly Monday night bingo sessions, the Wednesday afternoon teas and Mrs Whites' book reading club, the only major event is young Sandra Green's wedding reception. Her father is the man who runs the local taxi company.'

'Oh I think I spoke with him only last week when I telephoned for someone to take me into town. He sounds like a nice enough man, very well spoken.'

'Yes he is. I believe he went Lampton Grammar School when he was younger and was about to embark on a career as a trainee accountant when his father passed away, resulting in him inheriting the cab company.'

'Before I forget, there's an invite to the wedding reception on the mantelpiece in the front room. Sandra's mother Helen gave it to me the other day and asked me to pass it on to you. The wedding's on Saturday week at the local church with the reception in the village hall.'

'Oh thanks,' said Jane. 'That will be a lovely evening. We'll pick you up if you wish. That is, if John can get away from work.'

'Thanks.'

Dorothy placed two cups of tea on the table and opened a biscuit tin which contained several rock cakes.

'Please do take one Jane,' she said as she sat opposite.

'Oh, Dorothy. How am I supposed to watch my diet? Your cakes are just too tasty to refuse.'

Jane tucked into one of the cakes trying not to spill too many crumbs on the table.

'I guess you're helping out at the village hall next week?'

'Yes, but there's not much to do really. The Greens' have booked their own catering firm so all we have to do is to make sure the place is clean and tidy.'

'I do hope there's going to be some music in the evening,' said Jane.

'I believe they've arranged for some young lad to provide a disco. I expect they will play some loud music that no one can sing to or understand. '

Jane could tell from Dorothy's tone of voice that she didn't really approve of the idea.

'What's wrong with having a nice band? That's what I want to know.'

'I'm afraid us old one's are in the minority,' Jane replied laughing. 'Do we know who she's marrying?'

'Some young fella from Bath so I'm told. He's a builder. Got some fancy idea about buying one the old cottages at the other end of the village and knocking it about.'

Jane had a feeling it was going to be a long afternoon as Dorothy clearly didn't like that idea either.

95

The drilling and the hammering had stopped about an hour before Gary Knowles appeared from the tunnel entrance. Wesley knew something was wrong before the man spoke.

'What's up Gary? You look like you've seen a ghost.'

'I think you ought to come down on your own, Mr Wesley.'

Looking somewhat concerned, Wesley informed Adam to ensure that David and Harvey stayed up top and followed Gary down the steps, past the original gated entrance and down into the tunnel.

Two council workers stood by the opening where the wall had previously stood. As they approached, one of the men handed Wesley a lantern. Gary already had one in his hand.

'Tread carefully. It's probably really slippery down there. Damp too.'

Wesley nodded and beckoned Gary to lead the way. There were no further steps but the floor sloped away. As the daylight gradually disappeared behind them, the light from the lanterns began to cast flickering patterns across the stone walls. The passageway narrowed before it began to widen again and the height of the roof increased as they continued their descent into the black void.

Suddenly Gary turned to face Wesley.

'We're almost there,' he said nervously.

Twenty feet further down, Wesley noticed that the whole area had opened up into a huge cavern. He strained his eyes trying to take in all around him. They were stood in a square shaped room, some fifteen foot square.

Gary held up his lantern and pointed ahead. Two crossed swords, attached to a wooden shield were hung on the far wall but what caught Wesley's eye was the raised black marble tomb that stood in the centre of the room.

'I think you should read the inscription,' Gary said holding his lantern aloft and pointing towards the top of the tomb. Wesley moved forward as Gary walked around the other side of the tomb adding more light to the inscription. Wesley looked down upon the tomb and read the inscription aloud.

Here lies King Arthur and his Queen Guinevere. Rest in peace our Glorious King. Sleep at God's side our Lady

He read the inscription several times again to himself then looked across to Gary Knowles.

'You do realise what this is,' Wesley said.

'Yes, that's why I thought it best that no one else should come down here. History wasn't my strongest subject at school but being born in the town, the legend of King Arthur is engraved on my mind. This is the original tomb. It has been missing since the dissolution of the Abbey in 1539.'

The two men stared at one another for a few minutes, both trying to take in what they had discovered. Wesley ran a hand over his eyes and around his jaw.

'Well I wasn't expecting this son. A few skeletons maybe but not the tomb of the legendary King Arthur.'

'The thing is Mr Wesley,' said Gary. 'What do we do now?'

He looked across the tomb to where Wesley stood who seemed to be listening to something other than Gary's voice.

'You OK Mr Wesley?'

'Can you hear that?' Wesley asked.

'Hear what?'

Wesley tilted his head and raised his hand as if to say listen. At first, Gary didn't hear anything but then he became aware of the sound of running water. Although it was distant, the more they listened, the more apparent it became.

Wesley stood back from the tomb and turned to the wall behind him. He leant his ear against the damp stone as Gary did the same just a yard in front of him. They listened for a minute before Gary nodded with a smile on his face.

'The mystery continues,' he said. 'Are you thinking what I'm thinking?'

'The Chalice Well?'

'It has to be doesn't it? I just didn't think the Well spread this far wide.'

'I'm no expert son but I'm sure pretty sure the tunnel I was in wasn't this far away from the Tor or Abbey House.'

Suddenly a voice from back in the tunnel broke their thought.

'Are you two OK down there?'

It was one of the council workers shouting out loud.

'Don't let him in here,' said Wesley quickly moving back towards the tomb. 'I'll explain why in a moment.'

Gary sped back into the tunnel and for a few moments Wesley could hear a mumbled discussion going on. When Gary reappeared he looked flustered.

'Everything OK?'

'Yeah, except it's absolutely pouring with rain outside and the troops are getting restless.'

'The heavy rain may be the reason we can suddenly hear running water,' Wesley replied running his hand through his hair.

'It's running like a torrent behind that wall. What do we do next Mr Wesley? Once the press find out about the tomb, there will be thousands of people queued outside trying to get in here.'

'I think we should leave the legendary King resting in peace,' Wesley replied looking stern.

For a moment, Gary stood frozen to the spot. His mouth wide open.

'Surely you're not saying we should just close the tunnel without telling anyone of our find?'

'That's exactly what I'm saying.'

'Think of the tourists that will flock here,' Gary pleaded his arms outstretched.

'Think of the damage to the grounds and the Abbey ruins once thousands of tourists, archaeologists, and religious groups around the world descend on the place. It will also destroy the myth that brings so many people here already.'

'I can't believe what I'm hearing,' said Gary. 'We would be denying the world the knowledge that the legendary King is actually still laying here in state.'

'Gary, I hear what you say and I appreciate that the public may have a right to know. Right now, I'm conducting a murder investigation. I don't need thousands of people traipsing around the town, especially around the grounds of the Abbey or the Tor.'

Gary gesticulated with his arms and leant back on the far wall. For a few minutes there was silence between the two men. Wesley was the first to speak.

'Gary, listen to me. Can we come to an agreement?'

Gary shrugged his shoulders but nodded his head.

'I know that I have no jurisdiction over you in this situation but I'm going to ask you a favour.'

'I'm listening Mr Wesley.'

Wesley took a deep breath.

'Let me find Denise Wright and solve the recent murders. Then this discovery is all yours.'

'So, you're suggesting we just reseal the tunnel again?'

'Yes, for the time being.'

'And what do we tell the lads up top? '

'We say there's nothing here. That it's a dead end.'

'I'm not sure they're going to believe us. We've been down here for almost half an hour.'

'Then we need to convince them. Gary, I need your help here. Are you with me?'

The young council worker walked over to the tomb and rested his hands on the marble. Time seemed to stand still for a few minutes before he spoke.

'You're asking me to close the door on something that could change my life,' he said looking directly at Wesley.

'I'm asking you to help me save a girl's life,' Wesley replied.

'But you don't even know if she's still alive or where she's being held.'

'Evidence suggests right now that she is very much alive. For the time being in any case and we believe she's being held around here somewhere. I'll not give up on her whilst there's hope.'

Wesley knew how difficult his request was for Gary to understand. Of course, the lad's career would change for ever the moment the discovery was announced.

Wesley stood waiting in anticipation of Gary's response. When Gary looked up, Wesley feared the worst until the lad smiled.

'You're right Mr Wesley. The girl's life is more important. Come on let's get this place sealed up.'

He looked down again upon King Arthur's final resting place as Wesley patted him on the shoulder.

'Thanks son.'

96

After ensuring she had eaten, Denise's captor had left her on her own again. Even though it was just a small amount of food she had eaten, it would be enough to keep her alive. Although Denise had felt hungry, it was becoming more and more difficult to eat as each day passed. Being untied to go to the toilet was the only exercise she'd had in over a week and she knew she was getting weak.

Sitting back against the base of an old bread oven she began to imagine she was writing to her mother. She would reassure her mother that she was OK and ask her not to worry, telling her that everything would be alright. She would tell her mother that she loved her. Something she now realised she'd not said for a long time. She would ask if Timmy the cat was OK and whether her mother's arthritis was playing her up. She tried to picture her mother wearing her apron, in the kitchen preparing dinner. It was her mother's little domain where no one else was allowed. Denise could smell the Sunday roast and the pastries cooking. Sunday lunch was never eaten without rhubarb or apple pie for pudding. Her mother's pastry was the best in the world.

It was at this thought that tears appeared in her eyes and Denise began to sob. Trying to readjust herself from her sitting position she slipped and slumped face down on the wooden floor. As she lay there trying to compose herself, she suddenly became aware of a noise. She strained her ears to listen.

Although the sounds were muffled and sounded as if they were coming from somewhere outside, it slowly became apparent that she was listening to two people talking. She couldn't quite hear what was being said but it was definitely two male voices. Denise tried to call out through the masking tape that was wrapped over her mouth and she repeatedly raised both legs and stamped her feet on the floor but it was to no avail.

Within a few minutes she was exhausted. She listened to the voices until they began to fade, as if whoever it was began to walk away. Denise pulled herself into the foetal position before weariness overtook her and she fell into another restless sleep.

97

When WPC Alison Bolt arrived at Abbey House, the front door was wide open. She stuck her head inside and called out and waited for a reply. Receiving none she stepped inside the hall and closed the door quietly behind her. As she called out again she thought she could hear voices coming from the back of the property. She made her way towards the door at the far end of the hall and slowly turned the handle.

Peering around the door Alison watched and listened to the on-going argument between Penny and Michael who were completely oblivious to her presence.

'You don't even tell me you have a child and yet you ask me for help because you receive a bloody ransom note,' Michael bellowed.

'So who should I ask? I thought you were my husband. Isn't that what husbands do? Help their wives in times of trouble.'

'So I'm your loving husband now, am I? You didn't want to know me just an hour ago and it was only a couple of days ago you accused me of have an affair.'

'Something you know is true,' Penny replied prodding Michael on the shoulder. 'Oh you denied it, I knew you would but I have proof. You'll see,' she shouted in his face.

Michael raised his arm as if to strike out.

'I wouldn't do that if I were you,' said WPC Bolt as she strode across the room. Michael turned to face her, anger stretched across his face.

'Who the hell let you in?' he asked.

'I let myself in. The front door was wide open.'

She now stood face to face with Michael who was shaking with rage.

'I suggest you calm down, Mr Westbrook, unless that is you wish to accompany me to the station where we can discuss this matter in more detail.'

He tried to out stare her but Alison had far more experience in confrontational situations than he had vouched for. A grin came to his face and suddenly he started to laugh. He turned away before facing her again.

'You women are all the same. You make me sick,' he said and threw the piece of paper he had been clutching on the floor and walked out of the room.

'Are you OK ma'am?' Alison asked Penny.

'I'm fine,' she stammered. 'I'm so sorry you had to witness our argument and experience Michaels temper.'

'I've been in worse situations,' Alison replied.

Penny managed a smile as she wiped the tears from her face.

'Let's go through to the kitchen. I'll make some tea. God knows I need a drink.' She led the way out of the room, across the hall and into kitchen.

Alison excused herself, asking for the toilet whilst Penny made the tea. She used her time away to do a quick search of all the downstairs rooms but there was no sign of Michael. When she returned to the kitchen it was apparent that Penny had been crying again. Her eyes were red and swollen and her cheeks were flushed.

'Penny, come and sit down. Let me finish making the tea,' Alison said and directed Penny to a chair.

'Thanks, you must think I'm silly. I can't stop crying,' Penny said with a sigh.

'Not silly at all. In fact, if it was my daughter being held by someone, I think I would be hysterical.'

'Oh, how stupid of me. I haven't even showed you the ransom note.' Penny reached into her cardigan pocket and extracted the piece of paper that Michael had earlier thrown on the floor in the library.

Alison placed two cups down on the kitchen table and pulled up a chair opposite Penny. She took the note from Penny's shaking hand and started to read. After a couple of minutes she folded the note and handed it back to Penny, who was sat staring into space, holding her cup of tea with both hands.

'Have you any idea who could have sent this? Inspector Wesley will want to see it. Do you still have the envelope it arrived in?'

Penny nodded her head and pursed her lips.

'Yes it's over there on the Welsh Dresser.'

OK, let's leave it there for the moment; we'll get it checked out for fingerprints. The note gives the impression that whoever wrote it, believes you own a share of the estate, and assumes you're a wealthy woman.'

'Hmm. I guess it does,' Penny replied shrugging her shoulders.

'Is that not the case? I don't wish to be rude or imply anything but living here and being married to Michael must surely mean that you have no money worries.'

'We're comfortable if that's what you mean. But Michael has made some bad business investments over the years so we're not quite as well off as we may appear and when his father died there were several areas of the house in complete disrepair. As you know, the East Wing is still closed off for that very reason.'

'Are you saying that Michael has debts?'

Penny seemed lost in thought.

'Penny?'

'Oh sorry. I was miles away. I really don't know. Michael keeps his finances quite close to his chest but I've heard him arguing with the bank a few times about keeping up repayments or something or other.'

Alison paused for a moment thinking how she should change the approach to her questions. She'd already made a mental note to check Michael's finances.

'Penny, this may seem like a silly question but do you have any idea who may be holding Denise?'

'No. That's what frightens me the most. It's the not knowing where she is or who she's with. If I knew who she was with I think I could handle it better. I know that probably doesn't make sense but it's just the way I feel.'

'I think I understand,' Alison replied taking a sip of her tea.

'The Inspector has told me how you had Denise adopted but have made contact with her in recent years. Is there any possibility that Denise's father could have taken her?'

'I think we can rule that out. You see, when I split up with James, I never knew I was pregnant.'

She hesitated for a moment as if unsure she should reveal her next statement.

'I never told James that he was a father and he was the kind of the person who had no interest in being one either. He would have pressured me into having an abortion.'

She placed her cup down and rested her elbows on the table. Placing her hands over her eyes she sobbed uncontrollably as her whole body racked with grief for the second time that day. Alison walked around the table and placed reassuring hands on Penny's shoulders.

'It's OK. Let it all out. You'll feel better for it,' she said.

98

Jane opened the front door to find Jenny Stevens standing there with a suitcase in her hand. It was obvious the girl had been crying. Her eyes were red and mascara had run down her face.

'Oh my dear, what on earth is wrong? Do come in.'

Jane led the way into the kitchen at the back of the cottage, telling Jenny to leave her suitcase in the hall.

'Come and sit down my dear.'

'I'm so sorry for coming round without telephoning you first. I have no one else to talk to and there are things that people need to know.'

'Jenny I'm pleased that you chose to come here but shouldn't you be talking to my husband?'

'No, I mean, well, maybe but I thought you would understand better. I know you saw me leaving Kelvin's flat. I just need to explain a few things. I expect you have already told Mr Wesley that you saw me.'

'I did mention it to him. I thought it was particularly strange that someone would want to visit the poor man's flat, especially after his death and knowing that it was empty.'

'Not if it was your Uncle's,' Jenny replied clutching her bag with both hands.

Alison met Wesley by the entrance to Abbey House and brought him up to date with details of the ransom demand.

'Thanks Alison. I'll go and talk to Penny. While I do that, find Michael for me. I need to talk to both of them together while I'm here.'

'Sure thing.'

'Oh and one other thing. I want you to witness our conversation.'

Wesley found Penny in the library. She was standing looking out of the window across the landscaped gardens. He coughed politely.

'Oh Inspector, it's good to see you.'

She walked across the room and took one of his hands in both of hers.

'I assume Alison has shown you the ransom demand?'

'Yes, she has. Shall we sit down?'

Penny sat in one of the wing backed chairs that surrounded the small mahogany table whilst Wesley sat in the matching chair opposite.

'Penny, I've been involved in a number of kidnappings and ransom demands in my career and I've learnt that my initial instincts are usually correct. I honestly believe that Denise is still alive and that whoever is holding her doesn't mean her any harm.'

'Do you really believe that Inspector?'

'Yes I do.'

'Then why is she being held captive?' Penny asked clutching at the arms of the chair. 'Why would someone want to kidnap my little girl?'

'That we don't know but we will find out, we'll find her. I have most of the local force looking for her. Penny, listen to me, I'm more than convinced now that Denise is being held as a bargaining tool. Whoever is holding her knows that you'll do anything to get her back even if that means agreeing to what may well seem unfair or unrealistic ransom demands.'

At that point there was a knock on the door.

'Come in,' Wesley called out.

Michael was led into the room by Alison, who closed the door behind her and stood back.

'What the hell is all this about?' Michael demanded striding across the room.

'Mr Westbrook. Pull up a chair,' said Wesley without looking up.

'I've got better things to do other than...'

Wesley stood up and stopped him in mid conversation.

'That was an order Mr Westbrook.'

'Well it's damn inconvenient,' Michael replied grabbing a chair from the far wall. Wesley didn't reply immediately. He waited until Michael was seated before staring into Michael's face. The man seemed to visibly shrink under Wesley's stare.

'Kidnapping, ransom, murder, theft, fraud. I'm afraid they're all inconvenient but it's my job to investigate them. It's my job to find out who the guilty party is. It's my job to protect innocent people like your wife and that is exactly what I intend to do. My priority right now is to get Denise back safe and sound. I would prefer to do it with your help but I'm just as happy if you don't want to assist us.'

Michael sat with arms folded.

'I still don't see how I can help so can we get on with it?'

Wesley took a deep breath, trying to compose himself. His dislike of Michael Westbrook was growing by the minute.

'First of all, just for your information. I've already informed your wife that we're doing all we can to find out who is holding Denise and where.'

'Well it's good to know the police are doing something.'

Wesley ignored the remark and extracted a set of drawings from a plastic wallet he'd been carrying under his arm.

'Take a look at these items and tell me if you've seen them before.'

He handed one of the drawings to Penny and another to Michael and watched for their reactions. Penny looked at the drawing on her lap and Wesley could see the immediate recognition on her face. Michael glimpsed at the one he was holding and shrugged his shoulders.

'Pieces of furniture. What do you want me to say?' he asked.

'Do you recognise them?'

'Can't say that I do.'

'And you Penny? Do you recognise them?'

She hesitated, looking towards Michael before speaking.

'I think….'

'Oh come on,' Wesley interrupted. 'You both know that one of these items is standing in your hallway and in the other is in the front parlour above the fire place. I've seen them. One is a vase and the other is a tapestry.'

'I don't know what you're getting at?' Michael said pursing his lips. 'What have these things got to do with a missing woman?'

'That's what I'm trying to find out,' Wesley replied.

'I'll leave you with this thought shall I? Both items are artefacts dating back several centuries. Items that were believed to be lost when this area flooded over two hundred years ago and yet here they are in your house. Now we have a ransom note that suggests you have something of interest to someone. I do hope you can provide me with an explanation.'

Wesley stood to leave. He directed his next sentence to Penny.

'Penny, Alison will remain here with you until WPC Tredwell arrives later on. Please give some thought to what I've just said.'

He then turned to face Michael.

'Think about what I said. I'll expect an answer from you in the morning. Don't worry, Mr Westbrook, I'll see myself out.'

'I told you we should never have displayed those damn things in the house,' Penny shouted as soon as Wesley had left the room.

WPC Bolt was listening from the hallway having just left Wesley by the front door.

'You never did tell me where you bought them from. It must have been some dodgy dealer if they're historical artefacts. Why do you always have to deal with rogues?'

Michael started laughing which only fired her temper even further.

'How can you find this so amusing when the police are asking questions?' she screamed.

Michael wiped the smile from his face. His jaw tensed and he looked scornfully down his nose at her.

'It was your father who found the artifacts. It was your father who found them when we had the Chalice Well dug out. Now you have to admit that's rather funny.'

The colour drained from Penny's face as she stared in disbelief.

'I don't believe you.'

Michael shrugged his shoulders and walked across the room to stand by the bay window that looked out across the front of the estate.

'I'm afraid it's true, Penny dearest. Your father was as big a crook as anyone.'

She was about to interrupt but he waived his arm to silence her.

'Eddie knew this place and the grounds like the back of his hand. He ought to; he'd laboured on both for most of his life.

A few years ago, after excavating part of the Chalice Well which runs under the gardens, he struck gold. Well, what he thought was gold. In fact, what he had stumbled upon were four items that would have archaeologists appearing from across the world if the story got out. However, the objects were of no great interest to Eddie, all he wanted to know was what their value was.'

'And you stitched him up?'

'Penny, I actually did him a favour.'

'Oh yeah how do you work that out?'

'I paid your father a couple of thousand pounds and planned to sell them on. Well, he'd never had that kind of money before so as soon as I offered him the money, he gratefully accepted.'

Penny gave him an ice cold stare.

'And what's the true value of them?' she asked folding her arms.

'A million? A lot more than that probably but I couldn't let the items go on the open market. That would be too dangerous, it would start ringing alarm bells somewhere.'

'So what did you do?'

'I marketed the items abroad under a different name. They were snapped up within hours.'

'So why are they still here?'

'The tapestry and the vase are both in need of major repair but their authenticity is obvious with King Arthur's emblem emblazoned on them.'

'Do you mean you've sold part of England's heritage to some unknown foreigner just for financial gain?'

'Oh come on. Don't give me all that crap. I'm not the first person and definitely won't be the last to make a few bob from our predecessors.'

'You make me sick, so what are you going to do with these items that the Inspector has identified eh? Go on, answer that.'

'I'll just say they were a present from your father.'

'What?'

'Well they were. He found them. The Inspector doesn't have to know that I paid him any money for them and if he asks, we don't know where Eddie found them.'

'So if you've sold them, why are they still here?'

'Because I have to wait for the right time before they are released to the outside world.'

'Oh Michael, what have you done? You know the Inspector won't believe a word of this.'

Michael walked back across the room to where Penny stood by the fireplace. He placed his hand on her jaw and she felt the pressure of his fingers squeezing her face.

'He'll believe me because you'll back me up,' he sneered.

Releasing his grip he pushed her face sideways.

'Don't be foolish enough to tell the police anything different.'

Michael left the room and left Penny leaning back on the mantelpiece. She was shaking from head to foot and in desperate need of a drink.

He strode across the hall and out of the front door. He didn't see WPC Bolt stood by the kitchen doorway.

99

Wesley stood next to Carl Bradshaw. Carl was one of the best forensic guys Wesley had come across in all his years in the force. Carl and his team had just returned from Abbey House. Forensic tests confirmed that Denise and her captor must have gained entry below the East Wing of Abbey House via the tunnel. There was no evidence to suggest they had been anywhere else in the property.

Carl was now examining the blackmail note and the envelope that Penny had received.

'So what's your opinion?' Wesley asked.

'Well the print comes from a Xerox 4500 printer, quite an old one. It's the type of printer they used back in the mid to late nineties.'

'So it's used for large quantity printing. Is that what you're saying?'

'Yeah. That's correct Inspector.'

'What about the hand writing on the envelope?'

'That's rather confusing. My immediate reaction is that it's a woman's handwriting but whoever it is has tried to disguise it.'

'What makes you say that?'

'Take a look at the two N's in Penny. Now compare them with the N in Glastonbury. The Y's are different too. Someone is making a real effort to confuse us and to conceal themselves.'

'OK. Thanks Carl. Give me a call if you come up with anything else.'

'There's one thing I would suggest before you go.'

'What's that?'

'Contact Xerox. Find out if there are any local companies who had these printers installed. I know it's a long shot as we're talking several years ago but it's worth a shot.'

Wesley nodded.

'Good call. Yeah I'll do that.'

Back in the car, Wesley put a call through to the station and asked the duty officer to transfer him to the office. The phone rang four times before anyone answered.

'WPC Tredwell speaking.'

'Mandy. It's John.'

'Hi, Sir. How can I help?'

'I want you to drive over to Abbey House later. Speak with Alison and agree a time to take over from her. I want you to stay with Penny Westbrook for a while. She's in a bit of a state and Michael Westbrook isn't exactly helping the situation.'

'I understand. Yes of course.'

'Thanks. Right now though, I need information from Rank Xerox, the photocopier and printing company. I want to know if they ever sold any Xerox 4500 commercial printers to companies in the Glastonbury area. If so, to whom and when? It's a bit of a long shot as this range of printer was being marketed twenty years ago.'

'Sure thing Inspector. Anything else?'

'Yeah, make sure someone puts the kettle's on. I'll be back in half an hour.'

When he arrived back at the station he was advised that the press had been congregating outside Patricia Smiths house and the poor woman was becoming more and more distressed.

After contacting Bath HQ to arrange for two support officers to deal with the press he asked Mandy to pop in to see Patricia on her way to Abbey House.

100

Sally had read the note that David had left saying he'd gone to meet Inspector Wesley and would be back sometime in the afternoon. She went into the bedroom and reached under the bed grabbing the sports bag. A few minutes later, she had emptied the contents into the washing machine. It would all be washed, ironed and put away before David got home.

'Damn', she said to herself when she noticed the trail of mud around the flat. Taking off her shoes, she put them in a plastic bag and threw them in the wardrobe. Rummaging through her handbag she located her mobile to phone her mother. The phone only rang twice before her father answered.

'Hello.'

'Hi, Dad, it's Sal.'

'Hello darling. Where have you been? Mum's been worried.'

'I'm sorry but works been real busy. The days go so quick. You know what it's like.'

'But we even phoned you at the flat.'

Sally bit her lip and hesitated before answering.

'Oh, I forgot to tell you, because I've been working such long hours, trying to get this project completed, I've been staying at The Balmoral two nights a week. It's only one stop from Canary Wharf on the DLR.'

'Oh right. Sal, don't take this the wrong way, we know you're not a child any more but just tell us where you are and that you're OK. You know how Mum worries.'

'I know. Sorry Dad. Anyhow how is she?'

'She's fine. She's gone round to see Auntie Mary. Her neighbour phoned us yesterday to say that Auntie has had another fall.'

'Should she still be on her own?' Sally asked.

'Probably not Sal. I know the doctor has applied for her to go into sheltered accommodation but there's a long waiting list I'm afraid.'

'Oh OK. Listen, Dad, tell Mum I'll phone tonight. I won't forget and don't worry about me. I'm fine.'

'I know darling. Look after yourself. Love you.'

'Love you too.'

Sally hung up and tried David's number but it went straight through to his answer phone. She checked her watch, it was only just midday. David probably wouldn't be back for several hours yet. Sally thought she would give him a surprise and cook dinner so after checking her purse to make sure she had cash on her, she grabbed her jacket and keys and headed into town to buy food and a bottle of wine. Work had been unbearable for the past few days so she intended on making the most of her time back in Bath.

101

'Oh Jenny, I had no idea.'

Jane put her arms around Jenny as the young woman began to sob. It took her more than five minutes to calm her down. The poor girl was shaking and looked at the point of desperation. Jane handed her a box of tissues and left the kitchen to pour her a strong drink. She was just returning to the kitchen with a large brandy when Wesley walked in the front door.

'Blimey. You've started early today,' he said kissing her on the cheek.

When he saw the look of concern on her face, he knew something was wrong.

'It's Jenny Stevens. She's in the kitchen. She's really upset. It appears that Kelvin Ward was her Uncle.'

'What?'

'I know I was surprised when she told me.' Jane put her hand on Wesley's arm. 'Go easy with her John. She looks as if she could crack any minute.'

Wesley entered the kitchen to see Jenny sat at the table staring into space, her elbows on the table and her head resting in her hands. With puffed up red eyes and crimson cheeks she looked like a young child who had just been scalded by her parents.

'Hello Jenny,' he said pulling up a chair alongside her. She turned to look at him. There was vacant look in her eyes and despair written across her face.

'Mr Wesley.'

He put his hand on her arm and she automatically lent into him, her head resting on his shoulder. He looked up at Jane as Jenny sobbed uncontrollably.

'I'll go and make a bed up. I think it'll be best if she stays here tonight,' Jane whispered and placing the glass of brandy on the table left the room.

Jenny sat up and dabbed her eyes with a tissue.

'Have a sip my dear,' he said handing her the glass.

Jenny took the glass in trembling hands and drank a little of the brandy. She grimaced as the liquid seemed to burn her throat and gave a little cough.

'Thanks. I don't know what you must think of me. I mean, it's been weeks since Uncle Kelvin died and yet, it's only just sunk in.'

'It's not uncommon,' Wesley replied taking his tobacco out of his pocket.

'Do you smoke? I only have roll ups I'm afraid.'

'No, but thanks,' Jenny replied managing a little smile. She watched Wesley expertly roll a cigarette between his fingers.

'I used to watch my grandpa roll his own cigarettes. Nan would tell him off because he would never brush the flakes of spare tobacco off the dinner table.'

'I have to admit, it's something that gets right up Jane's nose,' he replied with a grin. There was an awkward silence between them for a moment before Jenny spoke.

'I think I owe you an explanation Mr Wesley.'

'There are a few things I'd like to ask you.'

'They can wait until the morning,' Jane interrupted as she entered the kitchen. 'I've made a bed up for you in the spare room. You can stay here tonight then in the morning, I'll leave you and John to have a nice little chat.'

'Oh I couldn't impose, really, it's OK.'

'Once Jane has made up her mind, there's no changing it,' said Wesley. 'Have a lay down, you look exhausted, if I may say so. We can talk in the morning.'

Jenny looked at Wesley then at Jane. A tired, beaten expression etched on her face.

'Come on love, I'll show you to your room,' said Jane. Jenny followed her towards the hallway.

'We'll talk in the morning Mr Wesley,' Jenny said stopping to turn around. 'There are things I need to tell you.'

Wesley nodded and watched as Jane led her up the stairs.

It was only seven-thirty in the morning when Jane entered the kitchen and she was surprised to find Jenny already stood at the cooker.

'Good morning,' said Jenny turning around and looking embarrassed. 'I was going to make breakfast for everyone but I couldn't figure out how to operate the cooker. It's different to the electric one at Abbey House.'

'Come on, move over,' Jane replied laughing. 'You make the tea and butter some bread and I'll rustle up some egg and bacon.'

'OK, you're the boss.'

By the time Wesley appeared in the doorway, still in his dressing gown, the two women had prepared breakfast.

'I was just going to call you downstairs,' said Jane as she placed his plate on the table. 'You can thank Jenny for the tea.' She winked across the table to Jenny.

'Good morning my dear.' He pulled up a chair next to her.

'Did you sleep alright?'

'Yes, thank you Mr Wesley. I didn't think I would sleep so well.'

'Well you obviously needed it,' said Jane.

The three of them ate in silence until breakfast was finished. Jane was the first to speak as she stood and gathered the empty plates.

'I'll wash up while you and John go into the sitting room where you can talk in private.'

'Are you sure Jane? I don't mind washing up.'

'Off you go, before I change my mind,' Jane replied smiling.

Wesley motioned for Jenny to sit on the settee as he made himself comfortable in his favourite chair.

'Tell me all about it.' Wesley began to roll a cigarette.

Jenny took a deep breath and sank back into the settee.

'As you now know, Kelvin Ward was my Uncle.'

Wesley acknowledged by nodding his head.

'So when did you first know your Uncle was living in Glastonbury?' Wesley asked lighting his cigarette and tossing the used match into a glass ashtray.

'He turned up one Saturday afternoon a couple of years ago at our home in Swindon. He'd fallen on bad times and asked Mum to lend him money. I heard them arguing in the kitchen.'

She paused for a moment as if recalling the scene. When she looked up there were tears in her eyes. 'He left by the back door that day. I never saw him again until last year.'

'Did you know he was living in Glastonbury?'

'Yes, he never made any secret of where he lived not to me in any case. I phoned him just over a year ago to tell him that Mum had passed away after a sudden illness.'

'I'm sorry,' said Wesley.

'It was a blessing in the end. She'd had a stroke. She was really a shell of the woman I'd grown up with. Then one morning the hospital phoned to say she'd had a fatal heart attack.'

Jenny ran her fingers through her hair and flicked it away from the side of her face.

'Kelvin was good. He paid for everything. You see, I was on my own. My own father disappeared when I was an infant. Anyhow, after the funeral Uncle Kelvin asked me what I was going to do. I had no idea at the time.' She shrugged her shoulders.

'Anyway, two days later he called me and said that the Westbrook's were looking for a housekeeper. The rest is history.'

Wesley sat forward and rubbing the remains of his cigarette between his fingers, dropped the few remaining tobacco flakes into the ashtray.

'Jenny, I know you've been through a tough time but I have to ask you if you know what your Uncle was involved in. I know he owned the bookshop. I'm not interested in that but I do need to know why you were in his flat the other day and what was his relationship was with Penny Westbrook.'

A smirk came to Jenny's face.

'Well, as far Penny is concerned, yes, they were seeing one another.'

She watched Wesley's reaction as he raised his eyebrows.

'Come on Mr Wesley, don't look so shocked. You've met Michael a few times. Can you blame her for looking elsewhere?'

'I can imagine he's hard to live with,' he replied.

'That's an understatement. He watches her every move, day and night.'

'That's an excuse for having an affair?'

Jenny grinned. 'No it's not but it would be a release from the prison he tries to keep her in.'

Wesley sat back in his chair, deep in thought. It seemed a fair enough explanation but there was something missing, something he couldn't put his finger on.

'You haven't told me what you were doing in Kelvin's flat.'

'I'll come to that in a moment. I noticed a change in Uncle Kelvin. Something was bothering him he seemed distracted, like he'd lost something or even stumbled upon something. Whatever it was, it certainly bothered him.'

'So what happened?'

'One afternoon I followed Penny out the house. I'd heard her talking to him on the phone. Her voice was quite animated.'

'Do you think Michael knew about Penny's relationship with Kelvin?'

'He knew.'

'You sound very sure about that,' said Wesley.

Jenny's face reddened. Wesley nodded in recognition of the situation.

'You told him, didn't you?'

Jenny put her hands to her face. When she looked up there was a glazed look in her eyes.

'Michael and I had an affair. It's over now but, yes I told him. I was angry. Angry because Penny was using Uncle Kelvin.'

'Using him? In what way?'

'Oh he thought she really fancied him and she laid it on thick but she was using him to find out what he had discovered about her family history.'

'Family history? Sorry Jenny but you've lost me now.'

'I can explain better by taking you there,' Jenny answered.

'Take me where?'

'It's a house in Havering. The place is empty but I found a clue there as to what Uncle Kelvin was looking for.'

'OK. Let me phone the station first. You grab your things. I hope this is important Jenny not just some idle ramble out into the countryside.'

102

PC Martin Philips was lent on the reception counter reading the local newspaper when Dorothy walked into the station. She gave a polite cough to attract his attention.

'Good morning, Mrs Hallerton,' said Martin looking slightly embarrassed.

'Oh call me Dorothy please. Is the Inspector in his office?'

'I'm afraid not. Can I be of help?'

She retrieved a bundle of papers tied together with a couple of thick rubber bands from her shopping bag.

'Are you any good at reading accounts?'

'Accounts? Well, err, probably not. What is it you're exactly trying to read?'

Dorothy removed the elastic bands and quickly flicked through half a dozen pages before stopping at a page where a yellow sticker had been placed.

'I found these in the back of our wardrobe. They appear to be Eddie's old accounts but what I don't understand is why he's put a line through some of the items. These ones here,' she said running her finger down the page and pointing to a line that was almost obliterated by red pen.

Martin squinted to try and read what the item read as but it was almost impossible to decipher.

'I'm sorry Dorothy but Eddie's writing is hard enough to read without a thick red line running through it. Why the interest though?' he asked.

'Because, whatever it is is repeated every so often and the amount is always the same.'

She flicked through several other pages where she'd placed a sticker.

True enough, the same entry was there but almost erased by a thick red line.

'Have you thought of asking an accountant?'

'Oh no, I don't think that would be a good idea,' she replied. 'My Eddie was always a bit of a wheeler dealer, if you know what I mean. I don't want some smart accountant to suddenly find something untoward.'

Martin smiled. He found it amusing that Dorothy trusted the local police enough to ask them to look at Eddie's accounts but wouldn't dream of asking an accountant for help in case Eddie had been involved in something dodgy.

'Oh well. I suppose it's nothing important. I mean, if Eddie owed people money, they would have asked for it by now wouldn't they?'

'I expect they would,' Martin replied watching for her reaction.

Dorothy tidied up the pages and rewrapped them with the rubber bands.

'I'll tell you what I'll do. Leave them with me and when the Inspector arrives I'll ask him to take a look. He's usually good at that sort of thing. God knows how he reads the finance stuff he gets given from Head office.'

'Are you sure? I don't want to be a nuisance. It's probably nothing but I do so hate not knowing if everything is alright.'

Martin reassured her that Wesley would be able to help and he put the papers into the Inspector's in-tray under the counter.

'Don't worry, I'll hand the inspector the papers myself. They're safe here.'

'Thank you so much,' she replied. Checking her pockets to make sure she had everything, she then hesitated for a second before saying goodbye.

103

The ten mile drive to Havering took nearly thirty minutes. The early morning wind and rain had blown leaves and branches across the country lanes. Jenny continually swore at other drivers as they repeatedly found themselves stuck behind someone who was dawdling along, either lost or looking for signposts or both. When they eventually pulled into the un-adopted road on the edge of Havering village there were pot-holes everywhere full with rain water. Jenny carefully avoided the puddles before bringing the car to a halt. Unlike her last visit, Jenny parked the car directly outside the cottage.

Opening the garden gate, she suddenly stopped and gasped, pointing towards the cottage. Wesley looked to where she was pointing. The small glass pane in the top of the front door was broken and the front door stood open. Wesley put his hand on her shoulder.

'Wait here.'

The wind had left leaves piled up on the doorstep but there remained distinctive footprints going in and out of the property. He tried not to disturb them too much as he gently pushed the door. He stepped directly into the front room, the staircase facing him. The room was empty except for a small table that had been upturned and one of the legs broken off.

Jenny appeared behind him.

'I'm sorry. I was frightened standing by the gate on my own.'

Wesley took a few strides forward and peered into the tiny scullery but it was also empty.

'I'm going to look upstairs. Please, wait here. You're safe in here.'

'OK.'

Wesley mounted the stairs, taking the bedroom to the left first. Again, there was nothing to be found. He crossed the stairs into the other bedroom and almost stumbled over the body.

He tensed as he immediately recognised the light grey overcoat. Bending down, he felt for a pulse before turning the body over. The sightless eyes of Harvey White stared into oblivion. Wesley felt again for a pulse but knew it was pointless. The body was already cold.

He slipped in his hand to search the inside pocket and withdrew it immediately as his hand touched something cold. Unbuttoning two buttons of the overcoat; he pulled the coat open to expose the handle of the knife that had been buried deep into Harvey White's chest. Hence there was little blood.

Wesley recovered the handle with Harvey's coat and stood up, reaching for his mobile phone. PC Adam Broad answered the call.

'Hi Adam. Get the SOCO team over to Havering. I've just found Harvey White, he's been stabbed,' he said giving the exact address. 'We'll need the place cordoned off to the public too.'

As he turned to leave the room, Jenny screamed.

She was stood at the top of the stairs, staring at Harvey's corpse.

104

As soon as David turned the key in the lock he could hear the shower running.

'I'm so pleased you're back,' David shouted knowing that Sally must be in the bathroom. 'I didn't expect you until tomorrow at the earliest.' He looked around the room.

'You've managed to walk mud right through the flat,' he said following the trail from the front door through into the lounge.

'Sorry,' Sally shouted above the noise of the shower. 'I'll hoover up in a minute.'

When Sally walked into the kitchen she found David preparing dinner.

'Sorry darling. I didn't know you would be home so soon. I thought you were going to meet Inspector Wesley then pop into town.' She reached out to kiss him. She only had a towel wrapped around her and her long black hair was still soaking wet as she wrapped her arms around his waist. She pressed herself against him as their tongues explored one another's mouths and she was soon aware of his excitement.

Un-wrapping the towel, she let it fall to the floor and led David into the bedroom.

'So what did you find by the Abbey?' Sally asked a short while later.

'Well I had planned to go into town but I spent longer than expected over at the Abbey grounds, in fact, we found an underground crypt.'

Sally stiffened a little and looked up.

'A crypt? Wow. That must have been exciting. Did you discover anything in it?'

'Unfortunately no. Well, Inspector Wesley and one of the lads from the council actually entered the crypt but they said it was bare.'

'Oh, how strange, but how did anyone know the crypt was there in the first place?' she asked playing with the hairs on his chest.

David explained the story about the Vesica Piscis and where Dorothy believed the crypt and the Well interlocked.

He also informed her about Harvey Whites interest. Sally pulled away from him and sat on the edge of the bed, staring out of the bedroom window that looked out across the university courtyard.

'What's wrong Sal?' he asked.

'It's nothing. I just had a nasty vision about a dark, damp, cold crypt.

Places like that scare me.'

'Sal, don't be silly. It's not as if you're ever going to be entombed in a crypt is it?' he laughed.

'Why don't you just leave this to the police? I know Colin was a friend but I think you're getting too involved.'

'Colin was a very good friend. I'll do whatever I can to help the Inspector to find out what bastard killed him.'

David threw back the bed clothes and made his way to the bathroom. It was the first time Sally had ever seen him angry.

105

Wesley was reading the pile of finance papers that had been dumped on his desk when Alison joined him and Jenny in his office. The young WPC placed a tray of tea and biscuits on the table.

'Where are the chocolate digestives then?' Wesley asked.

'Sorry but there are only bourbons left in the cupboard.'

Alison handed Jenny a cup which she gratefully accepted. The girl was still in a state of shock and her whole body seemed to tremble.

'Are you sure you don't want to see the police doctor?' Alison asked.

'No I'm fine really. It's just that I've never seen a corpse before, especially one with a knife sticking out of its chest.'

Alison grabbed her own cup and sat in the chair next to her, placing a reassuring hand on her arm. Wesley had lit his cigarette and sat blowing blue plumes of tobacco into the air. Alison gave a polite cough.

'Oh, sorry,' said Wesley sitting up straight and looking slightly embarrassed. 'I was just thinking over the morning's events.'

He had already brought her up to date in the corridor whilst Jenny had visited the toilet to be sick. Alison had only just returned from Abbey House where Mandy was now staying with Penny Westbrook.

'Jenny, I know this is difficult for you right now and that the discovery of Harvey White's body was a very unpleasant experience but I need you to tell me everything you know and why your Uncle Kelvin was using the house in Havering.'

'Before I do, who was Harvey White? What was he doing there?' she asked.

'Harvey White was helping us look for Denise Wright, the girl who has been missing for several days. Before he retired, he worked for the council's planning department and was a member of the local historical society. He knew Kelvin from their college days some years ago. He once told me that Kelvin had applied for permission to excavate a plot of land in Havering but this was refused by the council. We may never know what he was doing there or why. I was hoping that might be something you could shed some light on.'

'I'm sorry Mr Wesley but I've never met the man and hadn't even heard his name before today.'

'Hmm. Well it's something we'll need to investigate further. In any case, let's get back to our visit there this morning. When you entered the front room you exclaimed something was missing, a painting?'

Jenny took a sip of tea and cleared her throat.

'Yes. The last time I visited the house there was a painting hanging in the front room. It caught my attention because it was a painting of the property.'

'What was so special about that?' Alison asked.

'It wasn't so much the painting rather what seemed to be some sort of coded message written at the bottom near the edge of the frame.'

'What message?' Wesley asked sitting forward and placing his elbows on the table.

Jenny rummaged around in her handbag before extracting her diary. She leafed through a few pages before finding what she was looking for.

'Ah here it is. Southwest80mtrssoutheast50down2.'

Seeing the confused look on their faces she read it out twice.

'Let me explain,' she said. 'Like you, when I first read the message I couldn't make out what it was about, then it suddenly dawned on me that it was actually a set of directions.'

Seeing the blank stares from both Wesley and Alison she asked if she could draw a map on the wipe board behind where Wesley was sitting. Wesley obliged by moving aside as Jenny stood up, grabbed a marking pen and started to draw a basic outline of what she'd found on her previous visit. When she finished, she stood back to address them both.

'You see, if you go to the back of the property and walk for about eighty meters in a South Westerly direction, this takes you down the slope, across open land, before you enter Parsons Wood. Then as soon as you bear East, where the woods are at their thickest, fifty meters along you come to a steep drop.'

Wesley nodded to say he understood so far.

'Anyhow, I decided to climb down the slope at this point. I'd gone so far, so it seemed silly not to continue. Once I'd reached the bottom, after just a few yards I found myself in a clearing. It's almost like a valley as there are steep slopes on all sides. In any case, I'd only taken a couple of steps when I tripped over what I thought was a rock but after closer inspection I realised it was a headstone.'

'You mean, as in a graveyard?' asked Wesley.

'Yes. Although the bottom of the valley is quite flat it is somewhat overgrown. I started to clear away some of the foliage around me and within minutes I'd discovered another two headstones just protruding above the level of the floor. Of course I wasn't sure what to do next and didn't understand what I was supposed to be looking at.'

'I had wondered how you had managed to scratch yourself so badly,' said Alison. 'I mean, I couldn't help but notice the scars on your arms when we were in the toilet.'

'That's when I went down the slope. I slipped at one point and tumbled down the rest. Sorry Mr Wesley, I'm digressing. As I say, I found myself in the middle of an old graveyard that no one appears to have visited for years. It stands in a valley that sits above Glastonbury, just west of the town. I had no idea what I was supposed to be searching for when I suddenly thought of the coded message again. I then followed the same instructions from two corners of the graveyard and found nothing. However, it was third time lucky. This time, again following the same directions but from the West corner of the graveyard, I found myself standing in front of a tombstone that barely stood above ground level. It seemed smaller than most of the others around it and after getting down on my hands and knees to brush away the dirt and foliage, I found out why. The grave was that of a young child. A boy in fact, but the most interesting thing is the boy's name, Westbrook.'

'Westbrook?'

'Yes, Alfred Westbrook. I went to the Births, Deaths and Marriages place in town to find out more information. Apparently the boy died of polio when he was just four years old.'

'But why would anyone write a cryptic clue on an old painting, giving directions to a graveyard?'

'I've no idea Mr Wesley. I think that's a question you ought to ask the Westbrook's.'

'Hmm, perhaps you're right,' he replied opening his tobacco pouch.

Jenny placed both hands around her cup drank the tea.

'Are you aware that your Uncle Kelvin had a daughter?' Wesley asked watching for her reaction.

Jenny didn't answer immediately but stared across the table to where Wesley sat.

'Who said he had a daughter?'

'Harvey White told me that Kelvin had a daughter when he was in his teens.'

Jenny placed her cup on the table and ran her hands through her hair.

'He did have a daughter Inspector. You're looking at her.'

Wesley and Alison looked at one another in astonishment.

'But you said he was your Uncle,' Wesley replied.

'I grew up thinking he was my Uncle. That's what Mum told me. It wasn't until a couple of years ago when she passed away that I found out the truth.'

'Why would she say that?' Alison asked.

'Mum never really forgave Kelvin for walking out when I was two years old. I don't have any memory of my Dad at that age so when I saw him a few years later I had no reason to disbelieve that he was my Uncle. Mum always said that he had left because he couldn't handle the strain of being a parent.'

'So did you and Kelvin, I mean your Dad, talk about this?'

'Yes. One day just after she died he explained everything to me. He told me why he'd left home when I was a baby. I'd rather his reasons for that remain private.'

'I understand,' said Wesley. 'Did he ever tell you about his visits to Havering and what he was looking for?'

'No. I followed him and Penny there on a couple of occasions. I believe they originally used the place just to be alone.'

'But that doesn't explain the writing on the painting,' Alison exclaimed.

'I think Dad discovered the grave by accident and just thought it would be amusing to write down the directions somewhere. If he did it for other reasons then I don't know what they were.'

106

Jane had just returned to the kitchen when the phone rang.
'Hi,' said Wesley. 'How's my favourite girl?'
'Cut out the flattery. What do you want?' she asked laughing.
'You know me too well,' he replied coughing.
'Still on the roll-ups?'
He ignored her question.
'Jane, I need a favour.'
'You do surprise me. What is it?'
'Can you speak to Dorothy? I want to find out what it was exactly that Kelvin Ward requested Harvey White to authorise when he made an application for excavation work in Havering a few years ago. I believe Dorothy was part of the Somerset Levels and Moors Action Group in those days and being on the council committee too, she would have been party to the decision to reject Kelvin's application.'
'John Wesley. How on earth do I drop that kind of thing into a conversation?'
'I'm sure you'll find a way. You always do.'
He couldn't see the face that Jane pulled.

An hour later Wesley pulled the car up outside the terraced cottage and switched off the ignition. He made a quick call on his mobile to Jane informing her he would be home late.
Patricia Wright opened the front door in response to the continual ringing of the buzzer. The person Wesley saw when the door was pulled back had aged ten years in just a week.
'Mrs Wright. It's Inspector Wesley. I just popped by to see if you were OK.'
She stared at him for a moment as if she were lost in another world.
'Can I come in?' he asked.
'Oh hello Inspector, yes do come in. I'm sorry I'm not really with it today.'
She led the way towards the front room as Wesley closed the door. He was shocked to see the state of the room. The first time he had visited the house, the day following Denise's disappearance, he'd noticed how clean and tidy it was but today there were food wrappers, empty plates, newspapers and magazines littering the coffee table, settee and floor.

'Let me just make space,' she said moving a pile of washing from the settee. 'I'll put the kettle on.'

Wesley looked around the room whilst Patricia pottered around in the kitchen. It was apparent that the woman was struggling to come to terms with the situation. He made a mental note to arrange for WPC Tredwell to pay Patricia a visit.

When she re-entered the room it was obvious she'd been crying. Taking the tray from her, he made space on the coffee table and poured the teas as Patricia sat staring into space.

'What did you want to see me about?' she asked with a vacant look in her eyes. 'I know you haven't found Denise because you would have told me straight away.'

'No we haven't found her yet but we won't give up looking for her, you have my word on that.'

He paused, watching for Patricia's reaction. Holding her cup of tea in both hands she looked like someone who had admitted to defeat in that Denise would never be found. Wesley had seen a similar look on people's faces when they had just been convicted of murder. He knew he had to play his next move delicately.

'Patricia, what I've come to ask you about is something that happened in Street yesterday. I believe you were in the shopping centre. Am I correct?'

'Yes.'

'May I ask what the purpose of your visit was?'

'I don't understand.'

'Why did you visit the shopping centre? Were you meeting someone?'

Suddenly Patricia's cup dropped to the floor and she covered her face as the tears began to flow. Wesley put his own tea down and moved across the settee to comfort her.

'Oh Mr Wesley. I've been so stupid. I thought I would get Denise back.'

He handed her a handkerchief from his jacket pocket.

'Do you want to tell me about it?'

Patricia took a few moments to answer.

'Someone posted a note in the door.'

She extracted a piece of paper from her cardigan pocket. She handed it to Wesley who read the contents.

'Why didn't you tell me about this?' he asked reading the note.

Patricia waited for him to finish reading before replying.

'You saw what they wrote. If I told the police, I'd never see Denise again.'

Wesley could feel her body shaking.

'Patricia. Believe me, I understand what you're saying and in all honesty I don't know that I would have done anything different but you have to realise that you can't do this on your own. If you had told us, we could have watched from a distance and at least obtained video coverage if nothing else. There's no way we would jeopardise Denise's welfare.'

'I know Inspector but I'd do anything to get Denise back and I thought it was worth the chance. I'm so desperate to see her again.'

'I know from our chat on the telephone that you haven't heard from anyone since you left the ransom money in the litter bin. Two hundred pounds I believe.'

'Yes.'

Can you describe the person who collected the money bag?'

She shook her head.

'Only that it was some kid on a bike.'

'The person WPC Tredwell saw racing away on a bike was wearing a hood. Is that the person?'

'Yes.'

'WPC Tredwell was too far away to be able to confirm if it was a male or female. Although she did give chase, she lost the cyclist. The fortunate thing was that because she was off duty, she was wearing plain clothes, therefore even if the cyclist had turned around to see her, all they would have seen was a member of the public running after them.'

Wesley took hold of her hand as the tears started to well in her eyes again.

'Patricia, I will do everything I can to help bring Denise home safely but you have to trust me. Should anyone contact you, you must let me know immediately. Do I have your word?'

She reached across and wrapped both her hands around his.

'Yes,' she replied and closed her eyes as if she were trying to shut the world out.

'Yes I will.'

107

Denise stretched her legs. Each day now seemed to be more painful. The lack of exercise was beginning to tell on her health. She felt her pock marked skin, how the sores on her legs and thighs were now itching constantly and how her whole body ached continuously. Her eyes ached too, possibly due to the lack of daylight.

She reached forward to pick up the water bottle and raised it to her lips. It was empty. Her mouth was parched and the corners of her lips were cracked. She could taste blood.

Denise sat back against the wall and closed her eyes. She tried to think of warm sunny days and recalled her last holiday abroad in Zante where she spent a week by the pool, dressed all day in nothing but a swimsuit and flimsy clothes for evening wear. She remembered watching the entertainment team putting holiday makers through their paces in the mornings keep fit sessions. How the fat lady from Wales always fell over in the water when she raised her leg and the young girl from Swindon who was sunburnt after the first day.

A brief smile came to her face as she remembered Adrian. He was tall, muscular and the head of the keep fit team. She knew it was only a holiday romance and that he would be sharing someone else's bed as soon as she left but their time together was still magical. For her in any case.

108

It was 08:00am when Wesley entered his office. Mandy followed him in with a tray of teas and coffees. Alison, Martin and Adam were already seated awaiting Wesley's arrival. Wesley sat behind his desk and began to roll a cigarette whilst Mandy handed the drinks around.

He was just about to commence the meeting when a young cadet entered the room handing him a sheet of paper. Wesley read the contents and dismissed the young lad with a nod of the head. Folding the sheet of paper he dropped it onto his desk, his face grim.

'Bad news?' Adam asked.

'Yes,' he sighed. 'Patricia Wright was taken to hospital this morning complaining of chest pains. She's been kept in and is under observation.'

'Do you want me to go to the hospital?' asked Mandy.

'Yes, I think that's a good idea Mandy. You'd best call them first to check on her condition. Let me know what they say and if it's OK to see her then pop up this afternoon.'

'OK, before I go though, you asked me to find out if Rank Xerox had installed any Xerox 4500 printers in Glastonbury. Well we have one hit, the council offices. Xerox had a mega contract with Glastonbury council from 1987 to 1995 during which time six of them were purchased by the council.'

'Do they still have any now?'

'Apparently so. One still exists in the Records office. It's no longer covered by any maintenance agreement but according to the council it's still in use.'

'So do we have a list of employees who have access to the printer?'

'Hmm. That's the problem. Anyone can pay to enter the Records office to look at the microfiche or use the desktops to access archived information then print it off.'

'Yeah but there must be a record of people who pay to be granted access.'

Mandy smiled, holding up a wedge of pages.

'I've got a print out of the list here. It goes back as far as 1992 but the last page is the interesting one.'

She handed it across the table for Wesley to read.

Mandy had highlighted one name in particular. Harvey White.

After some debate amongst the team, Wesley continued.

'Have we had anything back from the lab yet?' he asked looking across the room to where Martin sat.

'According to Terry Austin, Harvey White died somewhere between six and eight a.m. yesterday morning. The stab wound pierced his heart and he would have died almost immediately.'

'Anything else?'

'Yes, Terry said he'd found coat hairs underneath Harvey White's fingernails.'

'Coat hairs?'

'Yes, apparently they match the coat Harvey was wearing. The strange thing is though, that there are none of these coat hairs to be found anywhere else in the house.'

Wesley sighed and ran a hand across his face.

'Anything else from forensics?'

'They've come up with little so far. There are no fingerprints on the blade handle or any of the furniture. It would appear that the murderer has covered their tracks well. What seems strange to me is that there's no sign of a struggle taking place. I mean, we all know Harvey White was no spring chicken and was bad on his feet but unless someone took him by surprise, he must have known his assailant.'

'Yeah, good call,' Wesley answered.

In the short time he'd known Martin; he was always the one person who seemed to be able to see beyond the evidence to date.

'So you believe that Harvey White knew his assailant?'

'Yes I do. Harvey was a big man and I don't think he would have let any stranger get that close to him. The forensic team have taken away the tools that were found in the bedroom for further analysis too,' said Martin.

'I still don't understand what Harvey White was doing there.

He must have spoken to someone, but if it wasn't Jenny, then who the hell was it?'

'Jenny said she never knew the man. Is that correct?' Alison asked.

'Yes, that's what she told me,' Wesley replied.

'In which case, one can only assume that Harvey White had previously followed either Kelvin or Jenny to the house.'

'Or knew where the house was to start with,' said Martin. 'Or even Penny. Didn't you say that Jenny had followed Kelvin and Penny there previously?'

'Yes she did.' Wesley leaned back in his chair and looked up to the ceiling. 'Also, when I think back, the first time I met Harvey he said that Kelvin had asked to be allowed to excavate in the village. I think that's something that requires further investigation.'

'What does that bloody Inspector want now?' Michael asked after Penny had replaced the telephone and explained what the call was all about.

'I'm not wasting time sat in the police station just because someone has been murdered and the local police have no idea who did it.'

'They want to speak with Jenny too.'

If Penny was looking for a reaction, she certainly got it.

'Jenny? Why on earth would they want to speak with her? She's never hurt anyone. She hardly ever leaves the house.'

'Why are you so damn protective of her? Or should I guess?'

'What's that supposed to mean?'

'You make me sick. You couldn't give a damn about the police asking me to go to the station. But oh no, not your precious, innocent Jenny.'

Jenny was stood at the top of the stairs, listening to their conversation. She returned to her bedroom and closed the door quietly.

109

Having spent an hour trawling through the internet, opening pages, dedicated websites and social network blogs regarding the Tor and Glastonbury Abbey, Wesley now stood looking at the wipe board. He knew there had to be a connection to the murders and felt sure there was a link to the missing girl but he just couldn't figure out what it was, or who it was. He read down the list to himself for the tenth time today.

Suzie Potter – University Lecturer - strangled
Kelvin Ward – Shop owner - throat cut
Eddie Hallerton – Maintenance man - broken neck
Harvey White – retired council employee - stabbed
Denise Wright – University student and part time shop worker - missing

He was deep in thought when Alison opened the door.
'Sorry to disturb you but I think you'll find this interesting.'
'What is it Alison?'
'There's a young woman in reception. Says she's just returned from holiday and has only just seen the news about Denise. She says she saw Denise standing opposite The Pilgrim public house on the night she disappeared. Says she was talking to a woman.'
Wesley jumped up from his chair.
'OK show her in.'
Alison returned a minute later introducing Gemma Yates.
The tall blonde haired woman was toned and tanned and impressed Wesley even before she spoke. She explained that she had flown out to Spain the morning that Denise had been reported missing and only arrived back in the country yesterday. Her mother had shown her the newspaper photograph of Denise just this morning.
She said that on the night that Denise disappeared, she and a group of friends had spent the evening in Glastonbury, mostly drinking in The Pilgrim. They left just after nine o'clock because Gemma and one of her friends had an early flight to catch the following morning.
'So you recognised Denise straight away?' Wesley asked.
'Oh yes, from the photo in the local paper. As soon as Mum showed me I recognised her immediately.'
'What made you notice her on the night?' Alison asked.

'To be honest I probably wouldn't have noticed her at all but for the fact that she was arguing with someone.'

'Arguing? You mean shouting?'

'I don't know if you'd call it shouting but there were certainly raised voices.'

'You say it was another woman she was arguing with?'

'Yes, older woman I would say.'

'What makes you think that?'

'The woman was wearing a headscarf and us younger girls don't wear them do we?' she replied looking directly at Alison.

'No, I don't suppose we do.'

Alison looked across the table to Wesley who was smirking.

'Could you describe the woman?' he asked.

'Sorry Inspector, but the answer to that is no. We only had a side view.'

'We?'

'Yes Helen Smith and I. Everyone else departed as soon as we came out of the pub but Helen and I stopped for a brief chat to confirm our arrangements for the following morning. You see, it was Helen who I went to Spain with. Oh, sorry I forgot to mention, she's still in Spain. She met up with this dishy young waiter and has decided to stay out there, for a while in any case. It probably won't last very long though. I'm afraid Helen is the type of girl who falls in love every time she goes on holiday. She just loves all the attention then gets bored.'

This time it was Alison's turn to blush. Wesley sat forward, resting his arms on the table.

'Gemma, is there anything you can think of that would help us identify this other woman?'

Gemma started to laugh.

'I'm sorry. What's funny?'

'No I'm sorry Inspector it's just the vision of the woman. It's not so much that she was wearing an old knee length mac, that's OK I suppose but what was strange were the plastic looking red boots.'

'Red boots?'

'Yes, that's what I thought,' said Gemma. 'They looked more like the kind of boots one would use for gardening.'

'Where did Denise and the woman go from there?'

'I have no idea Inspector. I said goodnight to Helen who left to walk in the opposite direction towards to the taxi rank and I walked to the other end of the town where my father was waiting to pick me up. Once we parted I didn't look back.'

There appeared to be nothing else to gain from further discussion so Wesley thanked Gemma for coming into the station and asked her to call him if she should think of anything else.

110

After waiting for the locksmith to open the front door, PC Martin Philips stepped into Harvey White's bungalow. Already several newspapers and a pile of mail were spread across the floor. He checked the mail for any personal looking letters but apart from a gas bill the mail contained mostly circulars. Throwing the mail on the small table where the house phone stood he knocked Harvey's private address book on the floor. Retrieving the book he placed it in his pocket to take back to the station.

The first room on the left was obviously Harvey's bedroom. Apart from a cardigan lying on the back of a standalone chair, it was clean and tidy. There was nothing to be found in the drawers of the dressing table and although the wardrobe was full of expensive looking suits and shoes, there was nothing of interest.

Coming out of the bedroom he crossed the hall to the bathroom where again apart from a large quantity of paracetamol there was nothing to be found. It was apparent that Harvey had lived well. The kitchen cupboards and fridge were well stocked with expensive foods.

I'm the wrong job, Martin thought to himself as he surveyed the range of cheeses in the fridge.

As soon as he entered the lounge he was taken in by the panoramic views from the back windows. The bungalows elevated position allowed for magnificent views across the Somerset levels.

The lounge was the only room that contained any photos. Martin studied the small assembly of photo frames that were lined up on the sideboard. Most were black and white and seemed to come from a bygone era. Groups of men and women dressed in pin striped suits and frocks. However, one photo stood out from the rest. It was a black and white photo of a young woman sat on a wooden bench. She was dressed in what appeared to be a white shirt and pleated skirt and was holding a collection of books on her lap. Something about the woman looked familiar.

It was the only other item that Martin took back to the station.

Martin walked into the reception area of the police station just as Alison came out of the back office.

'Hi Alison, where are you off to?'

'I'm just going to bring the car round to the front. Inspector Wesley and I are going over to Abbey House to interview Penny and Michael again.'

'Where have you been?'

'Over at Harvey White's place. Nothing to be found though except these.' He showed her the address book and photo.

'Who's the woman?'

'I don't know. Nearly all the photo's in Harvey's are black and white but this one looks older than most of the others.'

As he passed the photo over, it dropped on the floor, breaking the frame. He retrieved the pieces of the frame as Alison picked up photo which had landed face down. Alison examined the back, there was one word written on it. Dorothy.

'I don't understand,' said Alison studying the photo. 'Assuming this is Dorothy Hallerton, why would Harvey White have a photo of her? More importantly, why would Harvey have her photo displayed in his lounge?'

Wesley was just about to leave when his mobile rang. He checked the caller's number before answering.

'Well good morning Mrs Wesley. I assume you wish to speak with the light of your life. '

'Yes please. Could you go and find him,' Jane replied laughing.

'Love you too.'

The sudden change in tone in Jane's voice told him something wasn't right.

'John, I knocked on Dorothy's door on the way into the village but there was no reply.'

'Perhaps she's gone out?'

'But John, I told you. I popped round there yesterday too. There was no reply then either.'

'Could she have gone to stay with her sister again?'

'No. I mean, she hasn't. I called her sister just now. She says she hasn't spoken to Dorothy for several days.'

'Have you still got a key to the house?'

'Yes, but I can't just walk in. It's not right.'

Wesley rubbed the remains of his cigarette out between his thumb and forefinger. A habit that Jane constantly berated him about.

'Yeah I understand. We'll go over there this evening. I'm sure she's OK. Have you tried the neighbour?'

There were only two cottages at the top of lane then a gap of some two hundred yards before the next property.

'I didn't knock next door, although I did see Mrs Jenkins yesterday and she said that Dorothy hadn't turned up at the village hall the previous night to help with a charity event which she's involved in.'

Wesley had to admit that it all sounded a bit strange and knew that Jane was worried.

'As soon as Alison and I get back from Abbey House, I'll pick you up and we'll go over to Dorothy's.'

'Thanks John. It will put my mind at rest. You have to admit that it's strange that Dorothy has been missing since Harvey White was killed.'

Wesley stood looking out of the window. He took a few seconds to reply.

'I think it's just a coincidence Jane. I don't see what the connection could be.'

'I'm sure I don't know John.' There was a pause before she continued. 'So what's the reason for visiting the Westbrook's? Has there been a breakthrough?'

'I'd like to say there has, but nothing yet. I just want to ask Penny and Michael about a number of issues.'

'Oh OK darling. Take care. I'll see you at home.'

Wesley grabbed his coat from the back of the chair and walked out of the office. Pushing open the door to reception he almost bumped into Martin who was still in conversation with Alison.

'Take a look at this.' Martin showed him the photo.

Wesley shook his head, looking bewildered.

'I have a feeling it's going to be one of those days,' he said.

'What's up, Sir?' Alison asked.

He explained his conversation with Jane and the fact that Dorothy seems to have disappeared.

'Do you think it's just a coincidence? The fact that Dorothy is missing.'

'I don't know really but there are certainly a few questions that need answering. Like where is she? Why would Harvey have a photo of her in his bungalow? Finally, who the hell killed him.'

'This photo of her was taken when she was a young woman,' said Martin. 'I mean, it's not recent.'

'Well we know they worked together at the council many years ago and they both still belong to the several local groups. I'm beginning to wonder if there more than just a friendship between them,' Wesley commented.

'Do you think they were once an item?' Martin asked.

'You make them sound like a package,' said Alison, punching him on the arm.

Wesley sighed.

'Whatever term you want to use, I think there's more going on than meets the eye.'

Wesley handed the photo back.

'Was there nothing else to be found at Harvey's place?'

'Nothing. I checked everywhere. There were a number of personal items in the dressing table in Harvey's bedroom. I've got them in the car but there's nothing there of any real interest.'

'OK son, no worries. Hold the fort here for a while. Alison and I are going to have a chat with the Westbrook's.'

'Sure thing, see you later.'

111

As they were walking across the grounds towards Abbey House, Wesley took a call on his mobile.

'Hi, Sir, Adam here. I've just had Terry Austin on the phone from the lab. He's confirmed that Harvey White died from the stab wound, it pierced his heart. But he says he's confused as to the angle of the stab wound.'

'The angle of the wound? I don't understand.'

'That's all he said.'

'What about time of death?'

'Terry says he died around two hours before you found him.'

'So we only just missed his murderer.'

'It looks that way.'

Wesley stopped for a moment, deep in thought before answering.

'Right. Here's what we do. Get on to Bath HQ and ask for two PCs to meet you over at Havering. Carry out a house to house search. I know we've done it once but someone must have seen something. Havering is a tiny village of no more than thirty houses.'

'Sure thing.'

'Oh and something else. Contact all the local cab companies. Harvey White didn't drive, so someone must have taken him there.'

Wesley was getting impatient. They had rung on the doorbell twice and there was still no answer.

'I only spoke to Michael Westbrook a short while ago so I know they're expecting us,' Alison remarked.

Wesley banged his fist on the door and called out. They waited another minute before Wesley's patience snapped.

'Come on, we'll go around the back. There's an iron gate next to the Chapel that leads to the rear garden. Hopefully it's not locked.'

It wasn't. They entered a gravelled path that wound its way around the outside of the property, keeping the manicured lawn at bay.

'What's that noise?' It sounds like someone shouting,' Alison exclaimed as they rounded the corner of the house reaching the large patio area.

At the top of the steps, standing just inside the open French doors, Michael's raised voice could be heard. Just as they started to ascend the steps, someone screamed. Wesley and Alison ran up the steps towards the French doors. Pushing the left hand door aside, Wesley was the first to burst into the library.

'Over there!' Alison shouted.

Wesley looked across the room to the where the inglenook fireplace took centre stage. Michael had his hands around Penny's neck, choking her to death. He ran across the room and wrapped his arm around Michael's neck, using his weight to pull him backwards. Releasing his grip, Michael staggered backwards. In one swift movement, Wesley spun him around. A single punch to Michaels jaw sent him sprawling backwards into the mahogany book shelving. Taking a few steps forward Wesley stood looking down on the pitiful looking Michael as he sat on the floor cowering from what he thought was going to be another blow.

'Michael Westbrook. I'm arresting you for the attempted murder of your wife. Anything you say may be taken down and used as evidence in court. Do you understand?'

Michael sat on the floor with a frightened expression on his face.

'I said. Do you understand?' Wesley shouted. His face now just inches from Michael.

'Yes.'

In the meantime, Alison had sat a sobbing Penny on the settee.

'It's OK,' she reassured her, placing her arm around her shoulder. 'You're safe now.' She nodded to Wesley to say that all was OK who extracted his mobile from his coat pocket and put a call into the station.

Less than twenty minutes later, Michael was led away in handcuffs by two PCs from Bath HQ who had fortunately been in the area when the call came in.

Wesley and Alison were in the kitchen while Penny was being attended to in another room by her GP, who had arrived less than ten minutes after he'd been called.

'I wonder what triggered that?' asked Alison handing Wesley a cup of tea.

'I hate to say it but it doesn't come as much of a surprise.'

He took a sip of hot tea.

'Michael Westbrook is highly strung and is known to be taking drugs for depression and other illnesses.'

'I have to say; I was impressed in the way you got that punch in. You almost knocked Michael out.'

'Just luck Alison, he stuck his chin out at the wrong time,' Wesley replied with a wink. He then rolled a cigarette and sat silent for a few minutes whilst reflecting on the events of the past hour.

Alison returned to the kitchen after having had a brief chat with the doctor and provided Wesley with an update on Penny's condition.

'Alison, I want you stay here with Penny for a while. I'm going back to the station to speak with Michael. Give me a call if you need to speak to me or if there's anything else that Penny says you feel I ought to know about.'

Two hours later Wesley stood looking through the glass panel watching Michael Westbrook who was seated alone in the interview room. The man suddenly looked ill but Wesley wasn't yet convinced whether Michael was putting on an act or was really feeling the strain.

'Are we going in?' Adam asked approaching from the outer office.

'Yeah in a minute.' Wesley pointed to the roll up in his hand.

It was six pm and although it had already been a long day Wesley was in no mood to rush the interview.

'Any news about Dorothy?' Adam enquired.

'Nothing yet. Jane and I are going round to her place later to take a look. Hopefully she's already turned up.'

Rubbing the remains of his cigarette between his fingers Wesley nodded in the direction of the interview room and led the way. Neither, Wesley or Adam spoke as they sat at the table opposite Michael. Adam pressed the record button on the tape machine then read out the time and date of the interview and those present.

Wesley opened a file and shuffled some papers before looking up. Michael sat staring at the table. His head supported by his hands.

'Michael, you do understand why you're here don't you?' Wesley asked knowing that the police doctor had raised concerns about Michael's mental state less than ten minutes earlier.

Michael looked up. 'Eh?'

'I said do you understand why you're here?'

Michael stared blankly across the table.

'Michael, you have been arrested for the attempted murder of your wife Penny Westbrook.'

'Penny?'

'Yes. Can you remember what happened this afternoon?'

Michael muttered to himself.

'I'm sorry, I didn't catch that,' said Adam.

'Penny? She's my wife.'

'Yes we know that Penny is your wife. Do you remember what happened this afternoon?'

Michael sat back in the chair. Sweat was pouring down his face.

'We had an argument.'

'You were trying to strangle her!' Wesley shouted.

'She's my wife,' Michael replied folding his arms tightly around his waist.

'Michael, I'm ending this interview. We'll speak later,' said Wesley pushing his chair away to stand up.

He nodded to Adam who read out the time and date before switching off the tape machine. Once outside the room, Wesley asked the duty officer to take Michael back to the cells.

'I think he's lost the plot,' said Adam when they were back in Wesley's office.

'Or is he playing clever?' Wesley replied searching for his tobacco pouch. 'Either way, we'll find out. I'll get the doc to check him over again first thing in the morning. A night in the cells may change his state of mind.'

In the library at Abbey House, WPC Mandy Tredwell was having more success talking to Penny.

Penny had explained that she and Michael had started arguing about finances which was apparently quite a regular argument. Penny had started to press Michael about the lack of money in the bank and when he started laughing, she had slapped him across the face. This had angered him and he started shouting but it was when Penny then asked him for the truth about the artefacts that Wesley had recently questioned them about, that Michael suddenly made a grab for her throat. At this point Penny started to cry again.

'Penny, I know this is difficult for you, but you have to be honest with us. Is this the first time Michael has assaulted you?' Mandy asked.

Alison handed her a tissue. Penny wiped her eyes and rolled the tissue in her hand. She was trembling.

'I'll go and make us all a drink,' said Mandy. 'Do you take milk and sugar?'

'Just milk please,' Penny replied.

'I suppose you think I'm silly. It's funny really. Michael and I haven't had a relationship for a couple of years. Yes, we're man and wife but only on paper.'

Alison let her continue.

'We have been arguing a lot recently. Some of which has been my fault because I've wound him up but you have to understand that the Michael now, is not the Michael I married. He's terminally ill and drugs and depression have changed him.'

'That doesn't give him the right to assault you, let alone try to strangle you. It's not the first time he's attempted this is it?'

Penny buried her head in her hands and began to sob.

Outside in the hallway Mandy telephoned Wesley to provide an update saying that Penny was still very distraught and that she didn't think they would get much more out of her right now.

'OK. Give it just ten minutes more then drop the questions but make sure someone stays with her. You and I can visit her tomorrow. She might feel more comfortable and more relaxed at home, more likelihood of her then providing us with information.'

'Will do.'

'Has the doc checked her over?'

'Yes he has.'

'Thanks Mandy. Oh by the way, if she asks about Michael, he's staying here. We're actually arranging for a psychiatrist to see him in the morning but I would rather we didn't tell Penny that.'

'I understand.'

Mandy headed off to the kitchen to make tea.

Wesley returned to his office. He had a mound of paperwork to complete before he picked Jane up.

112

'So, no news from Dorothy?' Wesley asked as Jane got into the car.

'No. I phoned her about an hour ago but there was no answer. How did you get on with Michael and Penny?'

Wesley explained both a doctor and a psychiatrist were going to see Michael in the morning and that he and WPC Tredwell were going to have another chat with Penny tomorrow, as she was too distraught this afternoon.

'I do feel so sorry for Penny. She's gone through so much lately with losing her father and Michael's behaviour, and on top of all that the poor girl's daughter has been kidnapped,' exclaimed Jane.

'Yeah I know, it's amazing she's managed to hold it all together,' Wesley replied.

Turning off the main road, they drove half a mile down the country lane before Wesley pulled up outside Dorothy's cottage. He immediately pointed towards the kitchen window where a light was on.

'That's strange,' Jane remarked. 'Maybe, she's just arrived home.'

'Maybe. Stay in the car for a second. I'll go and knock.'

Jane watched him walk up the garden path and tap on the front door. For a moment, it looked as if no one was going to answer as Wesley tried again. He was about to walk round the side of the cottage when the front door slowly opened.

'Hello?'

It was Dorothy's voice but almost like a whisper.

Wesley looked down at Dorothy who was almost bent in half.

'Dorothy, its Inspector Wesley. Are you alright? What have you done?'

Ten minutes later, after Jane had made her comfortable, Dorothy was sat in an armchair drinking tea and Wesley was on the telephone to the local doctor.

Dorothy explained to Jane that she had fallen over in the garden the previous night when she had gone to get the washing in and had spent the evening sat in the shed, as she couldn't move because she was in so much pain. Although she had managed to crawl back into the house in the early hours of the morning she was virtually immobile by the time she collapsed in the armchair. She had heard the telephone ring on a couple of occasions but couldn't answer.

'Why on earth didn't you call us?' Jane asked pulling a chair up next to where Dorothy was sat.

'I don't like to bother people.'

Jane shook her head in disbelief as she watched Dorothy grimace as she held the cup to her lips.

'I've phoned your GP,' said Wesley as he entered the lounge. 'You really are a naughty girl, you should have called.'

He looked across the room to Jane who closed her eyes as if to say that she had already stated the same.

'We were getting worried about you,' said Jane.

With a considerable amount of effort, Dorothy managed to place her cup back in its saucer.

'Don't go fussing over me. You and your husband have enough to do without worrying about me.'

'So what actually happened,' Wesley asked sitting on the settee opposite.

'I tripped backwards after catching my foot on the pole that keeps the washing line up.'

She winced as she held her hand to her back. 'That's where I landed,' she said trying to force a smile.'

'Oh Dorothy, you really should have called someone,' Jane cried.

Having examined Dorothy, Alistair McKay, the local GP, entered the kitchen where Jane and Wesley now sat.

'What's the verdict Doc?' Wesley asked.

'I'm pretty sure she hasn't broken anything but she sure has one hell of a bruise on her back and a couple of others on her arms along with a number of grazes. I'd like her to have an x-ray but she's adamant that she's not going to hospital.'

'I'll go and make sure she's comfortable,' said Jane.

When Jane had left the kitchen, Wesley closed the door and pulled the doctor to one side.

'Doc, this may sound like a strange question but do you honestly think Dorothy sustained those injuries from simply falling over in the garden?'

The doctor shrugged his shoulders.

'It's possible. Why do you ask?'

Wesley looked out the kitchen window, his eyes fixed on the back garden.

'Just call it police intuition. I have a feeling something's not right here. I'm not sure what I expected to find but there's no visible sign of anyone falling over outside and there are no clothes on the washing line.'

'Are you suggesting she hurt herself somewhere else Inspector?'

'Doc, I'm not sure what I'm suggesting, it's just that a few things don't add up recently.'

'No news on the missing girl yet?'

'Nothing.' Wesley started to roll a cigarette.

'Back in London it's easy for a young girl to go missing but I find it hard to believe that someone can just disappear around here where nearly everyone knows one another.'

'The trouble is Inspector, is that for more than six months of the year the population around here literally explodes with the influx of tourists.'

'Hmm. That's a good point.'

'It's not for me to say but have you thought of checking CCTV footage at some of the motorway services heading in and out of here.'

Wesley lit his cigarette and blew a plume of smoke into the air.

'No we haven't but it's a good call. Have you ever thought about joining the police force doc?'

Alistair McKay laughed as he stood up to leave.

'No thank you, Inspector. I'm happy just prescribing medicines, taking surgery a couple of times a week and I often get to listen to some of the local gossip whether I like to or not.'

'I can imagine. Well if change your mind give me a call.'

Wesley stood up and they shook hands.

'I'll see myself out. Good day Inspector. I'll pop in and see Dorothy again tomorrow.'

'Thanks Doc.'

'Oh by the way. You ought to cut down on those roll ups.'

Wesley smirked as the front door closed.

113

The following morning, Wesley arrived at the station before eight. Jenny was already sitting in the interview room. The duty officer said she had arrived more than half an earlier.

'Good morning, Jenny. How are you?' he asked entering the room.

'Morning, Mr Wesley. I'm fine.'

Wesley placed a folder on the table then stood back to roll a cigarette.

'I know you've had a rough time lately, with Kelvin Ward being murdered and seeing poor old Harvey White with a knife in his heart but I have to ask you a few more questions.'

'Sure, I understand.'

Wesley sat opposite, opened the buff folder and extracted a couple of pages of notes.

'You told me that you came across a graveyard on the outskirts of Havering.'

'Yes.'

'I still don't understand the significance of what the clues to the graveyard are supposed to be telling us?'

'I do,' she replied calmly.

'Pardon me?'

'I know what the clue is telling us.'

'Would you care to explain?'

'I went to the Records office. There have been no males born in the Westbrook family since 1955. The last male was a boy named Alfred who died in 1959 when he was just four years of age.'

She could see the confused look on Wesley's face.

'Don't you see? Michael cannot be a Westbrook. Which begs the question as to who he really is and where he originates from?'

Wesley ran his hands across his face.

'OK. So let's assume that the current owner and occupant of Abbey House is an imposter.' He held his hand up before Jenny could interrupt. 'That doesn't explain who wrote the instructions on the painting or why?'

'I think I know,' Jenny replied. 'I believe Uncle Kelvin found the graveyard and then wrote the instructions on the painting.'

'But what was he doing there in the first place?'

'I think he stumbled upon it when he was checking the site for excavation.'

'You see, I found some old drawings in Uncle Kelvin's flat which I couldn't make sense of at first. Drawings of the Tor, the Abbey, and what I now believe to be the neglected graveyard. You see, it's an old burial site that was used as an overflow site when the Abbey grounds became full. I assume that because of its remote location it soon became forgotten.'

'That doesn't explain why Kelvin would want to excavate there.'

'Oh, that part is simple,' Jenny exclaimed.

'Please enlighten me and put me out of misery,' Wesley pleaded.

'You see, in those days, when someone was buried, they were often buried with something belonging to them or belonging to the family.'

She smiled at the confused look on Wesley's face.

'I believe Uncle Kelvin found artefacts that had been buried in the graveyard. Artefacts that were buried centuries ago. He was aware that Michael and Penny were in possession of a couple of items from the past. I took photos of the artefacts they have on display to show him. He said they were only part of a collection that were said to date back to King Arthur's time and according to local gossip the bulk of the collection were buried somewhere along with the last of the Westbrook family.'

'So he worked out where the graveyard was?'

'Yes, but he told me that he believed that both Harvey White and Dorothy Hallerton already knew of the location of the graveyard and what was supposedly buried there.'

'Oh I think I see what you're saying, because Harvey and Dorothy were both members of the Somerset Levels Preservation Society and members of the local council, they refused to allow Kelvin to excavate. Is that right?'

'Exactly Mr Wesley. They were both members of the Historical Society also.'

Wesley stood up and walked across to the window to look down on the street below.

'OK,' he said holding his arm aloft, 'But where does the house in Havering fit in to all this? Don't tell me. That's easy too.'

'The house belongs to Dorothy Hallerton but it's been empty since she married Eddie. It was handed down from her parents.'

'Why did she never sell it?'

'Because it's where she and Harvey used to meet.'

Wesley stood aghast. His tobacco pouch in his hand and a roll up hanging out of the corner of his mouth.

'Don't look so surprised,' said Jenny. 'Harvey and Dorothy have been more than just friends since they were at school together.'

'That explains something else,' he replied removing the roll up from the corner of his mouth. 'Only yesterday, one of my PCs found a photo of Dorothy in Harvey's bungalow.'

'I rest my case.' Jenny sat back with her arms folded, a smug look on her face.

'Not so quick young lady. Let's go back to what you said about Michael being an imposter.'

'I thought you would mention that Inspector. Michael was taken in by the Westbrook family as he was born in their house. Their housemaid, a Miss Reagan, bore the child when she was employed there, but being out of wedlock and having no contact with the father left her in a sticky situation.'

'However, the Westbrook family stood by her and even agreed to help to bring the child up. When Miss Reagan left her service at Abbey House at the young age of twenty-three she was already of ill health. She asked the Westbrook's if the boy could remain in their care as he would have a better chance in life. They eventually agreed so long as the agreement wasn't made public. That kind of thing wasn't viewed quite as agreeably as it is today. Miss Reagan died of pneumonia two years after leaving her post as housemaid at Abbey House.'

'Where did you find all this out?' Wesley asked.

'Ada Chapman. She works in the Records office. She said that part of the agreement was also for the Westbrook family to pay for Miss Reagan's medical needs. The poor woman was buried in a pauper's grave somewhere in Gloucestershire. Michael never knew his real mother. In fact, to this day I'm not sure he even knows he was adopted.'

114

David Hare was sat with his laptop trawling through the web searching for historical data when Sally came out of the bathroom.

'What are you looking for?' she asked.

'I was reading about the maintenance work that has been carried out on the Tor over the past century.'

'Oh David,' she shouted. 'You're becoming obsessed with that damn place. Why don't you let the police deal with the matter?'

David looked shocked by her outburst.

'I'm sorry. It's just that I find all this stuff interesting.'

'Yeah maybe but it's all you do lately. It's boring.'

Closing his laptop, he threw it on the settee and walked over to the kitchen area where he grabbed his jacket from the back of a chair.

'Where are you going?'

'Out.'

'But where? Why?'

'I need some fresh air.'

'But David…'

The front door slammed shut and Sally could hear his footsteps as he descended the stairs.

'Damn!' she said to herself.

David put his foot on the accelerator and gunned the sports car to its limits. Most people would have crashed the car in the first half a mile but he knew these country lanes like the back of his hand.

Taking the next bend at over fifty miles an hour left him little time to stop as a flock of sheep blocked the road some hundred yards ahead. They were being led across to the field into Barton's farm. He waited impatiently until the last of the sheep left the road followed by an old looking collie dog and a grey bearded farmer who gave him a disdainful look before closing the gate to the field.

With a screech of tyres he sped past the glare of the farmer heading west towards Wells. His eyes were watering as the wind swirled around the open topped vehicle. After coming to a fork in the road he took a sharp left to head uphill. An old Morris Minor was struggling to cope with the steep incline and slamming the car into third gear David overtook pushing the engine to its limits. Reaching the brow of the hill the car then picked up more speed as he started to descend the other side. Suddenly he hit the brakes as a tractor pulled out from in between the hedgerow some two hundred yards ahead. The brakes didn't respond. He stamped his foot on the brake pedal twice more but to no effect. The driver of the tractor only saw him at the last moment.

Within seconds, what was left of the car was laying upside down in the offside ditch. One of the back wheels was slowly turning, but the crumpled lifeless body of David Hare lay still.

115

It was just after midday and news of David's accident had cast a shadow over the whole team. Wesley had asked Mandy to locate Sally and bring her down to the station.

Adam had identified the body and was on the phone to David's father in Salisbury.

Wesley phoned Jane to tell her the news and to say he would probably be late home.

When Mandy arrived at the station with Sally, the girl was almost hysterical. The duty officer directed them to one of the quieter pleasantly furnished offices on the first floor and went to advise Wesley they were in the building.

Sally was inconsolable so Wesley made the decision to call in the police doctor. A mild sedative calmed her down but she was insistent on seeing David. Wesley said he would put a call into the pathologist to arrange a suitable time. He didn't tell her that he needed time for the body to be examined and tidied up.

The train from Salisbury pulled into Street just after three o'clock. Adam was there to meet Paul Hare. David's father. A retired civil servant, he wore a grey suit with white shirt and purple coloured tie. His black receding hair was combed straight back from the temple, showing tints of grey at the roots.

Adam estimated him to be in his late sixties or early seventies, even though he still stood tall and erect and carried an air of authority. Carrying a black rain coat on his arm he followed PC Broad to the waiting police vehicle.

'Was it an accident?' he asked catching Adam by surprise as they headed towards the station.

'I beg your pardon?'

'My son's death, was it an accident?'

'I can only say that from the witness's accounts we have received so far, it would seem that way.'

'You'll be doing more tests I assume.'

'Oh yes. The pathologist will carry out a full examination,' Adam replied without wanting to go into further detail.

'What about the vehicle?'

'The vehicle, Sir?'

'Yes, there will be tests carried out on the road worthiness of the vehicle I assume.'

'Err, oh yes, of course.'

After entering the station Adam escorted David's father upstairs to where he knew Sally was being comforted by the doctor and Mandy. Adam made the necessary introductions and left them alone in the room together while he went in search of Wesley.

'What? Do you mean to say that David's father believes this may not have been an accident?' Wesley asked.

Adam puffed out his cheeks and shrugged his shoulders.

'I don't know what he thinks but he sure enough asked the question.'

Wesley made his way down the corridor and knocked on the door before he entered.

'Good afternoon.' He held his hand out to Paul Hare.

'Ah. You must be Inspector Wesley.'

The two men shook hands.

'So what can you tell me Inspector? Was it an accident or was my son murdered?'

At the word murder, Sally looked up from the chair where she was sat with WPC Tredwell.

'Murder? What was that you said about murder?'

Sally started to become distressed as Mandy placed an arm around her to calm her down.

'Let's talk in my office,' Wesley said to David's father and gestured him outside.

They were seated at Wesley's desk before either man spoke again.

'So, Mr Hare, what makes you believe David was murdered?'

Paul Hare sat upright in the chair with his raincoat draped across his lap and his arms folded.

'David telephoned me two days ago to say he had been looking into Colin Dempster's death. He sounded excited. He said he had found something but wasn't sure what it meant.'

'What did he find?'

'He didn't say. He simply inferred that it was something important. Something that had been overlooked maybe? Whatever it was Inspector, he said he was going to check his facts then discuss the findings with you but I assume he never got the opportunity.'

Wesley shook his head.

'No he didn't,' Wesley sighed, 'but I still don't see what makes you think he was murdered?'

'Inspector, I worked for the criminal courts for over thirty years and read up on far too many cases than I care to remember.'

He paused for a while as if thinking of what to say next.

'I just believe that whatever David found could have resulted in his murder. It's too much of a coincidence don't you think?'

It was early evening and Wesley was sat at his desk. Mandy and Adam had taken David Hare and Sally to the mortuary soon after Terry Austin, the pathologist telephoned Wesley to say that the body could now be viewed.

Just then there was a knock on the door.

'Come in.'

'Sorry to bother. Just to let you know that Patricia Wright is out of hospital,' said Alison. 'The doc says she should make a full recovery, although she's going to need plenty of rest.'

'That's the only bit of good news I've had all day,' said Wesley. 'Thanks Alison.'

Ten minutes later, after receiving a text saying that Michael Westbrook had been admitted to a psychiatric hospital, Wesley was driving to Abbey House.

Penny greeted him at the door and showed him inside.

'Please come through Inspector. I've made some tea.'

'I hope you don't mind me saying but you seem very relaxed,' Wesley remarked. They were sitting in the library, the French doors where slightly open and Mozart was playing quietly in the background.

'I think I can safely say that's down to the tranquilisers the doctor prescribed. I should have started taking them before now,' she replied smiling.

'Michael....'

'Yes I know. He's been moved to the nutty farm. Oh don't look so surprised at my reaction Inspector. Michael should have been admitted years ago.'

Wesley put his cup on the table.

'So how many times has he assaulted you?'

Penny shrugged her shoulders before taking a sip of tea.

'I don't know. Four? Five? I lost count.'

'Why didn't you report it?'

Penny laughed, stood up and walked across the room, running her fingers along the bookshelf.

'I loved him once. You see, when you love someone, you tend to overlook, forgive and even try to accept. All those things.'

Wesley nodded.

'Michael has always provided for me. I think he actually loved me too. In the beginning that is.'

'So what changed?'

Penny ran her hands through her hair.

'Could I have a cigarette?'

'Err. Yes of course. Roll up, I'm afraid. I didn't realise you smoked.'

'I don't normally,' Penny replied watching him expertly roll a cigarette, 'but like a lot of things. I think it's time I started.'

After making two roll-ups, he passed her one and lit the other for himself. Penny put the cigarette to her lips, lit it and inhaled. Exhaling the smoke she coughed.

'They take a bit of getting used to,' Wesley remarked.

'Yeah, I guess they do.'

'What's Michaels' real name?'

Penny spun round, almost dropping her cup on the floor.

'You know?'

'I know the last born male Westbrook died when he was only four years old.'

'Reagan,' Penny replied.

'Would you care to explain?'

Penny sat down again. She wiped the tea stain on her skirt and took a long drag on the remains of the cigarette. She then gave the same explanation that he'd heard earlier from Jenny.

'Why didn't anyone tell me?' he asked.

'It's didn't seem relevant. Well, it's not is it?'

Wesley sat deep in thought with his hand over his mouth.

'Maybe not, but it would have been nice to know.'

Penny stood up again and walked across to the French doors.

'Come and walk round the grounds with me Inspector. They look lovely this time of year.'

Wesley let Penny talk about the plants in the garden and how Eddie used to look after everything but now she had started to read up on what was what and when it needed attention.

He knew there was never going to be a good time to raise the subject, so he bit the bullet just as Penny was in full flow describing one of the mature bushes that blooms this time of year.

'Penny, where did you obtain those two artefacts from? The two items we discussed before, the tapestry and the vase.'

She turned to look at him, a vacant stare in her blue eyes.

'I can't remember where we bought them. I think it was some antique fair in Somerset. Look aren't these petals such a delightful colour?'

'Penny,' Wesley touched her arm to grab her attention.

'It was Eddie who found those artefacts wasn't it?'

'Eddie?'

Wesley was beginning to lose patience.

'Penny! Stop playing games. Michael paid Eddie Hallerton to dig another access route to the Chalice Well. I've been down there. That much seems obvious. While Eddie was digging out the tunnel he found those artefacts and others. Am I right?'

'You know, you have quite and imagination Inspector.'

'Enough imagination to arrest you both for attempted murder.'

'What! How on earth do you work that one out,' she cried.

'Tell me who else is responsible then. Eddie Hallerton dies in the Chapel, either entering or exiting from the Well. The only other people who knew about the entrance to the Well from the Chapel were you and Michael.'

'You can't possibly think I had anything to do with that. Eddie was my father!' she screamed.

'Then why didn't you stop Michael from blackmailing him?'

Penny had a surprised look on her face.

'Oh come on, you don't expect me to believe you didn't know,' said Wesley.

'I had no idea.'

'But it was Eddie who found the artefacts. Wasn't it?'

Penny hesitated before answering.

'Come on Penny, it's time to come clean.' Wesley's patience had all but expired.

'Look, I knew Michael had asked Dad to explore the possibility of digging down into the Well. Michael was convinced that the tale regarding the Lake of Avalon was true that before it flooded, a number of King Arthur's artefacts were buried there. Dad told me he'd managed to tunnel below the Chapel but didn't say what he'd found. I have only ever seen the tapestry and the vase.'

'But you knew he found other items.'

'I never got involved. He and Michael kept things to themselves. I suspected they had found other stuff because one afternoon two guys turned up asking for Michael. He looked real nervous. They walked off into the grounds and were gone for some time. I was beginning to worry, however, when Michael re-appeared he seemed extremely pleased with himself. It was obvious he'd done a deal with them.'

'Selling items of which that he had no ownership rights,' Wesley remarked.

'Why would Michael blackmail him though? It doesn't make sense.'

Wesley put a hand on her shoulder. She was shaking.

'I think Michael saw Eddie as an easy target. Michael knew what he had done was illegal. He blackmailed your father for his silence. We know Eddie was paying large sums of money to someone. That someone we believe was Michael. The money paying for Michael's drug addiction.'

'You know about that?'

'I've seen enough people in my time who are drug addicts. Michael's behavioural swings and appearance speak for themselves.'

'OK, but I didn't kill him and I can't believe Michael did either.'

'In that case. Who did?' Wesley asked grim faced.

116

'Hello Dorothy. It's so good of you to come round,' said Jane leading her into the lounge.

'It's very kind of you to invite me. It's the first time I've been out of the house for two days.'

'I must say, you're looking better than when I last saw you.'

'I feel better Jane, thanks to you and your husband.'

'I still don't know how you managed to hurt yourself in the garden,' said Jane as she picked up a tray of drinks. 'I mean, you have cuts and bruises everywhere.'

'Not looking where I was going I'm afraid.' Dorothy looked down at the bruises on her arms and legs pulling down the sleeves of her cardigan.

'We were getting worried about you, you know. I tried to call you several times.'

'Oh Jane, I'm sorry. I probably need to go to the doctors to get my hearing checked. I keep trying to pretend that I'm OK when really I don't hear as well as I used to.'

'Make sure you make an appointment, otherwise you'll be walking out in front of cars next.'

The two women both laughed. Dorothy looked quite at ease as they spent the afternoon gossiping about local life.'

Dorothy had just put her coat on to leave when Wesley arrived home.

She looked surprised to see him.

'Hello Inspector. How are you?'

'I'm very well thanks. What about you? I hope all your cuts and bruises are healing.'

Dorothy buttoned her coat up rather hastily, looking embarrassed.

'Yes thank you Inspector.'

She retrieved her handbag from the sideboard and bade her farewells. Jane escorted her to the door and watched her walk in the direction of the village back to her own home.

'She still hurts,' said Wesley closing the curtains as Jane re-entered the lounge.

'Well, she's no youngster to have a fall.'

'Hmm.'

'John Wesley, what do you mean?'

'I'm still not convinced that Dorothy received all those cuts and bruises simply from falling over in the garden.'

'What are you saying? That she hurt herself elsewhere and is too embarrassed to tell anyone?'

'No,' he took a deep sigh, 'not too embarrassed. It's almost as if she's scared someone might found out exactly how she hurt herself.'

'Are you going to ask her?'

'I think I have to, but not right now. I'll pay her a visit tomorrow.'

'Surely you can't possibly believe Dorothy is involved in anything untoward?'

'Honest answer is I don't know, but with everything else that's been going on I just have a gut feeling that Dorothy isn't telling all.'

'If I'm totally honest then I have to agree with you. She told me earlier that she's having trouble hearing things lately but I spoke to her a couple of times when I was stood behind her and she replied straight away.'

Wesley laughed and put him arm around Jane's shoulder.

'You're becoming more like Jane Marple every day.'

117

Denise kept drifting in and out of sleep. She had no idea now whether it was day or night; each day now seemed the same.

She gingerly managed to sit up and stretched her back before rubbing her eyes. Her whole body was aching. She shivered as the cold damp air seemed to bite into her bones.

Stretching her legs she screamed as cramp shot like a lightning bolt through her leg muscles. With hands and knees both raw from rubbing against both floor and walls she crawled forward to where the water basin stood on the floor. Raising the basin with her tied hands she slowly drank the small amount of water that remained. It tasted dusty and had the smell of stagnant water that had been exposed to the air for several days.

Having placed the basin back on the floor, she sat back on her knees and began to cry. In between her sobs she kept telling herself to keep calm but she knew her nerves couldn't hold out much longer. The loneliness and uncertainty were oppressive.

There were times she thought she could hear running water, other times she heard the scuffling sound of some animal nearby. She tried to remember the last time her captor had visited her. Surely it was yesterday or was it the day before? Hunger was eating away at her and she bent forward to ease the pain in her stomach.

Sleep must have taken over again because when she woke she was still lying in the middle of the room and the light was now a shade darker. As she stretched her legs her foot caught on something.

Twisting her aching limbs around Denise saw the cardboard box by her feet. Her captor must have left it there whilst she was sleeping. With considerable effort, using her elbows she managed to manoeuvre herself so she was sat in front of the box. Looking inside, her desperation was momentarily lifted as she surveyed the bread, fruit, and two cartons of drink.

She had just taken a bite of the bread when she heard the faint toll of the church bells. She listened intently to the sound she knew so well. Although they seemed so distant, it was a welcoming sound and for a moment Denise felt comforted by hearing them. Recognising the sound of the bells brought her a little comfort but she knew she was far from being safe.

Long after they had stopped she sat deep in thought. The bells only rang out that particular toll on a Sunday.

Although her head was still in a muddle, she was able to work out that she'd been held prisoner for over a week. She finished eating the bread and drank the contents of one of the cartons. After rubbing her arms and legs to help with her circulation she crawled across the floor to one of the chimney recesses. It didn't take her long to find what she was looking for.

Scraping the piece of broken brick on the wall she managed to draw several lines. If only to help her keep her sanity she decided she would try to mark off each day.

118

After promising the vicar they would attend the harvest festival in the coming weeks, Wesley and Jane left the church and made their way to the Pilgrim public house.

Although there was a slight drizzle, it hadn't stopped the tourists from flooding into the town and Wesley had to queue at the bar to get served.

'I ordered you beef for your Sunday roast,' he said placing the drinks down on the table. They were sitting in a small alcove opposite the bar, next to a table where a young couple were trying their hardest to keep their baby quiet.

'There wasn't an empty seat in the church this morning,' said Jane.

'Hmm, I noticed, quite a few regular faces though.'

Wesley sipped his beer, his first of the day and he was hoping it wouldn't be the last.

'I didn't see Penny there. I suppose she could have been down the front,' Jane commented.

'No I didn't see her either. I think she's happy to be on her own right now. I guess the last thing she needs is to be confronted by someone who starts asking her loads of questions.'

'Yes, I guess you're right.'

The waitress appeared with two roast dinners just as a crowd of about twenty people entered the pub.

'I think you're going to have a busy day,' Jane said.

'Thankfully there's nowhere for them all to sit,' the young waitress whispered into her ear and winked as she walked back towards the kitchen.

Wesley put his arm around Jane. It was the first time in several days they were able to spend time together.

The following morning Wesley looked out of his bedroom window as the rain cascaded down from the guttering above. It had been raining heavily all night and the narrow un-adopted road outside their cottage was now flooded.

'A lovely day for ducks,' said Jane as she appeared from the bathroom with a towel wrapped around her.

'What's wrong?' she asked seeing the worried look on Wesley's face.

'I fear for Denise. I just pray to God she's not being kept somewhere where she's exposed to the elements. It's rained nearly every bloody day since that girl went missing.'

Jane stood behind him and wrapped her arms around his waist.

'You'll find her John. You'll find her.'

'It's good of you to talk to me, Mrs. Harper. I know one of my officers has spoken to you before but I'd like to just run over a few points again if I may.'

'Sure Inspector, it's no problem at all. I guess you've not heard anything from Denise?'

'No nothing, but we won't give up. The girl can't just disappear.'

He didn't want to tell her about the ransom note.

'Come into the back of the shop. I'll put the closed sign up for a while; it's nearly lunchtime in any case.'

Mrs. Harper moved several boxes off the two stools in the back room and filled the kettle with water.

'Take a seat Inspector. Do you take milk and sugar?'

'Yes, both please, just one sugar.'

'How is Denise's mother holding up?'

'As well as can be expected but the strain is beginning to tell on her. She was admitted to hospital for a while but they've let her back home now.'

'It's not surprising it must be awful for her.'

She shook her head as she poured the teas and sat next to Wesley against the small worktop.

'Can you take your mind back a few weeks prior to when Denise went missing? Did anyone come into the bookshop that day who Denise knew? I mean, the majority of your customers are tourists right?'

'Well it is a Tourist office, Inspector.'

'Yes quite. What I mean is did anyone come in just to speak to Denise? You know, a friend maybe?'

'Not that I can remember. One of your police constables asked me the same question. I don't think Denise has many friends.'

'What makes you say that?'

'Oh, it's just that Denise is different from most of the girls of her age. She only seems interested in completing her exams so that she can obtain a decent job. She seems too quiet and reserved to have a boyfriend.'

'What about girlfriends. Most girls of her age have a number of close friends.'

'Not Denise I'm afraid.' Mrs. Harper took a sip of her tea.

'I did ask her once why she never went to parties or to the local pubs like most of the youngsters around here. She said that she didn't like to hang around with the girls she knew from University. She said they just drank and slept around and it wasn't her scene.'

'Can you remember what she was wearing the day she disappeared?'

'Yes, she had on black cords, blue jumper and trainers. Oh, she didn't wear the trainers at work, she wore black shoes but always put her trainers on to walk home.'

'What about a coat or jacket?'

'I did check when your constable asked me. She was carrying her leather jacket, her black overcoat is still hanging up on the back of the door here,' She pointed to the door behind Wesley.

'Can I take a look?'

He took the coat off the hook and returning to the stool, placed it on the worktop. There was only one inside pocket which was empty, as was the left hand pocket. Feeling inside the right hand pocket he found a scrunched up receipt. He unraveled it and flattened it out on the worktop.

'What is it?' asked Mrs. Harper.

Wesley scrutinized the receipt, squinting as he tried to read the feint heading and details.

'Do you want me to read it for you?' she asked rather meekly, not wanting to upset him.

'Could you? My eyesight isn't what it used to be.'

Mrs. Harper peered over the top of her glasses for a few seconds. When she looked up, she had an excited look on her face. 'It's a receipt from the arts and crafts shop in the High Street. Tea and cake for two.'

'Is there a date on it?' he asked.

'Yes, it's from May 12th. Time stamped 20:23.'

She stopped in her tracks and stared at Wesley. 'Oh my God. That's the day before Denise went missing.'

Having left the bookshop, Wesley put a call into the station to ask if there were any updates for him.

'Hi, Sir,' said Alison, 'no calls for you. Just to let you know though, Adam has gone to see Sally. Mandy has just finished her shift so Adam said he would stay with Sally for a while.'

A smirk came to Wesley's face.

'I bet he did.'

'Sorry?'

'Oh nothing. Just thinking to myself. I'll be back in about an hour.'

'Has anyone spoken to David Hare's father this morning?'

'Not to my knowledge. He refused Sally's invite of staying in the flat so he's staying at a B&B just at the other end of Bath.

'OK, remind me to call him later. I'm just going into Glastonbury. I may have a lead on Denise's whereabouts the night before she vanished.'

The arts and crafts shop stood only two hundred yards from the entrance to the Abbey grounds. The front of the old shop was long and narrow but widened at the rear where it opened up into a small seating area. Wesley entered the shop and was immediately greeted by a middle aged gentleman who sported a large grey beard and little hair.

'Good morning. Are you looking for something in particular?'

Wesley showed his ID and asked if could take a few minutes of the man's time.

'Yes of course Inspector. Please follow me. We'll sit at one of the tables at the back.'

Wesley followed the portly gentleman to a small two seater table and waited whilst the guy asked one of the waitresses to keep an eye on the shop. Rejoining Wesley he introduced himself as Stan Clark and said that he had purchased the shop two years ago when it was a clothes shop.

'How can I help you Inspector?'

Wesley extracted the receipt from his coat pocket and handed it across the table.

'Stan, I'm sure you're aware that Denise Wright is missing.'

'The girl from the Tourist office? Yes, poor thing, it must be terrible for her parents.'

'This receipt was found in her coat pocket. Can you recall who she was with that evening?'

Stan scrutinized the receipt before answering.

'The simple answer Inspector is no. I don't work the evenings. I just come down and lock up when we close. We only leave the shop open for people who want tea, coffee and maybe a snack if we have anything left. It would have been Donna or Marie who would have served her that week. Unfortunately Donna no longer works here. She was only here for a few weeks. She wasn't the brightest spark, if you know what I mean?'

'I see. What about Marie? Is she here?'

'Yes, that's Marie,' he replied pointing to the young girl standing by the cash till. 'I'll take over from her and send her over to you. Would you like tea or coffee?'

'No, I'm fine thanks, Stan. All tea'd out.'

A nervous looking Marie joined Wesley at the table. She had long, blonde hair which was tied at the back and the darkest blue eyes that Wesley had seen in years.

'Hi Marie. I'm Inspector Wesley.' He showed her his ID.

'Don't worry, you've not done anything wrong, I just need to ask you if you remember seeing this young woman in the shop.'

He handed her a photo of Denise. Marie studied the photo for a few seconds before responding.

'Is this the girl who's missing?'

'Yes it is. Do you recognize her?'

Marie nodded her head.

'I'm not a hundred per cent sure but I think this is the girl who I served.'

'We found a receipt in her coat pocket that suggests she was in the shop on the evening of May 12th.'

He handed her the crumpled receipt. 'So it would confirm it was Denise.'

'I was certainly working that evening. I remember that, because it was one of the evenings that Donna didn't turn up for work. She was always phoning in sick.'

'So do you remember serving Denise that evening?'

Marie placed her elbows on the table and put her hands to her face in the shape of saying a prayer. She closed her eyes, trying desperately to think. Wesley thought he was going to draw a blank until Marie suddenly looked up.

'She came in with another woman.'

'Are you sure? Another woman?'

'Yes I'm positive. I remember now. There was only one other table in use, an elderly couple. Tourists they were. They said they were staying at The Pilgrim.'

'Can you describe this other woman that Denise was with?'

'I didn't pay much attention but I would guess she was older.'

'What makes you say that?'

'She had a shopping bag and when they left, she put a rain hat on. You know, one of those clear plastic ones that tie under the chin. Well I mean, it's not the thing a young girl wears. And it's only mothers and wives who carry shopping bags these days.'

'How long were they in the shop for?'

'Hmm. I can't be sure Inspector, I'd guess, around half an hour because I closed the shop shortly after they left, just after serving the other couple who asked for some cake to take away.'

'Is there anything else you can remember about them?'

'I'm sorry Inspector,' she replied shaking her head.

Wesley handed her his card.

'Marie, you've been a great help. If you think of anything else please call me.'

'Yes of course I will.'

Wesley left the girl sitting at the table staring at his card.

119

Wesley sat in the officer's mess room with Mandy, Alison and Martin.

'So what's the news on David Hare's autopsy?'

'Mr Hare died almost instantly. He broke his neck upon impact. Even if he hadn't he would have died from two punctured lungs. There was no trace of alcohol or drugs. At first it looked like a tragic accident, following a domestic,' said Alison.

Wesley and the other members of the team looked perplexed.

'What do you mean, at first?'

'We've just received the report back from the garage. It was no accident; the car's brakes had been tampered with.'

Wesley put his hands to his face and rubbed his tired eyes.

'You're telling me that we're looking at another murder?'

'Yes, Sir. I'm afraid David Hare was murdered. The car's brake cable had been severed.'

Wesley put his hands under his chin and looked around the room.

'So David's father was right. He told me he spoke to David just a couple of days ago and that his son was convinced he'd found something. His father said he didn't think it was an accident. He said it was too coincidental.'

'It's certainly beginning to look that way,' Martin remarked.

'The forensic team say they won't be finished with the car until tomorrow. They've stripped down what was left of it into about a hundred pieces,' said Alison.

Wesley had finished rolling a cigarette and was about to light up when he was reminded about the no-smoking policy by one of the canteen staff. His three colleagues all looked away, unable to hide the grins on their faces.

'I guess Adam is with Sally right now?' Wesley asked breaking the silence.

'Yeah,' said Martin. 'Sally's parents are on their way to Bath. They are going to stay at the Mayflower Hotel. The provisional date for the funeral is Thursday week.'

'Personally, I think for now, there's nothing to be gained by telling Sally that this was no accident,' said Wesley.

'For now, we'll keep it to ourselves. Whoever is responsible will expect us to announce another murder but if we don't, it may flush them out. I'll speak to David's father so he's aware of the situation.'

'What are we going to say to Sally's parents?' Alison asked.

'Nothing yet. They have their hands full looking after Sally without burdening them with information that we want kept secret.'

'How's Dorothy Hallerton now?' Mandy asked.

'She seems OK,' Wesley answered. 'I want to have another chat with her though. I'm not convinced she received all the cuts and bruises she appears to have just by falling over in the garden.'

'So where do you think she got the bruises from?' asked Martin.

'That's what I intend to find out. That and other things.'

'What things?'

'It appears that Dorothy and Harvey White had been an item many years ago.'

'You're joking,' Martin exclaimed, 'there's more to Dorothy than meets the eye.'

'Yeah I want to ask her what she knows about Harvey White's visit to the Records office too.'

Wesley jotted a note down for himself.

'What's the latest report on Michael Westbrook?' he asked moving on.

'Still in the psychiatric hospital. The doc says he's in quite a bad way. Doesn't want anyone to interview him, says he's not fit enough. It looks like he's going to be in there indefinitely,' Martin replied.'

'What about Harvey White?'

'Harvey White's body has finally been released by the pathologist. I don't know when the cremation will be. We still haven't traced any next of kin,' Mandy replied.

'What about Dorothy? I expect she'll want to go?' Alison pointed out.

'Yeah she might, although she made no comment about Harvey's death when I saw her yesterday and it's been in the local papers as you know.'

'Don't you think that's strange?'

'As I said, I think there are a few strange things about Dorothy at the moment. Martin, will you get on to the security company who control the CCTV cameras in the High Street. I want to see if there's any footage of Denise talking to anyone the night before she died.'

Wesley then handed a piece of paper over to Alison.

'This is Marie Fielding's contact number. She's the young girl who works in the shop. Can you arrange a time for her to come into the station to meet to meet Sandy Holman and get an artist's impression drawn of the woman that she saw Denise with in the shop that night.'

'Yes will do.'

'Final thing, this one's for Mandy. Can you pay a visit to Penny Westbrook? I think if she sees more as a welfare visit then she may open up a bit more. I'm going to see Dorothy. Any questions?'

There was an accepted silence around the table.

'OK. Let's meet back here at 16:00 hours.'

120

Wesley knocked twice. There was no answer. He walked around the side of the cottage but there was no sign of Dorothy. He never thought to grab the key from Jane.

He checked the back door and the garden shed but everything was locked up. He would call back later.

Penny opened the door looking bleary eyed as if she had just been woken up.

'Oh hello.'

As she stepped forward into the doorway the sun's rays caught the side of her face. Mandy couldn't help notice that the tear stains were still wet.

'Hi Penny. I just popped by to see how you are coping,' said Mandy.

'I'm OK thanks,' Penny replied. 'One has to keep going. For what do I owe the pleasure of your company?'

'More of a social visit rather than an official one.'

'Oh, how come?' Penny looked confused.

'I know what it's like to have a partner who isn't quite what he seems. I might be a police woman but I do have a life outside of the police force too.'

Penny seemed to study Mandy before she answered.

'Do come in. I don't suppose you fancy a walk through the grounds? It's quite a pleasant day.'

'Sure. Why not?'

Penny grabbed a cardigan and led the way across the hall and into the library where she opened the French doors leading out into the grounds of the estate.

'Not many people are privileged enough to have a garden of such size and beauty,' Mandy remarked.

'I suppose you're right. I do take it for granted, I have to admit.'

They crossed the vast lawn to the edge of the private woodland where tree roots and an abundance of woodland fauna replaced the cushioned grass.

'Mind your step, the woodland floor hides potholes galore,' said Penny. 'It's so lovely out here. My favourite part of the grounds really although I haven't walked through the woods for a year or more.'

They reached a small clearing where the sunlight seeped through and the floor was a sea of bluebells.

'What a marvellous place,' Mandy exclaimed. 'It's so peaceful.'

She looked sideways at Penny and noticed the tears in her eyes.

'What's wrong love?'

'Oh, it just brings back memories of when Michael and I were in love. You know, those early innocent days when you don't have a care in the world. We used to sit here amongst the bluebells and pretend that we were invisible to the world. Did you ever do that kind of thing?'

'Unfortunately no. Oh, we were in love, at least I thought we were. Then one day he told me he was already married. Not only that. He had children too.'

'I'm sorry,' said Penny standing there with her arms folded.

'What happened after you found out?'

'Oh, we stayed together for a few months but we both knew it was all over. It's just that neither of us wanted to be the one to say it.'

'Are you over it now?'

Mandy pursed her lips.

'Yes, I suppose so but it takes time doesn't it? I mean, Michael has been living two different lives hasn't he?'

Penny tightened her arms around her waist.

'How did you know about his affair?' she asked.

'Just call it a woman's intuition.'

Mandy continued walking; her hands thrust deep into her police uniform trousers.

'Did the affair with Jenny start as soon as she moved in?'

Penny started to follow, her footsteps leaving a trail across the carpet of bluebells.

'No, and it probably would never have flourished had Michael and I been living as husband and wife.'

'How do you mean?'

'Our relationship deteriorated from the moment I found out that he had been blackmailing my father. I can never forgive him for that. I knew Dad was in his employment and to be honest I knew they had been working on the Well. But I didn't know why exactly. Michael told me he wanted to explore the opportunity of drawing water from the Chalice Well to sell to the public. He didn't tell me that he and Dad were also looking for buried artefacts or indeed, that they had found any.'

'How did you find out?'

'We received a number of telephone calls to the house from prospective buyers. I never talked to them but I used to listen on the upstairs' phone. Of course, when I eventually tackled Michael about it, he tried to deny everything. Then one day I mentioned someone's name I'd heard over the phone. That was the first time Michael threatened me. He told me to stay out of his business affairs.'

She wiped a tear from her eye.

'He said that he was blackmailing my father because he was greedy like me. He said that Dad had wanted a larger share of the profits. In the end he told Dad that he would go to the police unless he kept quiet about what they'd found. Unless Dad paid him back the small amount of money he'd invested, he would expose Dad as a thief and deny all knowledge of the excavations.'

'That would explain the money that was regularly coming out of Eddie's account.'

'Yes.'

'Penny, I have to ask. Do you think Michael killed your father?'

Penny picked a small bluebell from its stem and put it to her nose.

'I want to think Michael killed him because I could hate him even more, but if I answered you honestly I don't believe Michael would have the guts to murder anyone.'

'So do you think Michael arranged for someone else to have him killed?'

'No I don't think he would. When we got the news of my father's murder, Michael looked just as shocked as anyone else.'

Wesley was walking back to his car when his mobile rang.

'Hi, Sir, Martin here. Bad news about the CCTV in the High Street I'm afraid.'

'Go on.'

'The CCTV wasn't working on the night in question.'

'What do you mean not working!' he shouted.

'A fault was discovered that afternoon on the control panel in the monitoring room above the bank and wasn't repaired until the following morning.'

'Shit!'

'Shall I go back to the station?'

'No. Carry out another walk through the town. Ask anyone and everyone if they remember seeing Denise.'

'But we've already done that.'

'Then you should be good at it. Do it again.' Wesley hung up.

His patience was wearing thin and he knew he was expected to start coming up with some answers. Selecting the contacts button on his mobile he waited for Superintendent Adams to answer.

121

Wesley was back at his desk. Dorothy had disappeared again and there was no CCTV footage to examine from the night before Denise disappeared.

What else could go wrong?

'Yeah what is it?' Wesley snapped as someone tapped on the door.

'Sorry to bother you but Superintendent Adams is on the line. Shall I put him through?' Alison asked.

'Wesley sighed and nodded his head.

'Yeah I guess so.'

For the next few minutes Wesley listened while his boss read him the riot script, demanding for Denise to be found and for a person or persons to be arrested for the recent murders. By the time he hung up, Wesley felt drained.

A short while later Alison informed him that a local taxi driver has just come forward saying he took Harvey White to Havering on the night he died.'

'Did he say anything else?'

'Sure did, said that he remembered Harvey kept asking him to hurry, as if he were meeting someone.'

'Is that it?'

'No, this is the interesting thing. He also said that he'd taken Harvey there on several occasions in the past few weeks. However, except for the last time, when Harvey was killed, he had been told to wait whilst Harvey went into the house, then he would take Harvey home again.'

'So we can safely assume that Harvey had expected to meet someone that night.'

'It would seem that way.'

'Why has the cab driver only just come forward?'

'I thought you'd ask that. It would appear that Harvey paid the driver for his silence. Each time they visited the house, Harvey would pay him additional fare to keep quiet about their visit. On top of that, he used to book the cab under the name of Hastings. It wasn't until the driver saw Harvey's photo in the local did he realise it was the same man.'

Wesley sighed.

'Did he say if Harvey ever took anything to the house or returned with anything?'

'No, nothing. The only thing the driver said was that he never saw anyone else on any of the visits and that Harvey was nearly always in a hurry.'

'OK, thanks Alison. Get a statement from the guy and tell him we may want to speak to him again.'

Deciding there was nothing to be gained by staying in the office; Wesley drove into Street heading for the Fox and Hounds, his local pub. Although he had to stoop to avoid hitting his head on the wooden beams it didn't deter him from stopping off for a half pint of his favourite beer and something to eat. After receiving his change from the barman he sipped the Abbot Ale as he walked across the flagstone floor and took a table near the window. The pub was fairly quiet with just one or two locals sat at the bar and a couple of young lads who appeared to have finished work early, playing darts. Half an hour later, having eaten Steak and Ale Pie and having finished his beer, the world seemed a better place. Mandy had also phoned him to provide him with details of her meeting with Penny. He tended to agree with Penny's comments in that Michael didn't kill Eddie Hallerton But at least they now had confirmation that Eddie was involved and that Michael was in fact selling historical artefacts.

Arriving back at the station he was surprised when the duty officer advised him that Jenny Stevens was waiting for him. Gathering some mail from under the reception counter, he wearily climbed the stairs. He opened his office door to find Jenny sat with WPC Alison Todd. It was apparent Jenny had been crying.

Alison stood up as he entered the room and beckoned for him to step outside.

'We'll be back in a moment,' she told Jenny.

'What's all this about?' Wesley asked once they were out in the corridor.

'Jenny has just admitted to the murder of Eddie Hallerton?'

'Pardon? Are you serious?'

'Yes, Sir. She says she murdered him.'

Wesley looked stunned.

'Do you think she's telling the truth?'

'I have to admit I do. I don't think she intended killing Eddie. She just wanted to warn him off but they got into an argument. She pushed him and he slipped.'

Wesley scratched his forehead. This was something he hadn't envisaged.

'OK. Let's hear what she has to say.'

When they re-entered the room Jenny had her elbows on the table with her head in her hands. She looked up as Wesley pulled up the chair opposite.

'I'm informed by WPC Alison Todd that you wish to admit to the murder of Eddie Hallerton. Is that correct?'

'Yes Inspector.'

'Before we continue, you do realise what it is you're saying?'

'Yes, I should have told you before. I can't keep it to myself any longer.'

'Do you wish for a lawyer to be present?'

'No, can we just get on with it?'

Wesley nodded to Alison who switched on the tape machine and read out the date and time along with the names of those present. Wesley then continued.

'Jenny Stevens, you have stated that you are responsible for the death of Eddie Hallerton. Is that correct?'

'Yes Inspector. I killed him.'

'Can you please explain what happened?'

'I saw Eddie Hallerton enter the Chapel next to Abbey House.' Jenny coughed before continuing.

'I then followed him into the Chapel where I found him sitting by the grated access to the Well.'

She looked across the table, tears streaming down her face.

'Then what happened?'

'I asked Eddie what he was doing. He told me to mind my own business. I told him I knew what he and Michael had been doing and that I felt that historical artefacts should be left where they were or at least not sold but put on display for the general public.'

'What was his response?'

'He stood up and took a step towards me. He started shouting that I ought to mind my own business. He said local folk were entitled to their share of whatever was found on their land.'

'Did he threaten you?'

'I was scared he was going to hit me,' she cried.

'Did he attack you?'

'He shouted at me and started to wave his fist.'

'What did you do next?'

'I punched him twice on the chest with both hands. The problem was he slipped backwards and hit his head on the marble floor. I thought he was just unconscious!' Jenny screamed. 'I didn't know what to do. I couldn't just leave him there! The Chapel was due to be opened in a couple of hours.'

'So what did you do?'

'I dragged him forward over the hole. When I had his head and shoulders over the Well, I lifted his legs and dropped him in. How was I to know he had already broken his neck? I just wanted him out of everyone's view.'

Jenny slumped forward, her head on the table.

Wesley looked at Alison and nodded toward the tape machine.

Alison read out the date and time saying that the interview was concluded and switched the machine off before the two of them left the room.

'Take Jenny down to the cells and make sure she's given something to eat and drink. I'll call the local doctor. She'll need something to make her sleep tonight.'

122

Following the short drive to Bath, Wesley parked the car at the back of the Mayflower Hotel. The place had seen better days. The tiled flooring at the entrance was broken in several places and the reception area had that musty smell that old buildings take on when they haven't been decorated for some time.

Wesley walked over to the reception counter where a middle aged woman was sat playing Sudoku on a pc. She looked up and peered over her glasses when Wesley gave a polite cough.

'Single rooms are £45per night. We've got two en-suites on the 1st floor or a room with separate bathroom on the 2nd. That one's only £37:50.'

'I'm not looking for a room,' Wesley replied thrusting his ID in front of her. 'I'm here to speak with a Mr Paul Hare who I believe is staying here.'

The woman squinted at his ID and then back at him before answering.

'I'll have a look in the book.'

She returned to her pc and saved what she'd done before pushing back her chair to stand up.

'What's the name again?' She opened a shabby looking register and started to leaf through the pages.

'Hare, Mr Paul Hare.'

'Oh here we are, arrived yesterday. Room 22 on the 1st floor. Do you want me to telephone his room? I Haven't seen him today.'

'It's OK, I'll walk up. Sorry to have disturbed you.'

She gave Wesley a disdainful look as he walked away.

He found room 22 just on the right at the top of the stairs. He knocked and waited for Paul Hare to answer. He knocked twice again before he heard movement in the room. A shuffling of feet and then the chain being unhooked from inside the door preceded a bleary eyed David Hare poking his head through the crack.

'Oh it's you Inspector,' he slurred.

Wesley followed him into the room and closed the door behind him. The room was a mess. Clothes were spread everywhere and two empty bottles of whisky stood on the small bedside table.

David Hare looked nothing like the man who Wesley had first met only twenty-four hours ago. His shirt and trousers were badly creased where he'd obviously slept in them. His hair was all dishevelled and he sported a day's growth on his face.

'Are you OK?' Wesley asked as he took everything in.

'My son's dead Inspector. I thought I could handle it but I'm not so sure now.'

He sat on the edge of the bed and waved his arms in a carefree motion.

'I've come to terms with losing my wife. You know stiff upper lip and all that but no one should have to bury their child.'

Wesley could see the tears welling up in the proud man's eyes.

Extracting a few items of clothes from Paul's suitcase Wesley handed them to him.

'Grab these. Once you've showered, we'll walk up the road and have a bite to eat.'

Paul Hare sat clutching his clothes as Wesley made his way to the door.

'I'll be in reception having a cigarette.'

Paul nodded in response.

When Paul Hare walked into the reception area some thirty minutes later he looked a different person. Having shaved and showered and now wearing blue cords with a white, short sleeved shirt, he had suddenly regained that assured composure that he'd carried when Wesley had first met him.

'There's a nice little café just up the road. Come on, I'll treat you to a cordon bleu delight,' said Wesley.

Paul couldn't help but laugh and followed him out of the hotel.

It was obvious that the man hadn't eaten for some time as he tucked into a huge fry up washed down by two cups of tea.

'Ah that feels better,' Paul said rubbing his belly. 'Thanks Inspector, I owe you one.'

'No problem,' Wesley replied as he finished his own omelette and chips.

'I feel quite ashamed at my behaviour Inspector. I was brought up to look after myself and ride out anything that I came up against but this has been a whole different ball game. Have you got a family, Inspector?'

'Yes I have, I'm married to a lovely lady.'

Wesley placed his cup down on the table and wiped his mouth with the paper napkin.

'I know what it's like to lose someone you love. My first wife was killed a few years back. At the time I didn't know that I could handle it. I wasn't even sure that I wanted to handle it. Don't get me wrong Paul, I wasn't suicidal or anything like that but nothing seemed important any longer. Nothing seemed to interest me and I didn't see the point of going to work, eating, or even getting up in the morning.'

'Do you know Inspector, I think you just described all the emotions I felt yesterday.'

'We're only human Paul, only human.'

'What brought you over here Inspector? Surely not to check on my health?'

'I came here to tell you that you were right.'

'I don't understand?'

'I'm sorry but there's something I have to tell you Paul, David's crash was no accident. The brakes on his car had been tampered with.'

Paul placed his elbows on the table and put his hands over his face. When he looked up there was a look of anger and disbelief on his face.

'I knew it couldn't be an accident. David was such a careful driver. He's probably the only owner of a sports car that rarely went over thirty miles an hour.'

'Well, we know he was speeding when the crash occurred,' Wesley said. 'I don't know if Sally told you but she and David had been arguing just before he drove off. She blames herself for what's happened.'

'I didn't know.' Paul looked down at the table. 'I'd like to go and see Sally in the morning. I have to meet her parents too. I need her to understand that she's not to blame herself for any of this,' Paul said sternly.

It was early evening and a tired looking Wesley was working his way through a mound of paperwork. He had just phoned a shocked Jane to tell her about Jenny's admission and to say he'd be home late when Alison knocked on the door.

'I thought you might want to view this,' she said handing him an A3 piece of paper.

'It's the artist's impression of the woman seen with Denise the night before she disappeared.'

Wesley studied the pencilled sketch while Alison waited for him to comment.

'Are you thinking the same?' he asked after a few moments.

'Dorothy Hallerton?'

'Exactly but I don't understand? Why would Dorothy be in Glastonbury at that time of the evening? More importantly why would she talking to Denise?'

'I don't know but you said yourself only this morning that you had some doubts about the woman.'

'I think Dorothy Hallerton has some explaining to do.'

'Do you want me to bring her in?'

'No. Thanks Alison. I'll pay Dorothy another visit tomorrow. She owes me a few explanations. I think it's time Dorothy and I had a long chat.'

123

It was only eight o'clock in the morning when Wesley, accompanied by WPC Mandy Tredwell, rang the front door bell at Abbey House. Minutes later a bleary eyed Penny Westbrook opened the door. She was still dressed in her dressing gown and her hair was bunched up like a bird's nest on top of her head.

'Oh morning Inspector, morning Mandy. Do come in.'

She stood back, allowing them to enter the grand hallway and after closing the door, led them to the kitchen.

'What brings you over at this time of the morning?' she asked as she filled the kettle.

Wesley and Mandy both sat at the kitchen table.

'Come and sit down for a second. I have something I need to tell you,' said Wesley.

Penny's jaw dropped and a look of horror came to her face as she raised her hands to her face.

'Oh my God. It's Michael isn't it?' she cried.

Mandy stood up and escorted her gently across the room and sat her at the kitchen table.

'No, what I have to tell you actually refers to Jenny Stevens,' Wesley replied watching her reaction.

'Jenny came into the station yesterday and admitted being responsible for your father's death.'

'I don't understand. What has Jenny got to do with Dad's murder?'

'It would appear that Jenny found Eddie in the Chapel just as he had removed the floor entrance to the Well. She challenged him as to what he was doing. When he confronted her she struck out to hit him on the chest, at which point Eddie slipped backwards, hitting his head on the marble floor. He was unconscious. Jenny panicked. Knowing that the Chapel was due to be open later that morning, she dragged his body towards the Well and pushed him down.'

Penny looked bewildered.

'She heard noises outside the Chapel and expected someone to enter at any time so she quickly locked the door and made her exit. That's why she never closed the grill cover. If she had closed it, we may never have found Eddie. Certainly not for some time in any case.'

'I don't believe this. Why? What had any of this to do with Jenny?'

'She has admitted to being in love with your husband. She says she was trying to protect him.'

Penny started to shake and laugh at the same time.

'What's so amusing?' Wesley asked.

'Oh, the stupid girl. Didn't she realise that Michael was using her. She was just his bit on the side, a distraction to his mental problems. A substitute for our loveless marriage, someone he could manipulate.'

'Would you mind if we take a look at her bedroom?' Mandy asked placing a reassuring hand on Penny's shoulder.

'No of course not. Empty it for all I care. I don't want the girl back in my house. Her bedroom is at the top of the stairs, first door on the right.'

Wesley made himself a tea and poured a black coffee for Penny whilst Mandy went to search the bedroom returning ten minutes later with a plastic bag full of items.

'Would you just sign to say I've taken these?'

'Are you going to be alright on your own?' asked Wesley. 'I can arrange for someone to stay with you.'

'Do you think I'm going to top myself or something?'

'No, but…'

'Inspector, I have to get used to the idea of living on my own. I'm not foolish enough to believe that Michael is ever coming home. You know as well as I do that he's going to be institutionalised.'

'If you need…'

Penny raised her arms in despair.

'If I need you, I'll call. I'd rather be left alone now if that's OK.'

Wesley looked at Mandy before nodding.

'OK, take care of yourself Penny.'

'You don't think she'll do anything silly, do you?' Mandy asked after they left.

'No, I think she's quite a strong young woman. Either way, I'd ask you to give her a call tonight. Just say it's an unofficial call and that you are just checking that she's OK.'

'Sure thing.'

124

'I've written to your mother. Your future is in her hands now.'

Denise looked up at her captor who was retying her legs after allowing Denise the comfort of changing into new clothes.

'You know who my mother is?' she asked timidly.

'I know everything about you.'

'Then you know that I've done nothing wrong. Please just let me go. I want to go home,' she pleaded.

'I'm sorry but that's not possible. You're my ace in the pack now. There's no turning back. I will have the King's items returned then we can all be at peace.'

'The King's items? What on earth are you talking about?'

Her captor ignored her question, shoving her dirty clothes into a bag. She began to walk away towards the trap door.

'I'll scream all night until someone hears me,' Denise cried.

Her captor dropped the bag and walked back to where Denise was crouched against the wall. She watched as her captor withdrew a reel of masking tape from a coat pocket, tore off a strip and thrust it on her face covering her mouth. At first Denise thought she would suffocate until she calmed down a little and started breathing through her nose.

'That will keep you quiet.'

Denise looked on in horror as her captor lifted the trap door to descend the steps below. The slamming of the door as it closed left Denise back alone in her silent nightmare world. A world she was beginning to believe she would never escape from.

125

Penny saw the envelope on the floor by the front door. Her heart missed a beat when she saw the handwriting and her hands were trembling when she ripped it open.

Return the King's treasure, that's all I want now and Denise will be returned safely. You will be told where and when.
If you value your daughter's life, no police.

Penny read the message several times. It was the same typing font as before. She moved into the library and sat on the settee trying to understand what it was that Denise's captor expected her to provide.
The King's treasure? What does it mean?
Penny toyed with the card Wesley had left her. Her initial instinct told her she should phone him straight away but was she putting her daughter's life at risk? How did she know if her daughter was still alive?
Her mind was racing with a million thoughts. She poured herself a large brandy and paced up and down the room. An hour and two more brandies later, Penny was slumped in the chair looking out of the French doors to the extensive gardens beyond. Her face was stained with tears. The letter still in her hand.
Penny woke an hour later with a heavy head. The empty brandy glass lay on the carpet. The sun had now dipped behind the far trees on the edge of the wood. It took her mind a few seconds to realise the house phone was ringing. She ran out to the hallway and picked up the receiver. Before she could speak, the line went dead.
'Hello!' she shouted. 'Please speak to me!'
Penny replaced the receiver, sat on the floor next to the small table where the telephone stood and sobbed.

126

Wesley found Dorothy picking her herbs in her back garden.

'Oh hello Inspector,' she replied with a startled look when he called across the garden fence. 'I won't keep you a moment. I'll just put these cuttings in the basket.'

'No hurry, I just popped round for a quick chat.'

Wesley stood by the garden gate whilst Dorothy placed her tools and basket of clippings in the shed.

'Looks like that was good timing. It's just starting to rain again. What brings you here?' she asked as she walked up the garden path dusting down her apron.

'I'd like to ask you a couple of questions about Harvey White.'

Dorothy stopped in her tracks and turned to face him.

'Harvey White? The man who was recently found dead in Havering?'

'Yes. How did you know about his death?'

'I read about it in the local paper. He was stabbed wasn't he?'

'Yes that's right.' Wesley followed her into the house.

He finished his cigarette by the back door as Dorothy went inside to wash her hands. After rubbing the remains between his thumb and forefinger he stepped into the kitchen. What caught his immediate attention were the red wellington boots that stood under the sink.

When Dorothy re-entered the kitchen she looked harassed.

'I hope I haven't called at an inconvenient time,' Wesley commented.

'Oh no, that's alright Inspector. I do have quite a busy day though. A thousand things to do and so little time to do them. I have some cakes to bake and still need to prepare invitations for the village fete which is just two weeks from now.'

'In that case, I'll keep my visit short. I was asking if you knew Harvey White.'

'Yes. I had known him for several years. We both used to belong to the Historical Society and were once both members of the Somerset Levels Preservation group, created to ensure that local areas of interest were protected and not destroyed by fanciful historians or people who simply chase legendary myths for fun.'

'Have you any idea what Harvey would be doing in a house in Havering? We know he didn't live there.'

'Tea Inspector?'

'Pardon?'

'I was asking if you wanted tea.'

'Oh, err, thanks, yes. So would you know what business Harvey had in Havering?'

Dorothy stopped what she was and turned to face Wesley.

'Inspector. I may be an old woman but don't take me for a fool. From your questions it's obvious that you already know that Harvey and I was once an item as everyone so rudely puts it these days. However, for your information, I haven't seen or spoken to Harvey for a number of years. We never had an argument or anything like that, it was just that he and Eddie didn't see eye to eye. I'm not prepared to expand on that any further.'

'Dorothy,' Wesley replied rather defensively. 'I wasn't suggesting anything. I just wanted to know how much you knew about the man.'

She placed two cups on the table and filled the kettle with water.

'Harvey was quite a recluse. He was always embarrassed at his disability. You know he suffered from polio?'

'Yes, I knew.'

'He was a very educated man. Someone who liked his privacy and someone who thought that history should remain untouched.'

He waited until she had poured the tea and had sat down at the table.

'Dorothy, I have to ask. Do you know anyone who would have disliked Harvey?'

She laughed.

'Oh yes a number of people disliked him Inspector. He wasn't always a likeable man. He had quite a short temper with people who he referred to as the uneducated but if you're asking if I knew anyone who disliked him enough to murder him, then I would say no.'

They drank their tea in silence for a few moments before Wesley spoke.

'We still haven't found the girl yet,' he said changing the subject.

'Girl?'

'Yes, Denise Wright, the girl who went missing over a week ago.'

'Oh the young lass who works in the Tourist office?'

'Yes that's the one.'

'The trouble these days is that the youngsters are so promiscuous aren't they? I mean, you hear all these stories about young girls running off to live abroad with some Spanish or Greek waiter.' 'Poor Penny, she must be distraught.'

She drank the rest of her tea and stood up, placing the cup in the sink.

'Well, I must get on Inspector.'

Wesley put his cup down on the table and stood up to leave.

'Whose were the clothes we found in the shed?'

'What clothes?'

'There was a bag full of ladies clothing in the shed. Who's were they?'

'How did you find them? You know I forgot they were there,' she replied. 'They were some of the clothes I collected from the village hall charity event.

They were to go to the charity clothes shop in Glastonbury. Can I ask why you're interested in them? I assume you have taken them.'

Wesley hesitated, trying to think of an answer. He couldn't tell her that Jane had been looking through her things.

'We found them by accident a couple of days ago when we popped round looking for you. Jane said they would go mouldy if they were left there.'

Dorothy didn't even query why.

'So you still have them?'

'Yes I'll drop them back.'

He turned to leave.

'One last question Dorothy if I may? Where did you get those red boots from? I'll have to buy Jane a pair.'

'Oh those. I bought them from the garden centre in the village. They have red, blue, green and even pink ones I think.'

'Have you had them very long, only I'm sure I saw a woman wearing them one evening in Glastonbury a few days ago?'

'No, I only bought these the day before yesterday Inspector. They caught my eye. A bit funky for my age though. Don't you think?'

'Err yeah maybe. Right, thanks. I'll take a look.'

Wesley headed for the back door.

'Don't worry, I'll see myself out. Thanks for the tea.'

127

Wesley pulled into the station car park just as Jenny's solicitor was getting out of his car.

'Hi Inspector.'

'Hello Barry.'

Wesley had met Barry Haines on a couple of occasions since he'd moved down to Street. Barry represented anyone who had been arrested who couldn't afford a solicitor of their own.

Wesley led the way into the station and up to the first floor to his office. He quickly ran through everything on the incident board to bring Barry up to date then had Alison escort Barry down to the cells to have a brief with Jenny.

Half an hour later, Jenny, accompanied by Barry and Alison entered the interview room where Wesley was already sat with PC Martin Philips.

Once they were all seated Wesley informed Jenny that the interview would be recorded. Martin switched on the tape machine, recording the date and time and names of those present.

Wesley advised Jenny that she has been arrested for the murder of Eddie Hallerton. She didn't answer. She just stared across the table.

After a night in the cells she looked dishevelled. She was wearing the same clothes as the day before and it was apparent from her red rimmed eyes that she had been crying.

'Jenny, do you understand what I have told you?'

'Yes.'

'OK. I'd like you to tell me again what happened when you found Eddie Hallerton in the Chapel.'

Jenny repeated the same story as she had given the day before. The only thing she added was that she thought Eddie Hallerton was going to attack her. That's why she struck out at him. She never intended him any harm and had no intention of killing him.

She said her actions were purely in self-defence.

Wesley then asked why she had not gone to the police in the first place, instead of tackling Eddie. Jenny replied that Michael told her that he was in trouble and that all she did was try to help him. She said she loved Michael and believed that Eddie was trying to cheat on him.

'Why didn't you come forward when you found out that Eddie had died from the fall?'

Jenny looked to her solicitor before replying.

'I was frightened. I was so scared. I didn't know what I was thinking. I'm so sorry. I never meant to hurt the man.'

'When did you find out that Michael was taking drugs?'

The question caught Jenny by surprise and she sat tight lipped until her solicitor spoke in her ear.

When she eventually answered, there was an air of resignation about her. She puffed her cheeks and sighed.

'Michael was taking drugs for depression but then he started to need something stronger. He gave me the name of a contact he'd found and I arranged to meet the guy once a week.'

'I need names and addresses,' Wesley replied.

'I only knew the guy as Mason. I used to meet him in the café at the bus station.'

'Can you describe him?'

'Sure.'

Martin wrote down the details as she read them out.

Wesley then changed his questions back to Eddie Hallerton.

'Did you know that Michael was blackmailing Eddie?'

'Yes he told me. He said he was only doing it because Eddie had threatened to go to the police about the artefacts they had found and that the money he got from Eddie was helping to pay for his growing need for drugs.'

Wesley made a couple of notes before continuing.

'Jenny, is there anything you want to ask me?'

She looked to her solicitor.

'No Inspector.'

'In which case, Jenny Stevens I am legally bound to inform you that you will be held in the cells until tomorrow morning when you will be taken before the court charged with the murder of Eddie Hallerton.'

Martin then announced the time and date saying the interview had finished and switched off the tape machine.

Alison led Jenny away.

'Do you think any of this is linked to the recent murders on the Tor and the murder of Harvey White?' Wesley asked Barry Haines when they were alone.

'I wish I had the answer to that John.'

'You must have a gut feeling?'

Barry took a deep sigh.

'If you want my honest opinion, then maybe.'

A smile came to Wesley's face.

'That sounds like a kop out answer Barry.'

'That's because it is. Off the record, I think Jenny was being used and honestly believed that Michael was in love with her. I think he used her the same way he used Eddie. Someone to do his dirty work.'

'What hurts me most is that it's such a waste of a life. She's still only a kid really,' said Wesley.

'I agree, but unfortunately in my job I see it all too often,' Barry replied.

128

'Hello. Who is it?'

'Hi Penny, its WPC Tredwell. Blimey you must have been standing next to the phone.'

'Oh, err. Yes. Hello Mandy.'

'Are you OK?'

'Oh yes. I'm fine thanks. I'm expecting a phone call from the building company who are working on the East Wing,' she lied.

'Are you sure you're OK? If you don't mind me saying, you sound rather nervous.'

'No really, I'm fine.'

'I just phoned to make sure you were alright. It's not an official call. I was just worried about you.' Mandy hated not telling the truth but she knew she would get a better response from Penny.

'I do appreciate you calling me, I really do but I'm fine thanks. I have to move on and get on with things. I might go up to visit Michael later, I have some documents he needs to sign but I have to phone first to make sure the doctors are happy for me to visit.'

'Alright, You know where I am if you need me,' Mandy replied still unconvinced.

'I do. Thanks again Mandy. I appreciate it.' Penny hung up and leant against the wall in the hallway. She looked at her hands, they were both shaking. Heading towards the library she needed a drink.

Less than a minute later the phone rang again. Penny ran back out into the hall, snatching the phone from its cradle. With a trembling voice she answered. 'Yes?'

She recognised the voice but her mind was racing.

'Tonight at eight o'clock, leave the tapestry and the vase at the bottom of the steps by the entrance to the ruins of the Lady Chapel. I know you have the King's possessions. Do not hang around. Once you have done this I will telephone you the details of where you will find Denise.'

'How do I know she is still alive?' Penny shouted. 'Where is my daughter?'

The caller hung up. She frantically dialled 1471 in an attempt to obtain the telephone number but the number had been withheld. Penny replaced the receiver and slumped to the floor. Tears streamed down her face as her sobbing racked her whole body.

129

Wesley stretched his weary limbs as Jane prepared the table for dinner.
'Did you get the chance to speak with Dorothy today?' she asked.
'Yeah,' he replied yawning.
'She said she was busy and really couldn't wait for me to leave.'
'Oh, what was she doing then?'
'Preparing invitations for the village fete, baking cakes etc. Oh, I did ask her where she bought her boots from.'
'Boots? What boots?'
'She had a pair of red boots in her kitchen. Similar to those that the person was seen wearing when speaking to Denise the night before Denise disappeared.'
'You mean like wellington boots?'
'Yeah that's right.'
'Did she say where she bought them from?'
'Yeah, from the garden centre at the end of the village.'
Jane placed the utensils on the kitchen table.
'The garden centre has been closed for more than twelve months. Don't you remember? It closed when the new shopping centre opened.'
Wesley suddenly sat up in the chair.
'What's wrong John?' Jane asked.
'Something that Dorothy said. It's been niggling me and I now know why.'
'What is it?'
'When I said we still hadn't found Denise, she said oh you mean the girl from the Tourist office. Then she said, poor Penny, she must be distraught.'
Jane shrugged her shoulders as if to say so what?
'Don't you see? No one apart from the people on the case know that Penny is Denise's mother!'
Wesley jumped out of the chair and ran to the house phone. There was no reply from Dorothy's place.
'Fancy a drive with me?' he asked Jane.
'What about dinner?'
'We can heat it up. Come on. I've a feeling this may be the breakthrough we've been waiting for.'

Wesley banged on the front door of the cottage but there was no answer.

Jane had walked around the side of the cottage to look in the back garden but there was no sign of Dorothy. Wesley peered through the letterbox but the whole house was in darkness.

'She's not here,' said Jane as she joined him at the front door.

'I tried the back door but it's locked.'

Wesley retrieved his mobile phone and called the station. Alison answered on the second call.

'Hi, Sir.' You OK?'

'Hi Alison, yeah good thanks. Who have we got on shift tonight?'

'Martin is still around and Adam is on the late shift. He's out in the patrol car now. He went to talk to a couple of kids who have been seen throwing stones at cars from the motorway bridge between here and Bath.'

'OK good. I'm over at Dorothy's but she's not here. I have a key so I'm going to take a look around. I'll explain why later. Give Adam a call and ask him to pick Martin up and head over to Abbey House. They're to wait instructions from me. They're not to enter until I arrive. Is that clear?'

'Yes, Sir.'

'By the way, where's Mandy? Is she off shift?'

'Yes, but I know she was going to visit her mother in Glastonbury tonight.'

'Do me a favour, Alison. Try to contact her. I appreciate she's not on duty now but she has been speaking to Penny Westbrook today. Ask her to make another call to Penny, unofficial like. I want to know what Penny's doing.'

'Ok will do. I'll get her to call you direct.'

'Thanks Alison. Stay close to the phone. I think it's going to be a busy night.'

Jane handed him the front door key and they let themselves in. Wesley ran upstairs to check the bedrooms whilst Jane searched the downstairs. With the lounge being empty she entered the kitchen. Switching on the light she stood aghast looking at the vast array of herbs and spices laying on the table.

Wesley joined her after confirming the upstairs was empty.

'What on earth has she been doing?' he asked.

'Well I can't be sure,' Jane replied as she examined one of the small glass jars lined up on one side the table, 'but if I were to take a guess, I would say she's been mixing herbs with some of this stuff.'

She held up a small glass bottle that contained a clear looking fluid, opened it and smelt the contents.

'To create what?' he asked.

'A sleeping drug?'

She opened the fridge and pulled out two plates of food, both covered in cellophane. On the same shelf were a number of syringes, all of them empty. Wesley stood next to her and peered into the fridge.

'What do you make of all this?' he muttered.

Jane stared in disbelief.

'Oh my God. You don't think she could be feeding these meals to someone knowing they were being drugged?'

'You mean someone like Denise?'

Jane put her hands to her mouth. Wesley tapped a couple of numbers on his mobile.

'Sir?' asked Alison almost immediately.

'Alison. Put out an APB for Dorothy Hallerton.'

'Dorothy Hallerton?'

'Yes, correct. I want all officers in the Glastonbury area to keep a look out for her. If anyone sees her, then follow but don't approach. I want to know where she's headed for.'

130

When the station phone rang, Alison thought it was Wesley again.
'Sir?'
'Oh good evening. I'm sorry to bother you. It's Sally Martin speaking.'
'Oh hello Miss Martin. WPC Bolt here. How can I help you?'
'Is Inspector Wesley there?'
'I'm afraid not. Can I be of assistance?'
'Well it may mean nothing at all but I have been looking through some of David's papers. I'm shredding most of his old stuff. However, I've just come across the drawing that he was working on just before he died and some papers that he'd come across. As I say it probably means nothing but either David or someone placed a large cross next to a building called the Abbot's kitchen.'
'The what?' Alison asked.
'The Abbot's kitchen. It's an old cone shaped building in the middle of the Glastonbury Abbey ruins. I don't want to waste the Inspectors time. I just thought he ought to know. There's something else too. The photocopy attached has a signature on it. The signature reads Dorothy Westbrook.'
'Westbrook? Are you sure?'
'I think that's what it is. As I say, it may not mean anything. I just thought the Inspector ought to know.'
'Thank you for the information Miss Martin. I'll make sure the Inspector is informed.'
After Sally had hung up, Alison wrote the details on a piece of paper and placed them in Wesley's in-tray.

131

Penny closed the front door behind her. She had wrapped the artefacts in a cloth and now held them tightly under her arm. The tapestry and vase she had removed from the front parlour. The other items she had taken from the West Wing where Michael had hidden them until they were to be sold.

She looked out across the grounds. Pockets of mist hung in the air, looking like ghosts patrolling their domain. Penny shivered as she walked out into the rain. She wasn't sure she was doing the right thing but she wanted her daughter back.

Quietly closing the wrought iron gates that acted as the entrance to Abbey House she followed the gravel footpath through the grounds towards the ruins of Glastonbury Abbey. Stopping by St Dunstan's Chapel she leant against what remained of the outer wall. She suddenly felt lonely and isolated but it was too late to turn back now.

Taking a shortcut across the grassy bank, she almost slipped on the wet ground. Clutching the items in both hands she made her way down the slope toward the Lady Chapel. With daylight fast disappearing, the Abbey grounds were now almost a black canvass and Penny couldn't see more than ten feet in front of her.

The Lady Chapel, badly damaged by war and time lay just ahead. Reaching the top of the steps that led down to where the entrance to the lower level used to be, Sally felt more exposed than ever. She slowly descended the steps. At the bottom of the steps she placed the collection of artifacts on the stone floor then stood listening for any sounds.

There was an eerie silence to the place, only the faint whispering of the evening breeze as it wound its way across the grounds. Retracing her steps she quickly made her way back to Abbey House. By now the rain had returned and a steady downpour had begun.

As she reached the gated entrance that led towards the Abbey ruins she almost jumped out of her skin when Wesley walked out of the shadows.

'What's going on Penny?'

'Oh! Inspector. You made me jump. I've just been for a walk. I usually take a stroll in the evening.'

'Alone in the dark? In the pouring rain?'

'It's alright. I know the grounds like the back of my hand.'

Wesley's bluntness caught her off guard.

'When did you receive instructions from Denise's kidnapper?'

'I don't know what you're talking about.'

'Penny, this isn't a game. I think you have been contacted by Denise's captor again. That's correct isn't it?'

'No, no-one has…'

'Oh come on Penny. Denise's life is at stake! For Christ's sake wake up to reality. Do you think someone is just going to return her knowing she can almost certainly identify them?'

Penny leant against the gate and started to sob.

'Oh Inspector. What have I done? I just want my little girl back.'

Mandy and Adam helped the distressed woman back into the house where Mandy removed her wet things before sitting her in the library. Mandy sat comforting her whilst Wesley went back into the hall to make a phone call to the station.

'Hi Alison. Listen, I need backup support in Glastonbury. I need the grounds to Glastonbury Abbey sealed off. I need a support team, everyone armed but in plain clothes. I don't want to scare anyone. I'm putting my phone on setting two. All communication is to come through this. Do you understand?'

'Confirmed. Oh, and by the way, Sally Martin phoned and left you a message.'

'Sally Martin?'

'Yes.'

'When was this?'

'About half an hour ago. She said to tell you that she had come across a drawing that David had been studying. The drawing shows the Abbey ruins but what Sally wanted to bring to your attention is that someone had put a cross by the Abbot's kitchen.'

'The what?'

'It's a building called the Abbot's kitchen. It's near the Lady Chapel.'

Wesley turned to Martin who had just entered the house.

'Martin, you're a local lad. Where's the Abbot's kitchen?'

'Just across the way. It's almost in the middle of the grounds, the cone shaped building. Almost still intact it is.'

Wesley spoke into the phone again.

'Thanks Alison. If my instincts are correct I think that's where we're going to find Denise.'

'There's something else Inspector.'

'What is it?'

'Sally says the other document she found is signed by one Dorothy Westbrook.'

'Westbrook? Are you sure?'

'That's what she said.'

'OK thanks.' He hung up.

Wesley turned back to Martin.

'Can you lead us to this place?'

'Sure thing.'

'OK. Give me one minute.'

Wesley re-entered the library where Alison was still comforting Penny. He walked across the room, leaving a trail of wet dirty footprints and knelt down in front of where Penny was sat.

'Penny, listen to me. I need to know right now what's happened this evening. Not only is Denise's life at stake but so too are the lives of several policemen who will be searching the grounds along with an armed support team.'

Penny told him about the phone call and where she had left the artefacts. Wesley turned to Martin.

'Martin, where is this in relation to the Abbot's kitchen?'

Both Penny and Mandy looked confused but Wesley didn't have time to explain.

'The two buildings are adjacent to one another.'

'OK, Martin you come with me, Mandy stay here with Penny. There will be two armed officers by the gates to the house so no one can get in.'

Mandy nodded in acknowledgement. As Wesley turned to leave, Penny called out.

'I'm sorry for all this mess Inspector but please bring Denise back home.'

Wesley nodded then turned and left the room.

132

Having caught the bus into Glastonbury, Dorothy walked around the perimeter of the Abbey grounds to the back of Abbey House. Making sure no one was around she squeezed through the hedge. A route she had made numerous times before.

Crossing the lawn she stood next to the tree behind the spot where Eddie had planted the new yew trees. She knew the house alarm wouldn't go off. She'd switched alarm zones four and five off several days ago. They were the ones that covered the outside of the building. It was only Eddie who knew how to operate the alarm system so neither Michael nor Penny had any idea.

She got down on her hands and knees and swept away the leaves and dirt that covered the entrance. Pulling back the metal cover, she retrieved her bag and checking her footing stepped backwards down into the hole. She knew there were twelve steps before she reached firm ground.

Once inside, she switched on a torch to light her way and made her way slowly to the next level down. At the end of the tunnel she located a stone slab in the floor where two iron grips protruded. Grabbing the handles she slowly slid the slab to one side. Inside the lower tunnel it felt colder and she relied on her torch to light every step. Passing the point where the roof opened up to expose a narrow set of steps, Dorothy laughed to herself. She thought it amazing that no one had ever traced her route since she had moved Denise from the room above several days ago. Descending further downhill going deeper into the Chalice Well she reached the inner circle where only a small ledge on either side allowed one to continue around the outside of the Well. In the centre, the Well dropped over a hundred feet. Dorothy knew the precise times when anyone could cross and with the heavy rain the area would soon flood.

Having navigated herself around the chasm she entered the tunnel on the other side and continued into the dark wet passage until she reached the steps that were built into the side wall.

She stood on the 3rd step, raised her arm and pulled back the bolt. Then with both arms she pushed back the cover to expose the interior of the Abbot's kitchen. Switching off her torch she waited for a moment for her eyes to adjust to the grey light before throwing her bag on the floor and climbing into the room.

Denise was sleeping in the recess of one of the huge chimneys. The drugs that Dorothy had administered on her food earlier in the day had once again taken effect.

She walked across the earthen floor to where the huge oak door stood. Extracting the wrought iron key from her coat pocket, she unlocked the door and then slowly slid back the iron bolts at the top and bottom. Many years ago, due to structural safety reasons and the fact that the earthen floor wouldn't stand up to processions of tourists, the Abbot's kitchen was boarded up and closed to the public.

It was during that time that Eddie had stolen the key and showed Dorothy how to access the building from the Chalice Well.

Peering out into the gloomy night air, Dorothy cursed the weather. The rain had increased and now swept across the open ground, soaking everything in sight. Listening for any sounds other than the wind and rain, she closed the door quietly behind her and staying close to the outside wall of the Abbot's kitchen she made her way to the back of the building.

The Lady Chapel stood a hundred yards down the slope. She checked her watch. It was eight-thirty. If Penny had done as she had asked, then the artefacts would be waiting for her.

Dorothy crossed the grassy slope and down the steps into the entrance to the Lady Chapel. What looked like a bundle of rags was laid on the floor. Dorothy quickly un-wrapped the cloth to inspect the contents. A broad but brief smile came to her face. Quickly tying the cloth she picked up the bundle in both hands and made her way back swiftly to the Abbot's kitchen.

Once inside the dome shaped building she relocked the door and placed the bundle by the trap door to the Well.

Denise was stirring. Dorothy crossed the floor to where she lay and grabbed her by the shoulder, shaking her.

'Denise,' she whispered. 'Wake up.'

Denise opened her bleary eyes to see Dorothy rummaging through the bag at her side.

'What are you doing?' she asked.

Dorothy didn't answer but extracted a small metal container. Denise watched as her captor opened the lid withdrawing a syringe.

'What are you doing?' Denise asked again. Her whole body tensed and she tried to move away but she was already up against the chimney wall.

'I have received the artefacts I wanted but I'm afraid I can't let you just walk away. You see, unfortunately you know me, so once the police question you, I'd be arrested.'

'Just let me go,' Denise pleaded. 'I won't say anything to anyone. I promise.'

'I'm sorry, I can't take that chance,' Dorothy replied as she started to fill the syringe.

She watched as Dorothy squirted a small amount of clear liquid into the air and tried to recoil as her captor grabbed her arm.

'Dorothy, don't do this. We can work it out.'

'It's too late, too much has happened. This is an herbal drug that I make myself. It won't cause you any pain. It will just put you to sleep. The herbal traces would have been absorbed into your blood stream by the time they carry out a post mortem.'

Dorothy aimed the syringe at Denise's arm.

'No!' Denise screamed and tried to pull away.

At that moment there was a thud on the door to the Abbot's kitchen, so loud, that it echoed around the cone shaped building.

'Dorothy! This is Inspector Wesley. I know you're in there. Open the door!'

Dorothy stopped in her actions and Denise grabbed the opportunity by knocking the syringe out of her hand.

'Damn you!' she cried.

'Open the door Dorothy or we'll break it down.'

Grabbing Denise by the hair she pulled her out of the recess and dragged her across the floor towards the open trap door.

'Stay away, Inspector. This is none of your business.'

'Murder and kidnapping are my business Dorothy.'

Dorothy extracted a knife from her coat pocket, clicked it open and held it to Denise's throat.

Denise screamed. 'She's got a knife Mr Wesley. Help me!'

'It's OK, Denise. Stay calm,' he shouted trying to reassure the girl.

At the same time he beckoned one of support team forward and whispered his plan before turning back to face the door.

'Dorothy, listen to me. No one else has to get hurt. There's been too much blood spilt already. Let Denise go and you and I can talk.'

'There's nothing to talk about Inspector. I have to return the artefacts to where they belong. It is my duty.'

'Dorothy I understand. I now know who your family are. You were christened Dorothy Alice Westbrook. Abbey House really belongs to you.'

Wesley waited but there was no reply.

'Dorothy, talk to me. We can work this out.'

'That's what David Hare said. The meddling fool found out that I was born into the Westbrook family. He sent me a letter saying that he didn't understand why I wasn't living at Abbey House. He even asked me why I was so poor when my family was so rich.'

'So you tampered with the brakes on his car, knowing that could only lead to one thing.'

'He was asking too many questions.'

Her chilling laugh sent a shiver down his spine.

'Is that why you killed Colin Dempster too?'

'That man was too clever for his boots. Collecting every bloody map he could find.'

'How did you get into his apartment?' Wesley asked.

'That was easy. I changed into a set of cleaners clothes and carried a broom and bucket along the corridor. No one takes any notice of a cleaner, do they?'

'Dorothy, it doesn't have to end this way.'

'It's too late Inspector. Can't you see? I've already killed. You know as well as I do you can't just let me walk away. I'll be sent to prison for life.'

'That doesn't give you reason to hurt Denise, she's done nothing wrong.'

'She's Penny's daughter. She was the only way I could get to Penny. She was the only way I could get the artefacts back.'

'OK but you have them now. Let her go.'

One of Wesley's men scurried forward to advise Wesley that heat sensors confirmed that Dorothy and Denise were in the middle of the building. Knowing that the Abbot's kitchen was a designated historic building owned by the National Trust, he couldn't afford to damage it without agreement from people above him. He knew there wasn't time for that, so after consultation with the support officer they agreed the best method of gaining access to the building was by systematically removing the screws from the wooden planks covering the three window recesses around the building. Once done, he would then give the signal to enter the building. Armed officers would then surround Dorothy.

As the cone shaped roof was deemed unsafe, the building had been boarded up and closed to the public for the past few years.

Any other form of gaining entry was likely to bring the whole place down.

'You must keep Dorothy talking for as long as you can. I'll give you the signal when we're ready,' he whispered.

'Dorothy, can you hear me? Who else did you kill?'

'That idiot Kelvin Ward. He wanted to steal the artefacts. That's what he wanted to excavate the graveyard in Havering for. He thought that my ancestors had buried some of the artefacts with them.'

'And they hadn't?'

Dorothy laughed again.

'No Inspector. Until Michael Westbrook had paid Eddie to remove them from below the Well, they had been there since the day King Arthur died.'

The whisper in Wesley's ear told him they needed another two minutes. The rain was incessant now and the driving wind made it difficult for them to see far. Dorothy was struggling to open the trap door whilst keeping hold of Denise when Wesley called out to her again.

'So who was responsible for the murder of Suzie Potter?'

'That was Michael.'

'Michael? Michael Westbrook?'

'Yes, he was already mental. He had been over to our house, pleading with Eddie to help him find more artefacts. He was convinced there was more stuff down there. He was already in debt. In any case, on the bus home he befriended Suzie Potter. He was desperate for money and Suzie looked as if she was the kind of person who had it. He needed a quick fix. He persuaded her to get off the bus near the Tor. He told me she was impressed when he said he owned Abbey House and all the grounds, so he said he would show her around.' Dorothy laughed again.

'Once on the Tor he tried to get money from her. She refused. The rest is history.'

The support team signalled one minute.

Dorothy was also playing for time as she pulled the trap door up and let it drop to the floor beside Denise. Wesley was getting impatient and when he heard the noise of the trap door being slammed on the floor he wondered for a second if they were too late.

'I'm sorry it has to end this way Inspector,' Dorothy called out, at the same time as Wesley received the signal.

There was sound of wood splintering as several of the wooden shutters were ripped away in unison exposing the gloomy interior of the Abbot's kitchen.

Denise screamed as the spotlights from the support crew were switched on showing her and Dorothy in the middle of the cavernous room.

In one swift move that defied her age Dorothy pushed Denise away and dived to the floor. Within seconds she had thrown the cloth bag containing the artefacts into the void and was taking backwards steps down into the Well.

Before any of the support team could squeeze through the window recesses Dorothy had climbed down several steps pulling the trap door down over her. The first man in the building ran forward leaping at the trap door but to no avail. Dorothy had already bolted it from below. A minute later after the second support officer had gained access to the building and shot the door lock to pieces Wesley went straight to Denise who was cowering on the floor. He quickly untied her hands and feet and held her close as she collapsed in his arms. All of the support team were now in the building. Two of them were trying to prize the trap door open.

A member of the ambulance crew wrapped a silver sheet around Denise's shoulders to keep her warm.

Suddenly with the use of two crowbars, the trap door broke away from its hinges. Seconds later there were several faces peering down into the void.

133

'She brought me here through the tunnel,' Denise said.

Her whole body was trembling and the ambulance team wanted to take her out of there immediately. As they placed her on the stretcher, she reached out to Wesley and took hold of his arm.

'Inspector, I'm sure I was kept in Abbey House and led here through the tunnel, so there must be an underground route from the property. I know we took a right turn to climb the ladder into this place but I don't think Dorothy will go back to the house. She intends to return the artefacts, deep down in the Well.'

Wesley leaned forward and kissed her on the forehead.

'Thanks. Get some rest now.'

He nodded to the ambulance crew led Denise out of the building.

'Go back the house and tell Penny the good news,' Wesley told Martin. 'I'm going after Dorothy.'

'Be careful, Sir. Remember she's carrying a knife.'

'Don't worry Martin,' he replied patting him on the shoulder. 'I'll be back soon. You still owe me a beer.'

Two of the support team took the lead, both armed. The LED torches on their helmets lighting the way into the tunnel. As they rounded the bend of the tunnel they spotted Dorothy's silhouette up ahead. Wesley called out.

'Dorothy, you can't get away. It's all over.'

'She's not stopping.' The guy at the front pointed forward to where the tunnel straightened out. Dorothy could be seen fifty yards ahead.

Suddenly the lead guy raised his hand to halt them.

'Listen.'

The three of them stood in silence. The sound of running water could be clearly heard.

'That's rain water running down into the centre of the Well,' said Wesley. 'The centre floods when there's a lot of rain. It may stop Dorothy getting across.'

They pushed on for another hundred yards then just as the tunnel took another turn they rounded the corner to see Dorothy just thirty yards ahead. She had reached the centre of the tunnel where water was now cascading down into the bowels of the Well. It was going to be treacherous around the ledges as they were now soaking wet.

'Dorothy!' Wesley shouted her name which now echoed around the chamber. She looked back, almost losing her balance.

'Don't be foolish. You'll never make it around the chasm. One slip and you'll be washed down into the Well.'

She turned to face them. A vacant stare on her face.

'Stay there Inspector. I'm returning the artefacts to their rightful place. Where they will be safe for further centuries.'

Wesley raised his arms with his palms showing, to show he was unarmed. Dorothy was standing dangerously close to the edge of the chasm.

'Come back this way. It's too wet. You'll fall.'

'Inspector. I don't intend on falling. I intend on guarding the artefacts with my life. She raised the cloth bag in front of her. For a moment she stared at Wesley before a brief smile came to her face. Then she turned and jumped into the chasm.

'No!' Wesley shouted.

He ran as close to the edge as possible and peered down into the void. The sound of the torrent of water now falling into the Well was so loud that he never heard her screams.

134

The following morning Wesley was sat in the library in Abbey House with Penny Westbrook, Alison and Martin. The police doctor had examined Penny the previous evening and had given her a relaxant which had provided her with a few hours' sleep.

Alison had made teas and coffees and everyone was sat near the log fire. A welcoming warm from the continued torrential wind and rain.

'I had no idea Dorothy was born into the Westbrook family,' said Penny clutching a cup of tea with numerous helpings of sugar.

'None of us did,' Wesley answered. 'It was only because the signature was found on the drawing that David Hare was in possession of, that we found out. It was fortunate that we did and since then our researchers have confirmed that Dorothy was indeed born into the Westbrook family.'

'But if Dorothy was born into the Westbrook family, why didn't she own this place? Or at least challenge Michael's father for the ownership?'

'We have been carrying out some investigations into that,' said Wesley. 'It would seem that Michael was Dorothy's younger brother. Even though he was actually adopted when his own mother passed away.'

Penny put her hands to her mouth. There was a stunned look on her face.

'However, having spoken with Messrs Gatting and Smith Solicitors, it appears that their father wrote Dorothy out of his entire will when she said she wanted to marry Eddie Hallerton. Their father wouldn't agree to the marriage and when Dorothy defied his wishes, he simply removed her name from the family will.'

'Michael never even mentioned he had a sister. That's what I don't understand,' Penny replied.

'From what I've been told, their father had such dominance over Michael, he may have refused to allow Michael ever to mention Dorothy's name.'

'So was this all about jealousy?'

Wesley sighed and shrugged his shoulders.

'Some of it yes, but not all.'

He paused for a moment to roll a cigarette.

'When Michael seduced Eddie into searching for artefacts on the pretext of them both making large amounts money, Dorothy viewed it as the ideal opportunity to get her revenge. She always saw herself as being the keeper, if you like. The keeper of the King Arthurs treasures. Long before she fell out with her father, he showed her all the secret routes around the house and the grounds and if my guesswork is right he also told her where certain artefacts were buried.'

'So when I gave Dorothy a tour of the house, she already knew where everything was?'

'I'm afraid so. I'm almost positive that she also used her visit to access the East Wing which is why we found footprints in the room when you took us there.'

'But for what purpose?'

'I think to ensure that she could always move Denise if she had to. She must have known the servant's staircase existed and probably with Eddie's help ensured there was an escape route both into the Chalice Well and back into the house if she needed one.'

'Why didn't Michael's father include his son in all this?' Martin asked.

'According to Michael's doctor, the old man always thought Michael to be too weak and even said more than once that he thought Michael was unstable.'

'Then why did he still leave his whole estate to a son who he had little faith in?'

'Because he viewed Michael as his son, his only son. He already knew that Dorothy could never have children but there was always the possibility that Michael would father a child.'

'And carry the Westbrook name forward.'

'Yes.'

'Did you not say that Dorothy had a liaison with Harvey White?' Martin asked as he spilled some of his tea down his trousers.

'Yes she did. You see, I believe she and Harvey White became an item long before Eddie came on the scene. We now know they were at school together and worked together in the council offices. Harvey insisted they should never marry as he knew he was afflicted with polio which was only going to worsen as he grew older and he refused to burden Dorothy with his affliction. However, they agreed to always remain friends. They were both members of the Somerset Moors Preservation Group amongst others and both had access to council archives as they used to write articles for the council and local businesses.'

'Oh, so the typed blackmail threats came from Dorothy too?'

'No. They were actually typed by Harvey White.'

'What?'

'It's true. Harvey still loved her and would have done anything to help her.'

'Then that raises the question as to who killed Harvey?'

'That did confuse me I must admit. But it was Jane who solved that one. There were only four people who knew about the address in Havering. Harvey, Dorothy, Kelvin and Jenny. Dorothy was at home on the evening Harvey died. Jane saw her and waved to her as she walked past her cottage. Kelvin was already dead and Jenny was with me.'

'But that only leaves Harvey himself,' Penny exclaimed.

'Exactly.' Wesley paused to look around the room.

'Harvey White took his own life by stabbing himself through the heart. There were no fingerprints on the knife because Harvey was wearing gloves.'

'Why would he commit suicide?' Alison asked.

'That is the one question I cannot provide a concrete answer for. However, in my opinion Harvey was not a well man. He already thought that he and Dorothy had gone too far. He had implicated himself in kidnap and murder. By taking the easy option, for him in any case, by ending his own life, I believe he thought that his suspected murder would waste valuable police time and continue to detract our attentions away from Dorothy.'

'I have another question,' said Alison raising an arm.

'What was Harvey doing at the house?'

'He'd gone there to destroy the painting. However, it had already been removed. Jenny Stevens had seen to that. Jenny had been to the house previously. She knew that allowing the painting to be found by someone else would implicate Kelvin Ward, her uncle. It was Kelvin remember who applied for excavation rights after somehow discovering that certain artefacts were supposed to be buried alongside the Westbrook family in the remote graveyard on the outskirts of the village.'

'Is that where Dorothy really injured herself?' Alison asked.

'Yes I think it was. That and her repeated journeys down into the Chalice Well and the Abbot's kitchen. There is evidence of someone having dug the ground next to two of the gravestones. There's no trace of any hidden artefacts now. I can only assume that whatever had been buried there has now been dropped into the Chalice Well by Dorothy.'

'Can any of these items ever be retrieved?' Martin asked.

'According to what I've been told this morning by the rescue team, they may never recover Dorothy's body let alone any of the artefacts. The chasm in to the middle of the Chalice Well drops over a hundred feet into a fast flowing underground river that emerges somewhere out on the Somerset Levels. They estimate the river to be some fifteen meters deep with more than two metres of silt and mud at the bottom. I think it's safe to say the artefacts will remain there for many years to come.'

Back in his office Wesley replaced the receiver and sat back in the chair. Having just provided Superintendent Richard Adams with a full report he now looked across his desk to where his team sat.

'What did he have to say?' Martin asked.

'Oh, he was pleased that the murders and kidnapping have been resolved. But you know son, that's not important. What is though is that Denise is now home, safe and sound with her family.'

Mandy stood up, walked across the room and placed her hand on Wesley's shoulder.

'I'll go and make the teas.'

135

It was mid-afternoon when Wesley walked into the tea shop in Glastonbury High Street. After hanging his wet coat on the coat stand he joined Jane who was already sat at a table near the window reading the daily newspaper.

'Hello my dearest,' he said pulling up a chair.

'Do you know this is the first time since we moved down here that I've actually purchased the local newspaper? It's really quite good. Lots of juicy gossip.'

'Now you tell me. You might have saved me hours of researching,' he replied with a smirk on his face.

Jane folded the newspaper and put it to one side as the waitress came over to take their order.

'How's Penny taken all of this?' she asked.

'Taking into account everything that has happened then I would say she's taken it very well. Her local GP is with her now. She's just been told that Michael is to be transferred to a psychiatric hospital in Wells. Although I won't pretend to like the man, I do sympathise. Apparently he hasn't a clue who's who right now.'

Jane tutted and shook her head. 'That's so sad.'

Wesley thanked the waitress who placed two teas and two scones with jam and butter on the table.'

'My calorie intake for the day.'

'Eat slowly because that's your dinner too,' Jane replied laughing.

'What I still don't understand is why Dorothy kidnapped poor Denise. Surely the girl had done nothing wrong?'

'I think there are two reasons. Firstly, from CCTV footage we have, we're pretty certain that Denise overheard Dorothy and someone else standing outside the Tourist office talking about returning the artefacts. It could have been Harvey White. We'll never know. That's as much as I can say for sure but whatever the remainder of the conversation, she must have heard enough for Dorothy to believe she could be a problem.

Secondly, knowing Denise was Penny's daughter, what better way to entice her over to Abbey House by saying I'll get you in so you can meet your mother without anyone else knowing. Using her knowledge of the house, Dorothy met Denise from work on the night she disappeared. She gained access to the back of the property using Eddie's maintenance keys and took the poor girl straight into the East Wing where she drugged her using herbs from her garden. The rest is history.'

'Oh that poor girl. What must have been going through her mind?'

'I don't think Dorothy had any real intention of killing her. Certainly not initially in any case. Denise was the only pawn she had.'

'Was it money that Dorothy was after?'

'No, she just wanted to return the artefacts to their rightful place and using Denise seemed the ideal choice, especially after Denise had overheard something she shouldn't have.'

Jane ate a piece of her scone but her appetite had faded.

'What about Denise? Where is she now?'

'She was kept in hospital overnight for observation. Mandy took Patricia Wright to the hospital this morning before they all returned to Abbey House.

Mum, stepmother and daughter are all there together.'

'Oh John. Do you think they'll be OK now?'

'Yes I think so. Penny informed me that she is going to ask Patricia and Denise if they want to live there with her. Well, it's a massive place to look after, and Penny is going to need some help around the place.'

'I do hope it works out for them,' said Jane.

She poured the tea from the teapot into two cups.

'I didn't tell you,' said Wesley. 'Jenny's solicitor has made a plea for manslaughter. I expect it could be a few weeks yet though before she goes to court. The courts are so busy these days.'

'I know this sounds selfish but I presume the bookshop should be closed up now?'

'Yes unfortunately, for a while in any case.'

'What about Sally? Have you spoken to her?'

'Hmm,' Wesley mumbled with a mouth full of scone.

'Yeah, I spoke to her earlier today. David's funeral is next Tuesday. His father has arranged for David to be buried next to his mother. I've asked Sally to send me the exact details. I'll arrange for some flowers to be sent.''

'What is Sally going to do?'

'She says she's undecided. She's not sure she wants to continue working in London and may give some thought to moving out this way.' Jane smiled.

'I don't suppose young PC Adam Broad would have any influence would he?'

Wesley laughed and reaching across the table took her hand.

'Hey, I thought you were after my scone,' she laughed.

'Well at least you can have a rest for a few days,' Jane said as they walked back to the car.

'There's just one more thing I need to do,' he replied. 'Wait here for me. I'm just going to pop across the road to the council offices. There's someone I need to talk to. I'll be two minutes.'

After showing his ID to the woman on the reception desk he was directed down the corridor to the far end of the building where the maintenance department was.

Wesley spotted Gary Knowles through the glass door. The lad was busy repairing the drawers on an old set of filing cabinets. He jumped up when he saw Wesley approach across the room.

'Inspector Wesley. How good to see you.'

They shook hands before Gary invited him over to where a couple of old chairs were standing underneath a workbench.

'I hear that the young girl was found alive and well,' he said. 'That is good news. A happy ending.'

'Yes, it's not always the case but I'm pleased to say she is back home now with her family.'

'I thought she only had a mother?' Gary replied looking somewhat confused.

'It's a long story, perhaps another day eh?'

'Sure thing.' Gary paused as if he had rehearsed his next line.

'I know that sharing knowledge of what we found to the outside world would make me a star for a while but it would also change a lot of things around here too. I think we have something special here already in Glastonbury. Let's leave it at that shall we?'

A broad smile came to Wesley's face and he stood up to give the young lad a hug. When Gary looked up to Wesley there were tears in his eyes.

'If you ever need anything you give me a call,' said Wesley.

Gary nodded and went back to work.

The real location of King Arthur's tomb would continue to remain a mystery. For now in any case.

Lightning Source UK Ltd.
Milton Keynes UK
UKOW052304230712

196453UK00001B/9/P